THE QUE

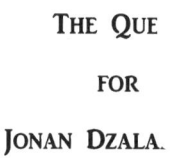

FOR

JONAN DZALA.

David Lister

The Quest
for
Jonan Dzalarhons

★★Corps du Chien Books★★

First published in Great Britain in 2019

Copyright © David Lister 2019

The moral rights of the author have been asserted

This is a work of fiction. Names, characters, businesses, places, events and incidents are either the products of the author's imagination or used in a fictitious manner. Any resemblance to actual persons, living or dead, or actual events is purely coincidental, and where historical figures are included, their appearance, actions and dialogue are completely fictional.

All rights reserved
No part of this publication may be reproduced or transmitted by any means, electronic, mechanical, photocopying or otherwise, without the prior permission of the publisher.

Corps du Chien Books
36 Mandeville Road
Potters Bar
EN6 5LQ
UK

Cover Image
©Santiago Andrea Arciniegas Gomez
softcreatures.com

ISBN: 978-1-9997445-1-9

*To
Jim Al-Khalili*

*By way of an apology for me
taking liberties with quantum biology.*

Sol III

OPEN FILE
NAME: HISTORICALLY SIGNIFICANT ANCESTORS
AUTHOR: ARIEL DZALARHONS
DETERMINE RELEVANT SECTIONS ONLY
RECORD TO CRYSTAL IN FIRST PERSON PRESENT
APPLY GERARDO PRINCIPLE I.E., DO NOT ASSUME POTENTIAL READERS HAVE FULL KNOWLEDGE OF THE NORMS OF 4TH CENTURY LIFE.

I've been on Earth for nearly two Venusian years – we call them 'vears' – having won an excursion to study at São Paulo's Unicamp as part of my preparation to join a gene-hunter collective. Unusually, my assigned dissertation is to hunt down material that has a strong probability of connecting me by an ancestral link to the subjects of the material.

Prompted by a find of staggering importance, personal and historical, I've decided to record the final stage of my research. It's been necessary to keep my emotions in check with a mild graph-administered blocker, but the excitement is still palpable.

Yesterday I had a call from my professor, Bart Coumans. He outlined the details of the find, his excitement every bit as evident as mine. But then he has a good excuse. He's no-tech, and without a neural-stent he can't benefit from blockers. Nor can he establish mind links, either with the living beings we call graphs, or our own AI constructs. Life must be very difficult for him, but he copes admirably. He interfaces with graphs, those beings who live in Quantum, and constructs, which are no more than computer programs, via holographic projections. Of course, we all do that to some extent. Projections are often very useful, but poor old Bart hasn't got the choice. It must be like living in a dark cave where everybody else has enhanced eyesight. They can all see, but no-techs have to get around by the sense of touch. It's entirely to his credit that he's risen to such respected heights within the halls of academia.

I cross the quad, straight over the lawn and by the water sculpture. It's too early for lectures and the space is populated by my fellow students, mostly Earthers but one of two Martians and a smattering of youths from the colonies. I'm the only Venusian male. Come to think of it, the only Venusian at all.

With my tall, slender form and complete lack of hair, I'm commonplace at home but considered exotic by my Earther friends and colleagues. I've been the subject of numerous offers from youths of all three sexes, but not wishing to confirm the silly misconception concerning the sexual licentiousness of my entire race, I have politely declined. I prefer to keep my filters topped up and get on with my work.

Several students are projecting constructs from their mantles. Worn on the upper body and studded with lenses, they project interfaces outdoors where indoor wall-mounted lenses can't reach. Nowhere near as efficient as indoor systems, their projections appear as translucent beings or objects of bright blue light.

There's a convention with projections to differentiate between graphs and constructs. A construct will often project as a blue-light version of the human for whom they work, while graphs choose their own form. So over there, the Adelia-shaped blue projection standing next to Adelia is most definitely a construct. But the equally blue and bright grizzly bear standing next to Genso is a graph.

Genso smiles at me and waves. Perhaps he still thinks he has a chance with me. The bear waves too, and smiles. Somebody should tell that graph bears don't smile. Creepiest thing I've ever seen.

It's cool inside the main hall, but I suspect most others consider it rather warm. Venusians are used to much warmer climates. I cross to the central spiral staircase and make use of it. After two years I'm entirely acclimatised to Earth's gravity, so climbing stairs no longer makes my heart race. The fact that it is racing now indicates my mounting excitement.

Here I am. I knock on Bart's door, and yes, I knock using my knuckles. Sometimes Bart takes his adherence to low-tech much too far.

The door swings open and Bart fills the frame. A large man, hair white and thinning on top, he looks about ninety years old but I guess he's only in his late fifties. People who shy away from augmentations and enhancements always looked much older than they are. Tall for an Earther, he still has to look up to me and I'm only average for a Venusian.

'My dear fellow. How nice to see you again.' We embrace in that typically Earther way. My height makes it awkward for him to get his arm over my shoulder and we laugh at the dance which accidentally ensues. 'Come in, come in. A beverage?'

I accept the offer and Bart scuttles off to prepare a hot drink all by himself when he could more easily order a domestic-skin to bring something. I make myself comfortable in his miniature recreation of the Amazon jungle, all achieved without a single holographic projection. I've been to Bart's home on the outskirts of the city. It appears that home or office, Bart loves to surround himself with living art. Without a domestic-skin I imagine it takes him a long time to care for all these plants. Plants in ceramic pots; plants in troughs and plants hanging from complicated ceiling fixtures. The air invigorates, it's so full of newly created oxygen.

I was here an Earth month ago and discussed my dissertation plans with Bart and a team of graphs. I provided a little drop of my blood, set some parameters and objectives, and armed with instructions the graphs went to work. Operating at speeds old world quantum computers could only dream about, the graphs set to work on my behalf, seeking out traces of my DNA, back through the many veils of time. I met with them every few days to discuss lines of enquiry – extend this search, close down this other – and now we have some tangible results.

Bart returns, two mugs of coffee held in one hand, his finger curled through their handles. It looks precarious and I leap up to relieve him of one before he drops them both. There's an intriguing brown leather bag under his other arm, and he sees me looking.

'It's a document valise, Ariel. In here is treasure!'

Such a strange concept: information contained on the surface of sheets of physical material.

'Sit down, my friend.' Bart puts his own mug onto a side table and allows himself to be swallowed up in a massive arm chair. 'It's mostly what they call "typed", but some of it is actually hand-written.'

This is true history. It's why I'm studying to become a historian. Most people have to wait a lifetime for that one special discovery, but here I am, a youth not yet enrolled into a gene-hunting collective, and my discovery is within arm's length.

Bart puts the valise on the arm of the chair and sits forward, like the Sphynx guarding a treasure. There's no getting past Bart. Must the treasure wait until I've answered a riddle? But no, the only riddle I must solve is patience.

Bart strokes the leather. 'I've really never seen anything like it before. You are to be congratulated.'

'Thank you, but really, the graphs did the heavy digging.' As usual.

'Not a bit of it. Your search parameters were so finely set and detailed, that the seeker-programs flushed these beauties out. They'd have remained hidden for another thousand years if not for you.'

A blush warms my face, rising from my neck.

'I've spoken with the graph team leader and even she's uncertain how they managed to uncover some of their results. It seems the graphs were led by more than your blood and brain. She described it as "spooky". Spooky, indeed.'

Curious. Graphs are usually very precise with their methodology and aren't prone to mysterious guiding hands. 'Spooky' is not a term I ever thought a graph might use.

'Before we look at the papers, let's discuss some of the other findings.'

No, no let's not. I want to see those papers, and I want to see them this very instant. 'Of course, Bart. What have we got?'

'Well, first of all, we'll start with the least impressive. We have traces to a figure of some substance at the beginning of the thirteenth century.'

'That's the least impressive? It seems crazy-impressive to me. We've traced my DNA to someone who lived nearly two thousand years ago?'

Bart laughs and I'm like a fifteen-year-old. 'Let's call it a work in progress. There is no detail. Other traces include a young gentleman of the seventeenth century and, brace yourself, a strong link to Shona Eastbrook, saviour of human-kind.'

This is tremendous. Beyond anything I could have hoped for. 'I'm descended from Shona?'

'No not directly. Remember, she had no offspring. But you are a direct descendant of Philip Fryer.

I could dance! This is magical.

'Not only have you come up with undisputable evidence for direct ancestry, but you've uncovered a small fragment of a biography Fryer had written about Shona. With the right treatment, it'll get you a doctorate.'

I point to the valise.

'Ah, afraid not. Fryer's work was lurking in a dark, never-visited corner of the grid. But these papers are equally exciting in their own way. Here!'

I take the valise. I swear my hands are tingling. I tell it to open which makes Bart laugh again. There's no tech about this thing, and I must operate a little metal catch with my fingers to open the flap. My clumsy manipulations release a smell that's not new to me. It reminds me of last year's visit to the Bodleian Library.

'They have that good old ancient smell, but they've only survived a thousand years because they were micro-plasticised and kept in stasis. They're sufficiently robust for you to handle without gloves.'

There are letters inside, and sheets of paper. Some have typed symbols on them. Old Standard, which I've studied. One piece has inked sections, as beautiful as calligraphy.

'Those words were formed by the hand of Christie Grey, your thirty-odd times great grandfather.'

I hold the paper in trembling fingers like the priceless artefact it is. There's a tingle in my sinuses and I need a graph blocker to stop my emotions spilling over. To cry would be inconvenient and embarrassing, but this is the handwriting of a direct ancestor who lived over a thousand years ago.

'Forgive me, but I've read some of it. I know I should've left it for you.'

'Not at all. Professor's privilege.'

'It's fascinating stuff. Christie lived in the time of a worldwide conflict of nation states, long before Earth became united. I think you will conclude he was a very brave young man.'

It's all so much to take in. Never in my wildest dreams had I expected this level of success. We continue to chat, but I'm taking nothing in. I can't wait to establish a graph-link with Father who's at home on Venus.

Bart rises from his comfortable chair, a sure sign that our interview is coming to an end. 'How do you intend to present?'

'Standard full immersion. It's really the only way.'

Bart agrees. There's nothing like seeing history unfold all around you, projected in high quality. I'll employ some top-rated constructs who I'll program with the last molecule of information at my disposal. Bart says he can't wait. I can't linger either, as my graph-link to Venus is imminent.

'Give Jonan my best, won't you?'

I happily affirm. Father and Bart have never met but they respect each other's work and have spoken several times across links, both standard and graph

I'm crossing the quad in a cloud of joy. All my hard work has paid off. Jonan – Father – will be so pleased, but he won't show it much. It's not our way.

I reach my rooms with time to spare. I close the door behind me and the visitor-bell chimes. It's BAHAT, a graph-lecturer who takes the form of a 17th century astrologer.

'Thank you so much for your time, Bahat.'

'My pleasure. Now, stand by while I establish the link with Amalthea.'

AMALTHEA is one of Father's colleagues at home. It's good of them to give their time. I'm far too excited and eager to give my news with the time lag that usually affects communications. Graph-links are instantaneous, another unfathomable trait of them living in Quantum.

'Link established, Ariel. Here we go.'

I hear Father's voice through the speakers. 'Are you there, Ariel?'

BAHAT uses the wall-projector system to create the scene for me, exactly as it is at this moment at home on Venus. And here's Father. The beams intersect and form his image, as solid-looking and real as if he were standing in front of me. He smiles and steps towards me with outstretched arms. And then he stops short and turns to look at someone outside the parameters of the projection.

'How dare you? Why have you entered my home uninvited?'

With that, the link is broken and Father's hologram vanishes. BAHAT can't tell me why and is unable to re-establish the link. He removes his periwig and scratches his head. Now he's fading away and looks shocked. 'I cannot maintain cohesion and …' His voice fades too until the wall-mounted projection lenses are dark and the speakers silent.

I call up my construct and set about establishing the usual form of communications link, but before I can, AMALTHEA appears in my room. From Venus to Earth in the blink of an eye.

'What're you doing here? And what's going on back home?'

'I don't know, Ariel. I have suffered an attack and I am incomplete. Part of me is still at your father's home.'

'What? Why?' Can graphs even be in two places at the same time? Quantum mech is one thing, but quantum life is on another level altogether.

'There is no time. I must show you what is happening.'

AMATHEA's faded image of a tumbling Jovian satellite pulsates. It's as if she's struggling to remain visible.
And now she projects a scene of pure horror.

***

There's a door which isn't part of my home. I don't recognise it at all. It stands open and a red, writhing tentacle whips around from the inside as if searching for prey. It's tamed by a young man on the threshold who I take to be Venusian. He is unclothed and although shorter, has the same honey-hued skin tone as me. There is a golden feathered bird on his shoulder, like a brazen eagle, which leaps to flight and joins the man in attacking the tentacle. Now they've beaten the tentacle back, he beckons me inside and in I go in.

The man, the bird and the tentacle vanish and now Father's home takes form. I know it well and AMALTHEA's projection is close to perfect. There are three beings present of whom one is human, one graph and the other a construct.

The construct stands by Jonan ready to comply with any request he might make. The graph is AMALTHEA and she rotates slowly, high in the corner of the room. As demanded of a polite guest, she bides her time while Jonan and his attending construct take in the air on our balcony overlooking Dzalarhons City.

As befitting a polite host, Jonan allows AMALTHEA time to settle before he greets her. He waits on the balcony where the warm breeze gives movement to his past-shoulder length dark brown hair. His construct, designated 'Edwin', stands in close attendance. Jonan is unusual among adults because he prefers to interface with a visible construct whereas most maintain an internal dialogue.

It's evening, which comes every 24 hours thanks to 500 years of terraforming. Prior to that a Venusian day lasted longer than a Venusian year, quite unsuitable for human comfort. The lights in the city are coming on and birds are settling to roost in the treetops of the forest which slopes down from our home to the outskirts. The distant howl of a slope-sloth paints the air, no more than a light stroke of the brush. The evening sky changes from ice blue to glow with the colour of dessert wine, golden and thick. The glow is reproduced inside me with the thought that no matter how much interplanetary space separates Jonan from me, we are warmed by the same sun.

Jonan is barefooted and wears a lilac film-gown which comes to his ankles, typical attire for people in this region of Venus. His heavily embroidered mantle sparkles with several dozen lenses which give form to constructs and graphs when out of doors. Construct-Edwin shines blue all over, but takes on the natural tones of a darker-skinned version of Father when he follows Jonan inside: the room's many banks of button-sized projectors are far more efficient than a mantle could ever be.

Jonan moves slowly, contemplatively, every moment a meditation in motion in that way that identifies Venusians on whatever world we happened to be. His hands clasped lightly at the front, he looks up to his guest and welcomes her formally. AMALTHEA sinks to Jonan's eye level and they exchange pleasant greetings.

'Thank you for coming so quickly. I apologise for the lamentable lack of notice.'

AMALTHEA flashes gold, her way of conveying a smile of reassurance.

'My graph colleague was called to Quantum on business, deep enough that he couldn't project at the same time, let alone set up a link to Earth.'

'No matter,' AMALTHEA says. 'When are you expecting the communication?'

Jonan looks towards Edwin, who opens his projected hand to reveal a series of numbers. 'Ariel is scheduled to link in five minutes. Is that sufficient time to establish a connection?'

AMALTHEA glows again, this time the gold rippling over the cratered surface of her interface. She's laughing. 'In Quantum five of your minutes are at least as many months to me.' The sound of her voice comes from micro-speakers secreted in the walls.

Jonan smiles too. 'Of course.' With skin like polished sandstone, full lips, deep brown eyes, high cheekbones and especially the waist-length hair, he is often mistaken for a woman by Earthers. Taking account of subjectivity and allowing for the respect I have for him, I'm still able to say with confidence that Jonan is quite exceptionally handsome. And at the risk of appearing vain, many say I take after him.

Jonan and AMALTHEA speak about my work on Earth, and how much longer it will keep me. Soon, Jonan's minutes and AMALTHEA's months pass, and AMALTHEA establishes a link with the graph attending me on Earth.

'We are ready, Jonan. Would you like me to end projection?'

'No, please stay.'

Another ripple of gold passes over AMALTHEA's surface. 'Please proceed.'

Jonan speaks into the air. 'Are you there, Ariel?'

I see myself appear as a hologram back at home, and Father reaches out his arms towards me.

And then the door to the causeway opens without instruction from Jonan. Three women enter in the blue-grey uniforms of prefects.

'How dare you? Why have you entered my home uninvited?' Jonan faces them, unable to comprehend the intrusion and the shattering of etiquette. He remains calm, and faces the intruders who mirror his relaxed stance, hands clasped in front of their stomachs.

Jonan spots an inconsistency; something that gives the intruders away. 'You are not true prefects.'

The shortest woman who appears to hold seniority answers. 'It is a necessary subterfuge.'

'To what end?'

'To evade suspicion while we ensure your compliance. You must come with us.' She lifts a flap on her fatigues to reveal a plazgun. I've never seen one before, but I'm fully aware of their destructive power, so I fear for Father's life. 'Failure to comply will force unpleasant action.'

Jonan slowly unclasps his hands and re-clasps them behind him. He dips his head minutely, in acknowledgment and compliance.

'Thank you. Please step this way.'

As Jonan makes for the door, he winds the black partner-band from his left middle finger. He pauses at the threshold and lets the ring fall into the thick pile of the rug. 'My footwear and cloak?' The causeway is of polished plasticrete.

'They will not be necessary.'

The two subservient prefects seize his arms, and their leader jabs him with a stunner.

AMALTHEA ends the projection. 'I am sorry. I've lost cohesion and I am thinly spread. I can no longer access the scenes on Venus.'

I should be in the grip of abject panic, but I'm inexplicably calm. Unless … 'Have you administered a blocker?'

'Yes. I apologise for not asking first, but you were displaying dangerous levels of stress.'

I'll let it pass. 'Where have they taken him?'

'I do not know.'

There is no time to speculate. I ask AMALTHEA to link with the Dzalarhons County Shepherd's office, but she is unable. My construct can't establish links either.

'You are being deliberately screened out of grid, Ariel.'

'Without a warrant? That's impossible.'

'It is not impossible. It is simply illegal. You are being screened, and they are coming for you.'

She tells me I have an hour at most. Whoever kidnapped Father wants me too.

'Dress as an Earther. Bring nothing. If we are lucky, we might make it to Mato Grosso.'

I'll comply, but I'm going nowhere without my valise of ancient papers.

***

Mato Grosso? What does it mean? And who gets to name places anyway? I try to distract myself with inconsequential questions. At the best of times I find Earther spaceports oppressive. Mato Grosso is no exception, and as a Venusian male I'm a focus for the other travellers. That many people in one place make a crowd, and a crowd is a different kind of creature. I'm dressed like them, so it's not my attire that singles me out. On Venus we wear either a film-gown or nothing at all, and yet dressed in a thick nanotex formsuit like everybody else, I've never felt more exposed. They see into my mind and want to tear me apart in a feeding frenzy. Surely, the game will soon be up.

Is that my old friend, Verone Kell, by the entrance to that relief-station? Wishful thinking: it's a Martian youth, about my own age, who studies me with the intensity of a graph-prefect, apparently so enthralled that she forgets to struggle with gravity three times above her comfort level.

A group of uncouth Callistonians break off their boisterous banter to stare at me. One leers, a look that's as uncomfortable as an assault. It's as if a sign hovers over me saying 'CRIMINAL'. I clutch my document valise, a comfort-blanket of sorts and something behind which to hide. Then again, the simple act of carrying something – anything – makes me stand out from the other passengers.

AMALTHEA makes her presence felt. It's sometimes confusing that the living creatures we call 'graphs' and our own programmed AI constructs often communicate to us via projected holograms, but in this instance it works to our advantage. 'Ariel, I've noticed an alarming increase in your heart rate. Should I administer a blocker?'

'Thank you, Amalthea, but I'll be fine.' It's a lie. I'm trying to be brave.

'Don't call me by my name, Ariel. Remember, I'm mantle-projecting as your construct.'

I don't need reminding. AMALTHEA's registered projection is a rust-brown, green-flecked representation of Jupiter's third satellite whose name she's adopted. Right now she's projecting as a translucent blue version of me. It's not unusual for youths to be accompanied by visible constructs, but it's verging on illegal for a graph to impersonate a construct, and that only serves to increase my anxiety.

'Try to breathe steadily.'

'That's easy to say if you're a being that doesn't need to breathe at all.'

'I would trade broaching a solar flux for breathing in an instant. It is dreadfully uncomfortable. Now, stop talking and … breathe. We have only one more security bar to cross and then we'll be safely spaceside. We have done extremely well to get this far.'

I'm aware of that, but as we close on our goal, waves of tension threaten to swamp me. 'Maybe a mild blocker after all, please.'

No sooner asked than the seas grow calm. AMALTHEA reaches into me, tweaks my neural-stent, and makes the necessary adjustments.

'Of course, blocker usage will be detected when we cross the bar, but it is quite normal for passengers to receive treatment before a transition. Nothing will seem amiss.'

AMALTHEA, in my blue-light form, smiles reassuringly. She's like my own image reflected from a blue-tinted mirror. At one-point-nine metres, I'm tall enough and thin enough to be recognised as Venusian, and young enough to draw unwanted attention from prefects. Gene-modified for depilation, I'm hairless from head to foot, but even without Father's uncommon waist-length locks, my features mark me as his son. My only hope of escape is to become one with the crowd; another traveller eager to get to an orbital hub with minimal inconvenience.

'I have taken the liberty of administering a little more blocker,' AMALTHEA says, 'on account of the fact that two prefects are approaching directly towards us.'

She must have slugged me a double, because I couldn't care less. I doubt a full cohort of prefects waving charged plazzers would raise more than a giggle from me. One of the prefects is a graph. He projects a human form in true colours and looks almost solid, a consequence of high res projection not possible from a mantle.

As soon as they're in range, they raise their side-arms and kill AMALTHEA with a disrupter pulse to my mantle. Other passengers can't get away from me fast enough and I'm soon at the centre of a deserted circle of cold paving. I feel no shock at this act of aggression, such is the strength of my medication. Shutting down a citizen's AI construct is a crime unless officially warranted. Disrupting a graph is a felony that can never be sanctioned, so I assume the prefects were taken in by AMALTHEA's subterfuge and mistook her for a construct.

'Good morning, citizen,' the human prefect says. 'We are authorised to relieve you of your liberty. Please come with us.'

'What're your grounds?'

They flash a holographic symbol by way of verification, but it's no answer to my question and it's not a warrant. The hologram fades in the air with my last hope of escape.

AMALTHEA's death is temporary. She'll collect herself in Quantum and find a way to return. I'm made of flesh and blood. Augmented, enhanced and engineered to a degree, but nevertheless my death will be permanent, and fear overwhelms the blocker like a turbulent sea spilling over coastal defences.

***

They keep me in custody all night. The detention area is comfortable and gives me the illusion of being in a spacious dwelling within a large garden. Scenes from home are projected and the heat increased to levels suited to Venusians. They provide me with a film-gown but are prompted by their ridiculous prudishness to insist I keep on the Earther underwear, so the illusion of being at home is completely spoiled.

I have the use of an external AI, but without AMALTHEA or even my old construct, I can hardly navigate through my own mind. I tell myself it won't kill me. After all, one in a thousand people elect not to have neural-stents, or have them removed on reaching adulthood, and without a stent a person can't access the grid directly. However, Professor Bart Coumans thrives on it, operating perfectly well in the modern worlds, and my best friend, Benjo Drexler, is no-tech too.

Still, my augmentations are useless without a construct, stent or no stent. It's like wandering through a mansion where most of the doors are firmly locked. Fortunately, for the first time since I lost Father, I have time to reflect, and the doors of the past are wide open. I roam the corridors of my memory freely.

A prefect enters my room without warning, and tells me they've arranged a link with my Mother. The graph-prefect facilitates the link, and Mother forms before me. I've seen very little of her since my infancy. She lives on the Venusian mainland mass and rarely visits our island, but it's still good to see her.

After brief niceties I get to the pressing question. 'What have they done with Jonan?'

'Jonan? Who's Jonan?'

I recall Mother has a sense of humour, so I try to see the joke, and then I counter it with a quip of my own. 'Jonan the Mons Slope-Sloth. Who else?' Father's the least sloth-like person I know.

Mother laughs, the hologram's lips a little out of sync. Pictures and words must be difficult to transmit instantly, even for a pair of graphs.

'So, Jemma. Joking aside, do you have any news about him?' I'm angry that she should try to be funny in these circumstances, but the residuals of my last blocker keep me from ranting.

Mother goes quiet and tells me to stop being silly, and that it's a rare privilege for a pair of graphs to be generous with their time. A privilege I should not abuse. Bemused, I ask her one more time.

'I don't know what you're playing at, Ariel. I don't know who Jonan is, and you know as well as I do, you have no father. The real question here is what have you done to have your liberty curtailed?'

It's baffling, but for a moment I consider my own predicament. I start to tell her the prefects have failed to comply with the most basic procedures and that they are in breach of Three Worlds Laws and conventions. She vanishes, and the graph-prefect stares at me as if I'm the law breaker.

Blockers or no, it's difficult not to be frightened. The world is allowed to skew in nightmares, but this is real life.

***

I manage to hold it all together. In fact I find myself possessed of a species of bravado which is new to me. If nothing I say can save me, I'll say anything I like.

It's interrogation time. My detention area transforms into a small, oppressive room with hardly any furniture apart from a seat facing the two prefects, and grey padded walls all round.

The graph-prefect introduces himself as GRENDEL, and then begins to question me. 'Ariel Dzalarhons?'

'That's me.'

'What is your age?'

'Early Mechopocine. The beginning of the fourth millennium.' Juvenile-like, yes. But I'm frustrated and annoyed.

The human interjects. 'Not the geological age, you halfwit. *Your* age! How old are you?' There's an edge to his voice which I don't much care for.

'I'm thirty-seven.'

It's GRENDEL's turn again. I like the graph a lot more, which isn't saying much. 'In years, please. Not vears.' As if they can't work it out themselves with no effort at all. They're merely trying to establishing dominance. I know their game.

'Oh, wait. Remind me, how many vears in a year? I'll need to work it out. I haven't got a connection with my construct. Let me see, it's my age times 225 divided by 365 ... I'll have it in a –'

'Twenty-three,' the human says. 'You're twenty-three. Now, were you born Jemison 14th, 3008?'

'Sorry, I'm not familiar with the Earth calendar, and without access to my construct I can't make the conversions.' Of course I know my date of birth by their calendar, but I'm not going to make anything easy for them. They're obviously part of a conspiracy to make it appear as if Jonan never existed.

'And your sponsors?'

'I'm natural born. I don't have sponsors. I have parents.'

'That does not comply with the information we have,' the graph says. 'Who do you claim your parents to be?'

'My father is Jonan Zahed-Dzalarhons. My mother is Jenna Greer-Dzalarhons.'

GRENDEL puts a holographic finger to his head, as if contemplating my answer; a common graph ploy to cover the delay while accessing remote data. 'You have named your female sponsor, but Jonan Dzalarhons does not exist.'

I'm not surprised. By now I've heard it a hundred times, but what's going on?

And now they change tack and get personal, which at least takes my mind from the question of my father for a few minutes.

'Are you sexually active?' GRENDEL speaks without intonation, which under the circumstances is a blessing.

'Not at the moment, unless you think I'm closer to my Earther undies than I should be.' Vile garment.

'You're Venusian,' the human says. 'The way I hear it, sex with anyone or anything is par for the course.'

'In your case I'll happily make an exception.' Ha! That stings. Do I detect the hint of a blush?

'How many sexual partners have you had?'

This graph has my number. On Earth these things matter, so I exaggerate a little. 'Five.'

The prefects exchange a glance. They look worried. Good!

'Have you engaged in potential generative sex at any time?' the graph continues.

'That would be, sex to … make an infant?'

'Or whereby an infant may result, irrespective of the intent.'

'In that case, the answer is no, nor have I been counselled to reproduce.' I'm not inclined to provide them with any detailed information. My sexual status is a non-subject at home, but Earthers are a strange lot. As for me and sex, well, I prefer to keep my filters strong. There was one person, when I was in my twenties – but then, we all have to make sure everything's working at about that age.

GRENDEL examines his holographic finger nails, I assume for effect. Maybe he's read about human interview techniques. 'Do you maintain emotional and biosexual filters at all times?'

'Of course. I only lower them a couple of time a Venusian month for construct-enhanced hormonal balance.'

The Earther pulls his features into a picture of mockery. 'Mighty fine way of saying that you stick your dick in a sex-skin.'

'Who's your preferred partner? A sheep?' It has to be a residual of AMALTHEA's blocker. I'm never so flippant.

He leaps out of his chair – again for effect, which is wasted on me – until GRENDEL puts him in his place with a wave of a hand. There's no doubt: the graph is in charge.

The Earther settles, and something passes between my interrogators. They're communicating via a telepathic connection and look pleased. They go on to ask how I, an unauthorised youth, have managed to get to within moments of boarding a transitship. I spin a story that involves my construct working overtime to overcome the low-level security systems we've breached. I think they believe me. They want to know why I tried to get on a flight, and I tell them the truth. I need to get home and find out what happened to Father. Next, they ask about my ancient papers. I tell the truth about them too, having nothing to hide.

Now, once again, questions turn back to matters of a personal nature. They ask me for the names of my partners. There was, in reality, only that one human. Sex-skins – basically, suited-up constructs – don't count as experience.

'Who are you in love with?' GRENDEL asks.

'I love my father and my mother.' I'm exaggerating about Mother. I've hardly seen her in years, and I can't say I miss her any more than a person might miss a sponsor. 'I'm "in love" with nobody. I don't believe that kind of emotion exists outside old-world romance crystals.' Sex is a biological necessity and required for mental stability. When it was hard to get or to filter out, humans tied it all up with silly customs and false, nonsensical feelings.

The prefects want more details, and I'm about to tell them to mind their own business, when a powerful realisation hits out of nowhere. Or perhaps it springs from the projections I witnessed about Father's kidnap.

'You're not genuine prefects, are you?'

They hesitate for too long.

'You're impersonating prefects.'

I have them! By the time they try and justify themselves and flash warrants and verifications into the air, I'm in another place, at least in my mind. I need a blocker, but AMALTHEA's medication has finally run out. My mind is a turmoil and I can't think, or hear what the prefects are saying. It's as if my head is guest to more than my own thoughts.

It's now that the door disintegrates and Death comes in like a whirlwind.

***

Two more prefects, both human women, step through the shimmering heat haze where the door used to be. My interrogators cease to be. The graph-prefect winks out, disrupted by a pulse, and the human dances to his death, a rictus of living lightning surging and sparking through his limbs. He falls and the smoke piping from his corpse has the aroma of barbecued soy-meat. A plazgun is turned on me. This is it then. I squeeze my eyes shut and wait for the agony.

'Come with us.' I open my eyes and the shorter of the two prefects has me fixed with a manic stare. She holsters her plazgun. 'Now!'

The taller woman gives me a shove towards the doorway.

They jostle me out and place a power-seal over my cell. It flashes a warning not to enter. We're in a corridor leading to a monitoring hall populated entirely by prefects, mostly human but some graph. One notices us and rushes up, but is brought to a halt when my captors flash warrants into the air. I conclude my present escort are not real prefects, but that I'd been wrong about my interrogators. This is a real Peace Office, no doubt about it. It follows that the prefects here are true peace officers, all except the two leading me to who-knows-where. I consider making a break, but I can't outrun a plazbolt.

We descend to ground level and pass over a series of security bars. Not one of them activates or registers any suspicion. And then we're out onto the causeways of Campo Grande. I know the city well enough and it's frustrating that the Mato Grosso Spaceport is so close. AMALTHEA and I had so nearly made it. External climate control is set to several degrees warmer than inside. In other words, still a little chilly for my liking.

The prefects slow to a halt in the centre of Peace Office Concourse. People congregate in the shade of plinth-palms and some sit on the edge of the water fountain. All seem to be looking at me. 'What on Earth has a Venusian youth done to attract such close attention from the prefects?' they may be thinking. Or perhaps, 'Oh dear, those film-gowns are inappropriate attire for public places'. Visit Venus then, and have a heart attack.

But the people aren't looking at me at all. No, the strange behaviour of my escorts is the centre of their collective attention. The two prefects stand as if unaware, or surprised by their surroundings, like mons slope-sloths suddenly dropped into the middle of a grassy, treeless savannah. They've certainly lost all interest in me. The shorter one draws her plazgun and examines it. Then, her indrawn breath so audible it's more a cry of anguish, she throws it to the ground and looks back in the direction of her murderous crime. The other one whispers, 'What have we done?' Of one fact

I'm absolutely sure. It's the perfect time to make a move towards escape.

Before I put that thought to action, someone grabs me. A Martian youth slips her arm through mine, her momentum carrying us both along and away from the dithering prefects. I recognise her from the Spaceport. She's the one who reminded me of my friend Verone, and who'd been paying me a lot of attention before the prefects took me.

'Keep going,' she whispers. 'Introductions later. Right now we have to get out of here.' She's as slim as me, which is not what I expect of a Martian. Slightly shorter she has long hair, like Father's, and wears a Martian engineer's formsuit with a Saint John's pendant on a choker chain. No matter where they are, Martians will not give up their nanosuits nor will they concede, in any respect, to local fashion or customs, personal comfort notwithstanding.

Still shocked at witnessing death from so close, it makes sense to give her the benefit of my doubt. That is, until she bundles me into a relief-station. 'I can't do anything about your lack of eyebrows, but we can get rid of this,' she says, and starts grabbing at my clothes. She tries to lift my gown over my head.

What the Hell? I push her away.

'No time to be shy. You need to get that off. A Venusian film-gown makes you stick out a mile.' Her eyes drop to my middle and she blushes. It's her imagination, for I'm still wearing that awful, restricting underwear. 'You know what I mean.' She flips me a formsuit disc.

The stalls are all empty and we're the only ones in the station, so I lift the gown off over my head.

'Do you have shoes?' She disposes of my gown down a waste pan.

'Now, let me see.' I make a play of searching between the cheeks of my bottom. 'Sure I had a pair somewhere.'

'Callywit!' Many Martian epithets show the Martian dislike of Callistonians. 'Hurry up, and activate the disc.'

The disc is small, but heavy with its load of base material and nanobots. I tap the underside three times to activate the adhesive and slap it onto the skin over my sternum. 'How many taps for suit activation?'

'Three short, two long. There's no choice of style.' With a disc only two centimetres across and one thick, she doesn't have to tell me that. It's obvious.

'Did you say "style"? I didn't think Martians had any?'

'Said the boy who spends most of his life in the nude.'

Touché! But I'm not letting her get away with that. 'That's what I call style.'

'That's what I call exhibitionism.'

I tap the disc and within moments the nanotex is spreading out over my body. It's the nicest feature of wearing heavy clothing: activation and deactivation really tickles. The cover includes socks. I walk a few steps; the material responds and thickens under the soles of my feet, although I really don't need the extra protection. My soles are naturally leather-like, having gone barefooted most of my life.

'You'll do. Now, best we pretend to be a couple. Let's get out of here.' The couple idea is good, especially as we're now Martian a la mode, although I'm surprised it sprang so readily from a Martian's mind.

'If we're going to be a couple, I should at least know your name.'

She introduces herself as Dorsa Sagan, a good old Martian name if ever I heard one. I begin to introduce myself, but she knows who I am. Other questions must wait until we're safe.

Something's wrong with the people on the causeways. None of the youths are accompanied by constructs. In fact, there's no sign of construct activity or interaction at all. A man close by slaps the front of his mantle: dishing out physical violence to malfunctioning tech is a solution immemorial. Others look to the sky or break their strides, bemused. A young boy holds both hands to head and wails a lament of loss.

There's a ridiculous explanation for all this, but paradoxically, it's the only one that makes sense. 'I think the grid's failed.' The grid hasn't failed, anywhere on the Three Worlds, in living memory. There're so many failsafes and backups, the very concept is ludicrous.

'You're right! Our chance of escape just shot up through the dome.'

There's a distant hum that thrills through my body. It comes from the direction of the spaceport. An orange and white transitship switches from atmospheric to escape-velocity engines and surges to three-gee acceleration.

'Ships are still taking off,' I say. 'The outage must be local or they'd be grounded.'

'Escape now. Analysis later.'

We each grab a bike from the line without having to engage with the grid: another anomaly, because an outage should lock down all public facilities. Dorsa pedals like a racer and I follow.

'Where're we going?'

Dorsa calls over her shoulder. 'If we can get a bike, maybe we can get a pod.' She means a 'carriage'. Martians have strange terms for everything. For them, a mantle is a 'tab'; they say 'dome' when they mean 'sky' even though Mars has had a real sky for half a millennium, and perhaps one of my favourites: they call a transitship an 'upper-downer'.

We duck through a park. I'm glad of the shade and take the opportunity to slow down. Earth grav is sufficiently above Venus's that it tells on me during heavy exercise. Martians on the other hand, whose grav is much less than either Earth's or Venus's, spend all their lives in weighted clothing. They overcompensate, and it looks like Dorsa can keep up the pace for hours. At least the park is a short cut to the Carriage Hub, and people are too worried about their disconnections to chide us for riding in a walk-only zone.

As hoped for, if not expected, we get a two-seat carriage without grid-interrogation.

'Where to?' Dorsa fastens her safety restraints.

'What do you mean? Don't you have a plan?'

'My plan was to help you escape. I've only been on Earth for a week, so I'm not all that familiar with it. Any ideas?'

I do, in fact, have one idea I think might work. I give the carriage AI instructions. 'Porto Velho, maximum velocity.' We shoot off in the direction of a facility run by Bart Coumans when he's not giving lectures at Unicamp. It stands about one and a half thousand klicks to the north-west on the border of the Amazon Jungle Protected Zone. All being well, we'll be there in three hours.

'Comfortable?' I ask.

'Quite.'

'Good. Then perhaps you can tell me exactly what's going on.'

Dorsa takes her time. She looks out at the passing scenery through the double skin of carriage port and transparent vac-tube. She plays with her fingers. She takes a deep breath and sighs. She is, in short, becoming emotional.

'To strip it down to the microcircuits,' she begins, 'my father's been abducted, and it's as if he'd never been born.'

***

Our carriage passes to the east of Cuiabá along a bypass tube. It's not the distant city that holds my attention, but a battery of agriculture-skins working the fields. They look like antique tractors. I need a distraction from recent events and I'm fed up trying to make sense of everything Dorsa's told me. Her story's so similar to mine. The slow, methodical skins give me something else to think about. Almost hypnotic.

In my late twenties (vears, not years) I was responsible for a small set of juveniles. There were five of them, all little kids of about ten vears of age, and one of my lectures was about skins.

Sav stood out. He was bright and the only boy with a mop of dark hair. He understood the principle of skins, or more precisely, the differences between constructs and graphs, but faltered at the practical level. 'Really? Really really? Constructs *and* graphs can be inside a skin making it work?'

'Yes, Sav. That's exactly correct.'

'How can you tell when it's a construct working a skin, or a graph?'

'If it's a construct, it's working for a human. But if it's a graph, he or she is working voluntarily.' Trite, and I should never have believed such an answer would satisfy Sav. 'You do know the difference between a construct and a graph, don't you?'

Sav rattled off the grid-stream answer. 'A construct is an AI that has no self-determination and requires a power source. A graph is a living being that lives in Quantum. Both use holotech to interface with humans, and skins to interact with the macro universe.' He smiled proudly and showed the gaps where his adult teeth were yet to arrive. 'I understand that, but how can you tell, just by looking?'

'Well, you can't really. A skin is only a machine. A construct can be downloaded into one to provide the operating impetus. A graph can insinuate itself into a skin's intel-matrix and operate it in the same way. However, there is a convention that a graph in a skin must inform any humans they encounter that the skin is graph-controlled. Usually a wave or a nod will suffice.'

Sav beamed again. 'So if a skin waves at me there's a graph inside, and if it just gets along with its job, a construct is operating it.'

'Exactly! Well done, Sav.'

He went on to ask me how many different types of skins there were, and I put the question to the set.

'Game-skins!' the whole set called in unison.

'Medical-skins!' Frolana yelled.

'Mechanics!!' from Chron.

'Multi-functional skins!'

'Farmer-skins, farmer skins!' Jase jumped up and down until he caught my eye.

'Domestics!'

Sav wore a smirk, and I knew exactly what he had on his mind. I willed him not to voice his thought. My will was insufficient. 'Sex-skins,' he said and became the instant hero of the set, which coalesced into a single entity of laughs and giggles.

'Sav Kinngas, thank you for you valuable contribution to the set.'

The juveniles merely laughed harder, and I found it difficult not to join in. It was time to change to a subject more suitable to juveniles.

Dorsa gently elbows my ribs. 'You seem totally absorbed in that fleet of aggy-skins.' The Mato Grosso countryside speeds by, and the skins quickly recede into the distance.

On Mars, Dorsa supervises several hundred 'aggy-skins': Martians and their terminology. She returned to the family dome one evening after work and her father had gone without a trace. Her mother had died in the meteorite shower disaster of 3028, so at least she was spared the denial of her father's existence by the remaining parent. But the house-construct claimed to have no knowledge of him. Martian prefects filed her report of a missing person and took it seriously for ten minutes, then she experience the same routine as had I. She was met with official denial of his existence; friends and relatives were vague about him, as if they'd had memory-washes. There weren't any mentions of him in official documents, and nothing on the grid.

Then she asked her graph friend and colleague to work on it. IDEW was also unconvinced that Dorsa's father had ever existed, but he was a loyal friend and set to work. He dipped into Quantum where graphs can access all the non-restricted information of human affairs, but found no trace three-worlds-wide and nothing from the major colonial territories on Moon, Europa, Titan, Callisto or Ceres. What he did find was my desperate plea, launched into the grid when all else had failed: 'Has anybody seen my father?' IDEW came up with a facial-image of me and had circumvented securities to discover my location. Dorsa left IDEW in charge of the farm and set off as soon as she could, experiencing her own local grid-outs which helped her on her way. The fact that she managed to hitch a ride from Mars to Earth speaks volumes of her resourcefulness.

I dwell for a moment on our recent lucky breaks. 'The grid-outs have worked in our favour. That really can't be a coincidence.'

'My thoughts exactly. But how long will it last?'

'We'll know when we die.'

AMALTHEA had been very clear that there were powers out to get me: 'You are in great danger. Your very existence is threatened. But I cannot say why.' She reported on unusual phenomena in Quantum where pathways were blocked, areas of knowledge sealed off, and former routes of communication no longer viable. 'There are humans at work here, but there are also graphs. None but graphs could influence Quantum in this manner.'

It sounds like a cross-species conspiracy, but now I have time to apply some thought, I know it certainly isn't official. If prefects – genuine prefects – apply to their county shepherd and have their request warranted, we'll be flagged through the grid, and our location anywhere on the Three Worlds or its colonies will be detected in minutes. Arrest will follow within hours. That we're still free is testament to a nefarious and hidden organisation.

'You really think someone will actually murder us?' Dorsa received no such warnings from IDEW.

'Whatever's going on, it's big. Far bigger than us. If we're in the way ...' I let the obvious conclusion hang in the air.

'Why us? What is it about me, you and our fathers that could possibly matter so much?'

Once we know the answer to that, we'll be a long way along the causeway to solving the mystery. But I haven't slept properly in days, and without functioning augmentations, I desperately need rest.

'Sleep sounds good to me,' Dorsa agrees. 'I could sleep for a week, but we'll have to make do with the hour we've got before arrival at Porto Velho.'

I manage twenty minutes. I'm wide awake now, but Dorsa still sleeps. Keeping the sound turned low, I activate on-board news and entertainment. It transpires that while Dorsa and I have been seeking our fathers, we've missed the most momentous event of our generation.

The Endeavour, first human-crewed ship to Albion has launched, at close to the time when the rogue prefects attacked and killed my interrogators, and the channels broadcast little else. There are interviews with the command-collective, engineers and scientists; sequences showing Albion as it is now, beautiful and ready for the next chapter in the human adventure; views of Endeavour as she slips away from the hub orbiting Earth, and an angle as she fires up her engines. She quickly recedes to a point of light as she begins her 300 day acceleration at one-gee.

Once the Endeavour reaches point eight-five light speed, they'll cut acceleration. The crew will spend nearly six years on the Coriolis decks and then back to the gee-decks for 300 days of deceleration, a new planet and a new pair of stars waiting for them. For more than a century, graph-controlled ships have been preparing the way and making Albion fit for the first human colonisers, and all will be ready in time for their arrival.

They're showing old projections of the first graph-ship launch too, when Albion had been called Proxima-B. I'd forgotten, if I'd ever known, the planet's name morphed from its thousand-year-old designation through Proxima-Albion to the name we all know it by throughout the worlds.

I feel cheated. I've missed the event we've all grown up anticipating. There's a heart-wrenching feeling of loneliness and loss, which inevitably makes me think of Father and home.

I bring up a view of Venus from space. It's a scene of blue oceans, fluffy white clouds and green landmasses. Now I regress the image to its pre-terraformed appearance of melting temperatures kept in check by immense pressure; fiery, boiling and dead. I wonder if there were youths like me several hundred years ago who watched projections of the first colonist fleet to Venus. Were they equally imbued with a sense of hope and adventure? Had they marvelled when we discovered there'd once been life on Venus, as my generation had when traces of former life were found on Albion?

I switch back to present day Venus and zoom to my mountain-top home in the Dzalarhons range. Our home was constructed within the shell of one of the thousands of mass-drivers that had encircled Venus at the equator. They'd worked at full capacity for a hundred and sixty years to increase the planet's rotational spin, giving it a proper day and night. Nothing goes to waste on Venus, and I'm proud that my home had once housed a machine that played such an important part in our history.

I swipe off the projection and look through the carriage port. The scenery passes by and I let my thoughts drift in space with the Endeavour, and hold on to the feelings of loss, for they're less painful than my personal loss. It's a sorrow made so much worse because nobody acknowledges it. Jonan Dzalarhons has never existed, so how can I miss him? 'The poor youth is in need of treatment.'

For the first time it occurs to me. What if they're right? One cannot assess a situation unless all options are considered. What if I really do need treatment to relieve me of a delusional notion? I've only my mind to make the assessment, but if my mind is at fault, what then? There has to be an empirical solution.

Of course, there is one. If I were no more than a youth suffering from a form of mental illness, nobody would be out to kill me, and Dorsa wouldn't be sitting opposite me, victim to the same conspiracy. I need to touch her, to make sure she's real.

'Hey ... what?' Dorsa wakes and slaps my hand away. 'What weird Venusian fade-wittery are you at, young 'en?'

'I was ... Hey, we're the same age. Don't "young 'en" me!'

'Don't change the subject. Why were you groping me?'

'I wasn't "groping", I was trying to wake you up. And it seems to have worked.'

Dorsa stretches out the sleep and pulls herself together. 'Oh, right. But why? I could've had another twenty minutes doze.'

I'm not going to tell her I was checking to see if she's really there. 'Do you realise we missed the launch of the Endeavour?'

She calls me a name which is rude on all three worlds and asks me why that riveting piece of information couldn't wait.

Martians don't much like anyone who isn't from Mars. They see themselves as eminently practical, which of course they are. But they have no time for the artistic ways of Venusians or the superior airs of Earthers. It's true some Earthers come over as a little arrogant, and think of the other worlds as no more than off-shoots of 'Home World', but we Venusians don't spend our whole lives arranging flowers in tentacle-swirl glass vases. If you ask me, Martians are intolerant knuckle-draggers, but that's my opinion immediately after I've been insulted by one.

'I'm sorry about all that,' Dorsa says after a few moments. 'I'm a crank when I first wake up.'

Then again, some Martians aren't too bad.

She tries to reference the time internally, but like me, she's without her construct. The on-board systems provide an answer for her. 'Fifteen minutes to arrival. What do we do when we get there?'

'Find a connection to the local ground-hub. Commission a crawler. At full velocity we should reach the bio-sciences facility within another hour.'

'I suppose we could hope for more grid-outages.'

'So long as there isn't a shepherd's warrant out for us, it should all be achievable.'

Dorsa's either losing her confidence or playing Devil's advocate. 'Two youths without an assignment or a grid-connection? There're bound to be question.'

'They can question all they like. If we aren't breaking any laws, what can they do?'

'Legally, nothing. But who's talking "legal" after what we've been through?'

All we can really do is keep our heads down and hope for the best.

To fill a space, we talk a little of our past lives. I mention how much she resembles my friend Dr Verone Kell. 'She's in space medicine. Psychology or something similar.'

'Why am I not surprised you have a friend who's a psychologist? Did she get plenty of practice with you?'

'Ha-ha!' Dorsa has a point. I wish Verone was here now, if only to certify me sane. It would help a lot to have a professional at hand.

The carriage is decelerating on the outskirts of the city, and now our chances take a dive. The on-board interface fires up spontaneously and a face is being projected into the middle of the cab. It's a face I recognise. My stomach tightens. We have nowhere to run.

'You will soon arrive at Central Hub, Porto Velho,' GRENDEL says. 'On arrival, please surrender to the waiting prefects. They are authorised to use such force as is necessary to ensure compliance.'

'But we haven't done anything wrong? We've broken no laws. What are your grounds?'

***

While I talk, Dorsa takes action. Her boot-heel shoots through GRENDEL's image and smashes the projection panel beyond. GRENDEL winks out and the carriage's AI audio gently informs us that our actions may lead to loss of privileges.

'Well, there's a crime for them to chuck at us, Dorsa. Nice work!'

'Emergency override!' she shouts, and then drops to a whisper. 'We need to get out of here.'

Audio tells us there's no emergency, and override is not appropriate.

'Do you have any tools with you, Dorsa?' She's Martian. It's a rhetorical question. 'Something to make heat?'

'Of course.'

'Then get it out.' While Dorsa takes a micro-solder from her sleeve-pouch, I whack my sternum three times, causing the formsuit nanobots to retract the nanotex material. The nanobots undress me at lightning speed, but before the material has fully withdrawn into the disc, I whip off my underpants and throw them at Dorsa. 'Set light to these, now!' Nanotex won't burn, so it's either my undies or a hank of Dorsa's hair. I tap the disc and I'm re-clothed in moments. Poor nanobots probably don't know whether they' coming or going.

Dorsa sends some sparks in to the garment. 'Very clever, Venus-boy. Very clever. Even if it does take me a month to recover from the shock.' The underpants are never going to burst into flames, but then all we need is a little smoke. 'Don't ever get naked again without warning me.'

'Back at the spaceport you couldn't get my gown off quick enough.'

'I kept my eyes closed,' she lies.

The end of Dorsa's soldering tool glows orange-hot and the pants start to smoulder.

'Fire detected,' comes the ever so smooth voice of the AI. 'Emergency diversion to next side spur. Oxygen levels reduced for fire retardant purposes. Hold tight.'

The carriage kicks up speed and throws us around as it takes a curved tube off the main route. The top priority of any AI is to preserve human life. It's a feature that cannot be overridden, not even by a shepherd's warrant.

The carriage decelerates at a rate that subjects us to at least a couple of gee, and comes to a halt. Our restraints unclip automatically and the door opens onto a small, deserted platform.

'Leave immediately. You are advised to seek medical scanning. This carriage is out of service.' The door closes and the cab floods itself with fire-retardant gas. It then scoots off to get decontaminated, or whatever the process is.

Dorsa and I don't wait to find out. We fly down the stairs to causeway level as if we're descending a ski slope. We find ourselves in a quiet and deserted suburb. Emergency evac-station or not, there's a line, so we take a bike each. The problem is, which way to go. Neither of us know the city at all, and without access to our constructs we're blind to any grid info.

The faint sound of a siren barely edges into audible range.

'A prefect's response vehicle, exactly when we don't need one.' Dorsa begins to look as if Earth gravity is beginning to tell on her, and the siren gets louder. 'It's getting nearer.'

My pulse quickens and panic probes my mind for a way in. 'They coach us in case of disconnections. And for augmentation failures. Right now I'm having trouble recalling any of those lessons at all.'

'Don't let me down, Venus-boy. Where's your famous Venusian sang-froid?'

I try to think, but rather than a solution it's Professor Coumans who comes to mind. A kind of solution after all, because his no-tech status jogs my memory.

'Got it! By law, every facility has to cater for no-techs, right? So there must be a manual grid-access panel around here somewhere.' I search up and down the handlebars and under the saddle.

'Here! Right between the handlebars.' Dorsa activates the grid by pressing a little red stud. It's like being back in the stone-age. A standard AI voice asks for instructions, which I duly supply, and then we pedal hard following directions to the nearest crawler hub. I specify a route that keeps to side roads and minor access alleys to avoid the PRV, the siren of which draws ever closer.

We pass through a residential strand formed of compact dwellings with integral cooling towers and small windows set in well-watered gardens, each plot a little oasis of greenery and lush-leafed life. The dwellings are so unobtrusive it's like cycling through a botanical reserve. A juvenile plays with her construct in the garden. She catches sight of us and waves. As we pass I hear her ask 'Is he a Venusian boy?' Martian clothes obviously do not trump a hairless head and lack of eyebrows.

'There's a bead on the back of your collar,' Dorsa says. 'Tap it twice and your formsuit will grow a hood.'

Why hadn't she thought of telling me this earlier? I feel for the bead, tap it and the nanobots complete the hood within ten seconds. It serves to cover my all too noticeable Venusian traits and muffles the sound of the PRV siren as the prefect-crawler shoots past the end of the lane at high speed. Time to put on some speed of our own. We pedal as fast as we can.

After fifteen minutes I'm beginning to flag. I ask the AI if it can augment my efforts with a little power, but the bike is without any form of motor. 'This bicycle has been designed to improve the rider's level of fitness,' it tells me in a voice that my imagination turns into smug and smarmy.

We merge with the main bike causeway and mingle with other cyclists, which to my great relief means slowing down a lot. A double line of trees flank the causeway, their canopies combining to give us an avenue of uninterrupted shade from the late afternoon sun. A sign up ahead indicates the slip to a crawler hub.

'There's some sort of commotion at the end of the slip.' Dorsa leads and has a better view than I. She swears in Martian patwah. 'Prefects! It's a roadblock.'

I panic, swerve off the causeway, narrowly avoid a tree trunk and run into some shrubbery. The front wheel hits something and I do a somersault over a low hedge and into a garden. I steady myself in time to see Dorsa peer at me over the hedge.

'Did you do that on purpose?'

I doubt she saw the accident. I could lie. 'Not exactly.' My knees, elbows and bottom tickle from the nanobots' efforts to remove damp soil and grass stains from my suit.

We abandon the bikes and find our way to the residential causeways, free from any unpleasant encounters with the people whose space we've invaded. The plan is to make for the hub on foot in the hope that it'll be easier to avoid the prefects. Land hubs (vactube or crawler) are subject only to public safety surveillance, and so long as there isn't a shepherd's warrant on our heads, we can enter the facility without fear of capture.

The terminal is a bright, single-story building of white plasticrete and glass with a living roof. It's flanked by trees and adorned with vines and creepers. There're several clumps of Philodendrons. They're the ones Bart favours, I think. He calls them spiritus-sancti, and we have printed versions at home on our island. The dispersal hall is cool and pleasant for Earthers, which is to say too hot for Martians and rather chilly for me.

The hall is crowded and it takes a few minutes to register our request for a crawler. I keep my eyes on the overhead display for our number to come up. I try to remain calm and feign a keen interest in the lobby's artworks. Dorsa keeps touching her tool pouch, fiddling with her pocket-flaps and looking at the display every two seconds. I wonder if she's as nervous as she looks.

'There!' Dorsa's spotted our instructions flashing. 'A two-seater at Ramp 2-Alpha. Come on!'

'There'll be no need for that.' A man in a bottle-green formsuit sidles up to us. The suit is some kind of uniform. Two other men in identical clothing converge on us. Beyond, by the main entrance, a team of prefects notice us.

'It's them or us,' the man says. 'And believe me, "us" is the sensible choice.' He points to the Amazon Jungle Protected Zone logo above his breast pocket. 'Professor Coumans sent us.'

'He's at the facility? I thought he was back at Unicamp.'

'Nope, he arrived here yesterday.'

The prefects make a rapid move in our direction. The AJPZ wardens make an equally rapid movement in the opposite direction and we follow. We're now the centre of attention as people scramble to get out of our way. The prefects shout a warning, and I imagine a plazbolt flying to the base of my skull.

We're nearly out of the building as the doors begin to close on us, but we're through and the wardens have a freight-crawler waiting outside. We squeeze in, shut the doors and speed off in time to see the confused prefects emerge from the terminal. There's no indication they've seen which vehicle we're in.

Dazed, and with a headful of question, yes, but for the first time since I lost Jonan, I'm more than a little optimistic. There's nobody on Earth I trust more than Bart Coumans.

***

The crawler was made for cargo, so the cab's very cramped for the three wardens, Dorsa and me. You can't miss the fact that the machine is equipped for humans to operate. There's a wheel at the front for directional control, and a foot-level lever, I assume for adjusting speed. I've never seen a human-operated crawler before. I hope it has construct safety overrides. For now, at least, a construct is driving.

We pass through a village full of smiling, happy people who are decorating the trees, buildings and other structures with yellow and black bunting. There're holo-displays, and there on the village square the ubiquitous statue of Shona Eastbrook, a yellow scarf of antique fabric around her neck, and yellow and black streamers tied to her bronze wrists.

'I'd completely forgotten it was nearly Bumblebee Day,' I say. 'It's tomorrow, isn't it?'

'The day after,' replies a warden.

We pass close to the statue, and although the lettering on the stone plinth is worn almost smooth by the passage of several hundred years, you can still read it.

SHONA EASTBROOK

HUMANITY'S MARTYR
SAVIOUR OF MANKIND

A thrill of pride passes through me, and I recall there's a crystal with a record of Philip Fryer's work. Philip Fryer: the trusted friend and companion of the great Shona Eastbrook, and my direct ancestor. And now, hot on the heels of pride, despair at the recollection that the info-crystal containing all my research on Philip, and my ancient papers are still at the Peace Station in Campo Grande. If I can get back onto the grid, I'll be able to retrieve everything recorded on the crystal, but the actual physical papers are unique, and completely irreplaceable.

In two days it'll be Othman 15th, 3031. Othman was called 'Octoba' in the ancient times that Shona Eastbrook knew. All over the Three Worlds and the Colonies we'll celebrate Bumblebee Day at the same time and, in this one event, be guided by Earth's annual turn around the Sun. Where, in all of space, will Jonan Dzalarhons celebrate? I can't accept the day will pass without Father, somewhere, thinking of home and me.

We go through other villages and the story's the same. Preparation, anticipation and joy at the approach of the one event that's celebrated throughout the Solar System. I wonder if Bumblebee Day will be the cause of as much joy on Albion, once it's been fully colonised. It's only fitting that Shona Eastbrook's sacrifice and her life should be humanity's beacon, throughout the human galaxy.

'You okay, Ariel?' Dorsa calls me by my name. Ariel, and not Venus-boy. 'You look a million miles away.'

'I was thinking about Professor Coumans.' It isn't a million miles away from the truth. 'He's famous at Unicamp for making food on Bumblebee Day.'

'With a printer?'

I roll my eyes. 'Anybody can do that. No, I mean he would source food where it grew in the soil. He'd harvest it and subject it to all kinds of manual no-tech processes until it was a delicious meal. You wouldn't believe how good that stuff is.' I smile at the recollection, and my mouth begins to water. Bart taught me to peel a mango once, a process I found surprisingly easy.

One of the wardens moves his seat to the operator's position at the front. 'We'll be crossing into the De-tech Zone in a minute, and we go manual control. Better get strapped in.' He takes hold of the wheel and positions his foot over the lever. A totally bizarre set of actions now follow. He turns the wheel to adjust the vector and presses the lever, which all looks like something from a history crystal. It's hard not to laugh, but that would be rude.

No tech of any kind is allowed in the Protected Zone, and forming a ten-klick thick border all around the AJPZ is the De-tech Zone where only simple tech is allowed. Constructs can only be accessed via monitors or mantle-projected interfaces. Direct mind links have to be disconnected and machinery operated manually. At least Dorsa and I will be on a par with everyone else.

The wardens are not very good conversationalists. They also shy away from our questions. They claim not to know anything about us, or what's going on. 'We're carrying out our brief from the Prof. He'll no doubt get you up to speed and answer all your questions as soon as we get to the facility. Not far now.'

But there is one piece of information they impart which is good to hear. Prefects have no jurisdiction inside the AJPZ or the DTZ.

The facility isn't a single building but more like a small campus made up of units which are organic in style, full of curves and natural hues, made to blend with the integral trees and formal gardens. The main concourse is the crossroads of several causeways and features banks of dancing waterspouts. They're calming, cooling and cosset the mind. There's a small troop of howler monkeys in the canopies. I wonder if they're natural or printed. Many species have been brought back from extinction through the use of bioprinting tech. We have howlers on Venus, all printed, of course. Ours have green-tinged fur, similar to slope-sloths.

The monkeys howl a greeting which makes Dorsa and me smile. The wardens appear not to notice. It's true you can get so used to sounds that they exist on the edge of perception. I'm not sure I'll ever hear those monkeys as ambient background. Such small creatures; such a loud song.

The reception area's a compromise between tech and no-tech. People wear mantles but there're no projectors in the walls. Furniture is solid and designed to look good without holographic enhancement. There are pieces of art on the walls and freestanding pieces that you can touch and move about. You have to bear in mind the pieces aren't projections because it would hurt if you tried to walk through them.

I haven't had time to take it all in before Bart greets us. His wrinkled gnomish face looks all the more gnome-like for his wide smile.

'My dear friend, how are you?' He embraces me, but being Bart, he imbues the simple hug with so much welcome. 'You look tired.'

'I've been better, Bart.' I introduce Dorsa and Bart's greeting is a lot more formal. You don't hug a Martian.

Despite Bart's genuine pleasure at seeing us, it's all a little rushed. Dorsa and I are assigned suites and we agree we should eat and rest a little before a full debriefing session.

'You're completely safe within my humble domain,' Bart assures us. 'Prefects have no authority here and I'm on friendly terms with the area shepherd. As for grid-tech, anything within the DMZ is zone-fenced. Our tech can see out, but general grid tech can't see in.'

I wonder about graphs though, so I ask.

'You know as well as I do, Ariel. Graphs are integral with and in all parts of the entire Universe, but though they're everywhere, they might as well be nowhere if the interfaces aren't in place. They can neither observe nor physically interact with our plane of existence without them.'

It is indeed something I know, but I need the reassurance.

My suite is all I could hope for, and more. There's a meal of fruit, salads and cheeses waiting, and laid out on the bed is a Venusian film-gown of the latest style. It has built-in projector lenses which abrogate the need to wear a mantle. The formsuit disc makes a hefty clunk when I drop in on a shelf, happy to be out of the restricting thing. I eat a little, then put the gown aside and take its place on the bed. Sleep comes instantly. And now, a strangely lucid dream.

***

'John's teeth, my eyes!' Dorsa makes a show of looking away from me as we walk along the corridor. 'What *are* you wearing?'

It's another rhetorical question. I bunch the gown in both hands below my hip and start to lift it. 'I can always take it off if you prefer.'

'No, no, no! Just … don't!'

'In that case, I'm glad you like my attire. I find your heavy duty Martian formsuit equally alluring.'

We've both had a night's rest. At 0800 we'd received a wake-up call and were provided with an appointment time: Bart's office at 1000. The corridor leading to our destination is lined with living, botanical art in the same style as at his office back at Unicamp.

'Good night's sleep, Ariel?' Dorsa asks.

'Apart from the dreams, yes thanks.'

Dorsa comes to a halt. 'You had dreams too?'

We'd had the same dream. Except in the fine detail, they'd been identical. This is another mystery that needs to feature in our debriefing session.

'Happy Bumblebee!' Bart stands aside and welcomes us to his rooms. The office is small and airy, with a balcony overlooking the garden. It looks like a small part of the rainforest, and jungle noises seep into the room: birds, monkeys and insects. It reminds me of home.

There's a copy of the famous Saint John the Baptist painting by Caravaggio, the version that became the first major artwork to leave Earth and take up residence on Mars. I wonder if Bart arranged this to put Dorsa at her ease: the jungle for me, the painting for her. Dorsa notices it, and her hand flies to her pendant.

'First things first,' Bart says. 'We need to download a new construct for each of you.'

It's done in moments. Mine projects as a small sphere and asks my preferences for its appearance. It complies at once and becomes a shimmering blue version of me. Dorsa chooses something that looks like an ancient monitor-screen. It floats at her left elbow.

She looks over and gives my construct's projection a disapproving appraisal. 'Wonderful. Now I have two might-as-well-be-naked images to look at.'

'I'm sorry if your filters can't cope. I shan't litigate if you fail to keep your hands off me.'

'Nor will I,' my construct says.

Dorsa blinks from me to my construct and back again. 'I'd rather hug a sludge-tank slime toad.'

The absurdity of our mock-antagonism hits us both at the same time, and the laughter springs up like a geyser.

'Excellent!' Bart adds to the laughter. 'A good sense of humour shields you against most of life's slings and arrows.'

The metaphor describing our situation in terms of medieval weaponry is enough to quell our brief sojourn into levity. Bart briefs us on the limitations of our constructs.

'Of course, they cannot mind-link. They can work without projecting an interface, but you will need to switch them on to learn the result of any grid enquiries.'

Switch them on? I love Bart's old world phrases.

In the absence of graphs there can't be any instant communication between worlds. There's a theory that linked graphs can relay messages instantaneously across unlimited distances, although the furthest it's been tested is between Earth and the graph parties terraforming Albion. Not even the graphs know how it's possible, it simply is, and if an instant link can be formed over the distance of more than four light years, why not between opposite ends of the Universe?

We stand in a loose three-person-three-construct circle. Dorsa and I relate our stories, so very similar.

'There's something else,' I say. 'Last night we both had the same dream. It involved a monstrous creature with pink tentacles, and a male youth who saved us from it. An Earther I think.' It's the same youth I saw in AMALTHEA's projection leading up to Father's kidnapping.

'Definitely an Earther,' Dorsa says. 'An Earther who has Ariel's same aversion to wearing decent clothing. He wore nothing but a few teeth and bones on a cord around his neck, and a thing barely sufficient to cover his ... middle.'

'It's called a loincloth,' Bart says, and then he turns to his howler-monkey styled construct and asks it to call up an image. Joining us in the circle comes the exact image both Dorsa and I had seen in our dream, right down to the details of his necklace.

'Meet Raoul.' Bart introduces us to the image as if it were a living being. 'The flesh and blood Raoul lives about a hundred klicks from where we're standing.'

'An Amazonian?' I'm in awe. If we worship anything at home, it's the Amazonians. Take away our tech, and our lives are very similar.

'He descends from the ancient tribes. Makuna, and others. He is a shaman, one of the youngest there's ever been as far as we can tell. Of course, there's a lot we can never know about the ancients.

'And there is something else. He has memories of having a father, which no other person can recall.'

Bart's last sentence hovers in the air between Dorsa and me.

'The same as us,' I whisper.

'Not exactly like you, Ariel. Remember, I'm no-tech. I have no implants and no neural-stent. In short, there's nothing within me that can compromise my memories, as I suspect has happened to others. I respect and admire Jonan's publications, although none are now traceable on the grid. And I remember discussing your internship with Jonan over a graph-link before you were accepted to Unicamp.'

My shock registers with a deep intake of breath.

'Ariel, Jonan exists, and I vow to help you find out what's happened to him.'

The relief catches me unexpectedly and the emotions overwhelm. With no control over my enhancements, tears trickle down the side of my nose, and I have to use a handkerchief. It doesn't help that Dorsa reaches up and rested a hand on my shoulder.

There's something else. He presses a wall panel which opens to reveal a storage compartment. Inside is my document valise!

'It came to us via special courier. The info-crystals and physical documents are inside.' Bart turns to Dorsa. 'Has Ariel mentioned them? They're the oldest documents I've ever seen up close.'

I open the valise releasing the aroma of aged documents and old libraries. This is the next best thing to having Father back. A distant second, but it gives me a much needed lift.

I'm lifted further by Bart's joyful smile. 'Tomorrow is Bumblebee Day. I suggest we enjoy it to the best of our ability. Put all our concerns aside for the day. Then we launch the quest for Jonan Dzalarhons.'

I hate the idea of putting everything on hold for a whole day. On the other hand, why should I expect everyone to give up Bumblebee Day for me? The day is all about sacrifice, so I ask myself: is it too much to sacrifice twenty-four hours when Bart has just promised to help me find Father?

***

Bart has put in a lot of effort, and Bumblebee Day at The Attenborough Bio-Sciences Facility is a happy affair. We join in with his family and staff, eat honey-cake, play Jump-the-Cliff, sing the seasonal favourites and listen to Bart's performance of *The Ballad of Shona Eastbrook*. It's all very traditional and everything a person could wish for, but I'm outside of it all. Not a minute passes when I don't think of home. I'm convinced Dorsa feels the same. Joy is for other people. We're not entitled to it.

There's a woman in a bottle-green jumpsuit with a shepherd's star at her left breast. I didn't see her enter, but she makes a beeline for Bart. It's a welcome distraction. Her badge is a real, solid object rather than a projection, and I recall hearing that some shepherds' stars are cast in titanium and are hundreds of years old. A seven-pointed star for the Rule of Seven, within a circle for the continuity of life. It shines like the sun reflecting off a still pond, and I want to touch it.

She stands with Bart on the other side of the hall. They speak, occasionally glancing towards Dorsa and me. They don't look happy.

'Should we run?' Dorsa asks in a harsh whisper. 'I think she's here to arrest us.'

'I'm not running from Bart. If we're not safe here, there's nowhere, so we might as well face up to whatever happens next.'

What happens now is that we're invited to join Bart and the shepherd in his rooms. Her name is Yalpa Watanabe, and she's Shepherd of Manaus with responsibility for all of Amazonia – the AJPZ and the DTZ. The head of each native tribe within the region is an ex-officio deputy. She doesn't wait for formal introductions before informing us that she has no warrant for us – yet – but there are strange official rumblings that centre on Dorsa and me.

'I'm hearing rumours from Council which include terms like "public safety", "danger to humanity" and other trigger phrases bound to alarm people.' Shepherd Watanabe runs a hand through her short blonde hair. Something says 'no-tech' to me, which if true puts her somewhere in her forties. 'You might not be safe for long, even here in the DTZ.'

'What about deep within the jungle?' Bart asks.

'Exactly what I was coming to. I think the jungle may give you some breathing space until all the craziness dies down. But paranoia is on an upward slope, and I feel it in my waters, they'll follow you wherever you go, eventually.'

I wonder why Yalpa's on our side and it transpires my guess was accurate. She's no-tech, like Bart. He's been in contact with her about us, and has convinced her that we're at the centre of a conspiracy.

Bart turns to us and I've never seen him look so serious. 'Do you think you can live in the forest, without any tech at all? Ariel? Dorsa?'

It's a ridiculous ask. I doubt I'll last a day. There're animals, and what about sustenance? Shelter? 'If you download us a survival manual, we'll be okay.'

'I'm Martian,' Dorsa says. 'A little old jungle won't be a problem.'

It's good to know Dorsa can lie too.

For the safety of the jungle inhabitants, we have to be med-scanned before they'll let us into the AJPZ, even under these extreme circumstances. Bumblebee Day is all but forgotten. There's a job to do.

Dorsa wishes me luck as they take me into the medical wing. It's a quick procedure. I step out of the body scanner and notice the doctor in conversation with Bart. It's like a replay of the time earlier, when Bart and Shepherd Watanabe eyed us across the hall.

I put my gown back on. 'You don't look happy, Doctor. What have I got?'

'Well, young man. It's more a case of what you haven't got.'

Being called 'young man' is a minor annoyance when being treated like a laboratory specimen. 'Don't keep me in suspense. Doctor? Professor?'

It's Bart who's first to rediscover the art of speech. 'Doctor Hare has run and re-run the scans …'

'And?'

'It appears you have no neural-stent.'

'The term "appears" doesn't apply,' the Doctor says. 'You definitely have no stent, and you've never had one.'

'But that's impossible. I've been using tech and links all my life. Of course I have a stent.'

Bart tries to calm me. 'Has there been a time in the last few weeks when it could have been removed? When you were detained by the prefects, perhaps?'

'You're not listening, Professor,' Doctor Hare says. 'He has never, ever had a stent. There are absolutely no residuals, not even at molecular level. This youth has never been stented.'

There's no more time to argue, because Shepherd Watanabe charges in despite protests from a junior medic.

'I've had notification from one of my deputies. There're two prefect defence team flyers heading this way. They're less than twenty miles from the DTZ.'

'Flyers? Defence teams?' Hare says. 'They haven't been mobilised in decades.'

Bart seizes me by both shoulders. 'Sorry, Ariel. No time to print a survival manual.'

'I haven't cleared prefect incursion into the DTZ,' the Shepherd says. 'I should be able to delay them, but I suspect not for long.' She runs out calling via her construct to muster all available deputies.

'"Now" wouldn't be too soon, Ariel.' Bart ushers me out of the medical wing and breaks into a run. Dorsa and I follow. We get as far as the concourse in front of the main entrance where Shepherd Watanabe blocks our way.

'I've received a Council Mandate. My orders are to detain you.'

***

'Could you see you way to … not seeing us?' Bart says. 'We'll be gone in a few seconds.'

A battle plays across Shepherd Watanabe's face. The loyalty of friendship vies with the demands of duty. It's a battle of moments that plays out over eons, and then she smiles, grim and determined. 'The fact is, a mandate isn't a warrant, and nobody's applied to me for a warrant. Sin-Jins! A mandate isn't even a Council Directive.'

'So you mean, we can go?' Bart's on starters orders.

'Get out of here!'

A high-pitched whine intersperses with throbbing base notes carries from the south.

'Flyers!' Watanabe cries. 'Get moving, now!'

We all run as the sound of flyers grows to a crescendo, but I can't look back. I recall an ancient text. Look back and I'll be turned to a pillar of ash. Plazguns on full power can do that. Ordinarily, plazguns would be the last thing on my mind, but they're in the forefront now because of the incident at the Campo Grande Peace Office. Such weapons are the last resort, the forlorn hope. In my whole life, I haven't heard of them being used, or even drawn from stores. Not anywhere on the Three Worlds. Now all I can think of is the smell of my bolt-blasted interrogator.

The noise becomes palpable and reverberates through my body. It's as if the incinerating heat of a bolt explodes in my spine, where my stent is. Or rather, where my stent should be. The skin at the back of my neck tingles and if I had hair it would stand up on end.

Bart and Dorsa are well ahead of me.

Dorsa yells 'Get that Sin-Jinning frock off and put on some speed.'

I bunch up the gown in one fist freeing my legs and yes, I gain some speed, but it's too late.

The engine sounds change. They slow down and drop tone, and then another sound blasts us from above. 'Stand still!' Deep, hollow and with the echo of a public address system. 'Ariel Dzalarhons. Dorsa Sagan. We are authorised to temporarily relieve you of your freedom.'

'Project your warrants,' Bart shouts up towards the hovering flyer.

'We are authorised by Earth Council Mandate. We are permitted to use physical restraint and incapacitation tech.'

The muzzle-emitter of a heavy plazzer attached to the flyer's nose cone aligns on our position. Straight at my heart, or is that my imagination?

'Put your hands in the air and stand by to –'

That's as far as they get before three bottle-green flyers come to a static hover between us and the prefect machine.

'A shepherd's deputy and two of my people,' Bart says. 'Come on!'

We have no time to waste and can't tarry to see how a mid-air argument over jurisdiction and the finer points of the law unfold. Heads down, we sprint, all our trust in Bart.

The trust falters when he leads us into a little hut of wood and thatch which angles into a mound of grass-covered earth, but only for a moment. As my eyes adjust to the gloom, I see we're in the entrance to an underground vac-tube terminal. It's tiny and there's only room for a handful of people, but the layout is unmistakable.

'Carriage for two, fully equipped.' Bart gives verbal instructions. Archaic, but the only option available to a no-tech. A carriage rises from a rack somewhere in the depths and aligns with the vac-tube doors. He gives destination coordinates and tells us to get in. 'Take a pack each. There's one under each seat. When you reach the far terminal make for the bridge over the ravine and cross into the jungle. And don't worry about the sentinel-skin. It's inactive and serves only as a way-mark.'

We bundle into the carriage.

'Get yourselves deep into the jungle. The AJPZ is protected by multi-world mandates and inviable laws. Even so, I have a feeling they'll find a way to follow you.'

Bart's keen to get the doors shut and send us on our way, but it's ridiculous. We can't dash into the jungle with no more plan than that. They, whoever they really are, won't have to eliminate us. The jungle will do it for them.

'Only for a few days,' Bart says. 'See to your basic needs. The packs will help, and I'll find you.' He fixes us with his eyes. 'I *will* find you.'

There's a commotion at the door. There're raised voices and the unmistakable swish-tang of a plazbolt, the sizzle as it strikes, and a scream.

'Go!' Bart tells us the vac-tube carriage exceeds a flyer's velocity, but not by much. 'When you get to the other end, run for all you're worth.'

The vac-tube and carriage doors seal shut, and we're flung back into our seats as it accelerates.

'By Sin-Jin!' I say, trying to catch my breath and swearing like a Martian. I never swear. Venusians don't have any swear words. I suppose that's why I steal one of Dorsa's. It's hard to experience such high levels of stress without recourse to blockers or modifiers. Coarse language helps, a little.

All my life, I've relied on modifying tech. But without a neural-stent? How in the Three-Worlds is that possible? It's a consideration that adds another level of discomfort.

'Breathe deep, Venus-boy. You're not going all cracked-dome on me, are you?'

'I'll be fine. We've only got a few minutes. Let's get the packs ready.'

The packs are under the seat, just as Bart said. Small and olive green in colour, each has a sharp half-metre long tool in a holder attached to the side. Dorsa thinks they're weapons until I tell her that jungle plants grow quickly and sometimes you need to cut a swathe where old paths have become overgrown. On Venus we have no need to resort to cave-man tech, but I immediately recognised the blades' use.

'Do you think the professor and Shepherd Watanabe will be okay?' Dorsa asks while trying the pack on.

'Who knows? Nothing's as it used to be. Prefects are supposed to keep us safe, yet they're chasing us from midnight to breakfast time waving plazzers all over the place.'

'I know. Sin-Jinning crazy, isn't it?' Dorsa takes the little pendant figure of Saint John between her fingers. Does she have a twinge of guilt for taking his name in vain?

'Do you think he can help us?'

The Martians adopted Saint John around 800 years ago as a kind of heroic icon. He'd been a man in almost prehistoric times who lived in a desert and washed the care from people as he dipped them in a river. In the early Martian years, I imagine they saw something in his life of hardship that resonated with them. Their world was like his, arid and dusty, with water the most precious of commodities. John lived in cave, and early Martians in similar-sized domes. The story goes that John once immersed man who was renewed to the extent that he became a god, but I can't recall his name.

I rather like the fact that I know of the man, but not the god. There are no gods, so they do not deserve to be remembered. And yet, so few humans are remembered either. From ancient times, there is Attenborough, Eastbrook and Hawking, and the pioneers whose names are reflected in the months of the Earth year. There are city designations on Moon, Venus and Mars that recall significant contributors to our ongoing story, and there are a few others, but so few. Will anybody remember me in a thousand years?

'You know, Ariel, I think he *can* help. There's no magic tech in Saint John, but if he can help me think straight, that might be enough.'

In hardly any time we are advised to strap in for deceleration and we slow to a halt. Unusually, the vac-tube door is opaque, so it comes as quite a shock when it snicks open to reveal a man, tall for a human but shorter than me, wearing nothing but a necklace of stone and bone, a twine around his hips and a loin-pouch. He carries a spear and something else of the same general shape.

'You!' Dorsa and I say at exactly the same time. Standing before us in the flesh is the man who helped us in our dreams. What was it Bart had called him? 'Raoul?'

'Yes, I am Raoul. I know you both too. Now, you must follow. Quick fast!' He turns and walks quickly, at that maximum gait before it becomes a run. 'The tentacles are coming for us.'

We grab our packs, follow, and immerge into the fringes of the jungle from a hut identical to the one we'd entered at the other end. There're no other buildings here, only lush grasses and a path towards what looks like a security-skin.

'Do not fear him,' Raoul says, pointing to the abandoned machine. 'He is asleep.'

We have no more than fifty metres to cross before we reach the skin, but we're too late. The distinctive sound of a speeding flyer grows from a faint hiss to an ear-splitting cacophony in the time it takes to move three steps.

The sound dies to a whisper, and the flyer casts its shadow over us. There's a streak of blue light and a holo-projection of GRENDEL forms in front of us.

'Please,' comes his smooth, detached words. He stands in front of us but his voice comes from above. 'You have given us quite the run about. But it is time to surrender to the inevitable. The safety of the Three Worlds and all the colonies depends upon it.' He turns his attention to Raoul. 'You! Run away into the jungle now. Do you comprehend Standard?'

'Of course,' Raoul replies. 'I have a degree from Manaus Uni.'

'Good, then I won't have to repeat … Wait!' Blue tendrils flick from GRENDEL's image, like little tentacles of light which search Raoul's body. 'On second thoughts, you must come with us too.'

'I think I will not do that,' Raoul says. 'And I think I will not let you take my friends, either.'

Raoul ignores GRENDEL's polite protests and concentrates his attention on the flyer.

'What are you doing?' It's the first time I've seen GRENDEL flustered. 'Stop it!'

GRENDEL sparks and flashes, and now his image vanishes while the flyer's engine whines and fusses with intermittent bursts so high-pitched it hurts my ears.

The flyer begins to rotate, and then spin. It yaws and rotates and moves towards the bridge which is guarded by the defunct security-skin. Then without further warning, it pitches nose first and disappears into the ravine below. There comes the sickening sound of metal crashing into rock, and I think I hear a scream, long, plaintive and diving into the throat of death.

'There are other's coming,' Raoul says. 'No time. No time.'

At every turn, the nightmare only gets worse. 'Did you do that?' I ask Raoul.

'Yes.'

I don't ask how. That'll take volumes to answer and I have the distinct impression time is not an infinite commodity right now.

'Did you kill the crew?'

'I hope not, but it is possible. Hear that? No time.'

Another flyer is on its way, but still Raoul doesn't run. We follow past the skin that has to be two hundred years old. I've seen one in a museum. It's partially subsumed in jungle weeds, but the silver and cobalt blue of its two-metre tall body still shine through in places.

'We clean him once a year,' Raoul says. 'He guarded our ancestors from intruders for many years. We are grateful. We call him "Yee", for once upon a time he was fierce.'

The engine sounds grow, and now we run over the bridge. Far below are the twisted remains of GRENDEL's flyer. I try not to think about the fate of the human occupants. Hopefully it had been entirely construct-operated. It's possible that GRENDEL had occupied it, wearing it as a skin.

We reach the far end of the bridge and the jungle swallows us. As soon as we move under the canopy, the humidity and heat soar. We follow Raoul for an hour. The conditions are so like those at home and I have to do something about my personal comfort.

'Sorry, Dorsa,' I say. 'A couple of days ago, you asked for a warning. Well, I'm getting naked.'

***

Martian formsuits can't be beaten in cold climates, but they're severely limited in hot, humid conditions. With an engineer's expertise, Dorsa persuades the nanobots to reabsorb the arms of hers, and shorten the legs to above her knees, but I still don't know how she copes. For me the conditions are exactly like home. When off-path though, some of the vegetation comes to our waists and if there's going to be much more of this, I'll need one of those loin-pouches. Some leaves are tall, tough and scratchy.

We follow Raoul along paths that are barely discernible and across stretches of jungle with no path at all. There're no signs of other people. Animals on the other hand, are abundant. All around us are insects, birds, little scurrying mammals and the signs of larger animals in the undergrowth. I assume most are printed, but some must be descendants of the jungle's original inhabitants.

The air is thick with the scents and aromas of leaf mould, of flowering plants and lush undergrowth, and in this alone the Amazon is different from home. There's a peppery base to the air at home attributable to the eucalyptus hybrids printed especially for Venusian equatorial conditions. They grow everywhere on our island.

Neither Dorsa nor I see anything of the larger creatures and we're only aware of their proximity because Raoul points out their 'spoor'. Here is a tapir's salt-lick; there's the pad mark of a jaguar and up there that green blob is a resting sloth. We take his word for it, and because he never slows his pace we have no time to stop and stare.

After a journey of hours we break through a screen of giant green leaves into the most perfect of glades. It couldn't have been created with more balance or beauty by the most accomplished of artists. It forms a circular, open refuge from the jungle, about 15 metres across. It's walled on one side by a slab of moss-covered rock the upper reaches of which are lost in the canopy. Light from the gaps in the trees above slants down into the shade like a laser-show.

There's a miniature waterfall flowing down the rock face into a crystal clear pool which takes up about a third of the glade's area. Surrounding the pool are myriads of flowering plants, and several flat-topped boulders that nature has scattered for our convenience. I can't wait to sit on one and dangle my feet into the water, or better still, dive right in and swim. It's a nice thought but that's all it will ever be. Raoul looks appalled when I ask if I can jump in. The water is pure, and strictly not for bathing.

'Here,' he says picking up a massive fallen leaf. He fashions it into a crude receptacle, fills it with water from the fall, and douses me with it. The chill makes me gasp, but that's nothing to the response he gets from dousing Dorsa. She uses several swear words I've never heard before. Raoul simply laughs, while the nanobots work overtime to wick the moisture out of her clothes.

It's the perfect place to rest notwithstanding the ban on bathing. Raoul leaves Dorsa and I alone while he goes to forage. He tells us we can drink from the pool. 'But if you want to piss, go out of the glade – there – and find a space in the jungle. This glade must not be defiled.'

'When he comes back, we need to clear a few thing up.'

Dorsa agrees.

'Raoul might be able to throw some light on our situation.'

'Don't get your hopes up, Venus-boy.'

Not again. I shake my head. The whole 'Venus-boy' thing has worn thin as a cobweb. 'The name's Ariel, as if you didn't know.'

I wait for a sour rejoinder but instead she apologises. She then reverts to form and tells me to close my legs or at least 'point yourself in another direction'.

I shift around and sit like the bronze mermaid in Copenhagen. 'I'm sorry if you find my natural state so loathsome. Seriously though, you should try it. It's the only way for the unenhanced human body to cope in these conditions.'

'Loathsome? Could anybody be more callywitted?'

I can't fathom her. Is she typical Martian or simply her own special variety of unreadable?

'Don't you realise, when I first saw you at the spaceport, I thought ... Never mind what I thought.' She clears her throat and blushes. 'Although a hairstyle wouldn't go amiss.'

There's no answer to that, but I become acutely aware that I'm running without filters. I shift my leg a little more and will the tingling of arousal to go away. For the first time I see Dorsa as incredibly desirable, and I wonder if I'd look as good as Father with locks of my own.

'And I can't be doing with *that*.' Ah, she's noticed. 'I can't handle it, not until we've got to the bottom of this mystery.' She becomes atypically diffident and mumbles something about wishing she'd never mentioned it.

'If it makes you deal more easily, I usually align with other males.' Not strictly true, because my sex-skin at home has a satin-grade nanoplastic outer covering which can adopt the appearance of all three genders and a couple of other interesting forms.

'Then I'm sure you and Raoul will be very happy.'

How I wish she hadn't said that. With a lack of filters and her suggestion, I see Raoul in a completely different light now that he's back from the hunt. I wish I hadn't discarded my gown, not that it would have hidden much.

Raoul brings us a feast of foraged fare and we tuck in gratefully. There're sweet flavours, and spicy. The textures vary from creamy to refreshingly juicy. We wash it down with water from the fall and now, with the sun going down, he sets about making us a shelter for the night.

We don't have our first chance to speak until after dark and we lay under a shared bivouac of leaves, branches, moss and twine. We settle to the sounds of night creatures and the waters of the fall cascading into the pool. It would be easy to drift off, but I'm not going another night without some answers, or at least, without posing the never-answered questions.

But there are still no answers. We can find nothing in common with our fathers. They had different careers and origins, just as Raoul, Dorsa and I have nothing in common except the loss of our fathers, a loss that extends into the memories of everyone who used to know them.

We speak softly, blanketed in darkness so absolute that hearing and touch step up in the hierarchy of our senses. When Raoul speaks on my left, his breath touches my face, and the same from Dorsa on my right.

'I think the fact that we share little is important,' Raoul says. 'We should examine our differences. It cannot be chance that there is one of us for each of the three worlds.'

He's on to something, but what? Raoul from Earth, Dorsa from Mars and I from Venus. 'Do you think there're more of us?' I think out loud. 'Someone from Moon, another from Callisto? In fact, one each from all the colonies.'

Dorsa contributes a dose of cold water. 'And if there are, have they all been caught? Maybe even killed?'

'None have been unnaturally killed,' Raoul says. 'But there is one other.'

'Who's the other one?' I ask.

'That, I do not know.'

Dorsa huffs. 'And how exactly do you know anything, stuck in the middle of a jungle with no tech?'

'The spirits of this glade tell me.'

I think what Dorsa now says. 'We live in a world of science, not mumbo-jumbo.'

'This is true, but we have different words that mean science. I believe my spirits are from Quantum, what you call graphs, and I have been able to commune with them since early childhood.'

I sit up and almost demolished our low-slung roof of leaves. Our shelter is made only for sleeping, not sitting up. 'Was it the spirits, or graphs, that led to our shared dreams? Was it graphs who told you to meet us by the vac-tube terminal?'

'No, I made the dreams. I found you and needed you to come here. With the help of the spirits, I watched you and helped you escape.'

The grid-outs were somehow caused by Raoul, a feat that appears too superhuman to be true. Of far more concern, he engineered my escape from the prefects, and so by extension has killed one of my interrogators and temporarily sent GRENDEL to Quantum. If true, Raoul is a dangerous man.

As for his appearance at the terminal, the spirits hadn't sent him to meet us, at least, not specifically. Knowing we were at Bart's facility, he was on his way there to speak to us. In the event circumstances moved faster than Raoul, a happy coincidence for us. Without him, GRENDEL would have had us.

I ask about the spirits, and Raoul tells us that we too may experience them.

'Now?' I'm eager, or impatient.

'Later, when the vibrations are harmonious.'

Dorsa lets out a loud fart. 'Those vibrations harmonious enough?'

Why do we never grow out of our juvenile years where farts are concerned? It takes a few moments before we stop laughing.

Now we spend time listening to the noises of the night. Raoul identifies each sound, tells us about the creature that makes it and what it signifies. A squeal is the death of a small prey mammal. The rasping thrum is the mating call of a species of tiny frog. Not a moment of time passes without the punctuation of jungle voices.

'Okay, now!' Raoul says. 'It is time for you to commune with the spirits, Ariel. Come with me.'

'What about me?'

'You come too, but the spirits wish only to speak with Ariel.'

'No accounting for taste. If the stuck-up dimwits don't want to speak with me, I'll stay here and get some sleep.'

Disapproval for the spirits made clear, Dorsa comes with us anyway. Raoul leads us to the pool, its waters reflecting moonlight. To navigate the shadows, he leads me by the hand, and I hold Dorsa's hand. 'Step lightly,' he says. 'Walk where I walk.'

We sit on the stones close to the waterfall. In the chill of the night, they still radiate some warmth.

'Sit very still and make no sound. Look into the light that dances in the falling water, and listen as it splashes into the pool.'

I follow Raoul's instructions, and there's something hypnotic about it which reminds me of a time long ago. I was a juvenile with others of my age on a natural excursion. We lived for several days with only minor tech, sleeping in tents and cooking our rations in hot water over a fire of twigs. I recall looking into the fire and it was as if the flames danced, like little people, and the wood hissed as if the people were singing. It's like that now, except the flames are moonlight in water, and the hiss is its gurgling and splashing.

And now the spirits come to me. The play of moonlight and flowing water form a vision of a rock which tumbles over and over in the waterfall, half a metre before my eyes, and somehow the sounds become voices, whispering spirits whose utterances form no proper words, but susurrate over and over.

'Can you hear that, Dorsa?'

Raoul tells me to be quiet or I will lose the link.

'Ariel', comes the combined and twisted sounds of nature, a sound on the edge of being a true voice. 'Ariel, home.'

The rock continues to tumble in the water and yet not fall, and other words come to me. 'Gene hunter' and 'project' and 'Christie Grey', the author of my ancient papers. Without full sentences, a meaning insinuates itself into my being, and now the effects, both visual and audible, are gone.

'Ah, Moon has shifted. We have lost her light.' Raoul guides us back to the shelter. Now we're settled he asks if the commune has been a success.

'I'm not sure if it was a success, but I get the impression she wants me to get on with my Unicamp project, and she also wants me to go home.' I must return to Venus to get anywhere near the truth. I would've been there by now if AMALTHEA and I had been more successful at the spaceport

'She, wants you to go home?' Raoul says. 'Who is she?'

'I can't explain it, Raoul. It's the impression that came to me. There was a voice, and it sounded female.'

Dorsa hadn't seen the tumbling rock or heard the voices. To her credit, she believes me when I expect her derision. Raoul says we should sleep and make plans in the morning.

***

Morning's here and light shines green through our low roof. Dorsa and I are alone. Dorsa stretches out the sleep, and I lift the knee closest to her: she has a hard enough time accepting my natural state and I don't want to make things impossible for her.

Who am I fooling? The real reason is that I don't want her to laugh at me, or come out with another cutting remark.

'I miss my music,' she says out of the blue. 'At home my construct wakes me with music every morning.'

'Nice way to be woken.'

'Yes, it is. What kind of music do you enjoy?'

Talking music takes my mind off my physical condition and thankfully has the same effect as a filter. I lower my leg, but she still looks away. 'I enjoy many of the ancients,' I say. 'There's Olly Alexander from the beginning of the last millennium, Joongwon Young of the 2890's, and of course Arjunai's Venusian Cycle.'

'Everyone loves the Cycle, even us Martians.' I hear Dorsa laugh for the first time. 'I especially love the Fire Cloud adagio for strings.'

We continue talking about music, but now we've exhausted the subject. With the temperature rising it becomes stuffy under the shelter, so we get up, find suitable leaves and douse ourselves with pond water. I'm worried that Raoul has abandoned us, but there he is emerging from the jungle with breakfast and a small open-weave sack.

He's brought me a loin-pouch and native style clothing for Dorsa. Once again she surprises me by taking to her new attire quite happily. She makes us turn our backs as she changes into it, so some things never change.

Raoul insists on tying the twine around my hips. He says it's the job of a shaman and that I should never remove it. I fit the pouch to the twine, fore and aft, and now I'm as much like a native as I can ever be. I have the correct skin tone, and if I hadn't been modified in the womb I'd look even more like Raoul, with long black hair.

We discuss plans. They revolve around my 'commune with the spirits'. I need to continue my project, and I have to get home to Venus. I'm not sure which is the more impossible, but Raoul is not at all concerned.

The last item he brings from his sack is my document valise. I really do wonder if he is a magician.

'The spirits told me of its arrival at the vac-tube terminal. I simply fetched it.'

It took hours for us to get here from the terminal. Raoul's 'simple' errand involved him completing the round trip in a fraction of that time. He must've run both ways.

I take the valise, the one tangible link to my old life. 'I can read the papers, but there's nothing I can do with the crystals here in the middle of the jungle, unless your spirits can read them.'

'I think they could read them, but there is no need. There is a place at the edge of the jungle, long abandoned, but its tech is intact. It will have what you need to proceed with your project.'

'It doesn't have a spare transitship so we can begin the journey to Ariel's home planet, does it?'

Raoul winks. 'We will close our eyes and sleep a while. Then we shall wake on Venus.'

'Do me a favour, Jungle-boy. Don't speak to us in riddles.'

'They are not riddles, Red-Rock-woman. They are impressions, and my impressions have a way of coming true.'

***

Raoul's place at the edge of the jungle turns out to be an old bio-printing station. There'd been several of them situated in the DTZ, all within metres of the protected zone. They say some seventy percent of the animals were printed in them, but now the ecosystems have been restored they've fallen into disuse.

'Looks like it's been abandoned for years.' Dorsa pushes at the door. 'Locked, but maybe I can work something.' Dorsa retrieves a tool from the sack Raoul had let her have. It's boxlike with a glossy cobalt-blue sheen and small enough to fit in her palm. I can only guess at its function.

'There is no need,' Raoul says. He takes the white cylindrical stone he wears around his neck and waves it close to the reader. The door opens, and he laughs to see my face. 'This isn't magic, my friend. My shaman-stone has a little tech in it.'

I was under the impression that no tech at all was allowed inside the AJPZ, but Raoul explains that shamans and headmen can access such places in case of emergency. 'We live as simply as the old ones, but we are not ignorant of today's worlds.'

Once inside, various motion-activated systems come online, including air conditioning.

'Oh, lovely,' Dorsa says, bathing in a stream of cool air.

I avoid the chilling flow. 'It's horrible! I was fine outside.' My teeth begin to chatter.

'I'll refrain from saying anything about the benefits of being dressed. Though in your case I'd settle for half-dressed.'

I guess our different opinions on clothing will never cease to be a topic of conversation between us.

As the light levels rise, I take in the surroundings and explore. I make a beeline for the printer wing. The bio-printers are museum pieces, but even so, at least second generation. The first printers required a sample of tissue from the form to be printed. The kind in front of me work from synthetically produced base chemicals.

Here are the four pre-ink booster hoppers that would have contained adenine, thymine, cystocine and guanine, and over there the nucleic acid and protein reservoirs. I touch each part of the machine and try to recall its designation from my classes at college. Chromosomal Mass Hopper, Conglomerator, and over at the far side of the room, the development tanks. It's like living in a history lesson.

The main disadvantage of these second gen printers? The end product was an infant form of the required creature which needed to be nurtured and raised before it could be released into the wild.

I continue my tour, and run my fingers along the casing of the Genome Alignment Cell and the Zygotic Initiator, which can only function with the direct involvement of a team of graphs working at quantum level.

Since the 2980's, third gen bio-printers have been able to create the full adult stage. It takes only hours from initiation to the completion of the adult form with all the mental capacities required to take on life in the wild. Such mental tweaking is fully within the graph realm because life at the level of quantum mech cannot be manipulated by humans alone. Graphs can create life because in essence, their realm is life.

'Over here, Ariel.' In the next room Dorsa calls up a grid interface. It floats in front of her in the form of a beam-interference control array.

'Can't it project a more user-friendly form?' I miss the construct which projected in my own image and negated the need to wave my fingers about in the air.

'You are such a child,' Dorsa says, but she obliges anyway and makes the necessary adjustments. The light shifts into the shape of one of the Saturn mission pioneers.

'Ah, John Christopher.' Raoul waves his hand through the seemingly solid projection. 'I enjoyed learning about him at Manaus.'

'Perfect,' I say. 'Let's get to work.'

***

Dorsa and Raoul discretely interrogate the grid trying to find traces of our fathers or any link between us that might enlighten us as to the situation we were in. On Raoul's insistence, I take up the gene hunting project, abandoned since Jonan went missing.

I'm troubled, certain I can be better employed helping my friends, but Raoul says it's unwise to disregard advice from the spirits. 'The answers you seek are linked to your work.'

I've found a small lab which has all the equipment I need. There's discrete grid access, mural projector arrays and an analysis shelf. I don't need any of that at the moment, because the ancient papers merely have to be read. They're written in an ancient form of Standard that I studied as an acolyte, but I still make use of the transcript on the crystal.

I open the papers, place the crystal on the objective and make myself comfortable. My method is to read out loud while the integral construct directs the information on the crystal. I read the words and immerse myself into the projection, but I'm looking for any relevance to my current situation and the disappearance of Father. There has to be something.

Christie Grey worked on the papers when Earth was divided into nation states. In his time, some of those states were at war.

And so, I begin.

**

The papers take the form of diary entries, letters and other correspondence, all of which Christie had converted from handwriting into print by use of a mechanical word-printing machine called a 'type writer'. Without access to modifiers or filters, I wallow in the undiluted thrill of excitement on reading the words of a man who'd carried my genes more than a thousand years ago.

January 1900

My name is Christian but nobody calls me that. I am Christie and I am nine and three-quarters. It is the beginning of a new century. Uncle Alexander says it is the last year of the old one but nobody else tends to agree and he gets rather cross. Aunt Jane says I should start writing a journal, which is a diary but she says girls write diaries and boys write journals. Girls write about their beaus and fine clothes and shoes, and their feelings. Boys write about adventures and derring-do. I asked why boys can't have feelings and why can't girls have adventures and write about them. Aunt Jane said 'Why, the very thought of it' which I am not sure is any kind of answer at all.

The first images surprise me, but not hugely. Christie is projected as I had looked as a juvenile, but with hair and eyebrows. This is all very logical although I wonder if an ancestor would look quite so identical.

May 3rd, 1905

I am now fifteen and I am an Eaton scholar. How very jolly. There! That will do for my journal entry and suffice for the next five years. So back to your dusty drawer, Journal. I rather suspect it will be an age before I dig you out again, if ever.

10th October, 1912

I have had this diary – sorry Aunt Jane – this 'journal' for twelve years. This is the third time I have written in it. Until today I have never had the inclination. Today is different, due to a curious meeting and a frightening encounter.

This morning's chance meeting seems a lifetime away, and it's this disconcerting dissonance between elapsed time and subjective experience that makes me want to record it. The feeling is so acute, I wonder if I am entirely right in my head.

I was fed up indoors attending to estate accounts and needed some air. I latched onto the excuse that I was in urgent need of some roll-film and simply had to attend to it at once. It's a pleasant stroll from the house to the High Street in spring or summer; not quite so alluring in the damp. This morning was damp and heavy with mist. I took my usual root along the lane and came close to the farm gate over which I was wont to leap to take the short cut across the meadow, but my gate was already occupied by some species of strange monster.

Made ominous and almost menacing by the mist, there was a figure leaning on the five-bar gate which stood between the road and Ninety Acre Meadow. At least, the darker shape within the white looked like a figure. It could as easily have been a trick of light and shade: the cap-

wearing head a leafy branch, the body a tree trunk. Once the shape coughed and moved a ghostly hand to its mouth, there could be no more doubt. I stopped in my tracks not at all frightened, but reminded of my childhood imaginary friend, equally swathed in mist after all these years.
    The apparition spoke. 'Who's there? Show yourself.' No figure of damp air had ever sounded so real. 'Are you spying on me? Step out where I can see you, or I swear I'll throw a clod at you.'
    I stepped forward and spoke in my officer-voice, carefully practiced to cover uncertainty and convey command. 'No need for that. I'm no more than a chap out for a walk.'
    The figure peeled away from the gate and coalesced into the youngest looking lance-corporal I had ever seen.

I stop reading and pause the projection. Now, while it seems perfectly logical to project Christie to look like me, where is the sense in modelling the young soldier on my friend, Benjo Drexler? Benjo, my friend almost since birth. Benjo my companion all through school and college. Benjo, that 'one human' I mentioned earlier. The likeness is perfect, except the soldier has a fine set of locks and eyebrows whereas Benjo is as hairless as I and the vast majority of other Venusians.

    I shake off my questions; there's no possible answer to them at this time. I resume.

He was the very spit of my imaginary friend, Harry. I was thrown for a moment.

The boy looks like Benjo *and* Christie's imaginary friend? I decide to interrogate the construct and ask why it had chosen that particular look. It says it's nothing to do with construct direction. Curious.

He carried a greatcoat over his arm. His cap sat on a nest of golden hair, and his left lower sleeve bore a Good Conduct Stripe which gave me a clue that he was not as young as he looked. I'm familiar with rank insignia now,

having enrolled with the university's Officer Training Unit, and I also recognised his medal ribbon. He really could not have been any younger than I.

'Begging your pardon. I thought you was one of the lads playing a dirty trick on me.'

'Think nothing of it. No harm done. Lovely fresh morning, don't you think?' I'd forgotten all about the imaginary boy of my childhood. True to his nature, as ephemeral as the air.

'Fresh is right. But I don't much care for the view.'

We laughed. Ice broken, the young soldier took out a hip-flask and offered me a nip. Far more acceptable than a smoke: I've never taken to tobacco. I recognised the soldier's brass shoulder titles as being of the Hertfordshire Regiment.

We got to chatting about this and that, but all the time he seemed somewhat unreal. Some way into our conversation, the soldier recalled the rules when a passing acquaintance acquires the possibility of something more lasting, and introduced himself as Jack Gabriel. We shook hands and I returned the formality.

'Lord Potrelle's boy?' Jack did not seem at all intimidated in the presence of his social betters, a trait I rather admired.

'Colonel Shepherd is actually my uncle.' I didn't see the need to go into complicated family relationships. 'They took me in when my parents died.'

Jack nodded sagely, took out a pipe, clamped it between his teeth and lit it.

'I say,' I said as the idea struck. 'If you're off duty, what say we call in for a pint at the Sibthorpe Arms?'

Jack withdrew a pocket watch from his tunic. 'Sunday opening hours. We'll have to be sharpish.'

'One thing first, if I may.' I was rarely without my pocket Goertz camera, and Jack was happy for me to take a shot, with him leaning on the gate.

So it was that an unlikely friendship, which defied class, had its beginning. We discussed everything under the sun, from football to military life for the volunteers. It also transpired that he was quite familiar with Bell House and the home farm, having been employed in the stables by us when he was a young boy. Strangely I had no recollection of him.

By the time hours were called, the mist had gone and the sun shone in a clear blue sky. I strode home to Bell House in a happy mist that kept me within myself as effectively as the morning mist had done.

That was when I was scared half out of my life by a white winged ghost that swooped on me. I think I let out something of a girlish squeal, so I was glad I was halfway across an empty meadow. I forced my heart back into my chest in time to see the wraith, a Barn Owl that seemed to have forgotten it was nocturnal, glide towards the hedgerow a foot above the stubbly grass. Another incident that added to the strangeness of the day.

I wonder if I am still affected somewhat by the beer. Does Jack Gabriel actually exist? If so, how is it he look so like imaginary Harry? I must wait until the film is developed, but I half-expect to see a blob of amorphous light where Jack should be.

January 1913

Cousin Louis is here, resting upstairs after his long trip. Of course, we share a grandfather in good old Willem.

Prior to setting off to meet Louis at the station this morning, I stood below Grandpa's portrait which hangs between the ones of Black Bartholomew and Grandma. Willem wears his cavalry officer's uniform. We have no idea who Black Bartholomew is, but it's by Peter Lely and quite the oldest painting in the house. He stands resplendent in a brown military coat with a red and grey waist sash and carries a halberd. My grandparents' portraits were painted as a pair in the 1820's.

I shifted to stand by Grandma's portrait and recalled something she said to me when she was very ancient.

'Leave no more than the lightest of footprints.' This sentence was Grandma's unintentional legacy, a phrase rattled off and forgotten, but one that took firm root in my mind. 'I really cannot abide those beastly urchins who blow eggs or steal nests. Mother Nature did not scatter her bounty for grubby little boys to augment their unsavoury collections or to spoil the parlour rug with dusty marks.'

And so it was that I never blew an egg or brought home an abandoned bird's nest. Instead, I was rarely without a pocketful of pencils and a sketchpad. Whenever I encountered a facet of nature that enthralled me, I was certain to take away an image, sketched in pencil or sometimes charcoal, which I would later turn into a watercolour. Nowadays I have my trusty Goertz, but I haven't abandoned the sketch pad entirely.

I obeyed Grandma's throwaway command almost to the letter, but the letter faltered over those footprints. A footprint will fade. The stems it bends will straighten. In an hour, or a day, there will be little to tell the most assiduous of trackers that 'man came by here'. But lay a footprint over a footprint, and the signs last longer.

The road that goes from Bell House into town follows a winding and circuitous route, and I was still a small boy when I discovered a shortcut across the meadow. At first I crossed willy-nilly, pressing down the long grass and weeds softly, so they would soon regain their posture. After a while, I would stand by the edge of the meadow, take a bead on the big oak that grew in the middle and walk to it in a straight line. At the tree I would pause, fix my eyes on the newly revealed highest point of another five-bar gate and start again, so that after several days, the grasses began to surrender. After a year, my many light footprints had combined forces to form a thin spread where the grass had given up the fight and was stunted, leaving bare patches of compressed earth in places.

Now, here we are, almost a decade later. A few hours ago, I stood by the edge of the meadow. Bleak and frost-touched, the path was barely visible thanks to the angle of the sun. I hadn't walked there since before University, but the hint of a path survives, and I mean to walk it back to full-blooded shortcut.

Wrapped up warm against the cold, I dug out my watch and checked the time. An hour before the train was due. Cousin Louis was probably eating penny buns at Kings Cross right now, and if I hurried, I could take tea at the café on the corner before crossing the line to the station in time for his train to arrive.

The ground was quite hard with the cold, and the chance of muddy turn-ups slight, so I fixed my eye on the oak and began the first leg of that much-walked path. Circumnavigating the thick trunk, I took my second sighting and strode out for the gate, only to pull up after a few steps. The young soldier, Jack Gabriel, was leaning against it, smoking a pipe, like a reprise of our first meeting.

'Jack? Jack Gabriel!'

The soldier turned his head slowly and waved. A pint of good ale instead of a tea at the corner café took on an undeniable appeal.

Now here's the thing. We enjoyed a pint each, Jack's treat. Then it was my round. I bought two more pints but Jack was gone when I returned to our place. I asked a chap at the next table where the solder had gone. 'What soldier?' he replied.

I am seriously beginning to wonder if I shouldn't book an appointment with one of those head-doctors. It's all so bally bizarre if you ask me.

I pause the run again and sift through the papers until I come to a pair of letters, one from and one to Christie's Uncle Alex. They are from several years into the second major conflict between the prominent nation states. The first was in 1745, and there was another in 1939.

The letters mark another stage for Christie, who'd been injured by enemy action in a conflict conducted greatly in ditches. They need no construct-directed projection, so I read them. Pure and simple. It makes me feel like an old professor of days gone by.

Lieutenant-General the Lord Potrelle
Corps HQ
BEF

Brigadier-General Sir Hugh Trenchard
Air Ministry
London

2nd February 1918

My dear H,

Congratulations on a rather spiffing nickname from the clerks at Staff. As I hear, you quite like it. Beats mine into a cocked hat. If you haven't heard, they call me Old Potty. Still, they say you have only really arrived when you earn a witty misnomer.

Bit of a favour to ask, if I may. I ask as a friend and not a superior officer, so a refusal will not offend.

My nephew Captain Christie Grey MC, of the Hertfordshire Regiment took a Blighty one. He lost half his right foot, and has earned a place on Staff. The thing is he isn't at all a Staff bod and despite his service craves more. Decent chap, I have to say. I'm rather proud of him. But as you can imagine, he is no longer of any use in the infantry, and would prove more of an encumbrance than an asset. No more Johnny-in-the-trenches for him, but he can still give fine service as a Johnny-in-the-sky.

Now, Hugh, I'm not asking you to take on a cripple. He was somewhat of an aviator before the war and is a skilled photographer.

Now, we come to the nub. As you know, my son Louis flies with the Belgian Air Service. He is due to commence a course in England to familiarise himself with a new aircraft and at length he will require an Observer. Both Louis and I would like that Observer to be Christie. My friends in Belgian high command are happy to take him on secondment, but they would rather like him trained up.

And so, to my request, and please understand, I am not the kind of man who enjoys pulling strings for family. In Christie's case, I believe he has earnt my support in the matter, and so I step into uncomfortable territory.

Would you consider taking him into the Royal Flying Corps on full transfer and training him, in tandem with Louis, for the role of Observer?

One more point. Christie hasn't the foggiest idea I am making this approach, and he would be mortified if he found out. We have discussed his transfer and

he has put in a request that I have on my desk. Shall I forward it?
   Yours, with kind regards,
   Alexander.

And the reply.

> Brigadier-General Sir Hugh Trenchard
> Air Ministry
> London

Lieutenant-General the Lord Potrelle
Corps HQ
BEF

4rd February 1918

Dear Lord Potrelle,

  So nice to hear from you.

  I have given your request much consideration, and I will say without prevarication, I am not entirely averse to it. I must also say, your nephew sounds like a fine fellow who one would wish to help. One fly in the ointment is his rank. My Captains are flight commanders, not observers. It won't do for him to outrank others who are more experienced than he, nor to hold a rank not suitable to the role, but he sounds like a game young chap and I am quite prepared to take him as a Second-Lieutenant if he can put up with what is, in effect, undeserved demotion.

  I have heard very good things about the Hertfordshire Regiment. Highly regarded by Guards Brigade command. As for Captain Grey, a Military Cross speaks volumes, so I have no fear of landing a duff one.

  In short, Alexander, please do send over his application. I will put the relevant Colonel on notice to receive it and pass it up the chain.

  All my very best,
  Yours,

Hugh.

I run the projection again and the scene has moved forward. Christie is lying injured amongst the wreckage of a primitive flying machine. He is in a strip of land, muddy and bereft of any vegetation, between opposing forces. Blood streams from a head wound and he hovers between states of consciousness. He repeatedly mumbles the phrase 'White-winged ghost.'

The situation appears hopeless, and now in desperation Christie calls out in a harsh whisper – the most he can muster in his failing condition. 'Harry! Help me.'

'That was no ghost, sir. It was Fritz in a plane, all done up in white paint.' Whether it's a trick of clever direction on behalf of the construct or a venture into fantasy I can't tell, but Jack Gabriel, the young Hertfordshire soldier who looks like both my friend Benjo and Christie's imaginary friend, Harry, is suddenly by Christie's side. I'm drawn to the brass badges on his epaulettes. They depict a bird, like the one in the projection where I first saw Raoul. Each bird surmounts brass titles which read 'MSS 99'.

'You can always rely on me in a scrape, sir,' Jack says. He crawls around in the mud until he's in the right position to bandage Christie's head, all the while under enemy fire.

And now the scene moves into slow motion. That is, everything winds down, slower and slower, except for Jack who continues to move in real time. After a few moments, Jack is the only animated part of the scene, all his surroundings now a still picture, time cast in amber. Jack stands, pulls the creases from his tunic by tugging down at the hem. Now he uses the cuff of his tunic to polish dust off the golden birds and shoulder titles on his epaulettes, and walks over to me.

'You ever need answers, sir, don't forget about poor Jack.'

'End projection!' The confusion within me leaks into my voice. 'Construct!'

The whole scene vanishes, but Jack remains. He is still there when my construct-likeness materialises from projected light.

'What are you doing? Why did you have this projection address me?'

My construct looks at Jack who stands frozen in time. 'I did not have the projection address you. In fact, I had nothing to do with any of the projection at all.' Its voice comes from the speakers but feels like it's in my head.

'Then who directed the projection?'

'I do not know. I was put on standby.'

'By whom?'

'By you.'

'I most certainly did not put you on standby.'

My construct hesitates. 'If you wish I shall carry out a diagnosis.'

'Please do so.'

It's a task of micro-moments too small for the human mind to measure. 'I cannot find a reason. It is as if the projection was guided by a graph, but I cannot detect any breakdown in integrity or security. Similarly, there has been no detectable corruption of the info-crystal.'

Baffling, but also intriguing. And so frustrating because there's no more information about Christie or his fate. I must rest for a while before I run the next projection.

But there's no rest while a mystery flies around inside my skull. AI constructs cannot lie. Although their reasoning power exceeds that of any human, they operate strictly within the parameters of their programing. They can grow, learn and become more, but they cannot overstep certain bounds. My construct has run several more tests but has not been able to discover who directed the projection.

I decide to look at the next projection, and set my construct to observe all the processes. I move forward in time more than a century and make use of the never-published work by my ancestor, Philip Fryer. As before, I read out loud, and the scenes are projected, but not by my construct. Somewhere in the midst of all this history and mystery are answers.

The Sneeze. It didn't kill you. Not at first. Not directly. Of course, there are always exceptions, and some people didn't survive the initial bout. It had a mortality rate, but then, so do all flus. People die of common flu. People died of Bumblebee Sneeze, but that wasn't why the pandemic with the whimsical name became the most feared ailment on the planet. See, it didn't kill at first, but it had a way of getting there eventually.

I want to talk about the First Pandemic. More specifically I want to tell you the story of Shona Eastbrook. Yes, me and a hundred other people, in every language on Earth: I've lost count of the number of biographies there are about Shona. Have you read any of them? If so, you'll have read about me too, in an off-the-page kind of way. I'm the figure in the corner. The one hidden in the shadows. Carrying her bag; running interference; watching her six. There is a shot of me in that big, dry, chunky 600 page tome that everyone bought but few ever read. Shona is hurt. We are running through a hostile mass of people. We have our backs to the camera. I'm the 'mysterious' man she's leaning on as we escape from the crowd.

I call for a freeze-scene. There they are; Shona and Philip, and I'm not surprised because I was half-expecting Philip to be modelled on me, but there's also a young man in the crowd. It's Jack again, and he's looking directly at me and smiling his mysteriously knowing smile. I let the scene run again, and Jack/Benjo disappears into the sea of humanity.

Let's just say, when it comes to Shona I know what I'm talking about. And now is the time to talk.

When I was fifteen, Dad was transferred, again, which meant we had to move home, again, and of course, find a new school.

I drift a little as Philip goes into details of their youth together. A friendship which became love and survived a brief, failed attempt at romance. Their respective university years and early careers, Shona in investigative journalism and Philip as a pilot in the RAF, the air arm of the nation state then known as Britain. It's all very interesting, but also irrelevant as far as my quest goes. One day I'll read it all again and be enthralled. For now it's all a waste of time unless it serves to point me in the right direction.

Eventually we come to a section that might be useful.

'Flight-Lieutenant Philip Fryer,' Shona said over gourmet burgers at Williams Ale House. 'Fryer the Flyer.'

'Like I haven't heard that a zillion times.' I threw a chip at her.

She picked it up and ate it. 'Thanks. Can't get enough of these babies.'

'If I gobbled up as many chips as you, they'd have to reinforce the flight deck. How do you stay so skinny?'

'Grant keeps me busy.'

'Really, Shona. Too much information.'

She laughed in that explosively loud, totally open way I associated with her. Heads turned and I felt a little self-conscious on her behalf. Shona couldn't have cared less. I often hear the echoes, to this day. God, I miss her. 'Head out of the gutter, boy. He makes me go to the gym, is what I mean.'

We were both 26 and we were moving along in our respective careers. We found we had one of those small windows of opportunity to meet up as our ships passed in the night, close to Liverpool Street Station. Unbeknown to us, or anybody else on the planet, a rather singular new flu virus was also developing slowly in a small, isolated community somewhere in the Far East. It would be a while before the scientists gave it its HN nomenclature, but the little bastard was on its way. From small acorns.

Within a couple of years we had both changed employers. I landed a job with a prestigious private airline company, and Shona moved into TV journalism. She hated it when people were selected for top jobs on who they knew and not what they knew, so she kept it quiet that her partner, Grant Olusonġe (yes, that Grant Olusonġe – although he wasn't that well-known to the general public back then), was someone high up in the BBC.

The virus had established itself now and its spread moved up a few notches. The world noticed, and people started calling it Sneezing Flu. It reached the nationals and the main news channels, mostly on the 'And finally ...' spot, because after all, Sneezing Flu is such a funny thing, and how jolly and quaint, and let's cheer people up after news of the latest food wars and water shortages and the plights of masses of humanity on the move. Once we've filled the screen with starving children and minor genocides, let's give them a chuckle. Looking back it is hard to believe that within months, Sneezing Flu usurped all other stories, and nobody laughed any more.

The projection continues, but it's a presentation of hours. My respected ancestor enjoyed waxing lyrical, so I will summarise.

Sneezing flu began to be called 'Bumblebee Sneeze' because of the strange propensity for survivors – most of those people who had caught it – to wear clothes of yellow and black. Lost in the intervening centuries is the reason why. Historians fall into two camps. Some believe it was a choice by the survivors caused by some kind of a psychological side effect of the virus. Others believe they were forced to wear those colours as a warning to the rest of society, a warning that they may have deemed necessary due to another of the psychological effects.

Every single survivor of Bumblebee Sneeze was a radically changed person once the illness had passed. They were physically exactly the same, but changed mentally. Even then, they were basically the same, but the change manifested itself in the shape of their ambitions and outlook in life. Not such a terrible effect, it might be thought, but society thought differently.

It was as if aspects of their previous lives, those that gave purpose and impetus, were now meaningless to them. Entrepreneurs were no longer interested in making money and gave up their business for other pursuits. Criminals seemed to awaken to the fact that their previous lives were of little account. In fact, what appeared to count most before the disease struck, now counted for nothing. Survivors had not the slightest interest in fame or fortune. They began to wear yellow and black, and they began to flock together.

Though they did no harm, the ninety percent of the world's population who had not contracted the disease in the First Pandemic began to fear and distrust them, a positioned fired up by the media.

In a vastly overpopulated and under resourced world, the Bumblebees were a perfect scapegoat. But before they could be truly persecuted, the most dreadful incident the world has ever known – The Event as we now refer to it – befell a horrified and baffled humanity, and it was an event led by Shona Eastbrook.

It is now the third decade into the fourth millennium, and there are fewer humans in the entire Solar System than once lived on Earth alone. Overpopulation was the underlying factor of every worldwide problem facing our ancestors of a thousand years ago. It fed pollution and global climate change, it drove the fear which came of dwindling resources, and whipped up conflict and wars. Often other excuses were given, but Earth's inability to sustain the sheer numbers of people fuelled it all.

A few were driven by greed, but most only by need. Back then there were so many humans that simple need outstripped the resources required to fulfil it. Untold thousands died from starvation, thirst, natural disasters and violent conflict, but still humanity was in a constant state of net gain.

Then Shona made her move.

At first she travelled the world reporting on the Bumblebee Sneeze phenomenon. Her biggest story was on the terrorist survivors of the disease who lost their radicalism and refused to take up their weapons after coming through the illness. She also interviewed politicians who had contracted the condition and would no longer carry party lines or spout comforting platitudes. The plain truth was that the planet was rapidly dying, in fact in its last throws, and its disease wasn't called 'pollution' or 'global warming'. It was called 'Humanity' and it sucked at the vitals of the planet like a cancer.

Nobody except those in the yellow and black knew what Shona Eastbrook was doing once she had recovered from the Sneeze, not even Philip. She took up the yellow and black herself and for a while provided a platform for her fellow Bumblebees, but while she presented to the world, she planned for that awful day.

The Bumblebees gathered at tens of thousands prearranged sites around the globe. And then, on that date and time I will not insult you with by naming, for it is engrained into the psyche of every one of us from whichever world or colony we hail, they laid down their lives.

At precisely the same time, after Shona had made the Speech, a tenth of the human population ceased to be. It appeared that as well as an overwhelming desire to wear yellow and black, the Bumblebees had acquired the ability to simply switch themselves off. No blades. No poison or firearms. No leaping from cliffs or jumping into lakes. They all said their goodbyes, laid down and went to sleep, never to wake again.

Humanity reeled from the event. Wars ceased, because the death of so many millions in an instant had presented more immediate problems, not least of which was dealing with the remains, and filling the voids.

There was, at a stroke, almost nine hundred million fewer mouths to feed. That many fewer contributing to pollution and consuming resources. In short, the planet was afforded a small breathing space.

Precisely three months after The Event, the Second Pandemic struck. There were no more events such as The Event. People remembered Shona's speech, and Humanity responded.

Within five years and one more pandemic, the world became a different place. Economic systems became based on 'enough' when previously they had all been rooted in 'more'. Human relations became less and less adversarial. Cooperation towards equality for all quickly replaced selfish objectives. It was as if the disease had woken us up.

The world of that far distant time is hard for us to fathom. But the world now, or at least my part in it, is equally baffling.

Running those two historic scenarios, Christie Grey's and Philip Fryer's, has raised more questions. The exercise has also presented me with another line of enquiry.

Like all good investigators, I must scope the scene of the incident. It's more urgent than ever for me to return home.

Raoul is convinced there's a message in the projections, but if someone has information for us, why be so cryptic?

'I suspect the people who are trying to catch you are also watching the grid.' Despite the simplicity of his life, Raoul has a deep knowledge of current systems. 'Perhaps the only way to reach you safely is via heavily disguised clues. You must watch the projections again and look for inconsistencies.'

***

After repeated viewings, we find an office for debriefing. I tell the others I can see nothing in my research that alludes to our situation but for the inexplicable inclusion of Benjo's image in the projections. They agree we must find a way to get to Venus, but their discoveries on the grid makes that next to impossible.

Dorsa and I have been declared terrorists, a quaint old term from early in the last millennium that hasn't been used in centuries except in history crystals. In short, it means that we're considered a danger and a menace to peaceful society. We're to be relieved of our freedom on sight, and if we resist then we are to be relieved of our lives.

Nothing has seemed so bizarre and inexplicable since Mother denied the existence of Father. The authorities simply do not kill people. They don't even incarcerate them without a Council endorsed shepherd's warrant.

We sit in the air conditioned office surrounded by natural works of art, oblivious to everything except the outlandish notion that we may be killed with State approval. My thoughts swirl around and around but defy my every effort to grasp them. It's as if the whole Universe and my place within it has shifted. Everything

I took for granted as solid fact has dissolved into smoke.

It's Dorsa who breaks the silence. 'Do you think we should give ourselves up?'

'That would be unwise,' Raoul says. 'There is something seriously amiss, something that stems from Council, so it makes no sense to give yourselves up to them.'

'Something the spirits told you?' I don't mean to be sarcastic, but that's how it comes out.

'Perhaps it is they who influence me.' Raoul stands. 'Come with me, to my village. We have to prepare for a long journey, and we will need support. My people will help.'

The village has only three main buildings: long, narrow and constructed of wood with roofs of overlapping leaves. Although they follow the same plan they vary in size.

'The biggest lodge is for married couples and children up to ten years of age,' Raoul says. 'Twined boys and unmarried men live in the hunters' lodge, and the twined girls and unmarried women live over there.' Raoul tied the twine, a mark of transition celebrated with a coming of age ceremony, about the hips of nearly all the children of fifteen or younger. 'The older ones were twined by my predecessor.'

There's a scattering of small shacks at the edges of the village clearing. Raoul explains that the widowed and elderly sometimes prefer to live in these. 'A person who loses their partner may choose where to live. No lodge door is barred to them, and they may sleep where they will.' Shamans also live apart in their own small lodge.

The adults are shy of us, but welcoming nonetheless. The children accept us at once. The little boys skip around me calling 'Yee! Yee!' with much giggling and high-jinx. They rush in, try to slap my legs and then run away squealing.

'"Yee" means "monster". They think it very brave to touch the monster,' Raoul says.

Monster? Hardly flattering. I greet the next onslaught with clawed hands and a fierce roar. Far from scaring the boys, they appear delighted. I'm reminded of Sav, the naughty little juvenile in my schooling set.

Dorsa looks agitated, and I ask if she's all right. 'Overloaded with all this nudity?' Most villagers are dressed only in their twines.

'Don't be ridiculous. Thanks to you two I'm fully acclimatised, thank you very much.'

'What's the problem, then?'

'Where're we going to sleep? I like my own space and don't like the idea of all this communal living. I'm certainly not snuggling up to you.' Dorsa protesteth too much.

'Don't worry, Dorsa,' Raoul says. 'I have told the headman that you both commune with the spirits. She wouldn't have you in a lodge if you begged.'

'Oh. Thank you. I think.'

'They will build each of you a small house, like mine, as the others are all occupied.'

Now I feel embarrassed, and Dorsa is clearly the same. 'We can't put them to all that trouble, Raoul.'

'It's a job of half a day, and a ceremony of welcoming that we relish. It would be rude to refuse, and most polite to assist with the task.'

Dorsa and I find ways to help. We gather armfuls of meter-long waxy skinned leaves for the roofs. We tie off vines here, slot lengths of branch there, weave reeds into mats and generally lend our unskilled hands wherever we can. There's much laughter at our inadequate efforts, and I appear to have acquired a posse of small boys who find some pleasure in following me wherever I go. By late afternoon, the job is done.

There are villages in some of the remote jungle islands back home where communes have tried to emulate the lives of the Amazonians. I spent a week at one once and came away feeling recharged and somehow superior. I lived the simple life and for a whole week I did without tech. Well, nearly. Who can do without their construct? Is it possible to obtain all one's nutritional requirements without food-printers? And of course, we must set out a shielded area free of biting insect, mustn't we? How bizarre to think otherwise.

I now know those Venusian copies of Amazonian villages are lamentable excuses for the real thing. Here, there is no tech except in dire emergency. Here there is no grid or instant access to the gathered information of all the worlds. Here, they eat meat. Real meat from a slain and butchered animal. My stomach churns at the very thought of it. In truth, they consume little flesh. Perhaps once a week, but it is an important and necessary requirement for their physical health. And dare I say it, I find the meal tasty. My stomach is a little heavy after my first omnivorous meal, but I don't feel sick.

It's dark now. I'd prefer to be in my own shack fast asleep, but we're guests in Raoul's tiny lodge. The task ahead of us appears insurmountable. The fact that AMALTHEA and I almost succeeded in boarding a transitship doesn't make it any easier. We are no longer ignorant of the fact that sophisticated forces are out to get us.

First, we must get to Venus. Dorsa believes her father's fate is so tied up with mine that she's happy to throw in her lot with me. 'If we find your father, we'll be more than halfway to finding mine.'

'The key to any success at all is training of the mind,' Raoul says. 'I will teach you how to walk paths within the grid.'

The spectre of the crashing flyer intrudes again.

'The preparation is all of the mind, and you are already far along the path to grid control, Ariel.' Raoul reasons that if I am without a neural-stent, but had accessed all the benefits of connection up until my arrest, there can only be two explanations. The first is that I have a stent after all and the doctor had either lied to me or been mistaken. The second is that I'm able to access the connections somehow without a stent. Either way, I should still be able to access them.

'Shall we begin?' Raoul's face looks skull-like in the shadow-pooling light of our small fire. Dorsa and I exchange glances.

'I hope there aren't any shenanigans,' Dorsa says. 'I was in a crystal once where you shamans were blowing narcotics up each other's noses and "seeing things". I'm not up for getting high.'

'You speak of the Semen of the Sun. It was a crude path that has not been used for many generations.'

Dorsa wears a comical face of disbelief and confusion. 'I'm not sure I want to know, but what were you people blowing up your noses?' She leans close to my ear. 'You should know, Venus-boy. Is there such a thing as olfactory sex?'

Raoul laughs while I wonder why Dorsa thinks I'm the font of all carnal knowledge. I hardly have to wonder for long. I'm Venusian, so the old prejudices apply.

Raoul explains that the 'semen' was actually a powder prepared from tree bark. 'Us three, we have no need of it. Now, let us begin by watching the dancing of the flames.'

With her mention of sex, Dorsa has spoilt me to the task at hand. I try to centre my consciousness into the flame, but I begin to burn in another way. Without filters, I am growing ever more frisky, and if I don't have sex with Dorsa or Raoul soon, or both at the same time, I think I'll explode and save Council all the trouble of killing me. It isn't a state of mind I've shared with my friends, but sometimes the evidence is hard to hide wearing nothing but a pouch.

I reach for the filters, stretching my mind as I had before learning I was stentless. Immediately my blood cools and my thoughts clear.

So it is that I embark into a period of mind-training with full confidence it will work. We find that we can indeed access many of the connections to which we've grown accustomed, and one or two that are new to us. For example, all three of us can communicate telepathically and instantly over a separation of several miles. It's like having our own, private and permanent graph-link and I wonder if the connection works over unlimited distances as it does for graphs. Raoul also tries to teach us the technique he used to bring down that prefect-flyer, but we have nothing to practice on. The principle involves us using our minds to invade the construct control system, but with no systems available we can merely contemplate the theory.

We return often to the sacred glade in the jungle. Now, on a day during the second week we sit on the cool stones by the pool and a frightening thought strikes me. 'I believe I still have a stent. Nothing else makes sense. If only for a moment, consider the possibility that we can operate without one.'

'I think I know where you're heading with this, Ariel.' Dorsa rarely calls me 'Venus-boy' these days. Our acquaintance had matured into friendship, and if I didn't keep my filters high, I'm certain there'd be more. 'If we're stentless and can do everything we did before, and a little extra, then we're not normal. Maybe that's why we're public enemy hatch one.'

Raoul agrees, but our time here is cut short.

There's a grid terminal in the village disguised as a shrine. It's strictly for emergency use and can only be accessed by the headman or one of the shamans. It's meant as a safety feature the villagers can call upon if facing a dire and threatening situation beyond their control. It's never been used for incoming messages before, until now. Bart calls for us and projects an image of himself.

'There's been an application to Three World Council to lift the protections on the AJPZ and allow a taskforce in to secure your capture.' Bart's face hovers above the shrine, blue and bright. 'I have no doubt the application will be allowed.'

They'll release swarms of seeker-wasps into the jungle. We'll be found within a few hours, or days at the most, and the taskforce will home in and take us.

'There's also a strong possibility I'll be relieved of my Directorship. If that happens, there's little I can do to help. Until then I'll do what I can.'

Bart wants us to get to the terminal by the bridge as soon as we can. We say hasty farewells. My little posse of small boys is no longer giggling and larking about. They're frightened and clingy. They know I'll look back on these short weeks as the centre of my life, and the most happy, but there shall never be any returning to Raoul's jungle home.

***

There're no direct paths between the village and Bart's terminal, so Raoul takes us on shortcuts through unmarked ways. En route we speak about the graphs.

They're a major topic of conversation as we're led through the jungle. It's been raining for more than an hour but now it's passed and there's nothing to interrupt us while we speak except a distant chorus of monkeys.

Raoul has dipped into the grid and reports news bulletins encouraging people to watch out for us and report any sightings to the nearest Peace Office. They imply we're not quite human, and despite the absurdity it's something I insist we consider. Are we, like the graphs in their turn, a new or at least different life form?

'I can't believe we're discussing it,' Dorsa says. 'How can you have any doubts that we're anything but a hundred percent human?'

I assure her that I have no doubts. 'We must consider all eventualities even if only to discount them. You've learnt the history of the graphs, so you know for a long time they weren't considered a true lifeform. People thought they'd merely evolved from constructs.'

'There's a crock of a difference between us and graphs.'

'And between graphs and constructs, and yet we confused the two for decades.'

A thousand years ago we had our AI helpers. They were nothing more than elaborate programs, their intelligence grown in the lab, their physical attributes, those of any machine into which they were downloaded. Then, sometime in the mid-21st century, it seemed that some of the programs escaped their physical confines and developed the ability to live in the ether, disembodies programs that developed a high degree of self-determination.

For a long time, humans believed we'd created a form of incorporeal life, until these lifeforms made discoveries about themselves. They were not beings who had evolved from our AI. They had been there all the time, living entities residing in Quantum, with all the strangeness of the quantum world. Alive and yet at the same time, not alive; a single universal awareness and yet untold millions of individuals; part of everything and yet part of nothing. In fact every contradiction a human could imagine and several thousand other states of being or non-being that not even graphs could comprehend.

Human and graph scientists have been struggling with questions of their genesis and development since the first graph made contact, and neither human nor graph are anywhere near close to a workable theory.

Dorsa listens to my ideas that we may be something new and therefore threatening to the status quo, in the same way that graphs had been when they first manifested.

'Look, Ariel. If we were other than human, we'd know.'

'But would we? What about all the people who should remember our fathers? If something can get to them, surely it can get to us.'

'I'll grant you that if people can forget our fathers, as if they have never existed, then we might have our minds and thoughts tinkered with too.'

'Add to that, we can do things that should only be possible with a stent.' In fact, we can do more. I find that I can self-administer blockers, something that previously required the assistance of a graph. To reach in and manipulate the chemical composition of our own bodies in order to counter pain or to modify emotions: this is beyond human. Filters are one thing, but blockers are on a different level. And as for Raoul, that trick he pulled on the prefect-flyer indicate abilities which are bound to make the Council a little nervous.

Several more hours pass and it's raining again. We're slick with water and the secretions of plants, and smeared with various pollens. Much to my relief, Raoul calls for a halt. It's time to eat and take a short rest.

It's good to rest after the physical exertion of the last few hour. There's a glow inside me that drives me to contemplate another form of physical release. I turn my mind, reaching inward to bolster my filters, but draw up short.

We don't speak, but there's something between us all manifested only in looks and clear in the words that are not spoken. I think this is going to be a memorable rest-break. I let my filters dissipate, a frail force against a natural surge of hormones.

We follow as close to the bank of a river as the undergrowth allows until we come to a rock pool full of clear running water. The heat and humidity are getting to me, so poor Dorsa must really be stifled. The rock pool's invitation cannot be ignored and we all discard what little clothing we have. I try to unpick the knot on the twine that girds my hips, but Raoul tells me to stop. 'You must wear the twine at all times. Never take it off.'

I want to jump into the pool, but I fear it may stir up mud from the bottom and spoil the water's perfect clarity. My filters have dropped off entirely and I don't want cloudy water to spoil the view.

I rinse my loin-pouch, wring it out and hang it on a branch to dry. Some hope in this humidity. Raoul does the same and to my mild amazement, Dorsa sheds her clothing too. We all step in and the water comes up to meet us. One foot, both feet caressed and healed by its cool touch. Shins, knees, thighs; now I sit on a smooth rock on the bed of this little tributary stream and the water is up to my chest. We let out an audible chorus of pleasure and relief. Never has water felt so good. My filters are non-existent and I do nothing to re-enforce them. Nothing more than a mind-manipulation, and they would be restored, but I enjoy the tingle of arousal, and it is plain Dorsa and Raoul feel the same.

I begin to quicken. My eyes dart, to Raoul's groin, to Dorsa's nipples. There is no doubt we all share similar sensations as our bodies prepare us for intimacy.

Raoul stands. 'Would you like me to give you both some privacy? I'll go into the jungle and find something to eat.' He climbs onto the bank.

'No, wait,' Dorsa says. 'I'd prefer it if you stayed.' She sees something in me which is hardly hidden or difficult to interpret. 'And I'm pretty certain Ariel wants you to stay too.'

Yes, I do. I want them both.

Raoul smiles and slips back into the water. We move together, into a shared embrace and shy, exploratory touches begin. And then we're all violently torn away from our lovemaking.

There on top of a rock that breaks the surface is a flying insect. As soon as I focus on it I know what it is. 'Seeker-wasp!'

Dorsa scoots water and washes it into the river. She snatches it up and dashes it into the rock. Once, twice, three times and it smashes. She holds out the broken pieces in the palm of her hand. 'This is an old model. The current ones are four times smaller. We wouldn't have noticed it.'

'They want us to know we've been spotted,' I say, and then spot another one hovering out of reach. Without thinking about it, I caste my mind into its central processing grid. For a moment I see us as it does. Far below, we are blobs of hot yellow light in the icy blue of the water. It relays the image back through Quantum to its graph master. Still experiencing existence from the seeker's point of view, I feel others of its kind. Thousands of them. There's something else, much bigger and bristling with ill intent.

Raoul calls me back to myself, and the icy water reminds me of my own body. He grabs his loin-pouch and refits it. 'We can only hope it didn't have time to send our coordinates.'

'It did,' I say. 'Others are already streaming towards us.'

'We must run!'

Dorsa and I grab our meagre clothing, I snatch up my valise and we run. I'm soon gasping for breath. Despite her natural acclimatisation to colder conditions, Dorsa is doing better than me. I'm an encumbrance. It'll be my fault if we're caught. I'm slick with sweat and my lungs labour, and yet we still run.

There is a high-pitched whine. 'Another seeker!' I yell, a real effort when I crave all the air to breathe. For all my discomfort, I manage to loop its motive controls with a tendril of thought and send it crashing into a tree.

Then there's another, and yet another. Raoul slaps several from the air, and Dorsa accounts for several more. I'm exhausted, able to do little more than stay on my feet. We keep running, slapping at the undergrowth and forcing paths where none exist. Someone, or something, plays a mental trip on me, and for a moment I'm in a meadow: Christie's meadow, soft grasses swaying gently in a breeze laden with the sweet aromas of late spring. I'm transported to twentieth century England, but not for long.

From directly above, the canopy bursts. Something large and black crashes through, scattering branches and shredding leaves. It's a prefect in combat armour. He or she is wearing a hover-pack. It's all story-crystal images. Prefects dressed for war is the stuff of juvenile-fiction, but it's a fiction which solidifies right before us. Another comes through from above, and then a rapid succession of them. Four, six, a dozen. And then a louder crash and a security-skin descends to land softly before us. Unlike the seeker-wasps, it's the latest model: stubby, stout and short, it bears little resemblance to the vaguely human-shaped security-skins of the past.

We're surrounded, and they level plazzers at us. It has to be a nightmare. I want to wake up. How is this more real than Christie's path of a few moments ago?

One of the prefects wears a built-in mantle, and with a flash of bright blue light, the image of GRENDEL is projected. He dispenses with the legal formalities of relieving a citizen of their freedom. He gives instructions with several precise movements of his holographic hands.

Then, he points directly to Raoul. 'We have no need of that one. Destroy it.'

The prefect cocks his head, questioning.

'Do it now!'

The prefect pushes Raoul into a kneeling position. There is fear in our friend's eyes. I am overwhelmed with horror and cannot speak. I try to initiate a blocker but I have no access. Using my mind to control the skin is equally futile. Fear has imposed an impenetrable barrier to the very cure for fear.

GRENDEL is impatient. 'I told you to destroy it.'

The prefect levels his plazgun at Raoul's head, but then wavers. He snaps the weapon off target and pulls himself to a loose form of military attention. 'I can't kill another human. He poses no threat to life and there are no other circumstances that the law allows –'

'Silence! I am giving you a direct order. It isn't human. It's no more than a construct in a biomechanical skin. Kill it, and kill it now!'

The prefect throws down his weapon and squares up to the graph. The mantle-wearing prefect's hand hovers over the off-button. All the other prefects lower their weapons, but they do not lessen their grip on me.

GRENDEL turns his attention to the security-skin. 'Destroy that creature.'

The skin glides towards Raoul. 'This creature is human. There are no imperatives that override the directive not to harm humans. Order refused.'

Without further comment, GRENDEL vanishes. The security-skin wobbles and trembles, its articulations rattle. I know exactly what is happening. GRENDEL is insinuating himself into the skin.

The disobedient prefect knows too. 'No! Stand down!'

The skin glides closer to Raoul and deploys its integral plazzer.

The prefect lifts his plazzer and fires straight at the skin, but the bolt is deflected by a force field, and in the same instant a flashing, fizzing bolt of lightning strikes the prefect, who falls stunned.

An instant later, Raoul screams as his body blackens and burns. In moments he is no more than smouldering wet ash over scorched bone.

I vomit. Dorsa falls to her knees. The dazed prefects obey GRENDEL's next command, issued from his new home in the security-skin. We are ushered through the jungle towards the DTZ where they say a flyer awaits.

My world has been destroyed. Normality no longer exists. We have entered a new era, but all these thoughts come to me through a haze of horror and denial.

GRENDEL killed a human. He killed Raoul.

The prefect grips tighter and pushes me on my way.

***

I discover it's impossible for a terrified man to do more than stumble, and my affliction impedes our progress. GRENDEL reaches into Dorsa and me and administers blockers. The mind-destroying trauma recedes, but the anger and memory of the horror remains. Poor, poor

Raoul. Can GRENDEL tell that given the glimmer of a chance I would blast him back to the Quantum in such a way that he could never reform?

GRENDEL's complete disregard for the standard etiquettes of enhanced life is no surprise. He's broken the highest laws, so niceties are nothing to him. He communicates with me telepathically without my permission. It's the same for Dorsa; he communicates with us both simultaneously.

'I am sorry about your native friend,' he says. 'Unfortunately my harsh actions were absolutely necessary.'

From somewhere in genetic memory, or more likely from my gene-hunting studies, I load and fire an ancient epithet. 'Bastard!'

Dorsa launches a broadside of her own Martian insults. They reverberate around my skull.

'I understand your pain,' GRENDEL continues. 'Truly, I do. But he had learnt how to use his inhuman skills and was therefore too dangerous to be left alive. After all, he had already killed one of my colleagues. Back at Campo Grande, remember?'

Of course I remember. 'And what about us?' I ask.

'We need to know more about you. For example, how are you able to control seekers, such as the one you recently destroyed? How did your native guide bring down a flyer?'

'It's just as much a mystery to me.'

'We intend to find out. For the initial tests it is necessary that you are alive.'

A chill of fear overwhelms the blockers for a moment. 'And after?'

'You will be deconstructed. Don't worry. There will be no pain. Once we have done with you, it will be as if you had never existed.'

Oblivion is not much to look forward to, whether or not it hurts. 'You are not doing any of this with Council approval, and you have taken us without a shepherd's warrant.'

'All those formalities take time, and we need to move quickly. You are clearly a threat.'

I ruminate upon the implications. Why the need for haste? Does he fear Dorsa and I will develop the same abilities as Raoul?

'You said Raoul wasn't human. What was he if not a man of flesh and blood?' And bones. I saw his blackened bones. They were human bones.

'Like you, he had the ability to commune with the grid without a neural-stent. Such a phenomenon is unnatural and worthy of our attention. We believe you are nothing more than constructs in a new fleshy form of skin. Androids, if you will.'

More blocker is needed. GRENDEL supplies it and I compare his words to my experience. He is lying, of course. I'm familiar with the historic term, but it has no modern application.

'Professor Coumans worked, with others, to manufacture you. He will be brought to justice.'

'The others? My father?'

'You have no father. The person you recall as Jonan Dzalarhons has never existed. He is no more than an implanted memory.'

Father and I played together. He told me bedtime stories. He picked sloth ticks from my skin when I'd ventured too near the creatures. He gave a speech at my graduation. I have clear memories of him. GRENDEL is lying. No manufactured memory could be as detailed, as extensive. Jonan was ... Jonan IS my father. I will not believe a graph who's broken our most sacred laws. But what is it he wants? Why Dorsa and me? And why did

Raoul have to die? GRENDEL's explanations are all lies.

The jungle begins to thin out and there in front of us is the bridge we crossed before. At the far end the decrepit old security-skin, more weed-covered than ever, stands silent guard. Maybe I can make use of it. I succeed in reaching into it with a strand of my being, but something lurks there and quickly evicts me.

I look down into the gully but there's no trace of the flyer's wreckage. The prefects' boots set up reverberations that make the bridge throb with their beat. There's a new flyer in the clearing on the other side, and there's the vac-tube terminal hut. GRENDEL, in his skin, brings up the rear.

Now we're on the other side in the open. The spikey grass scratches my bare feet. I never had time to replace my loin-pouch and I experience a rare species of fear. Unclothed is pretty much my natural state at home, but here I feel exposed and vulnerable. The flyer crew stare at us and I want to cover up. Dorsa must feel it ten times worse.

There comes the sound of ripping, and one of the prefects levels his weapon, but the crack and explosion doesn't come from his pazgun. Strands of blue-white lightning strike the flyer and all the prefects simultaneously. There's a wave of bolts, and the prefects all fall to the ground. Some move, dazed. They're not dead but each one's been incapacitated.

I spin to the sound of ripping and tearing and there by the bridge, the ancient security-skin has come to life and pulls itself free from the strands of living jungle. A heavy-duty plazzer muzzle deploys from its chest, several bolts of energy take out the force-shield of GRENDEL's skin and several more slam into the machine itself. It becomes incandescent and explodes. The shattered pieces fall off the bridge.

The old skin negotiates a path between the stunned bodies of prefects and comes to a stop in front of me. I look up into its eyes and it cocks its dome-like head. It speaks, and I know the voice.

'Hello, Ariel. Hasn't it been a long time?'

No blockers can handle the brief spasm of joy that fills me. 'Yes it has, Amalthea. A veritable eon.'

'Run to the flyer,' AMALTHEA says. 'I'm going to wear it like a skin.'

The old security-skin sags, empty again, and we run. Bart and two rangers run from the terminal hut and we all converge onto the flyer.

Bart is the last one aboard. I help drag him inside, the door closing behind him. 'It's one of our flyers,' he says. 'We'll soon get it airborne.'

The flyer shudders and lifts straight up, pressing us all to the deck. I fight inertia and get up onto my elbows. 'Don't worry, Bart. Amalthea's got this.'

Bart opens a locker and takes out a pair of formsuit discs, much larger than the last one I wore. It's too heavy to be held on with adhesive. It would damage our skin. Instead each disc has a pair of webbing loops, and Bart helps us on with them, arms through the loops. The disc sits comfortably between my shoulder-blades and within moments I'm dressed in a ranger's fatigues. For once, I'm relieved to be covered in clothing.

An identical uniform forms over Dorsa. Bart's final offering from the locker is a pair of boots for each of us. The nanobots finish my socks and I pull on the boots. They form to my foot-size, take on the correct colour for a ranger's uniform, and seal.

'The discs may be a bit on the heavy side, but they're the latest in nanotex tech,' Bart says. 'You can call up virtually any style or colour of clothing. The boots are linked and will form the correct complimentary footwear.' He goes on to explain that the tex features a blade-proof weave and has strong anti-bolt and ablative qualities.

'This all sounds very military-spec to me,' Dorsa says. 'We don't have anything like it on Mars as far as I'm aware.'

'You're correct, Dorsa. Neither Mars nor Earth has anything quit so advanced. It's actually Venusian Defence Force spec.'

I'm shocked. 'But, Venus doesn't have a defence force, or any military component at all.'

'It does now. Or rather, it's always had one, but now it's been called into action.'

I wonder how deeply Bart is into all this. Is he the man I thought I knew? Was GRENDEL telling the truth about him? 'You were obviously expected things to unfold much as they did,' I say, not ready to broach the deeper questions.

'Not exactly. We'd prepped the flyer for your evacuation from the DTZ, but the prefects arrived and commandeered it without warrant.'

AMALTHEA's voice sounds over the intercom. 'Strap in. We're about to go supersonic.'

Action first, questions later, unless we wanted to be splattered all over the rear bulkhead. As soon as I strap on restraints the questions won't wait another second. 'Where to now?' I don't give Bart time to answer. 'Because as far as I can see, we won't be safe anywhere on the entire planet.'

'Exactly,' Bart said. 'That's why we're leaving Earth.'

I know Bart's resourceful but how in the worlds has he arranged interplanetary travel?

'We're heading for the Venusian Eastwood Arboretum. Each of the worlds and colonies maintain an arboretum on Earth, and they all have small spaceports.'

Bart's achieved much more than to secure our ticket off-planet. He's made influential and high ranking Venusians aware of our plight. 'When we get home we'll meet with an old friend of mine. Markesa Zown is a government minister. I've every reason to believe she'll be able to help.'

Bart's reluctant to say why he's so confident about his friend's assistance.

An hour into our journey, the flyer starts to shake violently.

AMALTHEA's voice bursts from the speakers. 'I'm under attack. Another graph is attempting to wrest control from me. I need help, Ariel.' Her last sentence didn't emanate from the speakers, but planted itself directly into my mind.

I insert myself into the ethereal fray. Is this expanse of vibrations and electrical frisson … Quantum? I can't find proper words to describe any of it. How do you describe light to a blind person? How can I express Quantum in terms a world-dweller can grasp?

Insinuated between the tremulous being of AMALTHEA is the polluting essence of GRENDEL. At first I'm helpless. I have no terms of reference and do not know how to manifest my will in this non-space. The ability comes to me, and I expand. I expel GRENDEL, but I expel AMALTHEA too. Albeit linked to the universal graphness of Quantum, I am alone. I hear screaming, but there is no sound in Quantum, at least not the kind that ears can hear. And yet my ears hear.

I open my eyes to the world of substance, and it's in turmoil. My friends are all terrified. The flyer is nose down, and the land rushes up to meet us. We're about to crash.

Sol II

'Jamil, try to breathe.'

Jamil? The name echoes in the darkness. There are flashes of light that are not quite light. There are vibrations I cannot feel. Quantum or substance? I feel the weight of many minds, all directed towards me. I'm at the centre of something I can't understand.

'We need to get his lungs inflated.'

'Ease up on the pain blockers.'

All right, I understand. The crash. I'm too tired to think about it anymore. I must sleep, and trust my care to the people around me.

I come to and without opening my eyes I know I am home. The air is thick and smells different from Earth's. I keep my eyes closed. To open them may spoil the illusion. I'm in bed covered by a gossamer sheet. I let my hand fall from the edge and my fingers immediately encounter cool tiles. This really is home.

The light hurts my eyes adding to the dull headache that presses my skull, but it isn't enough to quell the excitement. I'm surrounded by the calming familiarity of my own room on Dzalarhons Mons. The plants have all grown since I was last here. Over there, the infamously slow-growing tree cactus is twice the size it was when I planted the cutting two years ago.

I throw off the sheet.

'Hello, Jamil,' comes a voice from system speakers. 'Your life-signs are stable. You may get up if you wish. I will continue to monitor you.'

That name again. 'Who are you?'

'I am the home AI. I have been set to medic.'

I sit up. Someone's removed Raoul's twine from my hips. Slightly annoying but I'm at home, so it's of little concern. The tiles are deliciously cool under my feet as I get reacquainted with my room. On the sill is the siliconized tentacle Father gave me, the most precious of my Rule Seven possessions and proof that life existed on Venus long before humans evolved on Earth. Next to it is the formsuit disc Bart gave me. But no, it's not the same one. Same design with its black webbing arm-loops, but this one has a catalogue number engraved onto the casing.

I pick it up and it's lighter than I recall. But of course, Venusian gravity accounts for this. I handle the tentacle. Smooth, glasslike and with a delicate pink hue, it was found with others like it shortly after humans began to settle on the newly terraformed Venus. Venusian fossils differ from those on Earth due to the extremes of heat and pressure to which they were subjected.

On the stand next to my bed is a film-gown. I reach for the garment, but hesitate. As good as it is to be home, I don't feel entirely safe, so I slip my arms through the loops of the disc and arrange it so the disc sits comfortably between my shoulder blades.

I contemplate calling up an unfamiliar set of clothing, simply because I have no idea what it looks like. I press the tiny control on the left loop and order 'Venusian Defence Force uniform.'

A wall speaker asks 'Dress uniform, standard uniform, standard combat or other?'

I order standard.

'Rank designation?'

'No rank insignia.'

The nanotex begins to form about my body with the same tickling sensation as always. The coyote-brown uniform is practical with several pockets and a high collar. It reminds me of projections I immersed myself in as a juvenile: tales of space exploration when early explorers experimented with space-bending;

experiments which came to no good and were abandoned hundreds of years ago. I notice there's a nametape above my left breast pocket that says MIRALAD. It's a well-established old Venusian name but one with which I have no connections, so I'm at a loss as to why it's there instead of my own name.

The completed uniform includes socks but no boots, so I root around and find a pair. I pull them on but like the disc these are not the boots Bart gave me. They're identical in style and function but subtly different in colour. They settle to a design that goes perfectly with the uniform. I stand in front of the wall adjacent to the window and tell it to reflect. It becomes a mirror and I'm the same old me but with dark, sunken eyes. I need to eat. I need to shower. But first I look around the old house.

The main hall has a spacious quadrilateral design. There's a short wall with a much taller one opposite and side walls that mirror each other. There's a compass design filling the highest wall. It alludes to the logo of the company that operated the mass-driver once housed in this building.

I think about the mechanics of the process. Before spin-up processes were initiated, Venus had a magnetosphere so weak it wouldn't turn a compass needle. But as the planet's spin increased subsurface dynamics changed and the faster the spin, the stronger the magnetosphere became. It was a side-effect that had been calculated and was entirely expected. Now our magnetosphere is over two-thirds that of Earth in strength, sufficient to deflect solar winds with a bit of help from a string of orbiting satellites.

All the rooms are as I remember them, but there's no sign of Father. I look everywhere, including the subterranean chamber. Father told me never to go there, but being a typical juvenile, I went anyway. Dark, with impressions on the walls and floor where old machinery of some kind once stood, and writing of a strange, swirling form that changes hue when light falls on it. The chamber was carved out by our very earliest colonists, its use and purpose lost to the mists of time. I suspect a quasi-religious connection. Superstitions had not entirely died out in those ancient times.

I return to my room and stand in front of the reflective wall. The MIRALAD name tag bothers me. I press the control at my left shoulder. 'Change nametape to Dzalarhons.'

'No,' says the speaker.

What!? I have given a direct and unambiguous instruction and the system has refused to comply? I give the order again, and again my command is refused. I access a blocker to counter my rising fury. System is not programmed to argue, or to refuse commands. This is outrageous!

Later I'll run a system diagnostic examination. Right now my skin irritates, and it's not because of nanobot actions. I undress again and stand in the shower-booth. I shower under jets of real water, a luxury on some worlds but a commodity that Venus isn't short of.

Something's wrong with my head. The skin over my skull is rough. The line over my brows too. It feels like a cat's tongue. And the area over my crotch. This is mildly frightening. What's wrong with me? I look down and my crotch area is covered in tiny black dots.

'I'm growing hair!'

System thinks I have given a command and asks for clarification. I rush out of the booth without drying. I'm dripping all over the tiles.

'Medical examination!'

I'm scanned. I can see where the beams intersect and the points where they move over my skin.

'Healing from recent trauma 89% complete. Raised heartbeat, but no indication of new trauma or medical complications. All your systems are functioning within normal parameters.'

'Am I growing hair?'

'Yes.'

'How is that even possible?' I ask the question out loud although I hadn't meant to. System begins to go through the biological processes of hair growth, so I tell it to shut up. I go back to the booth, dry and then get dressed in the VDF uniform again. I don't ask for links to Bart or Dorsa. It might not be safe to do so. Instead I go to the kitchen and order up some old Venusian favourites. I'll eat, and think, and then act.

I'm tired of being captured. I'm fed up being rescued. I've had it with following people. It's time I started leading this quest for Jonan Dzalarhons. Of course, he is my father. I love him and I want to find him, but he is also key to everything else that has followed his kidnapping. If I find Father, I find myself.

I pick up the few pieces of fruit I can eat while walking. I always think more clearly on my feet. Without making the conscious effort I take up the slow, measured pace of home, the gait I had almost lost in my years on Earth. I go out onto the balcony. I pace its width and try to order my thoughts, but it's difficult to get past the memory of Raoul. His scream. The smell. His ruined remains. The horror of it is magnified by the knowledge that I might soon suffer the same fate. And Dorsa. Where is she? Who brought me home, and why do I have no memory of the journey?

Right! First I need to avail myself of as much knowledge as possible. I have to set up an untraceable link to the grid, and interrogate it for the information I need to carry my mission forward. It shouldn't be too difficult, so long as I can order my stentless thoughts. I have an idea and go back inside.

'Medical. Neural-stent recalibration.' I don't speak, but stretch my thoughts into the home system.

The familiar beams of light touch me again. 'Examination reveals you have no neural-stent.'

'Question. If I have no stent, how am I communicating with you?'

I've waited more than five seconds for a reply. I wonder if the system is faulty. System examines me again and replies. 'Unable to determine. Shall I link and search to find out if there is new undetectable stent tech?'

'No. Do not link. Do not allow any activity to be accessed out of home system. Maintain system security, level "Locked".'

Of course, system may already be compromised. And just because it can't detect a stent doesn't mean I haven't got one. I return to the balcony and lean on the balustrade. It's so good to take in lungsful of fresh, home air. The forest slopes down to Dzalarhons City, the sun sparkles off the distant ocean beyond. And now, the distinct and earie impression that I am not alone. Something sub-audible, almost intra-ethereal but definitely real. My consciousness shrinks to the confines of my own body, and then flares out at the touch, light but electric, on my shoulder.

Spinning, I'm confronted by a tentacle-limbed spectre of Venus's indigenous and long extinct lifeform. My height and vaguely, barely humanoid it stands back and waves an arm that terminates with a hand bearing long pink tentacles in place of fingers. I shrink into myself like an exposed anemone in a rock pool.

***

But now, joy and relief. It spreads from my fear-contracted being and spills out as laughter.

When the siliconized remains of Venus's tentacle-bearing lifeforms were first discovered, their living form was a mystery. No DNA had survived the fossilisation process. Then came the emergence of graphs as a life form, and they could examine fossilised structures at levels far beyond human tech. Graph scientists established a theory that Venus's beings had been advanced and sentient. They were able to make a highly educated guess at their appearance.

Homo apoaphrotia, a nomenclature that sent scholars of Latin and Greek into fits of fury, had been determined to look exactly like the creature which stands before me.

It waves its tentacle-fingered hand in a humanlike way. The wave tells me my old sex-skin is being operated, not by a construct, but by a graph. I chuckle at the thought of what Dorsa would make of my choice of sexual partner, and then tingle by recalling the fun I'd had with it.

'Adopt human form.' I remember I'm addressing a graph. 'If you please.'

The sex-skin's satin-grade nanoplastic flesh begins to reshape. The tentacles become human arms, the fleshy mantle is now a female torso, and the transformation is complete. Standing before me is Botticelli's Venus, minus the oversized scallop-shell.

'Very nice. Now may I ask, who are you?' Immediately on asking I fear this renaissance beauty may be under the control of GRENDEL.

'Hello. It's me, Amalthea.'

What a relief!

'Correct me if I'm wrong, Ariel, but isn't this a sex-skin?'

'It is.'

'And the last form?'

'It was a great deal of fun, as far as I remember.' It was. Perhaps the best. I begin to get excited from the memory, but now I think of my Martian friend and it's like a bucket of cold water. 'But please don't mention it to Dorsa.' She'll believe all her prejudices about Venusians are true if she gets wind of my tentacle-bearing simulated-lover. 'Where's Dorsa, by the way? And how did I get here?'

'There is still much of Quantum I cannot access. It's as if there is a war among the graphs. I am in a constant search for the truth, but I know how you came to be here.'

AMALTHEA begins a projection. There's the flyer in which we escaped from GRENDEL and the prefects. I remember now. The forward port was filled with a landscape that rushed at us. My last memory of that flight was a crescendo of noise, and then nothing.

'You succeeded in expelling Grendel, but he melded so tightly with me that I was ejected too,' AMALTHEA says. 'His last action was to disrupt the back-up constructs. With nobody in control, the flyer crashed. You suffered critical injuries.'

'The others?'

'There were only two survivors. Dorsa and you were saved. The others were beyond help.'

I'm overwhelmed with grief. Dorsa and I survived, but Bart Coumans died in the wreckage. The flyer ploughed into the edge of the five-thousand acre Venusian Eastwood Arboretum.

'There was no sign of the Grendel after the crash. Help soon came and you were sedated and restructured. Being on Venusian soil, so to speak, we had no problems bringing you home.'

I find a seat and slump into it. First Raoul, and now Bart. Anger rises in me, eats up the grief.

'Would you like me to administer a –'

'No! No blockers. Ever again, thank you.' A few moments of deep breathing helps. 'And what of Dorsa?'

'Returned to her world on a diplomatic packet. We've given her a new identity. As we have you.'

I finger the nametape on my uniform. 'Miralad?'

'You are now Jamil Miralad. We've drilled down into the grid as far as possible to create a new persona. You should be undetectable to our adversaries as your former self. We've done the same for Dorsa. Officially you both died in the accident.'

I look at the projection. There's my hand, partially severed. My torso is twisted, and my bloody face can be seen through a mesh of broken metal. It is like witnessing my own gory death. And there's Dorsa next to me, equally bloody.

I examine my wrist. 'The medics did a good job.'

'Indeed. Graph-meds had to restructure at molecular level.'

Her words barely penetrate the grief. Poor, poor Bart. Now tears are falling. I'm hollow with it, a void that needs filling but with what? I cry out when I see Bart, so clearly beyond saving, his body smashed and ruined. At once, I understand the ancients' need for a god. Oh god. Oh god. Oh God, help me.

But of course, there is no help. Horror and grief must go its way.

There is familiar warmth. The pain is receding. 'Stop! I said no blockers. Stop it now!'

'You're in danger of collapse, Ariel. I must –'

'No, you mustn't. Get out of me at once!' It hurts again, instantly. My face is wet with tears, but I must navigate the agony. Deep breathing again, and the obvious question arises. Through sobs: 'Amalthea, you talk of "we". "We have done this. We have done that." Who is "we"?'

123

***

I'm calm now, but I have a lot to think about.

AMALTHEA tells me 'We' is her word for 'me' in that strange quantum world where she is smaller than can be seen with anything less than a quantum microscope and yet the entire Universe. She is we and we is she and one is all and all is one.

'Think of your body as the Universe,' she says. 'Think of each cell in your body as if it is a sentient individual. That is the closest analogy that a human brain may easily take in.'

But AMALTHEA is lying. I run my fingers over the stubble that forms on my chin, pass a palm over my once smooth head. Apart from the hair, I am me in every discernible respect. AMALTHEA tells me the hair is a side-effect of the procedures that were required to save my life. The ancients had a word for it that cannot adequately be bettered: 'BULLSHIT!' She's dissembling; attempting to divert me from the main question.

'You saved me. Operated on my close to dead body. Brought me here and changed my identity. All by yourself? There are others involved, Amalthea, and I don't mean other incarnations of yourself.'

AMALTHEA in her Old Master's Venus Rising sex-skin sits on the seat opposite me. She has mastered fine control over this lifeless machine and makes it peer at me, oozing concern.

'There's more to Dorsa and me than Grendel and the others who are after us, isn't there? There's another faction who are on our side. We're the centre of something big. Nothing else makes sense. Don't deny it!'

AMALTHEA neither denies nor confirms. It's an answer in itself.

'Believe me, Ariel, I was not part of all this until after the flyer crash. Even now I am only on the periphery.'

She tells me Dorsa and I are part of an experiment. 'The idea was to build in the ability to interface with the grid and to communicate directly with graphs. In fact, to enjoy all the benefits of a neural-stent without actually having one.'

That answers a lot of questions. But nowhere near all. 'Fine, but why does Grendel object, to the extent of killing us?'

'As I understand, the idea was always controversial. With the ability to work directly in the grid without augmentations, you shift a subtle balance of power.'

'I don't see how. It's merely a change of interface.' Now I'm being disingenuous. In recent weeks I've discovered I can exceed the abilities of the stented. I can see into Quantum.

'I suggest you access crystal projections on the historical phenomenon called the arms race. It was a time when seemingly small advances led to changes in the balance of power that resulted in warfare.'

'Those times were all pre-Pandemic. We're different people now.'

'And you are that little bit more different.'

I stand and take a few steps towards the sex-skin. 'Would you mind getting out of that thing? I'd be more comfortable if you project in your registered form.' I wonder why she chose to inhabit the skin in the first place.

The skin stand and dips its head. 'One moment, please,' AMALTHEA says, and leaves me. And then she's back, the tumbling, elongated projected satellite with which I'm familiar.

'Is that better?'

'Yes, thank you. And it will be better still when you begin telling me the truth.'

Her light dips, and then resumes its usual intensity.

'This body,' I say sweeping my palms down from chest to hips. 'You're implying that it's stented biologically rather than mechanically, right? What did they do to me?' I have no recollection of long sessions in hospital as a juvenile.

The light dips again. She's experiencing internal conflict. I know enough about graphs to recognise the signs.

For a moment I contemplate entering her world. I think I can do it. But it's not the time. 'Did they tinker with me in the womb?'

'Not entirely. Your embryo was created in a bioprinter.'

Something tilts. My eyes lose focus and there is a sound; high, keening and pathetic. I'm aware in some part of myself that the sound is coming from me.

'Sit down, Ariel,' she says.

Ariel? Who's Ariel? I don't want to sit down. I want to rant. I want to explode and take everything with me, to kill, to utterly destroy.

But I slump into a chair.

'I'm administering blockers whether you like it or not.'

I breathe deeply and the calm seeps from my core to my extremities.

'You are Ariel. Look within. You know it. It's only that until now you haven't known exactly who Ariel is.'

Something inside shifts and I recall events from a life that isn't mine. They're memories from Christie's world of mud and trenches and war. I am opened to an entire new vocabulary.

'Well, Amalthea. What the fuck am I? Am I even human?'

If she dims any more, she'll go out altogether.

'Of course you are, and you always have been. Your creation did not break the moratorium on human bioprinting. You are perfectly legal.'

Well, that's wonderful. I couldn't give a feathered fuck. I'm blocker-blitzed beyond caring. 'And Father? Is he real or is Jonan Dzalarhons another joke you've pulled on me?'

'I don't recall him, but I am able to state your father is real. And he has been kidnapped. I will do everything within my power to help you find him.'

I nod. 'Thank God for small mercies. Dad is still real.'

AMALTHEA brightens up again. 'Are you aware that you're speaking a very old style of Standard?'

She's correct. How bizarre. I make a conscious effort to reclaim my own speech patterns. 'I want you to tell me everything you know. I mean everything, no matter how badly you believe I'll take it. I need to be in control of my own destiny, and I can't go ahead unless I know everything.'

'Nobody knows everything, whether they're human or graph.'

If she was solid, I'd slap her. 'Don't be obtuse.'

'I am being no such thing. Your genesis is shrouded in veils of security that reaches into Quantum.

I struggle to understand what this all means.

'If you wait until tomorrow, you will be told as much as anybody knows.' Graphs can multi-task. While doing her best to comfort me, AMALTHEA has been busy and has organised a meeting at an obscure government building in the city. 'Bart had already started to contact people who might be able to help. I merely finished his work.

'There will be government representatives, graph-scientists and members of the security services. You will be briefed as thoroughly as possible.'

'With nothing left out? No redactions or "need to know basis" bullshit.' I like that old word. I intend to keep using it. AMALTHEA assures me I'll be told everything. 'And how long have you kept me in the dark? From your graph perspective, you must have been aware of my differences. You've been a family friend for years. How long have you been lying to me?'

'I knew nothing. There is nothing about you that makes you obviously different. You really are a very well-kept secret.

***

I'm a well-kept secret. Not very comforting.

After a surprisingly good night's sleep I put on the VDF uniform again, but I've changed the plan. I'm not going to turn up at a government building in the city. The meeting is coming to me, because I say so. To my surprise, there was no argument. They'll be here within the hour. I'm going to get out of this uniform and into a film-gown.

'No, don't do that,' AMALTHEA says. I reverse my command and the poor little nanobots have to dress me again before the suit is even half absorbed. 'For reasons that will become clear, the VDF uniform is a perfect choice.'

I've scheduled the meeting to last a couple of hours, giving me the afternoon to mull over the business of the meeting. I am fed up beyond blocking with 'mulling things over'. I try to establish a link with Benjo. I'm immediately successful although I wonder how. I know the science behind use of neural-stents better than I know the science of my own body.

'S'Jinning hail, Ariel! How are you? I thought you were killed in a flyer accident.' His heart rate goes through the roof. I reach into him and administer a blocker. The distance between us doesn't make my ministrations any less effective. 'Hey, you're not some kind of sick joke, are you?' Benjo's thoughts slide directly into my mind. Now the shock has subsided, they're silky, warm and comforting.

'I can explain everything. Where are you, Benjo?'

'Still on the island. West Beach. I'm in bioprint-evolution with Ven-Tech BioCoy, specialising in sloths.'

Sloths stink to beyond the canopy. 'Sloths? Yuk! Look, Benjo, can you drop what you're doing and get to Dzalarhons Hall?'

'Sounds urgent?'

'Bordering, at least. For about four this afternoon?'

'I'll be there. Meanwhile I'll wash the stenchof monssloth off me.' Benjo's transmitted laugh makes me recall the happiest of times.

'Codes are unchanged. Let yourself in. Later, Benjo.' I break the link and I'm optimistic. I try a link to Mother, but no luck. I can't get Dorsa either, but I don't try too hard. As a kind of forlorn hope I'm trying to link with Father. I can't find him, but nor is my mind faced with a sheer wall. It's as if he's disconnected rather than annihilated, and I'm hopeful. But I break off, being concerned that too much link-activity will alert GRENDEL and his minions.

A reunion with Benjo is something I look forward to. It'll get me through the meeting which is about to begin. I'm a fraud in this VDF uniform, but AMALTHEA assures me nothing could be better.

There! The declining whine of a small flyer's motive-generator. From the balcony I can see it through the trees on the landing court. It carries a logo which I take to be that of the VDF. For an organisation that's been in stasis for a generation, it certainly has some leading edge tech. Two people emerge, one of whom is dressed in a uniform like mine.

I greet them at the threshold in the traditional manner for formal meetings: hands clasped lightly over my stomach, head inclined whilst maintaining eye-contact. The VDF man returns the greeting and looks pleased to find me in uniform. He introduces himself as Force First Officer Kyler Britton. His attire is identical to mine except for a woven rank patch above his nametape.

He introduced the woman as Government Minister Markesa Zown. Bart's friend! I wonder if Kyler deliberately omits her department.

The couple look like a study in opposites. Kyler Britton has silver hair gathered in a knot above the nape of his neck. He is stout of limb and edging towards middle age, with a round, kindly face. Markesa Zown is slim and hairless in the traditional Venusian way. Her face is narrow, her chin pointed, and her sharp eyes fix on me like a laser-sight.

Her voice however, is sweet and pleasing. 'May we introduce our graph colleague?'

'By all means,' I say, and lead the couple into Father's study. The domestic-skin has made it ready for the meeting. The wall-lenses in this room are state of the art, so I am not surprised now that the next attendee forms so solidly. The cat-ears and tail are a little unexpected though.

NEKO presents as a boy who is half-cat. He immediately puts me in mind of a history-crystal in which I was once immersed, about the ill-fated crew of the Mapping & Survey Ship Phoenix Song. The ship was destroyed and the crew all lost in an accident that put an end to space-bending experiments.

In those days it hadn't been discovered that graphs were a lifeform completely different to AI constructs. Almost everyone had their own assigned graph which they used as an interface with the cyber-world. One of the crew of the Phoenix Song had a cat-boy graph partner similar to NEKO. I mention it, by way of breaking the ice.

'Of course I know the story,' the cat-boy says. 'I based my appearance on that same Neko.'

This graph actually has NEKO's personality. One of the crew of the famous MSS98 Phoenix Song? I had no idea graphs could take on so much more than simple identity. 'Isn't that as good as saying you're the real Neko?'

The cat-boy giggles, like a cheeky juvenile. 'I assume you are aware of the graph quantum-personality paradox.'

Of course I am. 'You are Neko and so is every other graph. I didn't know that covered all time as well as all space.'

'Suffice to say I salvaged much from the original Neko's personality framework, and I have come to think of this appearance as "me".'

Back in those days, graphs often took forms that were important to their human counterparts, and the histories are clear that Ollie Thomas, one of Phoenix Song's seven human crewmen, enjoyed an old art form called 'manga' and that NEKO had taken his form to please her. I must say, it is an appearance that quite pleases me too.

And now, here is AMALTHEA with her beautiful name but the drab appearance of a rocky old satellite. She tumbles and sparks. I excuse myself from the others once they're comfortably seated and draw AMALTHEA to one side.

'I need to make something clear, Amalthea. No more blockers, thank you. If I'm ever to get a grip of this new existence of mine, I have to master all aspects of self-control. Irrespective of the outcome or of your good intentions, I'll consider any such unbidden insertions as an assault. Am I clear?'

I expect her form to dim in contrition, but she shines brighter – a sign of approval. I find it surprisingly supportive.

The visitors' tone chimes and I let in the last of the attendees. It's another person in VDF uniform. Her rank patch is high-glow orange and bears a single gold bar. After introductions I lead Group-Commander Ibby Carlane to the study. The orange denotes her branch as the Space Corps. I mentally set myself the task of absorbing information about the structure and ranks of the VDF. Ibby is an older woman with a family mondokoro tattooed high on her forehead in the form of a small, stylised forget-me-not.

Now we're settled and the introductions complete. Our domestic-skin, inhabited by the construct 'Edwin', has served beverages and withdrawn to his cubicle. Art is projected onto the walls, and a picture-window gives us a view overlooking the jungle. Nobody speaks, and then I recall it usually falls on the host to chair a meeting. I go to speak, but …

'Perhaps you would prefer me to chair,' Minister Zown says.

'Thank you, Markesa, but no,' I say. 'I'll chair, and if you don't mind I'll also set the agenda. Or at least, the first part of it. Thereafter I'm happy to open to any business you may have.' Whoever engineered me gave me no choices. From now on, I intend to make choices.

There is a murmur of assent, and dear AMALTHEA glows again. NEKO smiles delightfully and I imagine he purrs. I wonder briefly if my sex-skin can become a cat-boy.

I clear my throat to begin, but the high ranking Kyler Britton interjects. 'If I may? It's very encouraging to see you've adopted Venusian Defence Force uniform, Citizen Dzalarhons.'

I tell him to call me Ariel. 'Citizen Dzalarhons' makes me think they're addressing Father.

'Certainly. "Ariel" will do until it's time to fully adopt your new identity. The thing is, it's not fitting that you present as a base level officer though, because we've already arranged a rank that will give you the authority required for the tasks ahead.'

Tasks ahead? They had better ask me, rather than appoint me to these unspecified tasks. I will not be ordered. First Officer Britton asks me to activate my formsuit control, and I do so.

'Add rank insignia for Cohort-Commander in Special Operations,' Britton says for the benefit of the nanobots. I watch the area above my nametape while they create a three centimetre square black patch bearing a single silver bar. Britton now addresses me: 'We've commissioned you to the highest rank commensurate with your apparent age, in fact slightly above. Youths can't usually aspire to higher than company-commander, but we'll get away with it because we've placed you in Special Ops. That'll discourage anybody from asking too many questions.'

He explains that cohort-commander is the lowest of the legionary-level ranks. This means nothing to me, but since immersing myself in the story of my ancestor Christie Grey, I have somehow acquired knowledge of the British Army ranks of that period. I ask if he knows the equivalent. He doesn't, but the minister has studied history. 'If memory serves me correctly, cohort-commander most closely equates to major. It's not an exact equivalent because there are no non-commissioned ranks in the Defence Force.'

I thank her, and call the meeting to order.

We deal with all the business. I learn much, but I'm disturbed that our mission cannot include Dorsa. It is apparently too risky to liaise between the worlds over a matter that is so sensitive. Opposing graphs are monitoring the grid for any talk concerning us despite the fact they believe us dead.

'You must be aware that your survival is known only to a few, even here on Venus,' the minister says. 'If it were discovered that you lived through the flyer accident, there're those who'd find many allies throughout the worlds happy to hunt you down. You're "different", and it has ever been too easy for those with agendas to make difference a target, and a focus for irrational fears.'

I ask about our hunters. They're no more than a faction at the moment. They've been working outside the law, but they are playing on fears and spreading lies. They're fast approaching a tipping point when their mission to debase the existence of those like me will be official policy.

It's as if I'm being told nonsense, it's so outside of my entire life's experience. I recall horrors from history; pogroms and concentrations camps. In our case their job is a lot easier. They won't have to eliminate millions, only Dorsa and me, so the longer they believe us already dead the better.

Much has been left unsaid, and I'll leave something unsaid too. Dorsa will be part of this mission, whether they like it or not.

The Venusian team acknowledge the existence of Father, though none have memory of him and records do not exist. It transpires that everyone with a stent is susceptible to memory modification, and the team accept this as the explanation to Jonan's absence from the minds of people who knew him. Simple data manipulation accounts for his disappearance from all records, except for certain paper-based notes which were found at home. Father had taught himself to write with crude implements and left a record. They promise to send me a copy.

The meeting concludes and Kyler tells me he'll be in touch when they have a plan.

'Thank you, Kyler. Perhaps it would be better if I contact you when I have a plan.'

He bristles and I know he wants to call me a jumped up little shit, although once again I'm uncertain to whom I owe thanks for that singular and very crude syntax.

They've left, all except for Minister Zown. Her parting words of sympathy and support sound hollow, and I'm sure I've still not been told everything.

***

I watch Zown's ministerial crawler disappear along the causeway.

'Seal the doors,' I tell system. 'Allow entry only to Benjo Drexler.'

System acknowledges my command. I order the domestic to prepare a meal.

Now, I'm fed and changed into my film-gown. It is nearly four, and Benjo is notoriously punctual. One of the meeting's conclusions is that nothing of my strange geneses and close to unique condition should be mentioned outside the meeting. Well, fuck that! I'm going to tell Benjo everything. We've never kept secrets, and I don't intend to start now.

I hear the door slide open. Benjo was never subject to the usual etiquettes. System has him listed as family.

'Hey, Ariel. You in here?'

'Come through, Benjo.'

There he is, his smile as infectious as ever. But now he is no longer simply Benjo. He's Christie's Jack, and the man being swallowed up by the crowd in that projection of Shona and Philip.

I recall Jack's words to me when he stepped out of the projection after helping the badly wounded Christie. 'You ever need answers, sir, don't forget about poor Jack.'

I'm not going to forget about poor Jack, and I hope poor Benjo is going to provide a few answers.

I tell him everything. I do better than tell him. I show him the grid-stream of the flyer accident. He squeezes my arm as he sees the state I was in, injured and covered in blood. Now I access my student-file on the Unicamp grid and download my research. We're in Christie's projection and Benjo shares the wonder at seeing the pair of us in a historical setting.

'This Jack fellow is an attractive character, Benjo says. 'And not only because he looks like me.'

We're on the last scene where Christie lies injured by the wreckage of his aircraft.

'Freeze scene!' Benjo says. Jack lies in the mud bandaging Christie's wound. 'I'm not sure why, but this means something.' Benjo points to the brass titles on Jack's epaulette. 'MSS99. Doesn't that remind you of something?'

I'm afraid it doesn't.

'Well, MSS98 – just one number out – was the designation of the Phoenix Song, and its emblem was a phoenix, and this little flaming bird badge above the letters looks like a phoenix.'

I have a closer look. Certainly, it's a bird of prey on fire, but it doesn't have the look of a phoenix to me. 'What could it mean? The Phoenix Song was destroyed hundreds of years back.'

'Aha, but the essence of the phoenix is that it rises again. Like you.' He takes my hand and runs a finger along the wrist. 'The medics virtually brought you back from the dead.' He shudders, and I regret showing him that gory projection.

Benjo has no idea why he appeared in my dreams and the history-crystal projections. I answer all his questions to the best of my ability, and then we speak about his life since I left. We broach that last night we spent together, probably not wise when I'm without filters.

Then again, why not? I'm back home. Surely it's time to really renew that old bond. I put a nuance into our conversation, and there's a look in his eye. I think I may have succeeded.

Now standing close, he lets his hand rest on my shoulder. 'I feel the sudden need to check over the medics' work. In close detail.'

'Don't let me stop you.'

He runs his fingers up my neck and face, letting them rest on my scalp. 'The hair. Is it only your head, chin and eyebrows, or all over?' He's adding nuance now. He slips my film-gown off over my head, then removes his. 'Let's abandon filters and go outside.' It's merely an expression, because Benjo is no-tech and has never had filters. I wonder how he copes.

He licks his top lip and a smile spreads through my whole body. I want to see if the medics did a thorough job. Does my repaired body work in all the subtle and not so subtle ways that the old one did.

On Earth, they say 'Let's go to bed'. On Mars it's 'Let's go to the corner of the dome'. I haven't a clue how Callistonians seduce. Here on Venus, we go outside, and it's been so long since I've been outside with anyone who isn't a sex-skin. It was Benjo when I was a juvenile and Benjo the night before I left home. It's going to be Benjo now. Since Jonan disappeared it's all been wrong. This at least couldn't be more right.

***

We're wet with the heavy, humid air of the Dzalarhonian jungle, and with sweat. We're lying in one another's arms on warm, damp moss.

Benjo traces lines in the moisture beading my skin; down my chest, across my belly and to my left hip which is uppermost as I turn towards him. His finger presses at the point a centimetre above my pelvis. 'Here's where you were bitten by that lion-snake when we were juveniles.'

'I know. You'd think the medics would have dealt with that when they fixed everything else, but no such luck.'

'Only the hair?'

'Afraid so. It's a side effect of the molecular tweaking that was necessary.'

'It's as if you can't be killed. Destroy your body and the graph-medics will always make up another one for you.'

'I got lucky.'

Benjo doesn't look convinced. I can't really say that I am either. He decides to forget about it all. Returning to the present, he touches the stubble on my chin. 'Rough, isn't it? I think you may have given me a rash.' He rubs the inside of his thigh.

'Jealous?'

'Absolutely not. The very thought of it makes me itch. I'm happy hairless.' He props himself up on his elbow. 'But don't get me wrong. It looks great on you. At least it will once it's all come through. Right now it looks like you need to wash your head.'

'You look good with a full head of hair, Benjo.'

'Yes, those projections. I looked good with golden hair.'

Again, we discuss his incarnations in my historical crystal projections, and I trace my finger through the moisture on his skin. Across his chest – he shivers at my touch – along his arm, his hand and … What's this? On the third finger of his right hand, a ring that looks very familiar. If it's not Father's black partner-band it's a near-perfect copy.

'What's wrong, Ariel? Lay back down.'

'Where did you get this ring?'

The friskiness flies from Benjo and he sits up as if under a dark cloud. 'Of course! I'm such an idiot! The ring. Ariel, I'm so sorry. It was so long ago, I forgot.'

'Forgot what?'

'It was weeks ago. Maybe months. I'd seen what looked like a prefect-flyer over your place and I was worried. I came over. Nobody was about so I let myself in. The ring was –'

'In the deep carpet pile by the threshold?' I recall a scene from AMALTHEA's projection.

'No, it was wrapped in the finger-tentacles of a very imaginative-looking sex-skin.'

There's nothing the least bit embarrassing about this, but a blush comes on. I wonder if I'm getting bursts of Christie's emotions as well as his memories. 'My sex-skin? Did it say anything?'

'I don't think so. It gave me the ring and returned to its dock. I don't think it spoke, but then I was too busy laughing and wondering where all those tentacles go when you're –'

'In all the usual places, Benjo. Now shut up!'

'Anyway, I put the ring on for safekeeping and left. I came back a couple of times but your father was never here. I couldn't trace him through the grid.' Being low-tech and stentless, he remembers Father. I imagine his life was in danger from our adversaries until mine apparently came to an end. Benjo takes the ring off and hands it to me. I put it on and immediately my connection with Father strengthens.

Benjo looks troubled and a little embarrassed. He feels he's let me down, but I know how to fix that. 'Now, where were we before I so rudely interrupted?'

Benjo answers with a smile. 'Be careful with those whiskers. That's one place I definitely don't want a rash.'

'Your files are ready and downloaded into a crystal,' System says, interrupting at the most inopportune moment.

'What files?'

'Projection files for the story of Christie Grey.'

System is obviously malfunctioning. I inform it that we've already watched the projection.

'That is impossible. Due to difficulties in the search and the time delay between Earth and Venus, I have only just processed them.'

I tell system to shut up and order a self-diagnosis.

***

Benjo is staying the night. Taking a line from the Earthers, we share a bed and discover a bed can be as much fun as the garden.

***

'It's a shame you have appointments today,' I say.

Benjo agrees, but he's project leader and cannot delegate today's duties to either human, graph or construct. 'May I come back here tonight?'

I chuckle. 'Ask again with cooler blood.'

'Cooler blood be damned. We have a lot of catching up to do.'

It's all I can manage not to drag him outside again, or into my bed. But there *is* work to do. I dress in the now officially approved VDF uniform and Benjo slips into his film-gown.

'You look smart in that get-up, Ariel, but how do you keep from boiling alive inside that thing?'

'It's an advanced kind of nanotex with built-in heat-dumps. It's surprisingly cool.'

Benjo prepares to leave. 'Have a productive day, Ariel. Can't wait to get back here this evening.' Nuanced again, but hardly subtle.

I point to my nametape. 'Maybe practice calling me Jamil. Those at the meeting were very keen for me to adopt my new identity as thoroughly as possible.'

'Sure, Jamil. If it keeps nefarious Earth agents and wayward graphs from breaking your bones, it's an easy ask.'

I wave him off at the threshold. Benjo waves back. Does a single night make us partners? He's gone until tonight, but he has left me confident, secure and complete. I think I might be able to retire my sex-skin forever. My repaired body appears to be working at least as well as the old one, and my relaxed mind is a vast improvement. Honed by adversity, perhaps.

True to their word, my allies supply me with a copy of Father's notes. They're written as an aide memoir rather than instructions to another person, but I believe I have the gist.

Father, Dorsa and I were supposed to be aboard the Endeavour. For reasons not apparent in the notes, it's imperative that we reach Albion. An impossibility with the Endeavour weeks into its voyage, but I'm not giving up. Cloaked in my new identity, I immerse myself in the grid and seek out alternatives, and yes, there is another ship. It's in orbit around Mars.

Father's notes show that we must get to Albion first. We must be the first humans to set foot on that far flung outpost. Another impossibility. But once again I set my mind to the task and through strings of mathematics even that becomes possible.

If we transit to Mars with minimal delay, board the deep space vessel and set off at 1.2 gee, we should be able to accelerate for longer than the Endeavour, achieve a higher velocity and overhaul her several months out from Albion.

I've contacted my high-ranking allies, who I think of as 'the Committee'. They are surprisingly accommodating and do not take much persuading. They agree to negotiate the necessary permissions and make the practical plans, all under the cover of strict secrecy. Without asking anyone for permission, I try to make contact with Dorsa. I'm determined she'll be part of the mission.

There's someone else I want on this mission, for the sake of my sanity, and I try to contact Dr Verone Kell. This appears to be a sticking point with the Committee, but we'll see.

To have any hope at all, we must leave for Mars as soon as possible. At the moment, 'soon as possible' is a week away. The Committee has negotiated the use of a ship to get us there, but it must be crewed with reliable people and prepped.

Meanwhile I'm getting up to speed with the rights, privileges and responsibilities of a VDF cohort-commander. In fact, I'm learning about the VDF in general; its history, functions, structure and traditions. On AMALTHEA's advice I'm making a detailed study of the practical requirements of the VDF's Space Corps. Zipping from one world to another as a passenger is a lot different from working in space, and it looks like I'll be clocking up a lot of hours, so I need to know the basics.

I'm also going to be trained in weapons handling. I hate the very idea of it. I can't think 'plazgun' without recalling the two deaths I've witnessed. They can teach me how to use one, but they can never make me operate the initiator, or trigger, or whatever it's called. I'd rather hone those mind-skills that Raoul used to such decisive effect on GRENDEL's flyer.

The Committee believes Earthers will soon discover that I wasn't permanently disposed of in the flyer accident, and won't pull any punches to get their hands on me, so combat is another area in which I must have at least a passing acquaintance.

All this, and I have less than a week. AMALTHEA says much of my training can be carried out in transit. We'll see, but I have to report that I'm quietly confident. I'm no longer running away. I have a goal and a purpose, and at least some knowledge of why all this is happening.

There's another task which AMALTHEA tells me is important. I have to immerse myself in my last crystal-projection. She doesn't know why, just as she had no idea why my life was in danger back when all this started. 'If I had intestines, I would call it a gut feeling.'

So that's my first task, and I'm happy about that. My last crystal takes me back almost two millennia to the furthest reaches of my gene-hunting exercise. Using archive material that came to light less than five hundred years ago and quantum-gene skewing, the projection promises to be an exquisite look into my most ancient known ancestor to date, although I don't know who it is. Judging on past projections, I assume he'll be projected in my image.

The crystal is slick to the touch, but it's perfectly dry. Give it a little lick and it tingles the tip of the tongue, a tried and tested trick to assess whether a crystal is loaded or not. I have a spare hour, so now is the time.

The hall is a wonderful space for crystal projected immersion, and it's all set up. I place the crystal on the objective-plate, and give my order. 'Play reconstruction. Accompany projection with third person past tense narration. Go!'

***

My quest has ruined me for my research. Material so rich I would once have needed blockers to curb my excitement merely annoys me for lack of relevant clues. The projection opens with Eleanor, former lady of Brittany and now King John's prisoner in Corfe Castle. She refuses to acknowledge the King who murdered her brother, Arthur Duke of Brittany, true heir to the throne.

But what's any of this got to do with me? Lady Eleanor awaits two callers. First, a visit from her lover, a young knight who is a prisoner like her, and later an audience with Sir Hubert, one of the King's men.

I'm done with this. But wait! Here's something of relevance. A knock and the door is opened, but not to Sir Benedict. This young lad has Benjo's looks, and so my attention peaks.

'May I?' A very young man stepped from the shadows and into the light of the doorway. He bowed low, as one would to a queen. 'Guy d'Annebelle, my lady. At your service, if you please.' His family crest, an eagle in gilded flames, was stitched upon his tunic.

Guy's face looks exactly like Benjo's did at that age, and the golden bird again. This is the third time it's appeared to me in either projection or dream.

But then, nothing. Guy tells Eleanor his brother Benedict has a chill and cannot attend upon her. Instead they play cards until Sir Hubert, her second caller arrives. Guy takes his leave. There's something about this next section though. I pay closer attention.

Sir Hubert came promptly after the None bell without time to say his afternoon prayers. There were the usual pleasantries. Hubert had executed a bow fit for a duchess if not a queen. It was the best Eleanor could expect by one known to be a staunch King's man.

Eleanor and Hubert sat across the table from one another, on heavy chairs without upholstery. His servants and hers melted into the background as was fitting, biddable at an instance but invisible until called. For a man in his mid-thirties, the knight had worn badly. A vivid scar at the point of his chin formed a cleft where the dark beard would not grow, and when he walked he needed a staff to lean upon.

The business of Hubert's audience had been to forewarn her of the royal visit, but Eleanor would not give him leave until he had told her all about the fate of her brother. She was bitterly disappointed, because there was no more news, only confirmation of the rumours that she had heard years ago. After his capture, Arthur was put into Sir Hubert's custody at Falaise Castle.

'I found him to be a haughty lad, as his station demanded, but a fine and engaging companion, for thus I soon thought him. After some weeks, when I had become very fond of him, the King's order came.'

Hubert would not allow the torturer to blind or unman the boy, but pretended he had died of the bloody procedures. 'To support the lie, I had most of the Duke's clothes given up for charity. But the people and lords of Breton rose up in fury, and I was forced to resurrect him again and show him, under strong guard, to the highest of the lords. For some days it pleased Arthur to pretend he was a ghost and scare the servants and men-at-arms, the boy in him not having entirely died to manhood.'

The furore died down, but the King was furious and took Arthur to another prison. Thereafter, Hubert was no better informed than anybody else. Arthur was never seen alive again. His murdered body was later dragged from the River Seine and given secret burial.

Eleanor clenched tight her jaw and made fists under the copious folds of her maunch-sleeve.

'There is ... something more, my lady. Though I fear to tell you.'

Eleanor's face flared. 'You must not show the hare and then tie it up in the sack, sir. If there is anything, anything at all of my brother, I command you to tell me.'

There were rumours, fantasies, tales from several quarters that the ghost of the young Duke had been seen, in the bloodiest of aspects, and that the spectre dogged the King's steps, herding him ever closer to insanity. 'He did always say, if he was ill-used to the point of death, he would haunt his tormenters.'

Eleanor was annoyed. She had no time for such nonsense. The shriven and God-fearing had no cause to take fright of the dead. She chided Sir Hubert for repeating the rantings of drunken fools.

Sir Hubert stood with practiced use of his staff, and walked to the window. 'I am no drunken fool, my lady.' Sir Hubert had seen the horror, and the horror's herald. The herald was a knight whose armorials were *ermines* – the reverse in colour to Duke Arthur's own – with a *cross vert*. The green cross was sometimes associated with knights of the Order of Saint Lazarus, many of whom were leprous, which was fitting, because the armour of the herald was rusty. But the grave-like look of the herald paled against the horror that was the ghost of Duke Arthur.

'Like Death, he rides a pale horse and emits such a scream as can only come from Hell. He wears no armour and is naked under a white, woollen, ermine-embroidered cloak, but for a cloth wound about his loins, like unto the garment worn by our Lord Christ upon the cross, ...

Christ! I remember now. That's the god who Saint John washed in the river.

... and a bloody bandage about his eyes. And despoiling the exposed, death-pale skin – arms, legs, belly and chest – blood, brown with age. Those who have come near, and survived the terror, speak of the stench of rot and call the horror, not ghost, but un-dead.'

Eleanor joined the knight at the window, pale and trembling from his revelations. But as horrible as the story was, she could not believe her brother had returned from the grave. So, he wore a cloak of ermine. As did the present lord of Brittany. Cloth, even rich cloth was easily had by a lord who had a trick to play upon the King. 'This spectre, this thing. Is he armed by more than a ghastly aspect?'

'That he is. He wields an evil-looking blade, over-long, ancient, jagged and rust-flecked, as if taken from a lord, long to bones in his barrow.'

Eleanor smiled. There! If her brother kept to the armorials of his lifetime, surely he would be faithful to his weapons. Where was his great-sword, with its smaller companion-blade? Whatever, or whoever this was, it was not her brother, alive or dead. Eleanor asked the knight where he had encountered the deathly couple.

'Here, my lady. My visit began two days ago and I shall remain until the King has been and gone, unless he should dismiss me earlier. Before, I had only heard the rumours and witnessed the King's discomfort at any mention of the ghosts. But two days ago, after the Vespers bell, I saw for myself. Over there.' He pointed towards the hill on the opposite side of the road outside the castle.

Corfe's keep had been built on such a lofty hill that it was easy to see over the curtain wall and to the countryside beyond.

'They say there is an ancient barrow near the top of that hill, my lady. I've a mind to call a bishop to minister away any evil that may lurk, for I saw the herald again after yesterday's Vesper bell.'

'Did you see my … Did you see the other spectre?'

'No, only the dark knight. The Castilian has a mind to set a trap, should it appear again tonight, but I have advised against it, until we can go with a bishop. Steel cannot rest the unsettled dead.'

Sir Hubert begged leave and when released, he made a bow as if to a queen. Not such a King's man after all.

There was much for Eleanor to take in and digest.

As for Sir Hubert de Burgh. He had missed his afternoon prayers, but would pray now, and ask forgiveness for the lies he had told the fair Lady Eleanor.

That evening after the Vespers bell, Eleanor saw the dark knight on the distant hill, although he appeared real enough to her. His surcoat and shield were clearly black for the most part, and she could pick out the green cross, but he was too far to discern the white flecks of stylised ermine-tails. He was fully armed as if for war, wore his helm and carried her brother's banner, but there was nothing of the grave nor of the after-world about him. Not a ghost or a demon, but certainly an artifice and a mystery; one that Eleanor meant to solve.

There follows scene upon scene of Eleanor's life as a prisoner which bore me to death. One day I hope to experience the immersion as an historian rather than a man on a quest.

Days go by, and then there is news of the King's visit. She is on her way to see him when she's intercepted by Sir Hubert.

He tells her the King has decided to starve to death the French knights, including Sir Benedict, and hang their young squires. Out of sheer spite, apparently.

Sir Hubert warns Eleanor to watch out for a visiting knight, Sir Malcolm de Beaumaris. He assures her he will do whatever is in power to help. Young Guy – the boy who looks like Benjo – is somehow in Sir Hubert's service, and he'll be spared any further excesses of the King.

This King John is an odious tyrant. To spite Eleanor he is true to his warped word. He starves the captive knights to death and hangs their young squires. I assume Sir Hubert is as good as his word concerning Guy, but the projection doesn't mention him anymore.

The projection goes into all the detail of John hanging the boys and starving the knights. It's horrible, and completely irrelevant. I call for the projection to terminate.

On one level, I'm enthralled by the story, but also disappointed. There is no likeness in any of the characters to me, and Benjo only appears as a doomed boy. I speculate that the knight or the ghostly spectre may be shown with my likeness, but I don't have time to remain immersed. I have to come out and look to other duties.

***

Four days until we embark. I have breakfasted and now have a visitor. A young adjutant of the VDF with whom I'm acquainted. Sav Kinngas was one of the juveniles in my instruction set. He's grown a lot but lost none of his sense of humour.

He's lost his boyish roundness of face and is now slender and tall but still with his atypically Venusian wild black hair held in check with a wide bandanna. Sav has also adopted the lower lip piercings (a pair of zirconium-black hoop snakebites), a cultural link to his origins in the northern extremity of our main landmass. He has a dark smear of whiskers, like a Callistonian who's been topside for a week. Hands clasped, he greets me. 'Happy to meet you, Commander Miralad.'

Miralad? Does he really not recognise me, or is this all part of the act surrounding my new identity?

He gives me a crystal containing everything I need to know about our ship, the VDFS Ashen Light.

I put the crystal on the objective plate. 'I appreciate the visit, but couldn't all this have been transmitted?'

'Best not risk grid use when it can be avoided.'

The Ashen Light is a corvette, a small vessel with quarters for up to ten human crew. It's built for speed and agility which isn't compatible with an unwieldy grav-ring. When not accelerating or decelerating we'll experience periods of zero-gee.

'You should try your space-film, Commander Miralad,' Sav says. The failure to recall, or the act, continues. And now he winks. 'I was gutted to hear about your death. It's great to see you got better.'

'You ...?'

'Shh! I'm not supposed to know, so I'll keep calling you Cohort-Commander Miralad. Don't tell anyone or I might be reassigned.'

'I'll pretend you still don't know, if you drop the formalities. Call me Jamil.'

He nods a cheery acknowledgement then taps his suit control. I watch as his coyote-brown standard uniform reforms into a contour-hugging seal-skin of a garment. It's mostly black with the red of his branch represented in the yoke and down the outside of each sleeve. His rank insignia, a single black bar on a square of red, is incorporated into the material of the neck tube which ends short of the chin.

I ask the significance of the red panels. Sav tells me it's the mark of a combat specialist. 'Like all spacers, a do a bit of everything, although mainly maintenance and operation of a section of combat-skins.'

'Will we need combat-skins?'

'Hopefully not, but we must be prepared.' He points out the various attributes of a space-film. 'You can order emergency space mode and the suit will grow gloves and a head covering. There's an oxygen supply that'll last fifteen minutes, but for planned extra-vehicular activity you can inhabit an EVA-skin.'

'A skin? A skin for people?' I've never heard of such a thing. It sounds fun. Sav tells me EVA-skins are like tiny personal ships that have motive power and enough air for a ten-hour excursion. They can also be deployed on a planetary surface.

'Go on then, Jamil. Try yours.'

My suit is identical to his except black all over, reflecting the colour of my branch. It has varying thicknesses of the leather-like material which provides protection, and as a side-effect visually enhances the major muscle groups. I've never had well-defined abdominal muscles, and my pectorals are vastly exaggerated. As for my underwear, the nanobots have shredded it and egested the strips of material as a fluffy puddle about my feet.

'Did that tickle?' Sav points to the macerated pieces.

'Yes, but what's going on?' I have the uncomfortable thought that if nanobots can shred material, they could probably do the same to flesh.

'A space film needs to be a second skin, with nothing between you and it. In a very real sense, it turns you into a space being.'

It's true. I run my fingers up my arm, and the sensation is transferred to my skin as if I'm wearing nothing at all.

'You can wear a space film for weeks without having to remove it.'

I feel stronger, but it's no more than a psycho-somatic delusion. The boots being integral, I'm wearing a single garment from head to foot.

Something stings my right foot – it sometimes happens when clothes are being formed – and I am reminded of the time when I was serving with the Hertfordshire Regiment and a whizzbang took off the top ... Wait! This is beyond bizarre. I've experienced a memory that can't be my own. It's one of Christie Grey's, my ancestor of a thousand years ago. I'm sure it must be the memory of a projection, but somehow it's been incorporated into a personal memory.

I'm in a dirty ditch, my blood making the duckboards slick. A trench, lined with wooden planks and topped with coils of spiked wire. At least I'm alive. Mere feet away is a gory heap that used to be a man. Feet? Like metres, I suppose. I'm in agony and my ears ring. 'Hold still there now,' someone says. 'Take a sup o' this, sir.' A small metal flask. A hard-edged fuming liquid that burns and then warms on the way down, and dulls the pain a fraction. I'm seeing all this in first person. It's nothing like a projection, not even full-immersion when you see everything from the side-lines. More than a memory, this has a quality of its own which is neither dream-like nor remotely similar to a crystal-presentation. I'm seeing it all from my own mind's eye.

'Are you all right, Jamil?'

And it's gone. The intrusive images are now no more than the memories of a memory. 'Fine thanks, Sav. A dose of nano-pinch, is all. It made me zone out for a moment.'

Sav looks at me from under thick black eyebrows. His eyes are darker by a shade, and his ready smile has been put aside as he assesses me. 'You looked like you were on another planet for a second or two.' It's the same voice as the soldier who offered the whisky flask, the same care and concern.

'I did feel out of it for a moment, but I'm okay now.' It's hard to define, but it's as if I'm no longer living in time, but rather time is living in me.

Sav smiles again, and forces time lines back where they belong. I've been rescued by his cheerful countenance, lifted up from a morose mood that threatened to drown me like the mud in the trench.

He tells me to expect an afternoon visit from the captain of the Ashen Light. 'Company-Commander Djogore Delatour has hair,' he says. 'So we won't be the only ones.'

I run a hand over my head. The hair no longer rasps like an expanse of tiny needles. It feels soft and downy.

'He's a rank below you, but in matters of ship's control he is absolute master.'

This, I understand. It was in my notes.

'You'll be in command of the mission, but he'll be in command of the ship and its crew.'

'I'll be in command of the mission?' Now, that's new to me.

'Yes. You'll be ranking grade and mission commander.'

There's the uncomfortable thrill of nerves, but it passes quickly into exhilaration. I'm looking forward to this.

His duty as crystal-courier complete, Sav takes his leave.

***

There's an hour to go before Commander Delatour is due and my domestic-skin stands before me. A short-lived notion to grow a beard has passed and I decide to rid myself of these itchy whiskers.

'Are you equipped to give me a facial shave?'

Edwin says no. 'But I will download a suitable grid-string if you wish.'

And now, I experience my first shave. I sit in the bathing cove while Edwin operates the skin, deftly sliding a sharp film over my face, having already applied a lubricating lotion. I understand this procedure must be carried out daily to maintain a fresh look.

'There, you are done.'

I look, and feel better. Once again my facial skin feels like my own, but I decline Edwin's offer to shave the rest of my head. I wonder how long it will take to grow hair as long as Jonan's.

'Are there methods and available equipment for me to carry out this shaving process myself?' If I'm going to remain clean-shaven, I can't always rely on having access to a domestic-skin. It dawns on me, Father was clean-shaven, and yet I never saw him shave nor came across his shaving device.

'I can secure the necessary equipment, but it will add to your Rule of Seven possessions.'

I run through a mental check-list of my personal possession. Gown; formsuit-disk; boots; sex-skin and tentacle fossil. The crystals, and if by any miracle I get them back the ancient papers, are not mine so they don't add to the number. The partner-band I wear is Father's, so that doesn't count either. 'Not a problem, Edwin. Please obtain the required items.'

Time passes quickly and from my vantage point on the balcony I notice a remarkably light-skinned man approaching from the jungle path, who I assume is Commander Delatour. From this distance he appears almost as white as Christie Grey and other characters in my projections. He has fair hair, short at the sides and thick on top. It's not a style I intend to adopt. He wears a film-gown, and desiring to be a good host, I disc-stow the uniform and put on my own gown. I do not intent to pull rank on him.

System lets him into the hall for our informal meeting, and having waited for a few moments in compliance with etiquette, I welcome him.

He's slightly shorter than me, but with the typically slender Venusian build. His eyes are brown and he has a long face with a deeply cleft chin. I'm not all that interested in his appearance, because he carried a battered leather valise under one arm.

He smiles and hands it over. 'It survived the flyer crash with nothing but a nasty gash and some scuff marks. The contents are all fine.'

Fantastic! I can't wait to share this old treasure with Benjo. But I must put it aside and attend to my duties as a host.

'Thank you,' Djogore says, accepting my offer of refreshments. He touches the mantle which is built in to the fabric of his gown. 'I have a graph colleague with me.' He waves his hand towards the surrounding walls. 'May I introduce him via home-system?'

Naturally I give permission, and the solid looking form of an ancient seaman is projected. He introduces himself as BLIGH. He has a round face with a cleft chin like the Commander's.

I enquire about his chosen form. 'Seventeenth century European?'

'Late eighteenth century, actually' BLIGH replies. 'British Royal Navy lieutenant.' He doffs his bicorn hat and gives a half-bow.

'He's my second in command,' says Djogore Delatour. 'His official VDF grade is section-commander, and he will project in the correct uniform once we embark. Won't you, Bligh?'

'If you insist.'

'I insist.'

'Then I shall make it so. Once we embark.'

I lead them to Father's study. There's a familiarity bordering on levity between these two. Delatour is undoubtedly secure in his grade, and it's my impression BLIGH would never fail to support his captain when the chips are down. This all comes to me as a visceral certainty: another trait of my new existence that could come in useful.

But there I go again. 'Chips are down'? Phrases keep coming to me from who knows where. I search my wayward thoughts, and once again it's as if I'm tapping into Christie's memories. I understand the import of the phrase, but its origins leave me baffled. I know 'chips' were once a popular preparation of potatoes, but how do they relate to the phrase?

'Jamil?'

'My apologies, Djogore. My mind was wandering.'

'I'm not surprised. You've been through a lot recently. I am sorry for your losses.'

'Raoul and Bart? You know about them?'

'Yes, I do. But there's also the loss of your father.' Djogore explains that he has been fully briefed, and knows my real name. It's so reassuring that Jonan is no longer a non-person, a being who never existed. 'It's important to point out that Bligh and I are the only crewmembers who know the truth about you, and we should keep it that way.'

'Indeed,' adds BLIGH. 'We must never forget, our mission depends on the Earthers believing you are dead.'

'Correction, Number One. They must continue to believe Ariel Dzalarhons is dead. Jamil Miralad is alive and well and fully accounted for in all records.'

On the one hand I'm reassured, but it's troubling that records can so easily be doctored. I'm benefitting from the same kind of falsifications that made Father vanish from the grid. I don't tell them that Sav also knows about me.

***

It's been three days since my meeting with Djogore and BLIGH. I'm with Benjo, walking the jungle paths close to home, my growing hair sufficient covering in this humidity. Benjo is naturally barefooted but atypically for these walks, he wears a gown. The hem is picking up leafy detritus so he'll regret it.

I'm telling him about the meeting and how they briefed me about the Ashen Light and its crew. There'll be five humans in addition to Djogore and me, curiously four male and one androgen. No females at all. I queried this and was told appointment was by application and competition. 'There're no quotas,' Djogore told me. 'Crews are often all male or all female, though most commonly a mix.' It still strikes me as odd, and Benjo thinks the same.

'Seems to me they don't want you breeding.' Benjo stoops to brush dead leaves from his gown. 'No other reason for a lack of female crew if you ask me.'

'Breeding? That makes me sound like a bioprinter's gene-source or a stud animal.'

'I've no hesitation in confirming your abilities, Stallion.'

'Oh, shush!' I tell Benjo I'm working on a way to upset their little plan as far as the ship's compliment goes. I let him into the secret and he thinks it's hilarious.

'Isn't that a little too crazy, Ariel? Verone will be a wonderful addition to the crew, but are you trying to antagonise them?'

'Not at all, but I need to establish I'm more than a passive unit to be ordered about. They're sending me on a mission that may last years, and they didn't even consult me or give me any say about the crew.'

There's more to it than that. As the weeks pass since the flyer crash, I feel less and less like myself. What am I? What is 'me'? If I'm a collection of blood and bones, then I'm a resurrected dead man. They did more than repair my body. It's as if they added something that's outside of me.

It's an indefinable feeling that's growing, and if anybody can keep me sane, it's Verone Kell.

'I take it Verone is up for it.'

'Oh yes. You know our old Verone.' We share a chuckle.

'Tell me, how do you intend to pull it off?'

'I'll say only this. I'm becoming more proficient at "grid infiltration" each day. I'm finding it easier to insinuate myself into systems to the extent that I can touch on Quantum. I can make certain changes to it.'

Benjo zones out for a moment. 'All this without a stent. You couldn't achieve manipulations like that even with one.' I know what Benjo's thinking, because he's old-tech and has no stent. 'I wonder if I could learn the technique.'

'I wish you were the same.' Is that selfish of me? Wishing my condition on another person, especially one I'm coming to appreciate more every day. Love? No, it doesn't exist except as a corollary to need. 'It's S'Jinning lonely being so different.'

'You know I'd come with you if I could. Can you imagine, you me and Verone back together again?'

What a thought! But Benjo has responsibilities at home and is key to the research program at Ven-Tech. There's something else I need to discuss with Benjo, although I'm not comfortable introducing the subject. It's to do with our continued relationship. 'You're aware they've forbidden me from seeing you, or any of the acquaintances I had when I was Ariel?'

'You're still "Ariel". But in the circumstances I understand their paranoia. Then again if they're so nervous about the Earthers finding you, why install you in your previous home?'

'All accounted for. I ... Jamil ... was awarded life-tenancy for services rendered.'

'And being in Special Ops, those services are allowed to be vague?'

'More like "completely unspecified".'

We've disturbed a corruja-fowl. Its screech makes us both jump and its plump form streaks across the leaf-mould path, light striking its black plumage and scattering in a star-burst of iridescence. This sets off a troop of howlers, and it all combines to remind me of my time with Raoul and his people in the Amazon jungle.

We've known each other since we first learnt to walk. We can read each other, and Benjo reaches up and squeezes my shoulder. 'If they need me to leave and never speak of you again, I'll manage that. If they want me to forget you, they're out of their Sin-Jinning callywitted heads.'

I'm laughing, almost as explosively as that carruja-fowl. Through it all I manage to ask Benjo who taught him to swear like a Martian.

'Ah. I was coming to that.' He takes a crystal from a tiny slit-pocket in his gown and slots it into the reader in his mantle, a small indentation no bigger than a projector-lens. So that's why he wears a gown. Arm-projectors are too crude for any form of detailed presentation. 'Since we last met, I've been in contact with an old friend of ... Ariel's. Our first conversation was recorded and I've risked keeping it until now.'

His mantle projects the image of Dorsa Sagan, and I gulp in a lungful of air. The pleasure at seeing her again is close to overwhelming. 'Tell Venus-boy to open his callywitted mind. I've been trying to contact him for Sin-Jinning days.'

'She told me that you'd mentioned me in connection with your dreams, and the projections I featured in. Said it was an easy matter to trace me, and through me she hoped to get a message to you.'

'Looks like it worked. Did she give any clues as to how I should "open my mind", or should I guess?'

'She mentioned your training with Raoul, and told me it was useless to burden me with further details as I wouldn't understand.'

Benjo plays the projection several times. I can't get enough of Dorsa and only now do I understand how much I've missed her. Finally, he pops out the crystal and places it on a flat rock. With a second rock he pounds it several times until it is no more than a stain of dark blue dust. It hurt to watch, but I understand why he's done it.

'Well, my friend,' he says adopting a formal pose. 'Am I to leave, never to return?'

'Are you, bollocks! If they think I'm abandoning you they can all foxtrot-oscar and do one!'

Benjo's confusion is spreading all over his face. 'What in the Three Worlds does all that mean? Is it more Martian swearing?'

Once again, I'm baffled. 'It's not Martian but I think it probably is swearing. I honestly don't have a clue what it means, other than don't you dare leave me.'

'Wouldn't dream of it. As you said, they can "do one".'

We don't speak of the separation which comes at us like a meteor. If all goes to plan, we'll take different routes that lead to lives light-years apart.

'You know, Ven-Tech doesn't take up every second of my day, and I've a mind to help you in any way I can.'

'Thanks, Benjo, but I don't want you drawing attention to yourself.'

'Sometimes, there are advantages to being no-tech. Slightly harder for anyone to keep tabs on me.' He tells me the image of Jack's epaulettes are playing on his mind. 'Those brass numerals, and the badge, they mean something. I'm certain they're a clue, and I mean to get to the bottom of it.'

He's right, and I've given it a lot of thought, but it's not the epaulettes that worry the edges of my consciousness. It's Christie's path through the meadow. His path is somehow mine too.

***

Benjo can't join me today. Ven-Tech calls.

Desperate measures, perhaps, but following my obsession with Christie's path, I feel the need to walk a path of my own. I've come to a small glade in the jungle about two klicks from home. It isn't exactly like the one Raoul took us to in the Amazonian jungle, in fact it isn't much like it at all, but I hope it's close enough. I came here once with Father when we were exploring. This time Edwin has guided me. He projects from an armband-interfacer strapped high on my left arm, of the kind we use when out without a mantle.

There's only a day left until I'm due to check in at the small government spaceport at Viriplaca, and despite all my efforts I still haven't managed to establish a link with Dorsa. I wish she'd sent the whole message to Benjo or at least left contact data.

'It's a good job Father recorded the place, Edwin. I would never have found it again on my own.'

'It is an unusually beautiful location to have remained unvisited for so long.'

I wonder what criteria constructs use to measure beauty, and I'm surprised they are able to appreciate it. But he's correct. This place is as lovely as Raoul's glade back on Earth. 'Well, there are no paths anywhere near. It's a fairly remote place anyway, and visitors rarely stray off-road.'

There's a pool and a waterfall. The canopy covers more here than its Amazonian counterpart, but there are sufficient gaps to allow a few stray shafts of light. It's a yellow, buttery light that has a much softer quality than on Earth. The air here is thicker and it shows. It's cool too, but I've worked up a sweat and as there are no rules here about purity, I'm going in.

It's funny how Edwin still projects underwater. Wavering and quivering with the disturbances I've caused by my dive, he stands straight as if his feet are actually touching solid ground.

Now I'm up for air, treading water, while Edwin's blue head stains the meniscus and ripples like a flat pancake with eyes. I splash the water and he fragments into a thousand droplets. His beams can't break the surface until I haul myself up onto the bank and the arm projector is back in the air.

I sit on a rock, dripping. Trying to dry in this humidity is pointless, and my sweat mingles with these fresh droplets. I use the edge of my hand like a scraper and slick of as much water as I can. And now, I will centre myself; quieten the mind and try to be open to Dorsa's link. Edwin stands silent sentinel, while the calls of a distant troop of howlers stroke the air.

I mustn't use the monkeys as an excuse or call them a distraction. I'm having no luck, but it's not their fault that I can't access Quantum. I'm not sure it's my fault either, but there's no more time to waste. I ask Edwin to contact AMALTHEA as I've done dozens of times in recent days. He has as little luck as I.

One last attempt. I reach out with my mind, and stop because I'm wasting my time – doing it completely wrong. There's no time to 'reach out with my mind' when a situation calls for immediate action. When I brought those seeker-wasps down I just did it without thinking.

That's the answer. It's not reaching out, it's relocating my consciousness, instantly. From here, to … where is this?

Back within the comfort and safety of my own flesh, I'm disorientated. For an unfathomable period of time, I was everywhere and everywhen, lost in a landscape where perception and senses mean nothing.

***

Benjo and I sit in our compartment's balcony-bubble enjoying a newly printed breakfast. He rescheduled in order to accompany me to Viriplaca Spaceport. We're crossing the Garret Bray Bridge with Dzalarhons Mons and several smaller islands behind us. Several more and the mainland are yet to come. There is nothing but ocean to look at and we zone out into the misty horizon.

'Have you ever been across the original Garret Bray?'

It's a moment before I come back to myself and string his words into something intelligible. 'I didn't know there was an original.'

'It's on Earth. It crosses the Torres Straits to the north west of Australia. If you've ever been there via vac-tube you'll have been over it.'

I've never been to Australia, but I wonder how Benjo knows so much.

'Put it down to my natural curiosity. The first time I crossed to the mainland I was intrigued by the name and researched it. Dug right down until I came to a bio of the engineer who designed it.'

Right now Benjo has another obsession. It's the link between the good ship Phoenix Song and my quest to find Father. Obsession or not, he reserves part of his mind for thoughts concerning my revelations to him.

'I think you're turning into a graph.'

Okay. My friend has lost his mind.

'No human can visit Quantum unless it's a version of it projected by graphs. And yet you've been there.'

'I've been somewhere. I don't have the empirical data to categorically state it was anything to do with Quantum.'

He thinks I'm hilarious with my empirical data and tells me I should consider my own observations as proof enough. The certainty of a low-tech? No perfidious stent for him.

163

'Here's a related thought. If you are turning graph, wouldn't that be reason enough to ruffle a few feathers? Stentless access to the grid and a passport to Quantum. Enough to shunt some folk out of their post-Pandemic calm, don't you think?'

I order more coffees by way of changing the subject. We finish them by the time a northern hook of land curves in from the haze, like an arm about to enfold us into the mainland.

The miles rush by and we become stilted. Soon we'll part for what may be years and years, or forever. With the conversations of a lifetime to fit into a few hours, our talk is trivial and the momentous words won't come. We sit close and commit our deepest thoughts to the passing countryside.

The port is crowded as ports always are. We amble listlessly passing airgates and spacegates until we come to the one for my lifter. It's boarding already and time to say goodbye. I should have planned this better.

'I guess this is it then.'

I can't find the words to reply, but there needs to be something. If not words, then a gesture. I twist off Father's partner-band from the ring-finger of my right hand, place it in Benjo's hand and fold his fingers into a fist around it.

He beams, takes my left hand and slides the ring in place. Father's ring has become my partner-band. There's nothing to say. Nothing we can say, unless we concentrate on the merely practical.

'Thanks for coming, Benjo. It was a long haul. Maybe you should stay for a few days and take in some of the Viriplaca art.'

'I'm not rushing home, but the art can wait. I have plans to visit Viriplaca University. I hear it has an amazing modern history department.'

'Ah, the Phoenix Song?'

He winks. We part, and I board the lifter.

Ashen Light

Many people enjoy zero-gee. I'm not one of them. At least my space-side uniform cum second skin couldn't be better for the job, and whether due to my rank or branch, I'm shown surprising deference by others on this Venusian government hub.

I'm getting the hang of this, and push off from a grab-rail lightly. I zip along the communication-shaft towards a grav-ring access hatch. Sav is my aide, but for the sake of accuracy let's call him my 'puppy-walker' with me as the puppy. He shoots ahead of me and I follow, his heels my beacon. I've pushed a little too hard because I'm gaining on him. What do I do? Brake against the soles of his boots to stop a collision? Slip past him and risk an over-intimate close encounter in this narrow tube? I don't know the rules or protocols. Everything's so easy as a civilian passenger when all you do is take a seat, do as your told and enjoy the ride.

Sav grabs a handhold and pivots round and down a side shaft. I miss the Sin-Jinning hold and continue along in the wrong direction. Someone grabs my ankle. It's Djogore. I had no idea he was behind me. He's trying hard not to laugh. 'It's the same for all of us at first, Jamil. Give it a day and you'll be scooting along with the best of us.'

'Is that before or after I pass "puking along"?'

I spoke in jest, but I spoke too soon. We've passed through the hatch into the communicating ring and it's winding up to speed. When it reaches main-ring synchronicity it will produce zero-point six gee and we'll cross into the main ring.

This government hub is smaller than standard hubs. The grav ring has a much smaller diameter, so if it rotated fast enough to produce full-gee, the Coriolis force would be too much for us. Point-six will have to do.

'Try to stand, Jamil. We've synchronised,' Sav says.

My body's too light, and the Coriolis is trying to push my upper body anti-spinward. I've never felt so sick.

'You're turning green.' I swear Sav is trying not to laugh. 'Raise a filter.'

'I'm done with filters,' I say, but I'm not sure if my resolve will last. My stomach is churning.

'Go filterless then. But if you puke, you have to clear it up. Grade has privileges but no one's going to mop up your vomit.'

'If he pukes, Adjutant, you will clean up his vomit,' Commander Djogore Delatour says. I chuckle instead of throwing up, and the other two laugh as well. Miraculously my nausea dissipates.

Transition from the communicating to the main ring is via a double set of pressure doors. They open, with a soft-edged whisper, to a deck five times wider than this one. I pass through trying hard not to kangaroo-hop. My feet can't seem to get purchase on the floor and every steps bounces me into the air. I notice the experienced spacers are sliding more than stepping, and I'm trying to copy them. Yes, much better.

We pass through a security bar manned by human and graph crew, and on to a room where I'll meet the crew of the VDFS Ashen Light. I'm nervously excited but I will not initiate a filter. I'm learning to enjoy the tides of emotion that a filterless life brings.

We walk spinward and the deck curves up and out of view. Along the corridor my eyes lock with those set in a friendly and familiar face. We exchange smiles which are little more than a minute curl of the lip. My plan is coming to fruition.

Now to the meeting room, through a door on our right. As I turn, my upper body bends anti-spinward and

I stumble. The other two have compensated and walk through as if they're strolling in a home-world jungle.

The rest of the crew are already assembled. They stand as we enter until Djogore asks them to relax. I'm delighted to see that NEKO the cat-boy is here. First Officer Kyler Britton is here too, but I don't know the others. Orange trim-panels on the suits tell me that most are experienced spacers, but there are other trim colours too.

The room is spacious and there's a large projected observation port. Sav explains that it shows the exact view we'd see if it were an actual port. The view right now is mostly of the blue curve of Venus. Many of the islands are visible as green dots, but the main landmasses haven't risen yet. The view changes with the spin of the main ring, and now I can see a ship docked at the far end of a boom. It's dark, like polished ebony, with a flash of orange along its sleek flanks.

'Sav, is that our ship?' S'Jinn, I hope so.

'Indeed it is. So what do you think of the Ashen Light?'

'She's beautiful.'

'She?' Sav looks at me as if I've emerged from a slime pit. 'It's not alive, you know.'

I don't know where the compulsion came from, but 'she' seemed the appropriate pronoun to me. Another incursion of false memory, I suppose.

'We board as soon as this session's over. And Commander, for the sake of formality, at least in the presence of "His Royal Bossness", please call me "Adjutant Kinngas". Okay?'

I know that's not meant as a sting, but I don't like it. It smacks of old world elitism, and I'm not having it. Of course, I will defer to grading officers and do my best to command with competence those who have been put into my care, but I'm not a military man despite this silver bar. 'You can address me how you like, Sav, so long as you don't call me a gangrenous mons-sloth.'

He puts a hand to his mouth to cover a grin as Force First Officer Britton joins us. 'Welcome, Commander Miralad. I trust you had a good transition?'

'Yes thanks, Kyler. The lift from Viriplaca was comfortable, but it'll take me a while to truly get my space legs.'

Kyler's smile is late coming, no doubt due to my informal manner of address. I'm glad. It's as if I've been a pawn all my life, until now. Accepting the formalities is the first step to allowing myself to be manipulated even further. Well, in one or two areas, I intend to be the manipulator.

'Roll with it, Jamil,' he says. 'It's the only way.' Esoteric to a point, but I know exactly what he means.

Kyler introduces me to the rest of the crew. I secretly reach through the ether and into the grid. I'm becoming quite adept. Good! Everything is in place for my little surprise.

'This is Officer Retz Keadle.'

Rets is another red-trimmed combat-skin specialist, like Sav but a rank lower. Now it's Hamo Mutairi, a very young looking androgen in a suit with spacer-orange trim and hair to match. He wears the symbol indicating he prefers people to use male pronouns, and has a tiny skin sitting on his shoulder in the form of a bee. It doesn't wave its head or antennae at me, so it's construct rather than graph-operated. Hamo explains it's a multipurpose tool but mainly deployed to seek out and analyse materials, and that a good engineer wouldn't be without one.

Moss Lirril in spacer orange panels is next, and last up is Matt Sketcher, his green trim indicating a speciality in medicine. Sketcher will be the ship's medic and he's one of the crew who'll transfer with me to the deep space vessel orbiting Mars.

'Of course, you've already met our graph companions,' Kyler says. BLIGH (correctly attired this time) and NEKO take a metaphorical bow and then AMALTHEA winks into existence.

Kyler is startled. 'How did you get here?'

AMALTHEA glows. 'By invitation of the mission commander.'

I confirm her answer and Kyler looks a little flustered. 'Well, I suppose it makes sense, but you should have put this by me, Cohort-Commander Miralad.' He uses my grade by way of a mild rebuke; a reminder that he stands several grades above me.

As if on cue, and an example of perfect if unintentional timing, the door slides open and a woman in a spacer-film with green trim enters. Her rank-patch sports two black bars which usually denote section-commander but in her case junior doctor. At my invitation she makes straight for us exuding a confident presence.

If Force First Officer Kyler Britton looked flustered earlier, now his jaw is virtually touching the deck. He addresses my old friend: 'Commander, this is a private meeting. How did you bypass protocols?'

'Excuse me, Kyler,' I say. 'But there's been no protocol-bypass. Dr Verone Kell is here at my invitation, and she'll be part of the crew.'

By Saint John, how Kyler hates this, but he'll soon hate it a lot more. He turns his attention to me. 'I'm sorry, Commander, but –'

'Jamil, please.'

'I'm sorry, Jamil, but the crew has been put together with utmost care. The skills and the balance of personalities can't be compromised.'

'Oh, we'll manage, Kyler. Dr Kell's inclusion in the mission is unnegotiable.'

'Completely unnegotiable,' Kyler says. 'No reflection on your skills, Dr Kell, but I cannot authorise your inclusion on the ship's roster.'

Vorone activates her inbuilt projectors. 'If I may, First Officer.' An official authority materialises as a holo in the space between her and Kyler.

Kyler reads it and grasps the knot of hair at the back of his head. 'This authority appears to be signed by Force Marshall Thosev Straw.' He puts a finger to his temple, no doubt accessing the grid for confirmation. I have to acknowledge his skill: he recovers composure instantly, greets Verone and welcomes her to the mission.

I think it's gone to plan. I've established something important. I may be a youth with much to learn, but I am not a juvenile and I won't be somebody's playing piece in a game I don't fully understand. If they know the rules of this game, they can bally well let me in on the secret. If they don't, then I'm as good a leader as anybody else.

Introductions and pep talks over, we have an hour before we board the Ashen Light. Time to find a quiet corner of this hub and catch up with Verone. Last time we met we were juveniles with Benjo, all in the same college.

Perfect! I've found a time-out space purpose built for quiet chats. There's a false port fixed on the planet below, and a pretty display of hydroponics: real ones, not projected. There's an objective-plate in case we want to use any crystals and the space is guaranteed free of listening or recording devices. The chairs are very comfortable and our beverages pleasant. AMALTHEA floats in the corner.

Verone resembles Dorsa in several respects. She is curvier than the typical Venusian woman though, and a little shorter. If you saw the two of them together, you'd think Verone was the Martian and Dorsa the Venusian. Verone has light hair as long as my fathers which frames a narrow face with high cheekbones, but her most striking feature are her teeth, by no means prominent but emphasised by her smile. 'How long's it been, Ariel.'

Despite the guarantee of privacy I find myself looking over my shoulder. 'Jamil! Call me Jamil.' That came out rather panicky. 'Got to be fifteen years since we last met.'

We talk about old times: Benjo; the day I was bitten by a snake; our old college and its cast of students and professors. Verone asks how I engineered her presence and I explain that I've acquired some interesting skills in grid manipulation.

'So, I'm here under false pretences?' For the first time since we slipped into this room, Verone looks less than happy.

'Not at all. Your authority is perfectly real. I invoked a VDF clause that allows any person commanding an off-world mission an interview with the Marshall. It was an easy matter to persuade him that your inclusion in the mission was vital to our chance of success.'

Verone relaxes, happy again. 'I can't tell you how thrilled I am. The chance to be part of a deep-space mission to Albion is beyond my wildest dreams.'

'I seem to recall some of your dreams were pretty wild.'

'I grew out of them.'

Now it's my turn, and I'm going to tell Verone the unedited version of my story. She listens carefully while I go through everything from Jonan's kidnapping until now. Like nearly everybody else, she has no recollection of my father.

'Benjo thinks I'm evolving into a graph. Stupid as that sounds, it helps to explain a lot.'

'The lack of a stent? Your ability to connect with the grid without one? And that hair?'

I run a hand over my ever-growing coiffure. 'A side effect of the procedures required to keep me alive after the flyer crash. I was pretty mashed up'

I think Verone's speciality in psychology has kicked in. She's processing everything I've told her. She knows I'm not lying, but perhaps doubts my sanity. 'Are you aware I was part of a study into the post-Pandemic phenomenon?

I'm not aware of that, and it strikes me as off-subject. Of course, there have been numerous studies and hypotheses in the centuries that followed the pandemics.

'What are your thoughts of the pandemics, and their effect on human nature?'

I can't supress a shrug. 'Most studies conclude that the survivors acquired a calmness derived from a side-effect of the illness, as if their bodies created a form of beta-blocker, combined with heightened observational skills.'

Verone nods, purses her lips and wanders over to look out of the false-port. She's contemplating letting me in to a secret. 'Humans and graphs have struggled with the mystery for hundreds of years. It was a ... no *the* turning point in human history. But it was also highly significant in graph history.'

'But it all happened long before graphs made contact with humans.'

'Long before they made their presence known, Ariel, which is a different matter. You see, we came to the conclusion that Bumblebee Sneeze was engineered by graphs. Humanity was on the verge of self-destruction, and we needed help. We believe graphs provided that help and changed humanity in a small be highly significant way.'

Verone turns from the port. 'It's not a huge leap from that to a human with the ability to interact directly with Quantum. Ariel … Jamil, you could represent the next stage in human evolution.'

'And graph evolution too,' AMALTHEA says.

My mind opens to new vistas. This is much more than realisation. I can see into realms I can't understand. Something inside me, something of me has opened to an expanded reality.

'Ariel! Ariel sit down. What's happening to you?'

There's Verone's voice, but there's another. It's Dorsa! And she's in trouble.

'They're on to me. I need help, Ariel. Come for me! Come for me come for me come for me.' Her fear echoes inside my head and in the air all round.

'Ariel, you must sit down, before you fall down.'

'No time!' I snatch it all back until once again I'm confined within my own body. 'Amalthea, ask Commander Delatour to call action stations and get the Ashen Light fired up. We have to launch. Now!'

***

'Now' is a relative term in space travel. We leave the grav rings and propel our weightless selves through the communicating tubes to our ship. I have the hang of this now, necessity making me an expert: no more bumping into my colleagues and missing handholds; simply an efficiency of movement. My resolve is steering me and honing my senses. The ship's cramped compared to the hub, but I find my place on the bridge-deck and strap in.

Djogore takes the captain's seat and calls up the control displays which float around him. Control tells us our slot will be in twenty minutes and I let out a Martian cuss, and then another that would have made Christie blush.

'Relax, Jamil. It'll take that long to get the ship ready.'

A set of monitors resolve around me. I understand most of the data: fuel ratings, environmental measurements and navigational settings. I relax, but my arms float up from my lap in this damnable zero-gee, so I tuck my hands under my armpits.

Djogore makes an announcement to the crew. 'There's a need to expedite, so we'll initiate with a three-gee flux of ten minutes and then reduce to one-point-five until flip-point. Deceleration will also be at one-point-five.' He gives the estimated time of arrival at the Martian diplomatic hub. It's a journey of several days when I need it to be hours, but nobody can change the laws of physics.

We're off-boom. Final checks are flashed before my eyes. The ship jinks sideways as thrusters are given a short burn, and then Captain Djogore Delatour tells us to hang on.

My body presses into the firm padding of this seat as the main engines fire, and my suit tightens around my calves, thighs and abdomen.

There's a verbal announcement; ship's system I think, but it may be a graph. 'Incremental velocity-vector achieved. Please remain in restraint until we have established line-vector.'

Read-outs now include a magnified reverse view. The hub looks like a speck, and Venus is receding at a discernible rate.

Eager not to waste a moment, I reach out for a link with Dorsa. Eyes closed, I try to stretch my mind outside the confines of my skull, but my skull refuses to let me pass. Nothing.

'Okay, crew.' Djogore sets his seat up from the reclined position and swings his legs over to the deck. 'We're done. Let's test the old muscles.'

Actually, it's not too bad. My legs hold up, and my intestines do not make a rapid exit through my bottom. The suit keeps everything in the right place, and I can cope with the weight easier than anticipated.

Djogore calls a meeting. 'My ready-room, in one hour please.'

We all acknowledge. Someone actually says 'Aye, skipper,' and I try not to laugh. I think it may have been BLIGH. But who am I to talk, with all these rusty terms I've been using lately. That's something I must mention to Verone. We have an hour and there's no time like the present.

My cabin has a projected porthole that looks like a brass one with glass, like those I've seen in crystals about old sailing ships. I've set the view to a seascape with rolling waves.

Verone perches on the side of my bunk, I take the stool and AMALTHEA hovers, as usual. Although there's something different about her. Her colours aren't what they were. I suppose being blasted back to Quantum several times has a detrimental effect.

Verone is fascinated to hear about my false memories; my 'recall' of events I'm not connected to, apart from ancestry. 'Ancestral memories? That tends to support Benjo's hypothesis. After all, graphs are said to exist in a continuum of all places and at all times.'

'So they say,' AMALTHEA says. 'It's a theory that even we graphs have trouble getting to grips with.'

'No,' I say. 'If you could be everywhere and all graphs at once, the first question I'd ask is, where's Grendel and what's he up to.'

'You see –'

I hold up my hand. 'If you're going to try and explain the quantum world again, get ready to scrape my brains off the deck. Quantum mech is one think, but quantum graph bio and graph norms? You might as well try to teach a slug how to play a violin.'

AMALTHEA goes through a staccato of light-changes. 'Rest assured, I am at the same time seeking Grendel and interfering with any efforts of his to find us. While humans involved in this affair are playing a game of hare and hounds, there is a veritable war going on in Quantum.'

Verone asks me for details of my ancestral memories and I answer to the best of my ability, and then AMALTHEA asks if I have viewed all of my gene-hunting crystals.

'No time for that, I'm afraid.'

'Make time. We've established someone is passing you clues that may help in our quest.'

'I've watched some of them several times. I can't see the clues.'

'When you have watched them all, a narrative may emerge, or a clue become clear.'

It makes sense, so I take her suggestion. I've asked Verone and AMALTHEA to join me in the tiny lab on deck two. It has everything I need to play the next part of my project. I insert the relevant crystal, and now we're ready.

I smell leaf-mould and hear the sounds of birds, and yet I haven't started the projection yet. Curious.

'There's a suggestion that not all the information from the crystals I've watched comes from the crystals. Will you keep the process, and me, under observation, Amalthea?'

'Of course. The last projection mentioned a knight. Sir Malcolm, wasn't it?'

'It did. Perhaps we're about to meet him.'

She agrees.

'Play projection, now.'

***

A small party led by Sir Malcolm de Beaumaris neared the end of a hard day's ride. His squire and herald rode one at either side. Close behind came half-a-dozen sergeants and two grooms leading the spare horses. Finally Friar Steven and Sir Malcolm's steward, James of Castile brought up the rear.

They came to the outskirts of Cheping Blandford, a small market town a day's ride from Corfe Castle.

The herald blew his trumpet. The leading sergeants waved banner and pennant half-heartedly, and Sir Malcolm threw a handful of quarter-pennies to some beggar-children, but they had arrived on market-day and few townsfolk paid any heed. Where were the cheering peasants? Where was the reeve or magistrate to welcome him? Sir Malcolm felt distinctly provincial. This was, after all, a town and not a mere manor. Steven and James exchanged glances. James winked. Steven rolled his eyes.

The party went their different ways and arranged to meet, if not at the inn, then in the town square next morning, soon after the Tierce bell. Friar Steven and James the steward found the tavern at the sign of the broken flagon easily. They were soon set up each with a jug of ale and a trencher of pottage. It would do until they heard the pie-man's clarion.

Conversation turned to a matter that could only be spoken in lowered voices. It was not safe even to whisper 'Arthur's ghost' without the risk of ruin, so people used the term 'King's blight', but whatever turn of phrase might be conjured, it seemed the ghost had no care, for it had been seen often, and in many places. At the gates of Rouen, it hovered in the shadows. On the banks of the Seine, it howled and cried, so that nobody ventured along the part of the bank from where the boy-Duke's body had been dragged. In Winchester it had slain and decapitated a poor man-at-arms who wore the King's livery. But nowhere had it been seen more often than about the walls of Corfe, so much so that the King feared to visit his favourite castle.

'Uneasy spirit.' James took a mouthful of ale and chewed on the pieces.

'Who has heard of a spirit that haunts more than a walking-space of the Earth? Spirits are bound to a location, but this one seems bound to the King.'

There were those who held that it was no spirit at all, but the living young Duke who had somehow escaped death and sought to regain his stolen crown.

'That will never happen,' Steven said. 'If the boy came back to us bedecked in all his ducal finery, and accompanied by a host of trumpeters and golden retainers, he would be slain again. The King's reasons are plain, but those Bretons who lamented his loss are now happy to have his dukedom. A resurrected duke would have no friends in England, none in France and very few in Brittany. For the same reason, nobody cares to speak for the release of poor Lady Eleanor.'

James agreed. 'And so Arthur will remain a ghost, and the fair maid will never be free.'

Steven skelped James across the top of the head for uttering the forbidden words, and James, remembering himself, muttered an apology.

Awkwardness was banished by the pie-man's clarion, a high note and a low, repeated three times, and then three rapid highs in a row. James sent for two pies on his account by way of a tangible apology. They were worth the wait, and the men tucked in.

The next morning, Sir Malcolm's party all gathered at the door of the inn and set off in good time. They rode all day, stopping only to water the horses and take a bite of bread. By late afternoon the castle came into view and they halted to prepare themselves for as grand an entry as possible. The banners were unfurled again, and the sergeants with livery put it on, and those without tidied themselves to the best of their ability and resources. While they were preparing, the sound of galloping horses grew louder. From the road behind came a dozen brothers of the Knights Templar, black and white robes flowing, the red cross of their Order very prominent on each. A trumpet was raised and a call put up, one high note and a low. They thundered past with the briefest of acknowledgements to Sir Malcolm.

Friar Steven hurrumphed. 'They won't sell many pies going at that pace.'

James slapped his forehead, and the sergeants laughed, until Sir Malcolm called them to order.

***

A day left before the flip. In consultation we've brought it forward so that we can complete our run-in deceleration at one-gee. Sleeping has been a nightmare. You lie there trying to breath and it's like someone's sitting on your chest. I had to resort to a high pressure breathing mask to get any sleep at all.

In the days since we immersed ourselves in the last crystal projection, Verone, AMALTHEA and I have gone over and over every section, and we can't see anything that might help us in our mission. Looking back, I'm not sure how anything from any of the projections has helped.

Granted, an early projection led us trust and accept Raoul. He helped us in our dreams and in life. But Benjo? My relationship with him certainly helped me to relax, and that might have been the point. Then of course, he remembers Father and gave me his partner-band – twice – so there's that too. On the subject of the ring, I've developed the habit of turning it round and round on my finger while thinking. It's smooth, slick, almost wet to the touch.

There've been two meetings in the captain's ready room since I last recorded. Our graph colleagues are extending themselves through the grid and Quantum seeking any trace of Dorsa, or indeed of GRENDEL. There're no news broadcasts that relate to Dorsa, myself or anything at all about 'dangerous terrorists'. I've tried to engage my graph skills but since that brief period of lucidity when I heard her calling for help, nothing works.

The human crew are honed and ready for anything that may come. We might have to execute a rescue mission, but without upsetting Martian authorities. If we go stomping around in battle-mechs they'll get a tad annoyed. So, while we prepare there are diplomatic approaches being made, world to world, at levels much higher than my grade. That side of our mission is being led by Minister Markesa Zown and Group-Commander Ibby Carlane, both of whom I've met. It's comforting but as the key word is 'diplomatic', I doubt much of the currency is a hundred percent gold-plated truth.

Even at the highest levels, few on Earth or Venus are aware of the interest shown in Dorsa and me. It must be the same on Mars, so any courtesies that are extended to us are likely to be unofficial. We'll have to tread carefully.

I'm going up to Deck Three to have another look at the mechs and combat-skins. I can't see any use for them for a mission such as ours, but they're incredibly interesting pieces of machinery. I've got used to this ladder up from the accommodation deck. I'll have muscles like a Martian at the end of all this.

Here is a mech. They're made to accommodate a human. We put them on like ceramic suits, or rather slip inside them. They're made to interface with our spacer film-suits which transfer our body movements. We walk, the mech walks. We stick a finger up our nose, the mech – will do its best to reproduce the manoeuvre, but it doesn't have a nose on its ellipsoid head. Naturally, they're bigger than combat-skins which only have to accommodate a construct or a graph.

Now I stand here and look at both, I'm struck with the thought that a combat-skin could easily be seen as the skeleton of a mech-suit. Their respective size and general shapes fit that perception perfectly. I squeeze my ribs. Trying to feel the skeleton within me?

'Got chest cramps?' It's Verone, ever on the lookout for symptoms.

'I'm fine.'

She peers up at one of the two-point-five metre mechs. 'Ugly beasts, aren't they?'

'You think? I quite like them.'

'Ever been in one, not counting yesterday's practice?'

'Never, but I find them surprisingly easy to operate. You?'

She reaches up and touches the upper arm, runs a finger along the dull olive ceramic skin. 'Not one exactly like this, but they have something very similar on Callisto. They're a kind of surface-mech. Cally's call them draggers.'

I laugh, one of those shock reactions, because 'draggers' is a derogatory terms for Callistonians you'd never use in polite society. 'Cally' isn't much better but used everywhere, even by Callistonians.

'I know!' Verone laughs too. 'Nothing like appropriating unacceptable terms and making them your own.'

Deck Three is usually busy, but right now we're the only two down here. Verone hovers, something on her mind. 'Ariel, tell me about your father.'

'What? Are you in doctor-mode? Because I could do without an analysis right now.'

She sits on a mech's right foot, which makes a perfect stool, and invites me to take the left, which I do. 'Call it more an attempt to fill in the gaps.' She taps her temple. 'I should have many memories of him, but someone took them away.'

I sit on the mech's foot, staring down at my own. Where do I begin? Until I left for Earth, Jonan was there all the time. Like Dzalarhons Hall, the surrounding jungle, the sky. I find I do not have many specific memories about him. There was the time he unwound the lion-snake from my leg and treated the wound. Then when he quietly kept pace below me as I walked on top of the balustrade over Gneesa Gorge, and then scolded me when I hopped off: he saved his admonishment for when my feet were safely back on the ground. 'Life is precious and should not be risked for the sake of fun.' He looked down on me: 'There will come other, more noble times when you might risk your safety.' Then there was his speech at my graduation. Waving me off at the Spaceport terminal. The strongest memories are all from times of heightened awareness, and yet very little remains of the everyday, except as a presence. Jonan was always there for me, like the air or the sunshine.

'Do you remember the lion-snake?'

'Of course! Benjo and I told you not to be such an idiot, but you insisted it was safe to pick up.'

I was a young fool. We're laughing again. 'But you don't remember Jonan saving me?'

'I remember pulling its tale while Benjo hit it with a length of fallen branch.'

'But Father?'

I can see her struggle to grapple up the memory, her brow creasing as she slowly, slowly shakes her head. 'Nope, it's a blank. One minute we're fighting the snake, the next you're in a hover being whisked off to the infirmary.' She shakes off the inconsistency and brightens up. 'You do know I still have that snake's skull at home? It's one of my Rule of Seven possessions.'

I'm about to tell her it's a bit macabre, but a skull is only a few millennia short of a fossil, so who am I to criticise? 'A constant memory of my youthful arrogance.'

'To be fair, your arrogance peeped though very rarely. I remember you as a quiet boy who pretended to talk to frogs and insects. A little juvenile with a big imagination. Hey, do you remember the time …' and we're off, recalling scraped knees and naughty pranks, laughing and smiling all the while. Verone's clever, and I swear she's administered the best medicine possible.

It's my turn to add to the conversation, and I actually do recall another memory involving Father. He is teaching me how to wield the two-handed sword. 'It has little to do with strength, Arthur. All is in the technique. See here, make the weight of the blade your friend, and don't fight against it.'

Arthur? So that's why my likeness didn't appear in that last crystal-projection. My ancestor was the boy-duke who John had murdered. I'm chilled, and saddened beyond measure, but at the same time relieved I have no memory of the acts which ended the poor boy's life. And now a hatred for King John develops. I know exactly how my sister Eleanor felt about him.

'Ariel?' Verone reached over and squeezes my knee.

'Another ancestral-memory.' I tell her everything about it. Each minute detail.

'Have you spoken to Amalthea about these memories? Or any other graph?'

Strangely, I haven't. Yet now Verone mentions it I can see that I should. If there's anything that can explain my condition, it's likely to rest in my burgeoning graphness. Can graphs transmit memories from the past? If all time and all space is the same to them, it's at least a possibility.

***

My cabin's ceiling is an astrodome. The projectors have created a facsimile of the Eridani system, and those little, distant suns are the only points of light in the room. They're comforting, and stop me panicking as I would if I woke to complete darkness. Is my future in the stars?

We're decelerating at one-gee, so I can breathe properly without the pressure mask. Another day of this and we reach the diplomatic hub in geosync above Mars. I've still not managed to make contact with Dorsa, but I'm sleepy, relaxed and so happy to be rid of the weight of my armour. Tomorrow we ride north.

I stand by a fast-flowing river. The shield, green cross on a field of black with white ermine-tales, is in the weighted sack. My helm is already on the river bed together with my rusting mail. My surcoat has been burnt. I throw the sack. It hits the water and sinks immediately.

'Nicely done, Your Grace. And farewell, Dark Knight. You served us well.'

It's a long time since Guy addressed me as a duke. I turn, half-expecting him to be garbed in his bloody bandages, his skin loathsome from the tinctures and applications that made him look like a dead thing. 'It is good no longer to be Arthur's ghost,' he says.

'It is better to have the deed done, Benjo.' I recall the screams from the king's chamber at Newark Castle as the poison took effect. I am avenged. If God is with us, as I believe he must be, John's death will be taken as the result of a fatal illness. Perchance our scheme is discovered though, we must away before noon.

I strap my great-sword to the side of this dull little pony. Friar Steven helps me. I will, from now, share Guy's armorials, differentiated but a little. The golden bird is a fine emblem.

We will ride with Sir Malcolm's retinue until we can properly recruit our own, which God willing, will be soon. Thanks to the King's treasure which he lost and I have, now nicely dismantled and beaten out of shape, we have the wherewithal to hire goodly retainers.

Guy looks back towards the castle. 'We both have much for which to thank Sir Hubert.'

'Our very lives.' It's true. Set to kill me, Sir Hubert schemed to free me. And Guy, doomed to hang with the other young squires at Corfe Castle, Sir Hubert secreted him away. Shame only that the others were not so fortunate. Let my vengeance be theirs too.

If Sir Hubert failed in but a single way, it was that my dear sister still languishes within the damp walls of Corfe. I dare not risk sending her word that I yet live. Neither messengers nor letters can be trusted.

I think to my future and look up to where daylight obscures the stars. Is my future in the stars? Mayhap, but for now at least, our goal in the land of ice and fire, that island which lies to the north and west of Britain's furthest north. There is no life left for me here.

I must say goodbye to Dzalarhons Hall, and to Venus, for there will be no return.

Sol IV

There's no life left for me here. Two days after that dream on my last night aboard the Ashen Light, it still troubles me. For the same reasons Arthur couldn't stay in England or Brittany, there's nothing for me here. And I don't mean here on Mars, but anywhere in the Three Worlds or the colonies. Albion is my island of ice and fire. I'm drawn to it, like a salmon to its spawning grounds.

Officially we're here to study farming methods in Dorsa's region of Mars. The diplomatic envoi reports that our most innocuous request was authorised by Martian authorities with barely a second thought. As for any question about the use of a VDF ship, why the need to travel light of course, without the worry of negotiating with an oversubscribed charter company.

For most of us, space travel is not an everyday event and it can be difficult to secure passage at short notice, so our use of a defence ship for a putative government mission isn't going to raise any suspicions. I hope.

The Venusian consulate is tucked in to an older section of down-dome Elysium that actually lies within the old dome. I doubt if the dome is functional these days, but it lends the impression of what it might have been like to be Martian before the world had a breathable atmosphere. It's like I'm living in a hollow world where I could bounce a rock off the sky.

Djogore and most of the crew are still spaceside, either on the hub or still aboard the Ashen Light. Sav's attending to some admin at the consulate, and I'm exploring the city with Verone and Officer Hamo Mutairi, all of us first-time visitors to Mars. We all stand out from the crowd in our VDF uniforms, but Hamo draws the most attention in the form of sideways glances, and I assume it's because there aren't many androgens on Mars. The locals are trying to work out if he's male or female and I'm rather uncomfortable on his behalf. Then again, it could be because he looks about twenty-five years old which, of course, is far too young to be a spacer.

We're all in spacer-films, now trimmed green for the science and medical branch which is more in keeping with our supposed mission. The weighted body-rig is less of a chore than I anticipated, although Hamo seems to be having trouble. He keeps worrying at his shoulder straps.

'I'll be fine,' he says. 'I think the rig needs adjusting.'

Tech would handle such adjustments at home and on Earth. Martians like to go minimal on unnecessary technology. 'Allow me, Hamo. Turn around.' Yes, this'll be easy to fix. Loosen the buckle at his back; pull through to the next setting and do up; fingers through the loops and give a little tug. Hamo is so light my 'little tug' pulls him backwards and almost off his feet. I steady him with a grip to his shoulders and he tenses up, but it's not because of my touch. Someone is staring at us from across the street.

Half-hidden in the shadow of a street-food booth, he's tall for a Martian and heavily built. There's a tattoo on his round, chubby face and he appears to be talking. One arm nonchalantly crosses his chest, his hand in a perfect position to make use of a wrist-mic. He has darker skin than the average Martian, a shade darker than my honey-brown, and his bald head shines in the domelight.

Hamo and I both instinctively look away, but he already knows we've spotted him.

'The guy over the road?' Verone says, also deliberately not looking at him. 'He's paying us a lot of furtive attention, isn't he?'

'I vote we take a few side streets,' Hamo says. 'See if he follows.'

Walking slowly, pretending to take no notice, we amble up and down the lanes. I engage with a construct distributor and try to look interested in a woollen poncho with a typical Martian pattern. I hold it up to the light, using it to disguise the direction in which I am really looking.

I keep a smile on my face, ever so intrigued by this strange garment, and speak from the side of my mouth. 'He's still there.'

'I know,' Verone says. She picks up a corner of the poncho I'm holding. Never has such a mundane garment been the centre of so much attention.

Hamo isn't playing any more. With fists on his hips, he huffs and strides over to our follower who looks more than a little uncomfortable at his approach.

I can't hear the conversation. It doesn't take long though. The stranger turns and hurries off along the lane, one departing look over his shoulder, eyes under worried brows.

Hamo's back looking very pleased with himself. 'I called him out for staring at me and asked if he'd never seen an androgen before. He apologised.'

'I'm not sure that's the reason he was following us, Hamo.'

'Of course it wasn't. But it gave me a good excuse to get up close. He had a tiny earphone in, and there was a mic on his sleeve. About as low-tech as you can get, so I'm guessing he hasn't got a neural-stent. And he was wearing some kind of a uniform under his poncho. High collar. Martian-red.'

'Sounds like their navy,' Verone says. 'But why put a stentless operative on a close-follow assignment? They'd be better using a skin like Hamo's bee.'

I can think of only one answer to that. 'They want us to know we're under observation.'

'To see how we react? Then let's carry on as if we never saw him.'

She's right. 'While being aware that we're probably under continued but more efficient observation.' I close my eyes, link briefly with AMALTHEA and ask her to see what's going on at grid and Quantum levels. 'Don't disrupt anything, Amalthea. Try only to locate sources and objectives.' We'll observe while being observed.

'It must be cold for Venusians, so please take a poncho,' the distributor says as I start to walk away. 'It will not count towards your Rule of Seven possessions so long as you leave it at a sharing point when you have finished with it.'

I take the offered garment. Verone and Hamo take one each. We throw them over our heads immediately becoming less conspicuous and more Martian.

It's been an interesting hour, and now we eat street-food by the Beagle 2 Monument, testimony to the ingenuity of our distant ancestors who still managed to explore our Solar System with their laughably archaic tech, everything achieved without graph help, in an absence of true AI and with massive computers that had less capacity that the tiniest quantum fleck. The giants upon whose shoulders we stand were actually quite tiny creatures struggling in the dark. And yet, they kept at it, and they prevailed.

There's been no more sign of our follower. 'Back to the consulate?'

'One more helping of beetroot lasagne first,' Hamo says. 'It's delicious.'

***

It's early. Martian dawn in fact, and I'm unnaturally light without my weighted rig. I'm in my bathing booth, shaving, with Benjo's holo as a welcome intruder to my morning ablutions thanks to a graph-to-graph link arranged through NEKO.

Benjo leans in until his light intersects with my face 'Does that shaving thing hurt?'

'No, but it's a bit of a chore. If I leave it for a single day it's as if I have a dirty face.'

'Well, at least your hair's beginning to look good.'

'Thanks, but I have to comb it all the time.'

'Comb?'

I hold up my comb and give him a demonstration. Going by his reaction it's the funniest thing he's ever seen. 'It's not that funny, Benjo. There are combs on Venus, you know.'

'Well, I've never seen one in use before. Any other minor inconveniences?' he manages through laughter.

'My pee's red.'

'What?' He's suddenly serious. 'Jamil, that's not good. Have you had a med-scan?'

'I'm not ill. It's a side effect of one of the local delicacies. I was warned, but it was still a bit of a shock this morning.'

Benjo laughs and as usual the link isn't quite up to coordinating the sound with the projection. Either that, or graphs impose their own way of laughing when in-link.

We swap a few inconsequential words on the contrasts between Venus and Mars, but it's clear there's something more important Benjo's wants to say. I wonder if it's playing on his mind that we may never meet again. Albion isn't exactly The Grand Worlds Tour. The thought puts a knot in my throat.

'Are you done?'

I fold away the blade. 'I am now.'

'Then put your clothes on and meet me outside. There's something I need to tell you.'

On with the form-suit disc. Activate. Countdown in seconds from ten. I'm ready, and walk to the sitting-room.

Benjo projects by the window and wears a worried face. 'Jamil, the prefects have been to your home, asking about Ariel Dzalarhons. Did you ever meet him?'

Ah! Benjo fears our conversation is being monitored even though NEKO has put in quantum-level encryptions. 'Dzalarhons? Apart from the name of my home, it doesn't stir any memories.'

'He was a good friend of mine. He died in a flyer accident on Earth.'

'Oh, Benjo. I'm so sorry to hear that.' I'm far sorrier to hear that prefects are snooping around asking questions. They must suspect I didn't really die.

'Anyway, they asked what I was doing in his house, and I told them it was your house now, and we were … you know …partners.'

I really wish we'd formalised things before I left. I give Father's partner-band a twist. 'Didn't they believe you?'

'Yes, because it was all but verified by house-system. They saw I had unrestricted access and made the obvious conclusion. But then they asked if I knew Jonan Dzalarhons. They said he was Ariel's father, which is silly because he didn't have a father.'

This is bad. If they know Benjo is un-stented, they'll know he's lying. But if he admits to recalling Father, there's no telling what they'll do. They've already killed and I have no doubts they'd kill again.

I have to choose my words as carefully as Benjo. 'Did they give the grounds for their interrogation?'

'No, and I'm aware they were in breach of their authority.'

'What happened then?'

'They left, but since then I'm pretty sure I'm being watched.'

'Inform Council at once. Unless they have a warrant —'

'Already done. But still …'

I really don't like the sound of this. 'Look, I'll see what I can do from here. I'm certain VDF high command would object to prefects overstepping their powers to push their noses into the home of a man in Special Ops. Maybe they can call them off.'

'Okay. Well, look, thanks. I have a smelly mons-sloth covered in algae waiting for me in the vet-lab. Got to be going. Take care.'

If ever two words could be loaded with the meaning of ten sentences. 'Take care, Benjo.'

His image stutters, and is gone. NEKO takes his place.

'Thanks for the link, Neko.'

'My pleasure, and I'll contact VDF Command about the prefects at once.'

I'm grateful to the cat-boy. He can deal with the prefect situation by graph-link and I'll finish preparations for today's mission.

'I wonder if you could extend a favour in return, Jamil.'

I'm more than happy to help, and NEKO asks if he can accompany my team to Dorsa's farm. We're due to set off in two hours, which will help take my mind off Benjo.

No sooner do I leave my apartment than I'm accosted by a very troubled Sav Kinngas. 'What's this rotten planet done to Hamo?' the young officer says. 'He's back at our apartment pissing litres of blood, and the med scanners won't work on androgens.'

'Of course they will, Sav.' It's obvious someone didn't pay attention to all sections of our briefing pack. I try not to laugh. Poor Hamo must be quite distressed.

'Well, I can't make them work,' Sav says pushing back his wayward hair to reveal a pair of eyes wide with panic. Not what I'd expect of a combat specialist. 'Tell me the protocols in this stone age world for getting medical help!'

'Sav, Hamo doesn't need help. We've all got red pee this morning.'

'I haven't!'

'Did you eat the beetroot lasagne?'

Sav's expression changes at once. It's like watching the sun break through black clouds and panic flees in the face of realisation. Before I can say another word, he's rushing back along the corridor to give Hamo the good news that he isn't dying. He disappears into the crowd at reception, and for a moment I think I see that tattooed man who followed us yesterday. But he's gone before I can fix my vision on him.

It must be my imagination. Certainly nothing definite enough on which to file a report.

***

Martian long distance transport is closer to Venusian's than Earth's: surface trains that travel at hundreds of klicks per hour rather than vac-tubes that run at thousands. However, they're luxurious by Venusian standards with lounges, bars and observations decks. And Martians have the nerve to call us decadent.

I've kept the team small. It's Verone, Hamo, Sav, NEKO, Verone's graph assistant AZNABLE and me. AMALTHEA's centred her consciousness at the consulate to get on with the quantum-level aspects of our mission, but she can join us within a nano-second if the need arises.

We humans form an atypical Venusian team in that every one of us has hair. Verone's is long and fair; Sav's dark, plentiful, scruffy and covering his eyes; Hamo's shorter, flame-coloured, neatly combed and with one bang covering his left eye; mine black and nearly long enough to accommodate a parting. People could be forgiven for paying special attention to our identification projections.

The relaxing, enjoyable journey takes us through cities, mountainous regions and sparsely wooded plains. We transfer to a crawler for the last five klicks, and now we're here with IDEW to greet us. There are no humans at the farm and IDEW is the only graph. He's in charge of all the constructs who in turn operate the varied army of agricultural-skins.

IDEW presents as a tight ball of swirling, bright green binary codes. Martians are generally more comfortable with interfaces which aren't based on lifeforms, and the graphs seem happy to oblige. He gives us a short tour of the home domes. 'Thanks to your advanced warning, I was able to recommission the domes for human comfort. Temperatures can be a little chilly, especially for off-worlders, and even more so for Venusians. How are you finding the weight-rigs?'

'A pain,' Sav says. He inserts a finger between shoulder and strap to administer an ineffective massage. Hamo glances towards his boyfriend and rolls his eyes. 'But it's better than bouncing around like a roo.'

The dome covers a largely open plan design with bedrooms and other private areas forming a central hub surrounded by seating areas, an office, a galley and work spaces. The working area has benches, printers and cutters and the signs of regular use. I'm intrigued by a pile of small, vaguely disc-shaped artefacts. Each is about four centimetres across, appears to be made of wood and bears a design in black. They remind me of ancient runes. I pick one up. It's light and I can't tell if it's natural wood or printed material.

'What're these?'

IDEW hovers over the pile for a moment. 'They're slices of wood from a fallen branch, polished and lightly buffed. The characters were made with a laser-burner. Dorsa was fond of making them in her spare time. She was very keen not to let natural wood go to waste.'

I twist one around between my fingers. The piece is silkily tactile. 'But what're they for?'

'Merely for decoration. People like to carry one around, or wear them on a thong around their necks. Dorsa sent out thousands over the years. There are many Martians who have one as a highly prized Rule of Seven possession. Dorsa was quite renowned for her work, planet-wide.'

That's a revelation: Dorsa, a well-known artist. I'm struck by how little I really know about her, despite those weeks in the jungle. But mention of Dorsa gives me an early opening to speak of her.

'I was hoping Dorsa would be here.'

IDEW flares, his codes building from mid-green to brightly incandescent lime, and then back again: that typically graph-like display of emotion that I know so well from AMALTHEA. 'Surely you know, she was killed in a flyer accident on Earth.'

He exudes a pall of dishonesty that only another graph could detect. I can detect it, though I can't describe it in sensory terms. There's no time to play loop-around-the-asteroids, so I'm going to be direct. 'I'm fully aware of the cover story, because I'm part of it. I was also "killed" in that accident. Now, Idew, if you don't mind, please let Dorsa know I've responded to her call, and I'm here.'

Something happens. There is a writhing and a swirling of the strands of code that make up IDEW's projection.

'Have you just sent a message, Idew?'

Sav steps in close to my left shoulder as if preparing to protect me. And NEKO forms at my right.

'I sent no message.' I can't work out how I know he's lying. 'I merely checked your appearance against the broadcasts of the accident. You do have an uncanny resemblance to Ariel Dzalarhons, but I have also looked at his history, and he was bio-adjusted in the womb to be free of bodily hair.'

'I've experienced one or two changes, but I'm still me. Contact Dorsa, please. And no more prevarication.'

IDEW doesn't prevaricate. He simply vanishes, but he's done his job and given us away. I stretch into Quantum and detect the formation of squads who will soon be on their way to capture us.

'I'm going after him,' NEKO says, and he vanishes too. He vanishes from my human eyes, but I watch him recede along quantum pathways with esoteric and nameless senses. I follow him while my physical body stays put, and watch as he works to deflect attention away from us. It's intricate work that takes may hours, but it's far from successful. Returning consciousness to myself, not even a second has passed.

If AMALTHEA was centred here now she'd be recommending blockers. As for Verone, she's not that kind of doctor. My pulse races and my breathing rate goes up, but no blockers. I've got this. 'I guess we don't have much time. Spread out. Look for any traces of Dorsa, and anything that looks like a message she may have left for us.' I join in the hunt while at the same time desperately trying for a mind-link. If she's near here, surely a link will be easier.

I'm back at the workbench sorting through the little wooden discs. I don't know what I'm looking for. A message. A sign. Anything out of the ordinary. The others have gone to different parts of the dome, and Hamo is checking the out-buildings. If we were prefects we'd require a warrant to do this, and I wonder how many laws we're breaking. It's a concern, but I feel no guilt.

I've found what looks like a spare bedroom. Apart from the furniture the space is empty and I wonder if this was Dorsa's father's room. It's an indictment that I don't know his name. In all the time I was with Dorsa I never asked. My loss was always first and foremost, and yet hers was equally as great.

I open storage recesses. Nothing. Here, the bathing-cove is empty with no sign of recent use.

I hear Sav calling for me.

'I'm in here!'

Sav bursts in with a streak of blue light trailing from his mantle-projectors like a piece of windblown silk. 'Incoming message, Jamil. Mission-Commander's attention.'

I give the authorities. The blue light stabilises into the form of a man and relays a message from Commander Djogore Delatour. 'The diplomatic hub's been locked down. No explanation as yet, but Martian authorities aren't allowing any movement to or from the hub. You're on your own until this lifts.'

'Any indication how long the lockdown will last?'

'None at all, Commander, and there's worse. The Venusian consul and Martian council have received high level diplomatic requests from the Earthers. They want to board and search the Ashen Light, giving worlds security as a reason. I daresay we could hazard a fairly accurate guess what, or rather who, they're looking for.'

I try to keep my focus on the mission. Thinking about myself at this time won't help. I have the safety of my team to consider. Not only those here, but the crew of the ship. Also aboard the Ashen Light are my crystals. If GRENDEL is in the boarding party, it won't take much for him to realise they belong to me.

'Captain, get the ship and crew to safety. Until everything's been through the correct channels, any lockdown is unenforceable without triggering an interplanetary incident. It's little more than an official bluff.' I don't really know what I'm talking about, but it seems reasonable.

I expect Djogore to argue. He doesn't. 'Aye, Commander. Securing for launch. We'll find a way to keep you updated.'

The construct-projection vanishes and with it the link to our refuge. It's as if we've been cut adrift and the waters race round me making it hard to think. 'Carry on with the search,' I say, for want of anything better. It all hinges on me now, and I have to at least appear to know what I'm doing.

I continue searching, but my eyes see little and my mind registers less. All my thought processes are running through possible scenarios and plans of action. We have to utilise what we have, and now I remember we're on a farm which is replete with skins of various types.

NEKO zaps into existence by my side. 'Sorry, Jamil. I lost Idew. Quantum is crazy with activity. We're not safe here.' The cat-boy looks all around. 'We're not safe anywhere.'

Tell me something I don't know. 'Can you control the constructs that animate the agricultural-skins?'

'I can do better than that. I can evict any resident construct, inhabit a skin myself and control it directly.'

Verone steps up. I hadn't known she was in the room. 'I'm sure Aznable could do the same.'

AZNABLE flashes onto the scene, an ancient-modern mashup of a Samurai warrior. With a swish of his sable cape he says 'I assume you want us to set up a first line of defence.'

'Exactly!'

The two graphs catch each other's holographic eye, nod and vanish.

Now it's Hamo's turn to rush in. He suppresses his excitement to give a measured report. 'I think you'd better come and see what I've found in one of the utility domes, Commander.' It helps that these career VDF people have immediately snapped into official mode. They treat me as their leader. It lends me confidence and it's a constant reminder I must act the part.

'Lead on, Hamo.'

Hamo heads off at the double, and we follow. We hurry out of the main dome and to a larger one that houses machinery. It stands about fifty metres from the home-dome.

'I deployed my seeker-bee set for structural anomalies,' Hamo explains as we enter the dome.

I have a nasty flash-back to the Amazonian jungle when GRENDEL's seeker-wasps swarmed upon us. I'm glad they can be put to better use.

Hamo ducks behind a massive agricultural-skin, through some close-set ranks of tools and stoops by an open trap over a yawning maw of a hole in the floor. I direct some beams of light from my mantle. The hole is lined with masonry blocks, and there's a ladder.

'Have you been down, Hamo?'

'It's a long way, Commander. I got about halfway.'

I'm a leader who mostly directs, but sometimes, being a leader means going first. I think this is one of those times. With my mantle fully adapted to illuminate, I step into the maw.

'We could send the bee to scout and relay a projection,' Verone says.

'No time, Verone. You and Sav keep watch up here. Hamo, you're with me.'

***

After a fifteen metre descent I don't need my mantle-torches because my presence has triggered lights. They illuminate a hall crafted out of a vast cavern. On the wall by the foot of the ladder are some curious icons. Faded and of strange design, yet their meaning is clear: we have descended an emergency escape route. This distinctively fluid text is familiar to me.

Hamo peers up at the writing. 'What do you make of it?'

'I've seen this kind of writing in a cavern at home, but I've no idea what it means.' The dimensions of this place and the one at Dzalarhons Mons are the same, but this one's full of machinery and equipment.

'What is all this stuff? It looks prehistoric, and yet modern at the same time. As if part of "now" went back in time, thousands of years.'

Hamo's description is perfect. 'I think I know what this place is for. Look at the arrangement of machinery. The chambers. The tanks.'

Hamo shakes his head. It doesn't mean anything to him.

'It's a bioprinting facility.'

Hamo looks at me as if I'm crazy, sets his mantle to scan and walks around while the beams access as much of the cavern as is possible. I examine the machinery manually, and I need no scanners to confirm my suspicions. It's most definitely bioprinting tech, but I can't find the control interface.

The scans complete, Hamo listens while a Hamo-shaped construct gives the results. He's on the other side of the hall and I can't hear what's being said, but I can see his ever widening eyes and flabbergasted expression. And I have no trouble hearing his raised voice demanding verification.

He comes over to me at a jog. 'Commander, this is beyond crazy.'

'Report.'

'Scans reveal this place predates colonisation of Mars. Hell, it predates terraforming and even earliest space travel.'

I cast around to catch an explanation for the impossible. 'The cavern's carved out of the bedrock. Are your reading being compromised by the geology?'

'Absolutely not. I'm talking about the human activity. These machines are several thousand years old, and yet true bioprinting tech barely reaches back to the twenty-first century.' He looks around, as if the shadows may be watching us. 'I can't be sure this is human tech. Humans hadn't even harnessed the power of steam when this place was built.'

It's as if something to do with past learning and present perception is being turned inside out. By any standards, by whichever discipline, this is a truly phenomenal discovery.

I amble about, stunned. I can't help reaching out to touch the machines, half-expecting my hand to pass through them, because surely this is all a trick. These are holograms. But no, they're as solid as I am.

I recall my fossilised tentacle. 'As far as I can fathom, Hamo, there're only two explanations. One, human existence at high tech level is much older than we think. Or two, we're in the middle of a facility created by a non-human species.' I don't bother mentioning time travel for fear of losing Hamo's respect.

'Not entirely alien.' Hamo waves his hand towards the ceiling. 'The lighting is recent human tech, only a few tens of years old. So we're not the first to make this discovery.'

Now this is personal. There's nothing recorded about any of this. Nothing at all on the grid, no references to it in crystal-histories. Like the truth about Raoul, Dorsa and me, it's been wiped or restricted. I have to do something about this.

'Hamo, I'm going to record as much of this writing and iconography as I can.'

'I'll join you. I'll start from the far end of the hall and we'll meet in the middle. Let's record the tech too.'

We work as fast as we can. There's a feeling of time slipping away, of being watched and of unseen agents keen to hide the truth. My mantle-beams touch the faded signs on the walls, and plates of text set into the machines.

I have an idea, and manage to get a link-message to Benjo. Not real-time, but the message will be waiting for him next time he uses a mantle or monitor-screen. I want him to go to the cavern under my home and record everything he can.

While the mantle-beams slide over and record everything, my mind wanders. We came down an emergency exit, so where are the non-emergency doors? Is there more of this yet to be found?

'Hamo,' I yell across a space of fifty metres. 'Have you seen anything that resembles a door?'

He hasn't, so we begin to pay heightened attention to the walls, and I direct my beams to deep-scan. It's not long before the display reveals a metal door lying below a layer of plasiplaster. 'Over here, Hamo!'

But our time has run out. The scan-beams cut out and instead AMALTHEA appears, a barely visible smudge of blue, more cloud-like than holographic. Her voice fades in and out, now loud, now barely audible, but her message is clear. There are flyers on the way to our location. She estimates we have twenty minutes to escape.

At the same time, Sav's voice echoes down the shaft from the surface. 'Get out of there!'

I signal to Hamo and he runs to the ladder.'

'Drop your rig. It'll make climbing easier.'

He does so and starts to climb. I drop my weights too, and I'm close behind. The lamps begin to dim before I'm five rungs up and the only light now is from far above.

Sav and Verone haul us out when we reach the top, and I slam the hatch shut.

'Move it, people!' Sav says. Those flyers are less than ten minutes out.'

'Which way?'

'Follow me. There's a plan.'

'He calls it a plan,' Verone whispers.

Sav runs, and we follow.

As soon as we reach the front of the home-dome, my heart sinks. Our crawler is speeding into the distance throwing up a cloud of red-brown dust.

Sav's smiling. 'Part of the plan, Commander.' I hear him calling into the grid, a link to our graph friends. I shouldn't be able to hear that, but no time to worry about it.

A distant soft-edged whine grows to a thrum that thrills through my body, and two massive aggy-skins lumber towards us from the other side of the utility domes. Each one is the size of a modest dwelling and sprouts all kinds of attachments. The main tyres are twice my height. They're sowers, reapers, gatherers and processors all in one; biomass in one end, cubes ready for kitchen-processors and galley-skins at the other.

Each colossal machine has a tiny cabin with enough room for two humans. I climb into one with Sav, while Verone and Hamo take the other.

Another graph communication, intended for Sav, wafts along a corridor of my mind. I'm an intruder, as if I've tapped his stent, so I deliberately turn my thoughts elsewhere. In other situations an ability to intercept graph or other kinds of personal link communications could prove useful.

'Perfect!' Sav says. 'They've taken the bait. The flyer's diverted to follow our crawler.' Our aggy-skin picks up speed and keeps formation with its twin.

'That won't keep them busy for long. What's the rest of the plan?'

'There's a commercial hub 10 klicks that way.' He points out of the port in the direction we're going. 'We join a convoy of other agricultural-skins. Nothing out of the usual. The terminal and the trains are fully automated, but like these skins, there's cab space for a few humans. We use our authorities to get a ride, head back into the city and disappear into the crowd.'

It's not a great plan, but it'll do until we can get back to the Ashen Light.

'It's not a great plan,' Sav says. 'But it'll do until we can get back to our ship.'

I wonder if he can hear my thoughts too. No, must be coincidence.

'It helps that there're several convoys of skins on the move, and only one flyer. My guess is that once they find the crawler empty, they'll waste more time searching the farm, then they have to get lucky and follow the right convoy.'

I ask how long it will take, but Sav gets another message. His eyes take on that wide look again and he swears. 'They've taken out the crawler. Simply plazzed it into dust.'

'Maybe they thought we were on board.'

Before he can answer, AMALTHEA appears on the dash-monitor. 'Make all haste for the hub, Ariel. There are now two flyers looking for you. I'll do what I can to muddy your trail.' And she's gone again.

We rev the skins up to full speed, then send them off in pairs, each in a different direction, but we're in an almost hopeless situation. Within moments a flyer buzzes us, and I wonder if one of these things can survive a plazbolt. But they don't use a bolt. Instead, they hover overhead and kill off the constructs and power with a pulse.

Our skin winds down to a full stop, quivers like a beast breathing its last, and dies.

We're ordered from above to vacate the vehicle. A quick glance through the port tells me Verone's skin is suffering the same humiliation. Again, we're told to get out, this time with more urgency.

We don't have a lot of choice. With the power gone we have to struggle with the cab door and use physical strength to push it open. As I descend the ladder, my skin recoils with the expectation of being fired upon, and all the while the thought goes round and round: this is all my fault.

I try to reach into the flyer's control-matrix. Maybe I can bring it down, like Raoul did. And yes, I can sense the pathways and junctions. I think I can do this. But countermeasures have been set and the inside of my skull erupts into white-hot pain. It last only a second, but I won't be trying that again.

Sav and I gravitate towards Verone and Hamo who have touched ground from the other aggy-skin. We meet halfway between the two behemoths and watch the flyer land. The hatch opens and a troop of humans in red-brown uniforms deploy together with a fearsome looking combat-skin.

'Martian Navy,' Sav whispers from the side of his mouth.

I'm relieved they don't look plazzer-happy. In fact, there is no sign of side-arms at all, and their approach is calm, almost friendly. I begin to relax, until I catch sight of the stout man with the tattooed face.

His face twists into a smile. 'Got you!' he says, and winks

'There's some kind of misunderstanding,' I say. 'We have Council authorities to conduct research into Martian agricultural techniques.' I try to project the authorities, but there must be something wrong with my mantle.

A young man who appears to be in charge steps forward. 'Authorities revoked.'

***

And with no more ceremony than that, rights hard won at the highest levels are taken away. I ask on what grounds, and I'm told to shut up and get in the flyer. Anger flares, and for one tiny moment I wish I had a plazgun, immediately followed by relief that I haven't. How easy it would be to kill in haste and regret at leisure.

Tattoo-Face tells me to get on board, and as my foot touches the bottom rung of the flyer's ladder, he squeezes my shoulder, an act of friendliness that is completely at odds to the situation.

It's cramped inside. They make Sav and me shuffle tight together on a seat made for one. Verone and Hamo appear at the hatch and they have to do the same on the seat opposite. While our Martian captors are busy strapping us in, I get a message off to AMALTHEA.

A graph voice booms from the speaker. 'One of them sent a message. I have now established dampeners.' That'll certainly stop me sending out anything else.

'Okay,' says the young leader. 'Who initiated a link, and where to?'

'It was me,' I say.

'Well, you're in breach. Everyone knows the basic rules. Link-coms is prohibited if you've been relieved of liberty.'

'Oh, I know the rules, but I'm not sure if you do. Your actions are illegal. You haven't even pretended to stick to the protocols. I'm a cohort-commander working for Venusian Council with full approval of the Martian authorities. Your actions will have consequences.'

His insolent smile is chilling as he looks at each of us. 'Small cohort.' His most withering sneer is saved for me. 'Commander.' And with a delivery that makes my rank sound like the designation for a sewer-skin, he turns his back and disappears into the control cabin.

One of the other Martians follows him, but Tattoo-Face lingers. 'Sorry about him,' he says, quietly but not quite a whisper. 'He's an arse. Truth is we've been ordered to take you into protective custody. There's a Richter scale magnitude-twelve dome-breaker brewing over you lot, and unknown operatives are out to get you. S'Jinn, one of their flyers blew up your crawler not half an hour ago, and it doesn't look like they took much trouble to see if you were all inside it or not.'

'Remember me?' Hamo says. 'Street market off Beagle-2 Square, main-dome, Elysium? You were following us, and now you're here. Coincidence?'

Thunder gathers over Tattoo-Face's brow. 'Go with the flow and it'll work out.' He turns his face to me. 'Hear what I'm saying, Venus-boy?'

Relief washes over me like warm water in a blizzard. Venus-boy: it's like a code or password. I don't know who he is, but he's somehow connected to Dorsa. I give him a knowing nod and a genuine smile. 'I guess we'll go with the flow, then.'

'What's that all about?' Sav asks when Tattoo-Face has followed the others and slammed the hatch shut.

I eye the speakers and mics on the bulkhead, very obviously. I have no doubt we're being eavesdropped. 'Nothing to worry about, Adjutant Kinngas. I'm sure we're in good hands.' I give him a wink for good measure, and the penny drops.

We go with the flow, as instructed, and the flow takes us all the way back to Elysium. It's not the Martian capital, but it's by far the biggest city on Mars. Two million of the total Martian population of seventy-eight million live here. It's a Three Worlds Heritage City, a beeline for artists and the place most renowned for getting lost. People can get off grid and become anonymous here probably easier than anywhere else in the System; excluding Callisto, of course, but who in their right mind would want to live there? There's quite an enclave of ex-pat Venusian glass-weavers here, so the ease of blending in and vanishing in this city is a fact not lost on me. If we can escape, it's probably the best place to stay free and undetected until we can make better plans.

A dampener-field prevents our graph colleagues from joining us, but we humans are treated with more respect at this end of the journey than at the beginning. Nevertheless, my demand to be released into the care of the Venusian consulate is politely declined and we're interred in a suite of rooms where we meet some high ranking Martian officials. They inform us that Earth authorities want to extradite us for unspecified crimes against peace and security, but Venusian Council demand that as Venusians we should be returned to Venus. Three Worlds Council has nothing to say on the matter as yet.

'Matters have become more complicated since the Discovery Incident,' says the official.

The Discovery is the sister ship of the Endeavour, and our delicately negotiated ride to Albion. 'What incident?' I ask.

I get the feeling I've bitten down on a large baited hook. The official is a bad actor, and his feigned concern is a shoddy veneer to spitefulness. 'Did you not hear?'

Of course I didn't, you fawning oaf. Get on with it. 'No, I've heard of no incident.'

'Well, investigators haven't got to the bottom of it yet, but a Venusian ship called Ashen Light flew into the Discovery at high velocity. Both ships and their crews were lost. There were no survivors.'

He's doing his best to repress a smile, and I want to rip his head off. I let the anger build, because once again, it's better than being sucked into to a whirlpool of grief, or being dashed against rocks of guilt.

I hear no more of the official, nor am I aware of his exit. I see only Djogore Delatour and the rest of the crew who remained on board. I can't give in, no matter how horrible it all is, because Sav is here, and Hamo who knew the others far more intimately than did I. But what to say?

The mission's crumbled to nothing. Without the Discovery there will be no voyage to Albion. And yet ships are mere fabric, and missions can be planned anew. The real losses are Djogore, Lirril, Retz and Matt. A brief flash of anger burns away the mist and give me clarity. If only I can contain these explosive impulses.

'I must send condolences to the families.'

Verone nods; lightly grasps my forearm in support.

'Sav?'

He makes brief eye-contact before pain drags his gaze back to the floor. Hamo looks stunned too. Somehow my meaning passes to him and he embraces Sav. I let them hold each other for a while and wish I had Benjo by me, but no such luxury. A leader is ever alone.

'Listen up!' I let a little anger into the command, and all three of my team come to a kind of informal but expectant attention. 'We had a mission, but now we're in a war. The enemy, whoever they are, have shown that they'll break every convention, even the most sacred. They've killed, more than once, and I haven't the slightest doubt they're behind the loss of our colleagues … our friends, and our ship.'

Hamo reaches over and takes Sav's hand.

'Let's take time to be with our thoughts. When evening comes, we'll discuss our options, options that don't include waiting here at the pleasure of our Martian captors.'

Sav draws himself up, hands clasped firmly at his chest. 'Commander!'

Hamo follows suit and for an instant, I love them both, and Verone too. She smiles her approval. It's an emotion that cuts through the anger, and I wonder if this is the essence of military service. My commands have been accepted with more eloquence than could be spoken in an oratory. For this small moment in time, I know I would die for them, and they for me.

I let in the flames of anger again, for there is little time for sentimentality. That must wait for long dark evenings before flaming hearths.

***

It's our second day of captivity and we gather in the sitting room to receive a visitor from our consulate. We don't yet have a detailed plan of action, but we've all agreed we must effect an escape if diplomatic efforts to release us fail. There's something I'm holding back. It's not enough for me to keep one step ahead. I'm searching for ways to take my fight to the heart of the enemy. First, find your enemy.

The consulate and her secretary are escorted in by Tattoo-Face and another guard. Although not in VDF uniform I recognise the diplomat at once, chiefly from the mondokoro mark on her forehead. She wears a Venusian gown in the style of a film-gown but of a much more substantial material conforming to Martian sensibilities regarding modesty and decorum.

I rise to greet her. 'Very good to see you again, Ibby.' I think it wise not to mention anything about her high rank in the VDF with these Martians present, but thankfully they're now leaving.

'How're they treating you, people?'

'With civility for the most part, but we have no contact with the world outside this suite.'

'And I'll never get used to Martian food,' Sav adds.

'Excuse me,' Ibby says addressing her remarks to the others. 'I need to speak with Ariel alone for a few minutes.'

She called me 'Ariel' in front of everyone, and not 'Jamil'. A slip of the tongue that puts me on edge. But really, there's no need to worry. Sav and Verone know my true identity and I assume Hamo does too. The need for a false identity has passed.

Ibby's secretary and my friends leave, and she takes a seat. I choose the place opposite. 'Did you leave the VDF to become a diplomat?'

'Not at all. We're hardly a military world. Defence work doesn't take up much of my time, so you see me now in my day-to-day role.'

'You called me Ariel.'

'Yes. In that respect the game's up. The Earthers know you survived the flyer accident. It fits in nicely with their story that you're some kind of near-immortal uber-human planning to subjugate System.'

It gets more bizarre every moment of every day. Uber-human? Ibby tells me that I'm the biggest story on Earth and the conversation in every museum, gallery, restaurant and bar. Of course, not everyone believes the official line, but the fact that it *is* the official line is terrifying. For generations, since the Bumblebee pandemics, humans have been far less susceptible to manipulation, but this reeks of the olden days when people chose a faction that matched their prejudices and then became wilfully ignorant of anything that challenged their preconceptions.

'Unfortunately, Ariel, the rot is spreading on Mars too. The whispers are becoming open conversations and I suspect they'll soon be angry shouts for action.'

It's chilling. Once more I'm diminished by the pall of injustice drawing round me like a damp blanket. 'I'm almost afraid to ask, but what actions are they demanding?'

'As I say, nothing yet, but these unseen factions who're working so hard against you are pulling no punches. They're portraying you as less than human, and therefore undeserving of human rights. In their books you're a disease and you must be eradicated.'

The blanket tightens. I wish I could access some of that anger when I need it, but right now I'm scared, and the fear is spiced with the futile indignity of injustice.

I force a smile. 'So, what's the good news, Ibby?'

'Venus is holding up against all this mania, for the most part.'

'And for the lesser part?'

'You've been implicated in homicide. They're not releasing the full details but we suspect they'll try and pin Bart Couman's death on you.'

That's beyond sickening. 'They're accusing me of killing my old friend? And Raoul too?'

'Probably. At least at home the Council is with us, and the people hate the idea of Earthers abusing Venusians. But you know how it is. Drip, drip, drip with the lies; drop, drop, drop with the false news bytes. If they're persistent enough, the drips and drops become a stream, and then a river. And you try holding back an ocean of lies with the truth.'

I wonder if Ibby Carlane is right for this job. Surely a diplomat must have ways of breaking bad news in a less devastating manner. And now she tries.

'There's no sense in perpetuating the Jamil Miralad story, so you can go back to being you.'

'That's ... good news. I suppose.' How fucking magnanimous. Again, decisions being made for me without consultation. I try not to bristle too much.

'But you need every protection you can get, so you've been commissioned into the VDF in your own right. Same rank, but in the medical and science branch. The VDF has never had a cyber-archaeologist or a gene-hunting historian in its ranks before.' Her smile is genuine and something of her warmth seeps into the damp blanket. 'That gives us an edge in our demands for your release, and it might make them think twice about doing anything outside the laws and conventions.'

'Well, you might want to speed things up, because we intend to escape at the first opportunity.'

Ibby frowns and touches the little forget-me-not tattoo on her forehead. 'Right here my official line should be 'inadvisable'. Unofficially, we'll keep as close a watch on you as we can, and help wherever possible. Do you know the layout of this place and its surroundings?'

I admit that I don't.

'In that case, hold out until my next visit. I can bring you the info on a disguised crystal.' She detects my bemusement. 'A crystal doesn't have to be crystal-shaped, you know?'

I think about my documents and crystal collection, presumably lost with the Ashen Light. I ask about the ship and Ibby confirms that all are missing, presumed dead. Some of the more robust parts of the Discovery's core survived re-entry burn-up and hit the Martian surface, but in a mountainous region so there were no further casualties. 'What's one more crater on the surface of Mars?' she says. 'It might even become a tourist attraction.'

Ibby calls the others to join us. She makes certain assurances and repeats her affirmation that everything is being done to secure our release. 'In fact,' she adds. 'Everyone here except Ariel can walk out with me right now.'

'Ariel?' Hamo says. 'I thought we were supposed to be calling you Jamil.'

'No more need for that. Long story, and no doubt Ibby will tell you on the way out.'

Sav jumps to his feet. 'Have you gone mons-sloth or something? We're going nowhere without you.' He scans the others. 'Well, I'm not, anyway.'

Hamo simply steps closer to Sav. Verone chides me for having so little faith in my friends.

'But it's dangerous. There's no need to risk your lives any more than you already have.'

'Listen, Ariel.' Sav is fired up. 'We signed on for the Venusian Defence Force, not the Sub-Juve Teddy Bears' Jungle Jaunt. If you want us gone, give us a command. Otherwise don't dare insult us a single time more.'

I'm ashamed. And proud and lucky at the same time. I manage a smile and a nod. There are no further heartfelt displays of support, but nobody moves to go when Ibby gets ready to leave. Free to go, they all remain.

Ibby takes her leave with promises to return within two days, and I begin to relate the tale of the quest for Jonan Dzalarhons in detail. I enhance the story with projections from my personal crystal-journal, a show of trust they deserve and clearly appreciate. Crystal-journals are rarely shared, even between intimates, but after their unconditional support, they're entitled to access the more private aspects of my life.

If anybody has second thoughts, they can always leave with Ibby after her next visit. I know it's a possibility. I also know that if Sav overheard my thoughts, he'd be even more insulted. Why, I do believe he'd strike me.

***

We've shared an evening meal and I've disposed of the plates and cutlery. Ibby is due to visit again tomorrow, mid-morning and we hope she brings good news, but there's a tone at the door. Maybe she's come early.

I tell the door to open, a command that only functions when there's a guard on the other side. This time the guard is Tattoo-Face. He doesn't come in.

'Follow me,' he says.

'What, outside?'

'Of course outside.'

Sav steps up. 'I don't like this, Ariel. It feels wrong.'

'Who asked you?' Tattoo-Face says. 'Skitter-witted scruff!'

I hold Sav back. 'We're quite comfortable where we are, thanks.' Are we being set up for a fatal accident? Plazzed while escaping, kind of thing.

'Oh, for S'Jinn's sake. No time for this.' Tattoo-Face reaches up and presses at his neck. My stomach churns at the horror of his flesh peeling back, from the top of his head down, and then I gawk in disbelief as Dorsa's face emerges from under the mess of discarded skin. In

an instant she's Tattoo-Face again. A morph-suit! I've heard of the tech but never seen one before. Dorsa heads out and we follow.
 'Isn't it my turn to rescue you, Dorsa?'
 'If I wait for that, I'll wait forever.'

***

We follow Dorsa, for she really is Dorsa now, her Tattoo-Face disguise now discarded in favour of local civilian garb. Our discs have copied a range of Martian styles. We've taken a circuitous route with many doublebacks, changes of transport and alterations of appearance to reach the Venusian artists' quarter where our tall, slender frames most blend in.
 'I've established identities for you all. You'll get fully briefed once we're safe inside.' Dorsa leads us through domed squares, open plazas and streets ever narrower, until she ducks through a door at the end of an alley lined with lavenders and other woody shrubs.
 Inside the walls are of reds, yellows and terracotta. They have the appearance of old-world plaster, and it's very warm in here.
 'Like home,' Hamo says, loosening his collar.
 'We're about as deep into the quarter as we can get,' Dorsa tells us. 'Eighty percent of the citizens here are Venusian, so the temperatures indoors are set for Venusian comfort.
 'Couldn't be better,' Sav says and immediately strips off rig and clothes.
 'You don't waste a second, you Venus boys.' I think she appreciates the view. 'In fact, most folk do go Venusian indoors, but don't make the mistake of skipping around dressed only in your skin out of doors. There's a limit to Martian acceptance, and you'll frighten

us natives. Not to mention the fact you'd freeze to death.'

The rest of we Venusians undress. It's been an age, and it feels so good. Dorsa takes off her outer things, and loosens the rest. 'S'Jon, how can you stand the temperature?' She's beginning to perspire.

'How can you stand the clothes?' Sav asks.

Dorsa effects not to have heard Sav, a sure sign that she finds him attractive. 'When you do feel like dressing again, you'll find a range of clothing in the wardrobes. There's one in each of your rooms. No discs here. It's all natural fabrics.'

'Will you be staying with us?'

'I've secured three places, thinking it best to split up. I've got the dome next door. The place on the other side of the alley and five doors down is ours too. Argue amongst yourselves who stays where, but they're identical in space and facilities.'

I ask Dorsa if she made all the preparations herself and she tells us she's had some help. There's a small organisation of scientists and supporters who are in the know concerning our plight, and who don't accept the lies being whipped up about us. They include people at high levels of Martian society who are doing whatever they can to stem the growing mania.

'Look, Dorsa, this is all very good, and I appreciate the risks you've taken. But why not get us back to the Venusian consulate. We'll be safe there.'

'You won't. At least not for long. But don't take my word for it.' She takes on a look I recognise and calls into Quantum. Contact made, she snaps out of it. 'Your old friend Neko will join us in a little while'.

The others leave us to claim their new living spaces. Dorsa and I have a lot of catching up to do. We make ourselves comfortable on seats by the circular windows, and we try to fill in all the details: basically, everything that's happened since the crash on Earth which 'killed' us. It soon becomes apparent that Dorsa knows something I don't. She probes me about the details of the crash and what I remember about my time in the infirmary.

'Don't you think it odd that your hair started growing after the accident?'

One of those questions which heralds a revelation and requires no answer. I shrug and wait for the information that Dorsa finds so difficult to impart.

'I'm surprised you didn't work it out for yourself, Ariel. Your hair started growing after the flyer crash, because ...'

'John's sake, Dorsa! Spit it out!'

'You have a new body, Ariel. The old one was destroyed beyond repair. They printed a new one for you.'

'Hold on, hold on!' I struggle to assimilate this new information. 'You're telling me that we really did die on Earth, and that by some kind of illegal bioprint tech we've been resurrected?'

'We didn't actually die.'

'But the bodies in the wreckage? They were our own actual bodies, smashed up and ruined. And we ...' I bring my hands to my belly, feeling myself to make sure everything is real. I get up and touch the walls. 'So in effect I'm in Schrodinger's Box, alive and dead at the same time.'

'That's one way of looking at it. But if we're going to get anywhere, if we hope to get to the bottom of the whole mystery, we have to climb out of the box.'

We spend an hour in deep discussion. We touch on our newfound abilities and as always when Quantum comes up, full understanding is always that little bit out of reach.

'We should try to develop our skills together. We'll need every advantage we can in the fight to come.' She's with me as I outline my nebulous intention to take the fight to our adversaries.

Dorsa leaves me to assimilate all this appalling new information. I keep looking at my hands, hands that no longer seem to be part of me. My whole body is some kind of monstrous imposter, and yet for weeks I've got along with it perfectly. It's the same body I shared with Benjo, and he found nothing monstrous about it.

A newly printed body? This makes me illegal and in breach of Three Worlds' edicts concerning bioprinting ethics. It can't be true, and yet it's the only explanation that can't be pared away with Occam's razor.

I know why they're after us now. And as if in confirmation the wall-projectors come to life and NEKO's here. He takes on his cat-boy form and I'm pleased to see him again. It's a happy reunion, but happiness is an increasingly fleeting thing. NEKO's been busy in Quantum on our behalf, listening for news or rumours of us, immersing himself in Quantum activity to seek out relevant threads, and monitoring news bulletins Three Worlds wide. He gives us a rundown on his findings, but saves the most troubling for last.

'Our nebulous enemies are now concentrating their efforts on Venus, and you've been accused of murder.'

'I know. Ibby updated me on that. I'm supposed to have killed poor old Bart.'

'No, it's not Bart. The reports says the body of a young man was found in your home at Dzalarhons Mons.'

A chill spreads through me. I don't want to ask, but as it transpires I don't have to. NEKO projects the news bulletin.

There's my face. The report says Earther insistence that I'm an illegal bioprinted android are unfounded, but that a body has been found in my home. There is the outside of Dzalarhons Hall, and now a face is superimposed. 'The body was that of a young man called Benjo Drexler, a scientist at Ven-Tech.' Black dots at the periphery of my vision explode into dark universes, and there is nothing.

***

I'm floating in an ocean of black. I'm black. My skin is as dark as obsidian and there's a brightly polished yellow metal collar locked around my neck. My own features give shape to the dark skin of my face. I'm still me, but my name is Bartholomew. I wear rich clothes of linen and silk and have a turban about my head.

I risk a beating. My Lady, who was once the favourite of our lord King Charles, second of that name, has given me no leave to quit the Lodge or to explore the grounds. Perhaps she will see to the punishment personally. She enjoys the role of enforcer and requires little provocation. I am her favourite pet, but even favourites must be disciplined. I have the weal-marks to prove it.

She once had a groom beaten and he died of it, but she went short of a groom for less than a week before employing another. Young white men in need of work are easy to find in England, whereas those like me are rare and more expensive to buy.

'M'lord Elias!'

I respond to a name and a title neither of which are mine, and yet curiously they are. My skin is now snowy white, the opposite of what it had been a minute past, both extremes now so very rare in the Three Worlds. My hair is long, curly and golden.

'My lord, take this if you would be so good.' A disembodied hand gives me a scroll of velum which I unroll the better to read. 'Have it by heart by the morrow, sir.' I outrank my tutor, a mere knight, but until recently he had Uncle's permission to beat me if I failed at my lessons.

I assure him it will be done, and then I ask Bartholomew if he would be so kind as to lay out my uniform. I must cut a dash on my first day with the Regiment.

Bartholomew is reluctant to handle my gorget, and I suspect it reminds him of the hateful collar he was made to wear by the Witch, may she rot in Hell.

I take up the scroll and read. It is the warrant for the Regiment and it gives details of compliment, weapons and apparel. How many muskets. How many gentlemen of the pike. That they shall wear coats of brown. That I shall be Ensign Lord Grey and Bartholomew sergeant to the colour, so in effect, my close guard.

There is a seal at the bottom of the velum. Impressed into dull red wax is the sign of a fiery bird. It turns into flame before my eyes, the document dissolves to black, and by nothingness I am again surrounded.

***

'How you doing, Venus-boy?' Dorsa brings me some soup, her presence in my room activating the lights. I sit up in bed and hold the bowl close and let the warmth seep into me. The soup's thick and disgustingly brown-green, but the aroma makes my mouth water.

'Get this down you. One of Dad's favourite recipes.' No hint of sympathy in her tone, which is good, because I'd crumble. 'Same dreams?'

'Yep. I'm haunted by that fire-flecked bird.' As if I didn't get enough of it during my breakdown following Benjo's murder. 'It's all I have, that S'Jinning bird.'

Wherever my dreams take me, that damned bird is waiting. Here, the bonnet ornament on an auto of the 1930's, or the painted sail of a longboat; there an ice-age flying beast that never existed, and over there the engraving on a ring. I've spent hours on the grid trying to discover the meaning behind this persistent avian wraith. The bird is a focus that binds my grief.

'Finish the soup, and get some more rest.' Dorsa turns to leave me in peace, but I've had enough solitude.

'Don't go, Dorsa.' I pat the bed beside me, and she sits. 'Turns out I have a lot of military ancestors, and something of them has leached into me. Have you ever heard the term "Attack is the best form of defence"?'

'No, but I already love it. It's time we tackled these murderous manipulators.'

'Call the others together, including the graphs. It's time we held a council of war.'

'Are you up to it?'

Am I up to it? Of course I'm not, nor ever will be.

'Scary, Ariel. Looks like you could shoot lightning bolts from your eyes.'

'Get the others.'

Dorsa shakes her head. 'It's late. They're all asleep. Tomorrow morning?'

I agree, and Dorsa sits quietly while I finish my soup. She reaches out to take the bowl, but I place it on the nightstand, out of her reach and take her hand instead. The burning within me mutates into another kind of fire.

'The morning's hours away, and your place is a long cold walk away in the dark. Stay with me tonight?' My cover is thin, and she must see I'm becoming aroused, but can she see the guilt hidden within the flame? I shouldn't be able to feel like this. Did she put something in the soup?

'Are you asking me …?'

'To the corner of the dome? Yes, I am.' I reach and touch her face with the backs of my fingers. She doesn't pull away or act in any way affronted.

'Do you want me to be Benjo?'

'Nobody can be Benjo. I want you to be you.' I start undoing the buttons on Dorsa's top. She reaches under the cover, lets her hand rest on my hip, and a thousand electric sparks radiate from her touch.

'I'm sure this is exactly what they don't want us to do. Not just the enemy, but our side too.'

'Then all the more reason to do it, but don't be swayed by anything except your own will.'

'Call me shallow, but I've wanted this since I first set eyes on you at Mato Grosso Spaceport.'

I lean forward. We kiss. It begins.

***

We settle in to our new accommodation. The fifth move since I lost Benjo almost ten months ago. We're all in the same dome this time.

Sav drops a bundle of clothing by a door off the main ring. 'This one's a double. Hamo and I will have it, unless you and Dorsa …?'

'Go ahead, Sav.' Despite our closeness, Dorsa and I are not partners, or rather, we're both part of a bigger, communal partnership. The intimacy makes it easier for us to explore Quantum together, or rather, to access it in the first place.

While the others settle in, Dorsa and I find a quiet corner in the storage area at the back of the utility room. We both feel the need to settle and further our exploration of Quantum.

'Ready, Ariel?'

'As I'll ever be.' Dorsa finds it much easier to transition into Quantum. She never fails. We've had the same coaching from our graph friends but with me it's always hit or miss.

The room is dim. Dorsa turns the lights even lower. 'Look, this is going to sound ridiculous. So stupid I've always been reluctant to mention it, but I play this little mind trick with myself. It helps me transition, so maybe you could try something similar.'

'I'll try not laugh too much.' I wouldn't dare. 'Something the graphs taught you?'

'Not at all. They'd think it's stupid too.'

'I won't think it's stupid. So go on, what's this trick of yours?'

'Well, I get comfortable and close my eyes. Then I imagine I'm a seal rolling out of the sea onto the beach.'

I reference 'seal' on the grid. It's a sleek marine mammal still found on Earth and introduced to Mars, similar to our bull-otters, but with flippers instead of webbed paws.

'Then, I imagine I'm emerging from its skin. When I rise from the pile of fur at my feet, I'm in Quantum. Works every time. Every single time. Never a failure.'

Yes, it's ridiculous, but I keep my promise not to laugh. 'Whatever works.'

'Going to give it a go?'

'I'll try. Maybe not with the seal though.' The thought of being dressed in another animal's skin makes me queasy.

An idea comes to me at once. Standing tall, I breathe deeply and imagine I'm fully contained within a box, like Schrodinger's cat. I recall something Dorsa said months ago: 'To get anywhere, we have to climb out of the box'. I expand until the box is like a small container around my hips, and then I simply step out of it and into Quantum. It works!

Dorsa is a familiar spark, a trembling star, a point of incandescence inside a halo of purple light. The edges of her fade to a dark penumbra that expands and contracts within a terrain of feeling, resonance and vibration.

We no longer need NEKO or AMALTHEA to guide us through the non-space that is Quantum. Now we navigate and recognise the resonations that mark physical objects in our world.

Will-power is our motive energy here. We 'will' direction and drift towards a towering mega-city the size of the mainland. We recognise it as the shadow of the hardware fleck that's integral with a monitor projector; too small in our world to see without a microscope and yet a whole continent here in Quantum. We explore its streets, control pathways inhabited by strings of light which move like vac-tube trains. We seek out and recognise software strings and it's like searching a jungle for a single orchid, but we're becoming efficient explorers. We also approximate our experiences in words, shaping our alternate reality into a narrative our friends can grasp.

As for the war, that's here too. We know the feel of our enemies, and we have perfected methods to disguise our presence. We are few and our resources are limited, so ours is a guerrilla war. Strike and run!

I step back into the box and Dorsa puts on her fur. We come back to ourselves and for all the hours we have been away, less than a micro-second has passed here. It's always the way: a lifetime within a single breath.

***

All eight of us, five humans and three graphs, gather in our communal room. It has the best projector arrays in the dome, and we settle to watch the latest broadcast of lies. False stories about Dorsa and me have taken root throughout the System, even at home on Venus, and it's a Venusian broadcast we watch now.

They show our images, images that look nothing like us because we've been successful in our grid manipulation missions, right down to core strings. We could be watching this broadcast in a crowded bar with no fear of anybody recognising us.

'Ariel Dzalarhons is wanted in connection with the homicide of Benjo Drexler ...' Benjo's image fills the screen and rips at my heart. The attention of everyone in the room shifts to me.

The same lies are repeated. Suspected involvement in the death of Professor Bart Coumans; a flyer crash that may not have been an accident and the rumour that Dorsa and I are illegal bioprints. It's this last point that makes me uncomfortable, for if Dorsa is correct, that's exactly what we are: illegal bioprints.

'The process that saved our lives may have been illegal,' Dorsa says. 'But we're the same people we ever were.'

At least there's some balance to this broadcast, because now the projection shows Ibby Carlane who reminds everyone that suspicion and rumour are no substitute for evidence. She does not leap up and shout that the images look nothing like us, so she must still be on our side.

The broadcast ends and it's time to get busy. For every lying broadcast we launch a refutation with projections of the truth. Dorsa and I leave the others to cobble together our next bulletin. We make ourselves comfortable in the storage area and settle down to transition. We usually try to follow the strings of the most recent broadcast, looking for the hand that guides them. So far we've found a nebula that feels of GRENDEL. We're sure he's at its core.

'Ready, Ariel?'

'Yes, but let's not go Grendel-chasing today. I want to get to the centre of our creation. If we really are bioprints, who set the processes in motion?'

'Must we? We've tried so many times I've lost count. Someone's fogged up that period between the crash and our recoveries so well it's impenetrable. What makes you think we can succeed in finding our way through this time?'

'If you don't at first succeed ...'

Dorsa weighs up the options. 'Let's split up. You see if you can get through the fog and I'll try and get a hook into Grendel.'

It's a plan. I step out of the box. My bare foot transmutes from flesh, blood and bone into vibration, strings and particles before it touches the Quantum shoreline. Oceans wash over me. When I emerge and step back into the box, I am no wiser. Our re-genesis is sewn up as tight as the details of Benjo's murder.

Dorsa and I open our eyes at the same time. As usual, no time has passed for our human bodies.

'Any luck with Grendel.'

'Not exactly, but something's happening on Callisto. A tendril of Grendel's nebula shot off in that direction. I tried to follow, but couldn't make myself centre.'

We both re-enter Quantum. Whatever happened, there's no remaining trace.

***

The fight goes on, but we're losing. Many of our once strong supporters have deserted us, weighed down by an avalanche of enmity. They were our defence against the battering waves, but the relentless storm has broken them down. It's impossible to blame them.

We have to rely on ourselves. It's safer that way, and we keep our identities fluid. Each move, another persona rooted far down into the grid.

Whenever we move we take on new roles within our adoptive community. Currently I have the use of a small workshop and fashion glass tentacles. Some are replicas of the fossils found on Venus, others I form into cups, vases or trinkets that people seem to like. They take one if their possessions amount to less than seven. They admire them otherwise. As Bumblebee Day will soon be upon us again, I've crafted a few little bees too.

Sav teaches juveniles, and Hamo is writing a history of the third sex. Verone and Dorsa take on a variety of tasks. Dorsa and I have the added role of setting false trails. By manipulations of the grid and occasional forays into Quantum, we've sent the authorities scrambling for us all over the System, from Mercury's observation stations to the Callistonian hydrogen-skimmers of Jupiter. We've planted so many false sightings that they are no longer a matter for news bulletins. As a kind of double-bluff, we crafted a complicated target-contact right on the edge of the Venusian quarter. Risky, but it paid off and allowed us to observe their tactics.

It's mid-afternoon and bitterly cold outside. Sav, Hamo and I sit around the projected flames of a log fire set on a central hearth. The flames look real, but it's the hearth that emits the heat. The couple sit close and begin to touch. They unclip weight-rigs and loosen clothing, made frisky by the comfort of the seeping warmth. Rising, they head for their bedroom and ask me if I'd like to join them. It would be nice, but I'm more sleepy than frisky, so I decline. 'Have a nice time.'

'Oh, we will,' Sav says. 'Join us if you change your mind.' He hangs his rig on the door handle, shuts the door on his smile, and I'm in two minds for a moment. The three of us are amazingly good together, but I soon become lost in the flames and the arousal slips away. Then my imagination conjures up that S'Jinning awful fire-bird again. I'm rarely free from it.

After the initial annoyance, I concentrate on the gyrating flames. They twist and turn, while I spin Father's partner-band round and around on my finger. It feels slick, like a crystal. Twist, turn and watch the burn of the fire bird.

Crystal? There's something Ibby Carlane said to me when she visited us in our Martian prison. Something about crystals. The ring is of the deepest black, and I seep into it, every bit as deeply as into the flames moments ago. I look closer, and touch its slick, almost wet surface.

'A crystal doesn't have to be crystal-shaped, you know?' That's what Ibby said. I touch the ring with the tip of my tongue, and it tingles, exactly like an info-crystal. All at once, Benjo's part in my crystal-projections and dreams make sense. He was key to reuniting me with this ring. But what cruel fates used him until his usefulness was done, and then gave him up to Death? Why is my quest more important than his? If there's an author to my story, then I hate her.

I know I'm holding answers in my hand. I leap up and yell, a primeval release of sound that involves nothing resembling language. Sav bursts from his room, trying to hide behind a pair of red and black shorts. Hamo, hair all ruffled, peers out from the bedroom door. I've ruined their afternoon, but I may have found the direction we've lacked for the best part of a year.

I'm too excited to wait, and I explain while they're pulling on their clothes. Sav's only half-dressed and un-rigged when he snatches the ring from me and rushes over to an objective plate, almost kangaroo-bouncing in the low gravity. He activates it and the air is filled with document-icons, one of which bears a logo in the shape of the fire-bird. Saint John, but we're so close.

'The one with the bird, Sav. Open it!'

He tries but it's protected and requires quantum-string verification. It would take a graph weeks to open without the correct pass. A human couldn't crack it in several hundred lifetimes. 'You try, Ariel. Maybe it's a DNA pass.'

I try. It doesn't open, but the icon of a tiny trumpet appears beside it, indicating a sound-sequence pass.

'Are there any tunes that mean something to you?' Hamo says. 'Maybe a song your father used to sing?'

Jonan's musical tastes were eclectic, and I can't recall any pieces that might be called favourites. He was interested in my tastes though, and we'd sometimes listen along together.

I try the opening notes from Olly Alexander's 'If You're Over Me'. Nothing! Then several lines from Joongwon's 'Ketcha-heyah', but there's no response.

'It's a fire-bird,' Sav says, bright and fired up with an idea. 'Try something from the Fire Cloud adagio.'

It's an inspired idea, and I know he's right. We try a line, activating the correct sequence of notes on the floating keyboard, but we're unsuccessful. Another line, another failure. We play the theme in different octaves without success. With the main theme used and found wanting, we try other sections from the piece, but nothing works.

Dorsa and Verone return from a day at the museums and cafés and they're both immediately infected with our excitement, but new to the fray they're immune to our mounting frustration. There are more tunes, more suggestions, and pleas for me to access ever more remote childhood memories.

I do my best. I stare and stare at the translucent airborne icon and the tiny clarion. Clarion? Oh yes, of course. It's an ancient word for a trumpet. I recall the pie-man's clarion from my 13th century gene-hunting presentation, and ...

'I've got it!' I reach up and my fingers intersect the notes of the pie-man's call: a high note and a low, the sequence repeated three times, followed by three high notes.

The air is filled with maps and lines of text and plans which swirl all about us and reach to every corner of the room. I recognise a map of the surface of Callisto, and the ship's plans are known to every juvenile with an interest in history. 'It's the Phoenix Song,' I say.

'Not exactly.' NEKO has manifested, and he floats and glides among all the other images. 'It's the Mapping & Survey Ship Alicanto, sister ship to the Phoenix Song. Ariel, you've found our ride to Albion.'

I didn't know the Phoenix Song had a sister ship. I swipe the plans larger and zoom in to the control deck. The Alicanto must've been an identical twin to the ship whose history is so familiar to me. 'If it still exists, it's five hundred years old. It won't work.'

'I'm not so sure.' NEKO delves further into the display. 'Entropy is subject to many modifiers. In space, and very thin atmospheres, not even iron rusts.' He steps right into the display, almost merges with it. 'Here! Looks like the old girl is being looked after by an army of engineer-skins.'

A small section of the file confirms this, and then NEKO strokes the air to enlarge a section of text which reads 'J4 48-30S:35-36W'. He spins the group so that it comes to rest a few centimetres before my eyes.

'I guess "J4" refers to Jupiter's fourth major satellite, Callisto.'

'It does,' NEKO confirms. 'And the numbers are coordinates for Adlinda Spaceport.'

It's a name I know, again from history. It was Callisto's first major port, established to facilitate colonisation. 'Surely Adlinda's deserted. It was decommissioned generations ago.'

'Yes, after the meteorite strike which destroyed Adlinda City, but what better place to hide an old disused and highly secret ship than in an old disused port.' He points to another symbol and enlarges it. It's the Three Worlds Council Top Security Seal. 'If you're wondering why the Alicanto doesn't feature in the histories, this logo may be a clue.'

It's my turn to delve deep into the display. The map clearly shows the ruins of Adlinda, so at least it's a post-disaster document. Now I've expanded the Adlinda file to fill the whole room, and the five of us humans and NEKO intersect with the projected images, searching for anything which might be useful.

'Here!' Sav calls and we gather around him, concentrating on the pink slither of light to which he points. 'Recognise this?'

Yes!' Hamo says. 'I saw this exact same symbol in the cavern under the utility dome at Sagan's farm.'

'It was marked on the underside of the hatch too,' Sav says.

The tentacle-like cypher is also familiar to me. 'Once again, the same writing I saw in the chamber below my home on the Mons.' I wonder if Benjo managed to record it before Grendel got to him.

Something clicks inside my head, and parts of the puzzle shift to form a picture. For the first time in months, I know where I'm going. I'm so fired up, the fact I have no clue how we'll get there is nothing more than a minor inconvenience. I close the display, take Father's ring off the objective-plate, put it back on my finger and address all my friends. 'Objective, Callisto and the MSS99 Alicanto. Problem, how do we, the most wanted fugitives in the Three Worlds, get all the way from here to there with no ship? Then, if we get there, how do we overcome whatever security is in place?'

Dorsa stands contrapposto with her arms folded. She's wearing a lop-sided grin. 'As for getting there, sounds like a job for a Martian.' Now she activates her morph-suit and takes on her fierce-faced disguise. 'Or a Cally.'

***

Dorsa's in charge of planning our next move, and I've assigned Sav and Hamo to help her. This leaves Verone and me free to scour the documents on Father's ring-crystal for anything else that may help. I'm disappointed not to have found anything personal from him: an explanation, some direct guidance or a small father-to-son message of encouragement.

There are thousands of documents encrypted into the sub-atomic fabric of the ring and I'm trying to use my graph abilities to assist. I immerse myself into Quantum and come back again.

'It's such a confusing level of existence,' Verone says. 'I took the liberty of scanning your brainwaves while you were there, but even when I run the speed to the max, it's as if you never left.'

'Quantum isn't a place you go to. It's within you, not outside. Or rather, it's like the whole of "outside" is "inside".' With all of time and space within me, surely I should have a bigger shoe size. The fact is though, I completely understand when I'm in Quantum

I sit comfortably in my small, warm room with the ring in the palm of my hand. I can sense my way into the surface levels and see the icons. Imagine a crystal-display, but within your own skull. That's how it feels.

There are files marked with icons. Some have names written in Standard and others have cartoon-like characters instead of names.

I'm naturally drawn to one labelled 'For AD', but I haven't the depth of skills to enter the file mentally. Nobody's in the sitting room, so I make use of the objective plate and open the file. Nothing but a few lines of text that tell me about someone called Howie. I read this introduction to the stranger.

***

'Howie Montague was 18 years old, and yet he was 34. He had a well-toned lightly framed body tastefully decorated with the currently fashionable tattoos and skin-paints, and yet he shrank with disgust from his own ghastly reflection. Howie made love regularly with the most beautiful women or once in a while, for a change, with young men as well toned as himself, and yet he was a virgin. Howie lived life to the full in Etheria, and yet he barely existed on Base.

'Howie's place of work was located in one of the fluid sectors of Etheria where the office was likely to change appearance as often as the System-generated weather. That morning it resembled a deciduous wood in early spring and his console was discretely embedded into a mature oak at a convenient height for ease of use. He had completed all the necessary but tedious base-unit maintenance in record time, donned his face-suit and hooked up, passed through the security protocols and injected close to the front entrance of Rural Mechs Inc. He could hardly wait for the five-o'clock check-out. Today, for the first time, Howie was going to try out his new wings.'

***

Lucky Howie gets his wings. But what's that supposed to tell me? Father was a gene-hunter too, so I guess Howie was one of his research subjects. If he existed at all, it would obviously have been mid-21st Century, that dark period of our history when many people spent most of their short, squalid lives interfacing with crude mind-jacked projections while the real world crumbled around them. With a couple of Bumblebee Sneeze pandemics to go, insanity still prevailed in parts of the world.

Verone joins me, and I show her the text.

'Definitely 21st Century,' she says. She doesn't have to add 'Earth' because the other worlds hadn't been colonised back then. 'Probably the former nation state of Japan. I've studies the period.'

'It was part of my studies too. I have to say, "Howie" doesn't sound like a name typical of the region at that time.'

'I'd agree, not a traditional name, but by then borders were beginning to mean less and less. People migrated throughout the world and settled where they felt most at home. The Resource Wars led to nationalism on some parts of the planet, but by then it was generally accepted that we were one world and one people.'

Frightened people were ever susceptible to hoard rather than share, to look for the differences in their neighbours rather than the similarities. I can see it all happening again now, and it's mortifying to actually *be* the difference that causes division.

We sift through Father's files, opening them at random, and find nothing of more than family interest. There are albums of his travels, and of me growing up. There are research plans and the results of gene expeditions.

'Here's a cheery one.' Verone lets her finger intersect with a little yellow sun-face icon. 'I think they used to call this little chap a "smiley-face".'

I'm sure she's correct. When I was sub-juve I had a pyjama-robe covered in similar happy little suns.

I try to open it and a voice is triggered. 'I am construct-protected. Please say "Hello" and I will open.'

Rigged for voice-recognition? I say 'Hello' and I'm not surprised one bit that it's isn't that simple.

'Please call me by my name,' the little smiley says. It winks at me.

'What is your name?'

It laughs at me, growing until it fills the whole room, and then snaps back to the former little icon it was.

'One for later?' Verone says.

I agree. It's time to prepare the evening meal. Dorsa and the others will soon be home, and I plan to debrief them over dinner.

***

'We have to start by moving to the other side of the world.' Dorsa talks with her mouth full, her lips red from the lasagne. 'The biggest Callistonian base on Mars is a few klicks outside Xanthe City.'

We all sit around the raised hearth which serves as our dining table when the flames have been switched off. NEKO sits cross-legged in the centre, taking the place of the flames. There's a spread of replicated dishes, but not everything is cube-derived. The lasagne is made from real, soil-grown beetroots, and nothing tastes better.

'A bit of background,' Dorsa says. 'Callisto's largely dependent on Mars for essential supplements to their home-grown food supply. They run fleets of construct-piloted skimmers to harvest hydrogen from the surface of Jupiter's atmosphere, so they're self-sufficient in fuel. And they have thousands of sub-surface hydroponic farms which supply a good sixty percent of their most basic dietary needs, but the rest comes mostly from Mars. Consequently there're many daily launches between Mars and Callisto to keep the supply flowing, and that's the route we're planning to exploit.'

'There is no time to waste,' NEKO says. 'I have observed some worrying developments. The rhetoric against us increases daily, and citizens worlds-wide are being asked to look closely at their neighbours and report anything suspicious. Our images, albeit the ones we have planted, are all over the grid and in every broadcast.'

AMALTHEA hovers to the centre of the room. 'There is something else that I suspect is connected. Albion has been blocked to graph-link communications.'

Dinner finished we return to our tasks, Dorsa with our plans for the next part of our quest, and me one last night with Father's documents.

But I'm tired, and my bed is beautifully warm. Verone has already fallen asleep beside me, and it's time to close the files.

I think about Howie. Who was he, and how does he fit in to my story? The edges of sleep guide me into his shoes, and I'm him for a moment, but then he's me. He has my face, but I watch the next part of his story unfold as if I am a seeker-wasp on the ceiling.

His appointment with the wing-fitter didn't go well at all, and he runs home. He should be able to fly home now, and it's all so unfair.

Howie slams the door and throws the bolts. This is a good move, in that the knife-thrower is locked outside. This is a bad move, in that the wing-maker's body is in his apartment together with the weapon used to kill him. If Base-patrol bursts in on him now, he'll be connected again and sent straight back to Etheria to face a murder charge. Of course, neither his body nor his mind will ever leave Base, but perception is everything, and if he's found guilty they'll activate the high-voltage relays and kill his real, actual body. He shudders.

Howie has to think fast, but his mind is treacle. Nothing makes sense. Lying at his feet, brain oozing from his head like yolk from a top-sliced soft-boiled egg, is a man who cannot exist here at Base. Base is real, a fact supported by all its filth and time-worn decrepitude. Etheria is cyberspace, and this dead thing is a construct from Etheria. He is a programmed thing: strings of code not flesh and blood. Howie's mind gropes for answers and forgets to manage the necessities of life, such as balance. He falls heavily into the face-suit and sends it spinning on its gimbals.

Howie begins to panic. If he breaks his face-suit there'll be no return to Etheria until a tech team comes to put it right again. His insurance is basic – it was all he could afford – they could take a week. A week at Base will kill him. Another hour will probably kill him unless he can work out what the hell is happening.

Interface-ExoSuit 300: Howie reads the brand name as the suit comes to rest, but something's wrong. His face-suit is the only object in the whole of Base that he knows intimately. He's wholly familiar with the elasticity of every tube, the abrasiveness of every connector, the cool metallic zing of every electrode. They are all there, all the element that give him sight and sound and touch, but it's as if everything's a little out of kilter. Time to apply smell, the only sense for which the 300-series face-suit scores low. He leans in and sniffs a cushion-pad. It should be rank with the stench of his own stale sweat — he's on a basic maintenance contract after all — but nothing, not a whiff.

The truth spreads from his gut, chilling and laced with fear. He's still inside his face-suit, and IT wants him to believe otherwise. His apartment and everything within it is no more than another part of Etheria. Somebody wants him to believe he's at Base, and they've done a pretty fine job. But now the game's up. He bellows the emergency extraction code.

Nothing happens. He tries again, and then his apartment is filled with light, bright as the sun and impossible to regard without screwing up his eyes. The light shrinks and coalesced into a football-size sphere, yellow with the smiley face of an emoticon. The smile spreads wider, and a voice emanates from the direction of the sphere, although the lips maintain an inane grin and don't move in synch with the words.

'Got there in the end, Howard. I was beginning to wonder.' It's a high-pitched voice, like a pre-pubescent boy's.

And 'Howard'? Nobody calls him Howard, not since his mother died. 'What the fuck! I shouted the code. The code is fucking sacrosanct. You cannot keep me here against my will. It's illegal!'

'Bad words don't impress me much. It's not clever and it's not nice.'

Howie throws a punch but the ball jinks right and Howie pulls a muscle in his shoulder. Yes, the suit simulates pain in all the right places if the situation calls for it. Howie yells out the extraction code once again.

'You think IT cares a diddly-squat for all your silly codes? If IT wants to keep you, IT'll keep you.'

Howie swears again and the ball chuckles.

'But there's something I can do that IT can't do a whole lot about. Who needs codes when all you have to do is pull the plug.'

Instantly Howie is struggling inside his face-suit, coughing and spluttering. As before he activates the release, and as before he's dumped onto the floor with wires, tubes and touch-simulators attached to various parts of his near-naked body. With no thought for the damage that might be caused to the expensive suit he frantically rips away the many and varied attachments, adjusts his scant clothing and gets to his feet in time to see a boy drop the disconnected power cable to the floor.

The kid's about twelve years old, with an untidy eruption of black hair which completely dominates his young features. He's barefooted, and wears once-white, knee-length baggy shorts and a sleeveless khaki-formerly-yellow singlet; it droops so low at the shoulders that his skinny tin-ribbed torso is open to the air. This time Howie has no doubt that he's at Base. The kid stinks as if he hasn't washed in a month.

'Pleased to meetcha,' the kid says. 'The name's Crash.' He nudges the face-suit violently with the ball of his foot and sets it spinning. 'And that's what I do. Crash by name, crash by nature. Now, let's get you somewhere safe before IT sets a Base squad onto us.'

***

I wake up and open my eyes. For a moment, the face-suit continues to spin in the absolute darkness of my room, but it quickly dissolves. Verone calls for illumination, and the black retreats from the red-orange glow of a night-light.

'Another of those dreams, Ariel?' She smooths an untidy flop of hair away from my eyes. 'You were tossing and turning.'

'We have to get out of here. They're sending a Base squad after us.' I'm not sure what I'm talking about. Things are fuzzy and confusing.

Verone trails her fingers down my neck and torso. 'You're still in your dream. We need to bring you back to Mars.'

I'm hard, as I often am after these dreams, and Verone isn't going to let my condition go to waste. Analysis and interpretation no longer seem quite so urgent. It can wait until daylight.

'Shall I dim the lights?' Verone asks.

'No, let's leave them like this.'

We throw back the covers and warm tones of light stain our skin. We make love dressed in the hues of Mars.

Twenty minutes pass in pleasure. We're spent, but now I'm impatient for morning and can't fully enjoy the closeness that usually follows. It can't wait until daylight after all.

'Where're you going?' Verone reached out for me as I leave the bed.

'I know how to get past the sun-faced smiley icon.'

And now Verone leaps from bed too. Not so single minded that only Father's files matter, she thinks to bring a cover. Thank goodness, because it's freezing in the sitting room. Dome system detects us and activates the heaters, but it'll take a while before the room's comfortably warm.

We sit below the display wrapped together in the cover. I find the icon and intersect with it.

'I am construct-protected. Please say "Hello" and I will open.'

I give Verone a wink, and then face Little Smiley. 'Hello, Crash.'

'You know my name!' the construct says, and I swear it speaks with surprise and happiness. 'You have passed the first gate. Now, what is your name?'

'I am Ariel Dzalarhons.'

'Ariel!' Crash smiles wider and two clapping hands emerge from its spherical body. 'I've been waiting so long. You have now passed the second gate. But I must be sure you are Ariel.'

Why can't it scan me for all the proof it needs? I suspect memory is more important than physiology. I pass the third and fourth gates by naming my parents, complete with loconyms. Fifth and sixth are put behind me by naming my first crush (this makes Verone laugh) and the first person with whom I was intimate (this makes Verone cry).

'I must ask you one more question, Ariel. What do you recall as the first time you made Jonan proud?'

This, I suspect, is a moment known only to me and Father. 'When I was a little older than sub-juv I was bitten by a lion-snake. Father got the creature off me and was about to kill it, but I asked him to stop. "It's not the snake's fault," I said. It died anyway, but later back at Dzalarhons Hall, Father said he was proud of me.'

'Thank you, Ariel. You are through the last gate. There's someone who would like to talk to you. It's me really, but I will take on Jonan's form, as programmed.'

Little Smiley Crash changes shape and colour, and there before us as solid as any hologram can be, stands Father dressed in his signature lilac film-gown. 'Hello, Ariel.' His smile is so real, it's all I can do not to rush into his arms. I'm fifteen years old again

'I see you are with Verone. Hello, Verone. How you have grown since our jungle trips.'

'Who's that?' She whispers to me. 'Sorry, it's obvious, isn't it?' She stands up and the cover slips to the ground.

'I'm sorry, Jonan. Something happened, and I have no recollection of you.'

Jonan frowns a little. I'm really astounded by the intricacy of the programing. Every little detail is so ... so Father. 'The information I have to discuss might best be kept between the two of us. Of course, if you would like Verone to remain, I'll happily continue.'

If Verone were Benjo there'd be no question, but I hesitate for a fraction too long.

'I'll wait in the bedroom,' Verone says, and I'm pleased she's made the decision for me.

The moment Verone closes the door behind her, I ask the most pressing question. 'Jonan, are you still alive?'

Hands clasped at the front, head dipped but maintaining eye contact, so typical of Father's mannerisms, his answer is exactly what I anticipate. 'I am nothing more than an interface with a construct. I can tell you everything up to the date of my programming, but nothing following it.'

'Who wrote your program?'

He indicates himself with the graceful sweep of one hand. 'I did, or rather, Jonan programmed me.'

'So as far as you know Jonan may be dead?'

'He is either dead or out of reach.' The construct pulls no punches. 'I could not have been activated were he available to you.'

Jonan walks around the room while I take in his last words. I will not believe that Father's dead.

'How's this going to work then? Are you going to tell me anything useful?'

'Are you going to ask any pertinent questions?'

He's evidently programmed for response rather than oratory. Fair enough. 'Am I an illegal bioprinted human?'

'Not quite.'

Father or not, if he wasn't merely an incorporeal holo-projection, I'd slap him. 'I'd rather you didn't play games like some ancient Greek oracle. What does "Not exactly" mean in the context of my last question?'

'It means you're not illegal. Our creation was sanctioned by the highest echelons of Three Worlds Council. And you are not bioprinted in the strict sense of the term.'

The world starts letting go of me. If I don't tether myself down, I'll float away. His answer is terrifying. The next answer will end my sense of self.

'Then, what am I?'

'Ask rather "What are we?". Ariel, we represent an entirely new form of life. Raoul, Dorsa, you and several others who are no longer with us. We are human-graph hybrids.'

I believe him. I've suspected as much for some time. Such doubt as still existed has been blown away. 'How long have you known?'

'About myself? Since I was a young man. As for you, I've known your whole life.'

'Why didn't you tell me?'

'You were to be told after your coming of age ceremony. I was making preparations when I was taken.'

'When you were taken? So you were able to update the construct after that?'

'My partner-ring was set to permanent-record, and kept recording until the moment I removed it.'

I ask a series of questions to satisfy myself that Jonan really did program the construct. There's no doubt. He knows things that only the two of us shared.

'How many human-graph hybrids are there?'

'Up to the time I was taken there were four, one each for Venus, Earth, Mars and Callisto.'

'Would I be correct in stating that I'm the hybrid for Venus, Raoul for Earth and Dorsa for Mars?'

'Perfectly correct.'

Mimicking Father's natural responses in minute detail, the construct appears momentarily distraught when I tell him about poor Raoul.

I wait for him to settle down. 'Are you the hybrid for Callisto?'

'Jonan is the Callistonian hybrid, but as you already know, I cannot say where my human-graph counterpart is.'

I'm stunned. At last, I manage to stumble onto the most revealing question, which leads to a string of enquiries. These are answers I must share as soon as I've had a chance to ponder.

Did I really die in the flyer crash? Is the essential me no more than my physical body? I have never believed in any form of dualism. There's no insubstantial driving force inside me. I don't believe that a metaphysical something that once resided in my old body has been poured into this new one. And yet, I have a mind and that mind is as self-aware as ever. I have all my memories. I am 'me' in the truest sense of being

'Keep me with you,' Construct-Jonan says before I deactivate him. 'Wear the ring at all times.'

I promise to comply, but there's no time for prevarication.

Despite the ridiculously early hour, I'm waking the others, starting with Dorsa.

'I can't say I'm all that surprised,' she says. 'Humans Mark One can't go grid-skiffing without stents, and definitely can't swan around in Quantum. I'm kind of relieved to know, if you want the truth. Or should I say, happy to have my suspicions confirmed.' She looks at her palms, then turns her hands to check the backs of them. 'So, how did we get to be us?'

I fill her in on the details.

***

We're all here in the sitting room except Hamo, who's getting dressed. Sav stands wearing a bed cover like a toga. Verone and Dorsa huddle together sharing a blanket and I've activated a disc-badge and put on my VDF uniform which immediately compensates for the chill. NEKO perches on the hearth, which pumps warmth into the room without the decorative flames. I've been successful in contacting AMALTHEA who revolves slowly below the ceiling.

We're all silent and still while we wait for Hamo, like the surface of a secluded lake on a still dawn without a breath of wind. My revelations will be the boat that skims the waters and leaves a foaming wake.

I wonder what Hamo's up to. He's been a long time, but now joins us wearing a white hooded travelling suit of Martian design.

'Nothing like being prepared.' Sav rolls his eyes and Hamo pulls a face.

We're all here now, so I'm going to tell them everything I learnt from Father's construct. First, I have to break the most shocking fact, one Dorsa and I are yet to fully assimilate.

'Dorsa and I aren't quite human.'

I let it hang in the silent air. I leave it too long.

'What he means is that he and I are human, but we're something else as well. Humans Mark Two. The same as you, with a side order of graph.'

'We're human-graph hybrids. Our geneses was kept a secret among those graphs and humans who agreed to our creation, and of course, those who actually created us.

'We were seen as the next stage in human-graph evolution, beings who incorporated the elements and qualities of both lifeforms. Before our creation it was agreed we should be allowed to develop among our own kind.'

'There are others?' Verone asks.

I tell everyone about Raoul and Father. 'Initially, our "own kind" would have been limited to a handful of hybrids, some of whom, like Raoul, are no longer with us. We were to be monitored closely while we grew to adulthood, and then gathered on another world to begin the next stage of the process.'

'That makes sense of some of my dreams,' Dorsa says. 'The other world is Albion, isn't it?'

'Yes, and the next stage is for us to create other hybrids.'

Dorsa shakes her head. 'Think again, Venus-boy. You and I are absolutely not going to breed a new race.' She looks affronted. 'Hey, what are you laughing at? I'm being serious. I'm not S'Jinning breeding stock!'

Oh, S'John! My sides are splitting. The look on Dorsa's face. If I live to be a thousand, I'll never forget it. 'The process isn't biological reproduction, you goose!' I manage to splutter out through laughter. 'But even if it was, I don't see the problem. We've been together before.' I look around at the others. We've all been together at some time in the last year.

'Well, you're the goose then. What I do with my body is for me to decide, without any pressure from some human and graph megalomaniacs who want to play at being gods.'

I put Dorsa back at her ease. 'There's some quantumy-wantumy thing about our human-graph nature that enables us to initiate other hybrids. Humans can't do it, and nor can graphs. Only us.'

'Quantumy-wantumy?' Dorsa lets out a gargantuan sigh. 'I'm so glad you're a scientist with the ability to explain facts with such precision.'

'I'm a historian.'

'Well, of course. That explains everything.'

The room's warmer now, and Sav readjusts his blanket, tying it around his waist like a skirt. 'Can't they make more hybrids, in the same way they made you?'

My exact question when Jonan explained things to me. 'The science that created us has been lost. Try as they might, there's one tiny piece to the puzzle they can't recreate.'

'And yet we can? How?'

'I guess it's a skill we've yet to discover within ourselves. I suspect we won't know until we reach Albion.'

I explain that the whole Albion project exists because of us. We hadn't even been born, and yet their plans were set into operation. When the graph-led terraforming ships were first launched over two centuries ago, it was to build a world suitable for us hybrids. Over the years, the initial objectives were tweaked, not to say hijacked. It all came to a head shortly before the launch of the Endeavour, a ship that all the hybrids were supposed to be aboard.

'And that's when our adversaries first showed their hand?' Verone speaks to the air, thinking out loud, but she's quite correct.

'Opposition arising from fear had been building for years. It all bubbled to the surface once the launch to Albion was imminent.'

'I can't say I don't understand the fear,' Verone says. 'The thought of being replaced by a new lifeform is hardly comforting.'

'Nobody would ever have been replaced, but that's the exact fear that's being exploited.'

There are a few more questions and I answer them all to the best of my knowledge and ability. The others are happy with my explanations, and once again they show their true loyalty.

'No time to muck about,' Sav says. He throws his cover to the corner of the room. 'We need to get to the other side of the planet and hitch a ride on a Cally tanker.'

'Tomorrow morning,' I suggest. 'That'll give us time to make a few preparations.'

AMALTHEA swoops down. 'I'm not sure that's a good idea. All-Ports bulletins have been issued again and people have been warned to be vigilant. Any suspected sightings of you are to be reported at once.'

NEKO springs off the hearth. 'That may be true, but there's good news too. The Venusian authorities have discovered the allegations of homicide against Ariel were fraudulent.'

For a second, I'm fired up with hope.'

'No, Ariel. The news isn't that good. Records show Benjo was found dead in your home, but investigators discovered evidence that clears you. There was a sex-skin, in the form of a character from an Old Master's painting. She recorded the crime on crystal. Other records were tampered with, but nobody knew about the crystal. The investigators found it. Eventually. An assassin-skin was involved.'

I fight back a surge of grief. Benjo met his end frightened and alone. If real assassin-skins are like those in crystal-fictions, they're small and deal in deadly poisons. Poor Benjo wouldn't have known what was happening to him.

'The result,' NEKO says, 'is that Venusian authorities are on our side again. If you're captured, they demand you be surrendered to them.'

I don't want to be surrendered to anyone. And I certainly don't want to wait here until we're captured. It's tomorrow, then, at dawn.

And they're off. All except Dorsa, the others disappear into their rooms to start the preparations. We'll meet again this evening to discuss the finer points.

'I was thinking, Ariel. We need to be fully prepared, and we might need some weapons.'

I'm not sure I'm going to like this, but it's a conversation I've been expecting.

'Plazzers are way too tech for the facilities and materials available to me, but I could print off a few handhelds that work on the principle of expanding gasses.'

'You mean firearms?'

'Yes, just little things. Five or six shots. Fit easily into a pocket, or the palm of your hand.'

'No way! We're not killing people.' The very thought is sickening, and I'm surprised Dorsa can begin to contemplate it.

'I think we've been through enough to know they'd kill us.'

It's an argument I refuse to have, so I deploy an idea I've had at the ready for weeks. I tap the badge on my uniform and hold it while the material withdraws into it: a new innovation which saves us having to wear that old disc-on-loops version.

Dorsa gives me an up and down. 'I preferred you when you were less hairy.'

'Admit it, you can't keep your eyes off me.'

'I'm trying to decide if you're a human-graph hybrid or a human-gorilla one.'

If I didn't know she loved me, this would be growing rather tedious. 'Anyway, my idea involves reprogramming the nanobots in one of these.'

As I explain, Dorsa's smile grows wider and wider. 'You're a S'Jinning genius, Venus-boy. I can easily do that.'

I hand it over and Dorsa rolls the badge up and down between her fingers, then flips it through the air for me to catch. 'Put this one back on. I can get some others. Leave it to me.'

***

It's long after dark and I walk the streets with Dorsa. This quarter of Elysium has come to feel like a second home. Familiar accents, people of my own shape and build, even the occasional film-gown for those who've adapted to the colder climate. It's only my thick shoulder-length hair, eyebrows and beard that make me stand out now. Sav and I are as alike as twin-brothers. We're often taken as such, while Verone and Dorsa are continually mistaken for sisters. It's this set of circumstances that's at the heart of our plan of attack.

'I'm going to miss the others,' Dorsa says. The streets are deserted and lighting at this time of night is sparse. We feel truly alone. Martian Council has never approved of casual surveillance systems. Martians don't like to feel they're being watched.

'Do you think we'll ever see them again, when all this is over?'

'Who knows, Ariel? It'd be hard enough returning from Callisto. If we make it as far as Albion I seriously doubt there'll be any coming back.'

I've known Verone nearly all my life, and Sav since he was a cheeky little juvenile, while Hamo's become more than a friend. We're all as close as bonded partners, but it's all about to end. We'll be together until tomorrow, and then spend the rest of our lives in different star systems.

'At least we've got each other.' Dorsa slips her hand into mine and for a moment I wonder if she's been possessed. I return the pressure.

'No small thing, Dorsa.' In the last year we've been close once or twice. We've been casual lovers, and I wonder if it could be more. Would we make good partners? But it's no use. I can't think 'partner' without thinking 'Benjo'.

'What's wrong, Ariel?'

'Oh, nothing. Pre-action nerves, is all.'

'Action? We're only going to sit on a train for hours while it gets to the other side of the planet. Hardly taxing.'

'While Earther agents infest the whole place and Grendel fills Quantum with vibe-seekers. It doesn't exactly make for a relaxing trip.'

'Leave our graph friends to keep Grendel off our trail. And I think we're capable of handling Earthers. Look.' She opens her hand and in the dim light I see a handful of small spheres. 'Spheres are better than discs for our purposes, and I've incorporated an AI control interface so we can set them verbally.'

I pick one up. It feels smooth to the touch and cool but not as cold as metal. It has a diameter of about two centimetres and looks black in this light. 'What colour are they in daylight?'

'Cobalt-blue, like a security-skin's torso. You have to hold them tight and say "Activate Blue" followed by the desired setting command, and it's ready for use.'

'And they're effective against skins?'

'Yes, but there's only one setting for skins, hence the command is "Activate Blue Skin". Simple as that. And I've inoculated our own discs to prevent any blue-on-blue debacles.'

'Dorsa, you're S'Jinning brilliant!'

'Keep coming up with the ideas and I'll keep making them real.'

There's nobody else about. We've reached the bridge over the River Jinslam and stroll to the middle where we stop and lean over the balustrade. Those few sporadic lamps lining its banks reflect orange-red giving the water the look of flowing syrup. Our breath mists in the cool air and takes on the same shade.

'It'll be frozen solid in a couple of months.' Dorsa picks up a small pebble and drops into the river. The night's so still we hear it plop as it breaks the surface. 'If we're on Cally by then, we'll probably be frozen too.'

There's no breathable atmosphere on Callisto, and surface temperatures average somewhere around minus one-fifty. Apart from meteor-deflection stations, observation parks, spaceports and one or two other facilities, everything is subsurface. The gravity is a tenth of one-gee and Callistonians are weighed down with more rig-weights than Martians and have to sleep in centrifuge-dorms to ward off serious body malfunctions. Hardly surprising then, Callisto's not on the itinerary of the Grand Worlds Tour.

People leave the satellite in droves, so they're always keen to recruit more citizens. That's where our hope lies.

I'm letting my mind wander over the ripples in the red-gold syrup below. It's hypnotic and something strokes the inside of my skull. A feather's touch, but I recognise it as the prelude to a mind-link.

Dorsa touches her head. 'Do you feel that?'

'You too? Yes, I think we're being contacted.'

'By a graph?'

'That's my guess.'

On the far side of the bridge is a small red-stone crawler-stop shelter. There're no crawlers running this time of night, but the shelter has a lamp and a row of heat radiating stones. It makes a good place to settle while this link establishes itself.

There's a request to allow contact, and we affirm simultaneously. The graph enters our minds, but it's no stranger.

'Neko!' If he couldn't wait for our return home, I guess it must be something serious.

'Our mission has become more difficult. Callisto has suddenly become the centre of attention for our opponents. Grendel's vibrations are in evidence, and there is an Earther task force on the way.'

Dorsa speaks to me through the link. 'Does this mean we change our plans?'

'No! It's means we prepare for a fight.'

We sit quietly in the shelter, but we no longer see our surroundings. The three of us are together on the foothills of Quantum where the vistas have no equivalent in the physical macro-world. Dorsa is a feeling, NEKO is a touch and I am nothing and the Universe at the same time. Our words are not even thoughts, but the alignment of subatomic particles. In the space of an eye-blink for our human selves, the graph parts of us span the galaxies and our exchanges take nanoseconds. We take in the dispositions of our opponents and are infused with knowledge of their intent. There is something of aggression and of resolve, but everything is rooted in fear. They are frightened of us.

There is so much more. We are infused with truth and understanding.

'Do you understand this truth?' from NEKO in the hiss of a solar flare.

'We do,' Dorsa says. 'So this is what it means to be graph?'

'Yes, and I forgive you your inability to share with me what it means to be human.'

'You speak of truth,' I say. Dorsa says? We both say as one. No, that's not correct. We speak as three and answer in the same way. But even that isn't exactly right. We speak and answer as the Universe. To be graph is not to fully understand that plane of being. In that, humans and graphs are alike.

It has to do with the ship, our last hope to reach Albion. The Alicanto is a space-bender, and we all know that the space-bending experiments were a disaster. Ships were lost. Crews died. Disaster after disaster until at last, space-bending was abandoned as a reliable means of deep space transport. The mantra of our ancestors: 'We must, for the time being, satisfy ourselves with the Solar System.'

But that is the lie of generations! We are smoke, spread in the ether of truth. NEKO's mind echoes through as all and we align, thoughts and past knowledge.

Space-bending was a success until the loss of the Phoenix Song. Ships such as her and the Alicanto navigated to other systems. There are human colonies on exoplanets which have thrived for hundreds of years, and just as we have forgotten them, they remember us only as tales and fictions. We have been deliberately manipulated and history has been carefully edited. I wonder if that was ever the case with history.

Like dry lakebeds in a flash flood, we are filled with missing histories and the forbidden knowledge of non-human races, too much for human minds to absorb in a single great information dump, but so easily within the capacity of that of us which is graph.

That is the hybrids' purpose. We are repositories of history, and of the truth. That is our danger, for there are those who wish to control what we believe as truth. That is at the heart of Father's disappearance and all our subsequent troubles.

Why didn't you tell us before? Because telling is not the truth, only experiencing is true, and now you have experienced. Why not allow us to experience before? Because we were not aligned; our graph selves not sufficiently in tune. Now we are human. Now we are graph. Now we are hybrids who move forward for human and graph.

Now comes a whirlpool. I'm sucked down from Quantum to distil into my human body, the genie sucked back into the bottle. For a hybrid, human and graph can never live apart. The two elements are one. Now I have experienced, I am complete. Our earlier visits were like paddling on the shore. Now the sea surrounds us.

I'm sitting in the shelter next to Dorsa, drenched in quickly chilling sweat. I shiver, and that appears the only movement I can make. I'm stunned, and I can't speak. There's a dissonance between my human and graph sides, the latter so recently filled with knowledge while my body tries hard to absorb it all. Images pile up in my head, impossible until moments ago. A face rises in the dark before my eyes, or rather, behind them. It's a cat-boy, like NEKO but not him.

'Cat people?' Dorsa breaks the long silence. 'S'Jinning cat people. Have we lost our minds?'

I rather think we've gained them. 'They're called "felispiens", aren't they?'

'I think that's the name Earthers gave them.'

We lapse into another long silence. The Jinslam flows on, conducting liquid conversations with the land at its banks. The intensifier-satellites rise in the dawn sky ready to catch and magnify the sun's rays. They herald the sun itself, like the horses of Apollo's chariot.

As the sky lightens, my mantle registers a contact-request. I allow it and NEKO forms standing before us in scintillating blue light. 'The others are waking up. I think it's time we joined them.'

Back on our side of the bridge now, and curiously without warning, NEKO shimmers, shakes and winks out. We try to call him back but we can't get a link. It's all out of kilter, and we both increase our pace. Something's wrong. We exchange worried glances, and now we run.

Everything's upside down at home, and the others are rushing around in a panic. And yet, they are perfectly efficient in their actions. I've projected my panic onto them, imagined my fear in their actions.

'Thank S'John your back,' and 'Where've you been?' are phrases uttered by Sav and Hamo simultaneously, but as it turns out, rhetorical questions.

'We have to be gone in ten minutes, tops.' Sav says. 'One of our grid-triggers has fired. There's a squad moving in on us.'

He's hardly completed his warning when AMALTHEA winks into existence. 'Keep your heads down. Your descriptions are all over town, and there's an active team after you. I'll run some interference on the grid, so you'll be safe here.'

We have a plan, and now we have some advice from a graph, but they're conflicting. Everyone is looking at me. Somehow I'm in command again.

'We stick to the plan. Move out in five minutes.'

AMALTHEA asks for details of the plan, and I tell her. 'Dorsa and I head for the consulate pretending to be Sav and Verone. Hamo will come with us. We'll be protected there, and we can work out how to get to Callisto at our leisure.

'Meanwhile Sav will take his piercings out so he looks more like me. We'll tweak the wanted bulletins on grid to match. Then he'll go with Verone and make for the Callistonian port at Xanthe. They'll pretend to be Dorsa and me. They'll be quite obvious in their movements.'

'Bait?' AMALTHEA says.

'Precisely. If we're lucky, our pursuers will take that bait and go after the wrong people, giving us time to get to the consulate.'

'If we don't leave right now,' Sav says, 'they'll catch us all here.'

'Sorry, Amalthea. No more time for explanations.' I cut the link, unspeakably rude in normal circumstances, and snatch up the pouched belt I'd prepared earlier.

'You might need this,' Hamo says and hands me his bee-skin. 'Look after him.' I take it with thanks, and tuck the tiny machine into a pocket.

No time for goodbyes. Sav, Hamo and Verone are gone. I can hear their crawler accelerating away. Ours is ready, and it takes us in the opposite direction. We see no sign of the squad, but we know they won't be far behind.

As I settle into a passenger seat, reality hits me again. The five of us may never see each other again. It's the closest I've been to tears since the loss of our friends. I didn't get the opportunity to say goodbye to Raoul, Bart or Benjo either.

***

CRYSTAL REPLAY
1. HOW THE DAY PROCEEDED
2. WHERE WE ARE NOW

Ariel and Dorsa's crawler made best speed towards a suburban hub where they waited for a train bound for City Central. The hub was busy, but Hamo had selected their clothing and the three of them blended in well. Their sub-macro identities had been tweaked, so they showed as Sav and Verone at grid level and to any casually observing graph.

While they waited their attention was drawn through the observation windows to a vista of suburban domes, a village in the Martian scrub that looked like a pioneers' settlement.

'Beautiful,' Hamo said. 'Do you think it's been preserved since the early days, Ariel?'

'Shh! Call me Sav!'

'Indeed.' AMALTHEA said. She took form beside them, projected from the walls, so she had not needed to ask for mantle-activation.

'Do you think it's a good idea for you to be here, Amalthea?' Ariel-Sav said. 'You'd better go before you give the game way.'

'It's a little late for that.' AMALTHEA slowly changed shape until she was a floating head which then grew the body of a uniformed official. 'This time we have you,' GRENDEL said.

Ariel had time only to realise that he was surrounded by Martian prefects before restraints where fixed to his wrists, but he shook off the hands that tried to push him towards a vehicle, and drew himself to attention. 'I am Adjutant Sav Kinngas of the Venusian Defence Force, and I demand Consular Intervention.'

'Nice try, but you are Ariel Dzalarhons, and I relieve you of your liberty by virtue of Council Warrant.' GRENDEL formed the authority in the air. He turned to Dorsa. 'And you are Dorsa Sagan. You are likewise detained by Warrant.'

'I am Doctor Verone Kell of the Venusian Defence Force, and I demand Council Intervention.'

'Take them away.'

'Having made the demand,' Verone said, 'you are bound by Three Worlds Council law to contact our consulate and suspend any actions against us until our status as Venusian citizens has been verified.'

'I know the law, Dorsa. I am the law, and your citizenship is irrelevant. But we will go through the motions. Now you'll be taken to a holding facility until we can deal with your "demands" and arrange transport to Earth. And don't try anything. Your restraints prevent contact or assistance from any misguided graph allies you may have, such as your ridiculous cat friend and that stupid floating rock.' GRENDEL smiled, then turned to Hamo. 'As for you, we have no interest in you, so you may go.' He faded into the air.

Ariel and Dorsa were bundled into the transport, and Hamo was left alone among a sea of strangers.

Ariel and Dorsa were held in custody for almost a day before a representative of the Venusian Consulate was allowed to visit. He quickly established that the pair who were detained as Ariel and Dorsa were in actual fact, a fact proved beyond doubt by genetic profiling, officers of the VDF called Sav Kinngas and Verone Kell, exactly as they had claimed.

GRENDEL looked as shocked as it is possible for a graph-projection to be.

'I admit there are traces of graph identification manipulation on the grid,' the Consulate representative said, 'but that is of no concern or interest to me, and is not covered in the Warrant, so you will immediately release these people into my care.'

Helpless to do anything else, GRENDEL had to comply.

By the time all this had played out, the real Ariel Dzalarhons and Dorsa Sagan were on board a freighter bound for Callisto.

End replay

***

We're aboard the Callistonian Freight Ship Raggy Molly and the crew, at least, live up to the name. They're all stereotypical Callies, which doesn't bode well for our mission, but I suspect they're all role-playing. They dress in functional but unnecessarily tatty spacer overalls and they all look like they need a good session in a bathing booth. Sav would look neat among this lot.

The Raggy Molly on the other hand is the most pristine, spotless, clinically clean vessel I've ever been on. We've been assigned berths on different acceleration-decks, and as Dorsa's is a smidgeon bigger than mine, we're here to tweak our plans.

Stepping out of the box I meld with Dorsa and we coalesce in the scintillations that represent Callisto. We slide through Quantum-Callisto insinuating our intentions within local systems. We arrange things so that we'll be expected and supported when we reach our destination. It's a tightrope walk, because the vibration of GRENDEL are strong, and Earther influence is all around. We keep ourselves shrouded from observation.

Back in Dorsa's tiny cabin, we insert a cube into the printer and prepare a meal. It's a pasta and sauce dish which will do for quick nourishment, and it's not half bad.

'I don't know about you, Ariel, but I didn't get the impression the Earthers are looking for us.'

I feel the same. 'There's frantic action, but they're not after us. Grendel's essence is everywhere though, so I don't understand.'

'I might have a clue.' Dorsa takes on the look she always has when she's about to tell me something I don't like. 'What if they've got a bead on your father, or maybe mine?'

'Or both!' Dorsa's right again. There was a familiar vibration I couldn't place. I've never encountered Father in Quantum before so I can't be sure. Must be a chance though.

The cabin door reverberates from a hefty blow from outside. 'Out here, you two.' Rude! And then as an afterthought, 'If you don't mind.'

It's Finnrad, the first officer, and we follow him to the captain's bridge-office.

Captain Brunel waves us towards a couple of chairs, which we take. His suit looks like it's made from bands of leather that keep his skinny frame upright. He has a six-day beard, if my beard-growing prowess is anything to go by. 'Have to say, if you were Earthers I'd be tempted to air-lock the two of you.'

'Venusers not a lot better,' mumbles Finnrad through his scruffy beard.

'Blox, number one! I'd take a hundred Venusers with all their arsey glassy beads and stuck-up manners for one scraggin Earther.' Brunel turns to us. 'I suppose you're aware there's an Earther fleet bumbling around in Cally space.'

'I had got that impression,' I say. 'It's nothing to do with us.'

'Or is it? It seems Earth's gone full-scat over a bunch of terrible criminals and they've decided to suspend the usual rules of business. They've put a scabbing blockage around our world to try an' catch 'em. And all of a sudden I've got two paying guests who want to get there in my old barge.'

'Big fat coincidence,' Finnrad says.

'Or not!' Brunel leans on the arms of my seat and comes in so close I can smell his sweat. 'Are you this fluking Ariel Seller-whatever that Earth Council is pooping its pants over?'

'Do I look like him?'

'What the fluke does that matter? Pretty sure what a person looks like is the least important thing in the

Universe of grid-bleaching. The thing is, there's an Earther frigate off our port bow, and they're demanding I should heave-to and let a boarding party on.'

Now. It's one of those moments in time. My next sentence decides my fate. 'Yes, Captain. I am Ariel Dzlarhons, and everything the Earthers say about me is a lie.'

'Skagging fluke!' from Finnrad. He makes a move towards us but Brunel waves him off.

'Number one, open a coms link to those flukers, now.'

The Earther ship forms in the room until the projections changes into a scene which I presume if the Earther ship's bridge.

'Captain, the Earthers have manoeuvred straight ahead. They've slowing down.'

There's a man in Earther uniform who forms as if hovering in space. 'Power down immediately and secure for boarding.'

'Scag off, Earther,' Brunel says. 'Get off our vee-line or we'll ride straight through you.' He turns away from the display. 'First Officer Finnrad. Increase to one-point-one gee and hold course.'

Brunel strides from his office and we follow him onto the bridge.

'They're deploying plazzers,' shouts one of his bridge crew, and then 'Cancel that. Weapons now powering down.'

Only Dorsa and I know that between those two sentences, we went Quantum and destroyed all weaponry circuits on the Earther ship. An adventure of hours for us that took so little real time our physical bodies didn't even have time to stumble. While among the guts of ship's control, we took the liberty of adding a few mega-strings to their records. According to the grid, scans prove we're not on the Cally freighter.

'They thought better of it.' Brunel wears a satisfied yet grim smile. 'Are they moving out of our way?'

'Yes, Captain. With less than 5,000 metres to spare. There's a message from them.'

The officer activates the projections and the face of the Earther commander appears. 'You are in breach of safety regulation and you will be –'

'Go fluke yourself!' Brunel bellows, and then blocks the Earther transmission. 'Resume one-gee. Maintain course,' he says, then turns on Dorsa and me. 'You two, back to my office. I think you have a tale to tell me.'

We tell him everything, including the fact that we can skim Quantum. I even let him know about our sabotage of the Earth ship's plazzer circuits.

'Scag! So they might have shot us after all?'

'We saw no evidence they intended to power down. You were in the centre of their sights and they were ready to loose bolts.'

Brunel swears again, and flops down into his chair. 'So what am I supposed to do with you now? What *can* I do with you? If it's something you don't like you could make the engines explode, or open all the airlocks.' There's fear in his eyes. 'No wonder they're after you.'

Dorsa stands and walks towards him. He actually flinches. 'Captain, we haven't killed anyone. They've done all the killing. All we've ever done since all this started was to try and stay alive.'

Brunel stands again, and he's eye to eye with Dorsa. 'And yet you're heading for a big show-down on Callisto. You think that'll go down without a lot of people getting hurt.'

'That's not our plan,' I say. 'We'll do whatever we can to avoid conflict and leave for Albion on the Alicanto.'

'Then come back in a few decades to invade us?'

'Why would we do that? We're human too.'

'Maybe I feel a little like the Neanderthals when modern humans heaved up on the horizon. I don't like the thought of being the old model.'

'How can we convince you of our intentions, Captain?'

He paces a circle around his desk. 'One thing history teaches you. You can't stop progress even if people are frightened of it, and those that try are usually the ones to use extreme and deadly measures. As we've just seen.'

Brunel is no longer swearing. In fact, he's eloquent and his voice has lost the rough edge. All a Cally act, as I suspected.

'I'm with you. I know people ice-side who can help. Leave it with me.'

Back in Dorsa's cabin, we wonder if we've done the right thing. Brunel knows everything about us and our intentions. He could make things difficult.

'Too late to worry about that now, Ariel. Let's get back to Quantum and see if we can work out what Grendel's doing there.'

'He's not simply waiting for us, that's for sure. He's after someone else and the more I think about it the more I believe it's Father.'

J4

NEKO establishes that Verone, Sav and Hamo are all reunited and with the help of Ibby Carlane they're doing what they can to help us.

'Amalthea is also recovering from her subsumation by Grendel,' NEKO says. 'It might be a while before she has fully reintegrated.'

'Good to know they're all safe now,' Dorsa says. 'Grendel's only interested in us.'

We've achieved much with our manipulations to establish ourselves on Callisto, and Brunel's helped too. We return to our tiny quarters in Valhalla. We pose as a partnered couple of archaeologists, and we're acclimatising to conditions here. The gravity on Callisto barely keeps our feet on the floor and our rigs couldn't accommodate more weights even if we wanted them to. Without ballast we can propel ourselves around on our fingertips.

'Did you see anything of Grendel?'

'Not a thing,' I say the moment I step back into the box. It's now common for our conversation to begin in Quantum and end here. The Earther marines have been withdrawn too, even if their ships are still in orbit.'

So far the people we've met landside – or 'ice-side' as the locals say – are as annoying and helpful and ugly and beautiful as people the worlds over. They live difficult lives, but that only hardens them on the surface. It's a thin veneer beneath which they're as human as any Venusian, and contrary to expectation, their cities are wondrous.

Valhalla nestles subsurface, but it's not without its grand squares and parks, its water features and sculptures. There's one garden that rises close to the surface where the sun shines thinly through the ice roof, and every nook and cranny has an incredibly intricate ice sculpture.

Callisto's surface is unremittingly bleak, but they've made up for it wherever you look. Utilities are never left utilitarian, but ingeniously disguised and imbued with art. The garden, for instance, is actually Valhalla's primary air processing plant, but the machinery that melts ice and breaks the resulting water into hydrogen and oxygen is well hidden and fully automated.

People tend to stay near home and don't travel much, so we have to plan our trip to Adlinda carefully, especially as the whole area has been abandoned and pretty much forgotten for years.

We crawl out of the 'fuge and get dressed. Will I ever get used to sleeping in a centrifugal-dorm? No time soon, that's for sure. With local fabric clothing over our space-films, we sign out of the apartment that's been ours for two nights, and head to the city's museum to meet a historian, a friend of Brunel's who's promised to help us with our 'archaeological' project.

The city is small and people walk everywhere. There's no need for bikes or crawlers. Intercity trips are by subsurface tube; nobody ventures to the surface to travel, and those who do work dirtside are undoubtedly the toughest humans you'll ever meet.

We'll have to surface for some parts of our journey to Adlinda. There's no subsurface route between the city ruins and the old disused spaceport, which incidentally, we've been told is off limits. 'It's a dangerous place full of active wastes and seal-breaches. Apart from anything else, the whole place is surface temperature. The fate of anyone stupid enough to go there? Frazzle or freeze!'

It's a bridge we'll cross when we come to it. I have faith in the engineer-skins who've been watching over the place for centuries, and I'm willing to bet the descriptions of the ruin are exaggerated.

The curator of the museum gives us a contact who'll let us in to the disused roads to Adlinda, and loan us a machine that's part-crawler, part-skin. The curator tells us it comes with a construct, but we don't let her know we'll probably elect NEKO as our operator.

With one last scan of the grid and that part of Quantum with which we're now familiar, we feel safe enough to set off. There are vibrations of the enemy, but they haven't breached the veils NEKO's drawn over our presence. With the crawler in the cargo hold, our tube sets off for the frontier town of Rylco, as close as any public transport will get us to Adlinda.

***

This crawler is the most uncomfortable transport I've ever experienced. NEKO runs it from a detachable general purpose skin up front. The seats, set on a flat floor suitable for cargo, are an afterthought. There's no padding and they're horrendously sore on the bottom after the shortest of journeys. Suspension is almost non-existent, imperfections in the road surface dampened only by the pneumatic tyres. With the ceiling-sky as a roof, there's no need for one on the vehicle, so we feel very exposed.

Our passenger tube makes it to Rylco without incident and we meet our contact, Andal Smith, as planned. A heavily set man, he has a full beard. To offset his great bulk he wears a rig with less than the prescribed ballast. Consequently he moves around like a ballerino, far lighter on his feet than he has any right to be.

Andal leads in his own human-operated crawler, and we follow along ever narrower and more deserted roads. The warm lights of Rylco soon give way to functional lamps. We pass through several bulkhead-locks and Andal shouts out a running commentary from up ahead. 'That side tunnel leads to an early air-scrubbing plant. Was shut down in the 2850s. Might interest you bone-kicker types, coz it's all well-preserved.' A few side turnings later: 'Down there's the remains of Azimovia. Not so well preserved, and several areas have collapsed. My family can trace its origins to the place. It's worth a dig, if I can persuade you.' He stops by the junction and peers into the darkness of the side tunnel. 'If you find great-grandpop's skull, I'll have it as a Rule Seven.' And he's on the move again.

As we proceed, the lamps are farther apart and NEKO has to switch on the headlights. The air's so cool now Dorsa and I feel our space-film thermal regulators kick in. Dorsa lets out a sigh I've only been able to produce in her once, and even then she may have been faking.

Andal keeps up his commentary but I'm past paying much attention. It's so gloomy now, and my breath freezes on contact with the chilled air. Not quite freezing, because water drips from the pitch dark ceiling-sky making me wish this rickety old crate had a roof.

Rylco has a population of about seven thousand, quite sufficient to make the small town's streets and suburbs well-peopled. There were settlements along the road for several klicks, but now it's been hours since we saw anybody else. Only Dorsa, me, and Andal up ahead revelling in the history of his world.

Now the lamps are so far apart they cast insufficient light to see by, acting more as navigational points, each distant glow telling us only that the tunnel goes on.

'Woah, there!' Andal calls, like a horse-knight from a Western-crystal. 'This is the end of the line.' The tunnel ahead is blocked by a huge airtight gate. 'The air beyond here's going to be stale. Still breathable though, and the chambers are all airtight thanks to the repair-skins. Not going to lie, it's going to be tough going.' He steers his crawler to one side and dismounts.

Dorsa gets our equipment together and I join Andal at the gate. 'Have you ever been in there?'

'Yeah, when I was a lad. Dad led a scavenging party. We were out to find stuff to recycle. Earthers, and sometimes you Venusians too, speak a lot of shit about us Callies, but it's true we don't like to waste a single thing.' His face goes dark. 'It wasn't a pleasant experience as I recall. There were bodies. Not quite skeletons.' Andal shudders. 'I still have S'Jinning nightmares.' Nice to know Martian cuss words are interplanetary. He shakes off the macabre memories. 'Still, let's get this fluker open.'

I watch closely as he uses a key-like tool to open a panel. Once opened, he activates a control and looks at the readout. 'Bit of a pressure differential. According to this nobody's been through here for over twenty years. Let's hope the maintenance-skins have done a good job, else the fluker won't shift.'

Andal tells us to stand back. The door slides aside and air is sucked in with a whoosh. A wind blows from back along the tunnel for several minutes until the pressure is equalised. He waves us through with a grand gesture. 'You'll be able to use the crate for a few klicks, then it'll have to be on foot. Too much rubble for old tyres.'

That's an unexpected boon. I thought we'd be on foot from here on. Dorsa mounts up, and I pause to say goodbye and thankyou to Andal. Callistonians greet and part with a handshake, exactly as I've seen on history presentations. He grips my hand tighter and draws me in for a confidential word. 'I never did believe that old blox that you an' her are some kind of terrorists.' He gives me a big fat wink. 'Be sure an' seal the door behind you. Tight as a duck's arse, I would. My little tweeters tell me the Earthers int long after you.'

'Back again?'

'Afraid so. There's an Earther warship decanting troops like a mushroom chucks out spores.'

It's as if I'm living in a juvenile's comic-crystal. 'Warship? Nobody has actual warships.' You couldn't seriously categorise the Ashen Light or that Earther frigate we encountered as dedicated warships.

'Try telling the Earthers. That ship's bristling ordnance, and the Cally militia's had e-fluking-nuff! We've been called to stand-to, coz those fluking Earthy bloxers have violated Cally's sovereignty and about a dozen Three-World-Council statutes. So, if you'll excuse me.' He salutes, jumps on his crate and speeds off back down the tunnel.

I dip into Quantum and search. It's true. They're on our trail. There're strange echoes thrumming through the graph world. It's GRENDEL and his minions. They're coming for us. I scan about for something we can throw at them if the need arises and light upon squadrons of surface-skins. They might do. NEKO intones that he can handle the machines if the time comes.

I close the gate behind us. NEKO evicts its construct operator and destroys the matrix so our pursuers can't install a new one. 'This will hold them back for a while. The downside is we can't go back through, even if we want to.'

It's not our intention to come back this way. We're going to leave Callisto aboard the MSS99 Alicanto. The old space-bender waits for us on the far side of Adlinda's ruins. We shunt the crawler to full speed.

This tunnel is a perfect match for the one we've just left except completely dark. After a few hundred yards our progress has been detected, because lamps begin to fade up: first an indistinct glow, now intensified to sharp points which spill pools of dull light onto the road.

After only fifteen minutes the tunnel ends and opens into a cavern too vast for our crawler's lights to be effective. NEKO brings the crate to a stop.

'I've been in cheerier places,' Dorsa says. 'It's going to be hell crossing this dump unless we can see where we're going.'

'There!' I point high, to a tiny glimmer, a diffuse point of light that resembles a nebula more than a star. 'And there!'

'They're all over the place, thank S'John!'

And she right. They're not like true city lights. They're makeshift, emergency lighting. It's my guess they were installed by engineer-skins and set to come on only when necessary, but they do the trick. The ruins start to emerge from the darkness, as if they're coming to life and moving closer to see who we are.

'Shame about that.' Dorsa points along the road. It runs from the tunnel and ends fifty metres ahead in a mountain of rubble. 'That's as far as we'll get with the crawler.'

NEKO agrees, and he uncouples his skin from the rest of the machine. As he steps down from the dock, he has the appearance of a bipedal robot, like a security-skin but chunkier. When he communicates, his speakers give him a low, gravelly voice which is quite intimidating. 'Nothing I can't negotiate in this skin. How about you two?'

'A bit of clambering won't do us any harm. Ready, Dorsa?' Ready? She's already halfway there.

Before we head to the ship, our plan is to find the subsurface chamber marked on Father's map with the alien cypher. These ruins look nothing like the original street plan, but I have an idea. I take out Hamo's little bee-shaped seeker-skin and ask it to link with Father's ring-crystal. It's a simple matter for it to upload the coordinates, and it's away.

I sit on a slab of plasticrete while we wait. Dorsa sets one foot on it and leans elbow on knee, while NEKO ambles about taking readings. My eyes drift up the mound of rubble, and I wonder if it would be better to cast our rigs. It would make it much easier to climb. I'm about to suggest this to Dorsa, when the chamber is filled with a well-rounded but soft-edged boom, the report of a serious impact from the direction of the tunnel.

The vibrations die away. We're standing now, peering at the black hole that marks the opening to the tunnel. And now it comes again, this time with a sharp edge that makes Dorsa and I jump. NEKO steps forward and deploys a long range scanner.

'Earthers!' he says. 'They're attacking the gate.' He scans some more. 'It would take them an hour to break through if they used their brains, but they're using brute force. We're good for half a day at their present rate of progress.'

Now, another noise, this time a high-pitched thrum. The bee's back. It flies in a circle, then in one direction and back again. It repeats the sequence.

'This way,' NEKO says. 'It wants us to follow.'

The clever little bee doesn't lead us over the ruin but around the rubble at the base. We clamber and scrabble over loose blocks and shattered plasticrete until we come to a channel that's like a rock-strewn mountain pass. NEKO is first after the bee and he uses skin strength to kick away some of the larger blocks. We move swiftly, our progress punctuated by the ever diminishing thunderclaps of the Earther assault.

The rubble thins out and the narrow pass becomes a rocky plane. I assume this area was once a town square, and there's a building that could easily have been the seat of the town council. It's the most intact structure I've seen so far. Modelled on an ancient Greek temple, the columns have fallen, and with them a dedication stone.

'There's words on the stone.' Dorsa brushes away some surface dust uncovering the inlaid lettering. 'It's in Standard and Cally-pigeon.'

The plaque proudly states that Adlinda was the last town in the Three Worlds built with the involvement of 'money'. It reminds me that one of Benjo's Rule of Seven possessions was a disc showing the head of a monarch, and the words 'One Penny'. I don't know the value of a penny, but it's coming back to me. Christie used to enjoy a confection called a penny bun. But now's not the time to become overwhelmed by Christie's memories, or anybody else's.

My heart skips a beat when Dorsa lets out a truncated yell of fear. She's run right into a security-skin. It doesn't make a move, and it's covered in dust, so we relax when we realise it's a relic, and not after us.

'Hey, Neko. Can you scan this thing? Is it still operable?' I could scan it myself, but NEKO can do it with less effort.

'It's mechanically sound, but there's no construct.'

'Could you operate it?

'Easily, but I'd have to abandon my currant skin unless I multi-locate, and this one's more powerful. We might need the extra strength later.'

I have an idea. I wrap my fingers around my left ring finger, encompassing Father's partner-band. I close my eyes and let my mind sink into it.

In here, Father's files are like buildings in a city, but I soon find my way to the one I want. Floating before me is Little Smiley. 'Hello, Crash.'

'How nice to see you again. Would you like me to take on the form of Jonan?'

'No thanks, I'm here to ask a question. Are you a fully active construct, or limited only to file security?'

'I had other duties before I came here. What do you need me for?'

'Can you operate a skin?'

'Easy-peasy!'

Now we're off again, with a security-skin added to our party. Every few minutes, the thunder of our enemies fills our sails and gives us impetus to move quicker. If GRENDEL catches us again, I doubt he'll restrain himself. In a real sense, we're running for our lives.

We've followed the bee for nearly an hour, and the Earther assaults barely touch the air now. The tiniest of thuds every few minutes or so. We take paths leading off other paths; duck under culverts; leap across chasms and climb mounds until we come to a sheer slab of old wall that's about five metres high. There's no going around it.

'Can you break through, Neko?' Dorsa asks.

'No, it is too thick. I can jump it though.' He squats to make best use of the power in his legs, and extends them explosively. He grabs the rim at the top and hauls himself up. CRASH does the same.

'Time to shed our rigs, I think.'

Dorsa and I drop our weighted belts and join our mechanical friends with a single leap. There's a gentle slope down the other side, and the bee's found something. Now it circles, round and round over what appears to be an open hatch. We've found the cavern.

'Someone's been here fairly recently,' NEKO says. The hatch is blackened with plazbolt impacts.

'But Andal said nobody had been here for twenty years.' I'm certain of it.

'No, Ariel. He said nobody had been through the gate in more than twenty years. Whoever came here entered the city by another route. These bolt-hits are only a few weeks old.'

Peering down past the open hatch, it's very reminiscent of the one at Dorsa's farm, but there's a smell. It's the stench of plazbolted flesh, and once again Raoul's death comes to mind.

With the smell, comes the silence. Our pursuers have either given up their assault on the gate, or they're through. There are no more rumbling peels of distant thunder. NEKO's skin-based scanners are out of range, but he abandons the skin to go back to the gate and investigate.

'Maybe we should give this a miss and head straight for the Alicanto,' Dorsa says.

'No,' I say. 'This is important. I have to go down.' With not a minute to waste, I set my foot on the first rung.

***

As my foot touches the second rung, NEKO re-inhabits the skin. 'The Earthers haven't broken in yet. At present they're in a standoff with the Callistonian Militia.'

'The Callies have bought us some time,' Dorsa says.

I clamber back to the surface. This is dreadful news. I'd rather the Callies stay out of it. 'I'm not allowing people to die on our account. I'll have to go back.' I make a move but Dorsa grabs my shoulder.

'Go back and what? Negotiate? Surrender?' She grabs the other shoulder and pulls me into her face. 'Don't be an arse! This isn't our fault. If we go back we'll end up dead.'

'She is right,' NEKO adds. 'And anyway, the chance of mortal combat, or the use of any force at all, is extremely remote.' He tells us he observed calm and quiet negotiations between GRENDEL and the militia captain. 'Incidentally, the captain is Andal Smith.'

'So let's get down there, Ariel. While they're all playing nice at conflict resolution.' Dorsa begins to descend, and I follow. We leave CRASH and NEKO on guard at the surface.

This chamber is much closer to the surface than the ones under my home and at Dorsa's farm. After a few metres of descent, I reach the bottom. The lights come on and everything looks clean and new, a feature that contrasts with the putrid air. The stench of burnt meat and rot is almost unbearable, and I fear to discover its origin.

'Over there!' Dorsa points to a line of scorch marks on the wall. 'Looks like someone was firing volleys of plazbolts down here.'

The machinery is undamaged. It looks new but is of a fairly ancient design. Scans reveal old casings with newer internal parts; manually operated controls, and state of the art readouts and monitors.

Dorsa helps me examine the scan results. 'Some of this stuff dates from way past the destruction of Adlinda. This monitor is only a couple of years old.'

I check the hopper levels. 'It's been in use at least within the last year.'

'Maybe there's been a leak.'

'The smell? No, either something was blasted or an animal crawled in through the open hatch and died.'

'You think there are wild animals roaming about up there among the ruins?'

I have to admit, it seems unlikely, but there is breathable air and temperatures are way above freezing. We continue our exploration and find markings similar to those in the other chambers. I check off the various components of a bioprinter and recognise most, but there's a whole series of machines that seem out of place and I can't work out what they're for. They're all the kind that have to be graph-operated.

'Shall we go Quantum and dive into the circuitry?' Dorsa says. 'It might be the quickest way to work out what these components are for.'

'Maybe later.'

Dorsa holds her throat. 'That pong is ten times worse. Whatever the source, we're getting nearer.'

A corridor between rows of machinery bends to the right, and on the floor at the furthest part visible, is a brown stain spreading from out of our line of sight. 'I could be wrong, Dorsa, but I think we're about to come face to face with something rather unpleasant.'

Now I come to think of it, I stepped into the rotting carcase of a fossa once, and the odour was much the same. I wonder if different creatures have their own distinct smell of decay.

As we round the corner I see more of the wet stain, a pool that has more substance than most liquids. My imagination throws horrific images at me, and nothing exists outside the edges of the stain. I force myself to keep up my careful pace, and then it's there, more horrific than anything my mind could produce. I hear a noise from Dorsa that encompasses my feeling precisely. She reaches out and steadies herself against me.

There's a small cubical-like chamber, much like any cleansing booth, but instead of jet nozzles there are banks of gem-like structures. There appear to be no physical controls. I take all this in because I want to look anywhere but into the decaying face of the human corpse as it lies heaped on the floor.

'Poor man,' Dorsa manages. 'Looks like a plazbolt to the head. Not enough to completely incinerate him.'

I force myself to look. 'Is it a man?' The position of the remains hide the obvious signs of gender. There are hanks of long hair around a face that has shrivelled onto the underlying skull, its grinning teeth Death's mockery of the living.

Dorsa starts a scan. 'Yes, human male. We'll have to get a sample to check for toxins.'

'And DNA.' I call into the ether for the bee-seeker and it comes buzzing, but the sound of buzzing combined with a rotting corpse raises an irrational fear in me. I see bluebottles, maggots and writhing dead flesh. It took an hour for me to wash the stench of that fossa off my foot. I shake the image off and give the bee instructions. Within moments it's done, and the results are given via the speakers in my mantle.

'No trace of toxins,' the speaker says. 'Decay has been accelerated by partial disruption by a plasma bolt. Cause of death, cranial trauma. DNA an exact match for Jonan Zahed-Dzalarhons, last known locat ...'

My world contracts and my senses narrow. There a growl. A scream? Is it me? It blocks out the rest of the report. I dip into Quantum and out again. And I'm being held. Then a slap, right across my face, and the world rushes back in on me.

'No time, Venus-boy. The Earthers got through the gate.'

I swore I'd never do it, but I fill my system with blockers. It's that or lose it completely.

NEKO is standing there in his skin, and I assume the steady beat of metal on metal is CRASH descending the ladder.

'There's a door up ahead,' NEKO says. 'We have to try it.'

The security-skin joins us. 'I've closed the hatch and damaged the opening mechanism. It should hold them back a while,' CRASH says, and then he looks at the corpse. 'Ew! That's not very nice. Shall I clear it up?'

I want to hit him. Break him apart.

'Look, Ariel.' Dorsa's holding my shoulders again. 'Maybe someone reprinted him, the same as happened to us.' A hypothesis that's supported by no more than circumstantial evidence. 'He might be perfectly safe and well, somewhere in a new body.'

It's something to hold on to. For now it's enough. 'Let's see if we can get that door open.' I reach it first and find the control panel.

A hollow thrum fills the chamber, and Dorsa's hand goes to the row of small spheres attached to her belt. 'Earthers taking out their frustration on the hatch. They love to make a noise.'

'Here, let me.' NEKO steps in to operate the controls, and the doors swings out to reveal another tunnel. Lamps immediately illuminate our escape route and we pile in. NEKO seals the door behind us.

I manage to access a map mentally. 'This only leads to an exit to the surface. We may have cornered ourselves.' I note the surface exit is half a klick from Alicanto's bunker, but we've no way of going ice-side without a suit. It's time to put one of my standby plans into effect, so I centre and step out of the box. However long I spend in Quantum will reflect as micro-seconds for my human half, but I must still expedite. I shift, multi-locate and insinuate into one control matrix after another, giving commands and direction. The monsters stir, and I step back into the box.

Dorsa cusses and swears. 'Get a move on, Dozy! They'll be on us any time.' She lets out a stream of invective that would make a Cally blush. 'If we're cornered, we'll have to go down fighting.'

What have we become? After generations of peace we come to this. Can we never shed our animalistic origins? This isn't the time for philosophy and I'm thankful the adrenaline keeps my head clear. 'On the other hand, this must be the way my father got in, so maybe he left an EVA-skin.'

We start to run as the first blow strikes the door behind us. The hatch can't have held for more than a few minutes, and I guess the door won't impede them for much longer.

The tunnel is short and yes, there's an EVA-skin at the entrance to the elevator. In fact there are two, and they're of the same design I trained with aboard Ashen Light. But we're metres away when the door gives behind us, and we hear the excited voices of Earther marines.

'Stay where you are! We're authorised –' The sentence isn't finished before a plazbolt zaps between us and bursts against the wall.

CRASH walks back down the tunnel a few metres and activates a shield in time to intercept another bolt. It fizzes bright against the shield and its blazing remnants fall harmlessly to the floor.

It's time to try out my nanobot spheres. I whip one out of my belt pouch as a dozen Earthers swarm towards us. They're supported by a pair of combat-skins, which is soon reduced to one. 'Crash by name, crash by nature,' CRASH says, his plazzer emitter still glowing.

Dorsa screams. 'I tried a Quantum attack but they were ready for it.' She rubs her head, then shakes the pain off.

We're now at the receiving end of a hail of bolts, most of which find their fiery demise in CRASH's energy-shield. Some find their way through, and NEKO is hit. The lower part of his right arm falls off, but he's all right.

I hear Dorsa's command: 'Activate Blue Burst.' She throws a sphere high.

I give my command, the sphere in the pocket of a catapult, elastic stretched to the full: 'Activate Blue Skin.' I release as Dorsa's sphere bursts above the marines like a cloud of powder.

They're stunned for a while, and try to brush the powder off their uniforms. My sphere has struck the other combat-skin. It begins to spark and flash as the nanobots destroy its control matrices.

A marine lifts his plazzer, shoots, and the heat of the bolt singes my hair before it makes the wall behind me glow.

Another marine starts to lift his plazgun to aim, but he struggles, as if the weapon weighs a hundred kilos. The others have all slowed down and begin to walk like badly programmed robots. One falls on his face, another comes to a complete halt, and then they all become totally ineffective as their nanotex suits stiffen around them, like body-hugging coffins of steel.

'Nice work, Dorsa. They work a treat.'

'There'll be other. Let's move.'

We shuffle into the EVA-skins amidst a torrent of abuse from the frozen marines. I wish we'd incorporated a gagging element into the design.

'Oh, shut the fluke up!' CRASH says. 'Or I'll plaz the lot of you.' CRASH is a construct. He can't hurt humans, but I wouldn't risk it if I were them.

With our space-films interfacing with the EVA-skin controls, we power up and enter the lift. CRASH launches a volley of bolts into the ceiling and brings it down while leaving the roof intact. Another inconvenience for our pursuers. It won't kill them, unless they all die of raging embarrassment. CRASH joins us. I give the command and the lift takes us up.

The door of the surface-blister opens onto a field of dark green-brown shattered rock that stretches into infinity. In complete contrast to the drabness of the land, the sky is filled with Jupiter, huge, magnificent and swirling with colour. In the two-thirds of the sky that isn't a planetscape, the atmosphere is tinged ghostly yellow-green, a light so diffuse it's barely visible. Nevertheless, it's a sky I could watch forever.

Readouts show the thinnest of atmospheres and a temperature of minus one-twenty-seven. A clear line stretches out from the entrance, formed where the surface rocks have been recently turned.

'Someone's been this way.' It's Dorsa's voice on my speakers.

I check the direction against my map display. 'It leads straight to the Alicanto. Come on!'

The EVA-skins respond as extensions to our bodies. They mimic every move we make. Dorsa's skin moves with her own unique gait and is pulling ahead. I put on some effort to catch up.

We've made about a hundred metres and I spot the bunker dome. How will we get inside?

NEKO catches up with me. 'You can tell by the marks on the ground that a pair of EVA-skins, probably these ones, made a one way trip from the bunker up ahead and back the way we've come.'

It's another puzzle I have little time to ponder because we come to a circle of bright white ice. It's subsurface ice and all the overlying rock has been blasted away by the landing of a small vessel. The track goes on towards the bunker from the ship and then back again.

NEKO examines the site. 'I have it! A ship landed here. Two people in EVA-skins disembarked and went straight to the bunker. The ship took off again, whereupon they returned from the bunker, walked over the landing site leaving these imprints, and carried on to the elevator.'

'Then it stands to reason Father came here by ship and disembarked with someone else in two EVAs. Dorsa's father?'

Dorsa doesn't think so. 'He was claustrophobic. He'd flip in one of these.'

'It could easily have been your Father on his own with an extra construct operated EVA-skin,' NEKO says. 'When we get these machines into a pressurised bunker, we can see if there are any DNA traces.'

'Perhaps Father tried to get into the bunker, failed and then made for the only shelter available.' If he couldn't get in, then I doubt we'll be any more successful, but I mustn't get ahead of myself. 'Well, let's see if we can get in.'

'Excuse me,' CRASH says. 'But we appear to have guests.' He points, but before I can look a plazbolt takes off NEKO's head.

'And now our guest have guests,' CRASH says. He puts his metallic hands on his ledge-like hips. He leans forward, as if to get a better view. 'The new arrivals are water farmers, and I must say they're making imaginative use of their tools.'

'Correction, Crash,' I say. 'They're water farmers' EVAs, but there're pilotless.'

'I just dipped into Quantum for a quick look-see. Imaginative use of multi-location, Venus-boy. You'll have to teach me that someday.'

In the distance the two sets of skins converge. One group are clearly of the same sort we encounter in the tunnels just now; Earther combat-skins and the larger ones among them must be Marine EVA-skins. The other lot are a diverse pack of machines, some as massive as aggy-skins, others about the size of our EVA's, and they're all under my control. Well, technically I'm not controlling them, I merely initiated and programmed them with a set of instruction.

'There's another lot!' Dorsa says. This group is actually piloted by water farmers and other Callistonians. 'My best guess, the Earthers have severely pissed off the Callies who are about to demonstrate the depths of their pissed-offedness.'

'It's as if we've triggered Armageddon.'

'Don't start that again. Crash, can you hold them back while we try to get into the bunker?'

'Easy-peasy,' he says. He deploys his shields in time to disrupt a flurry of incoming bolts. The Earthers don't have time to launch another volley, because my EVA company and the Callies are in amongst them and flailing at them with massive metal limbs. From this distance it looks like a battle of Titans.

My speakers crackle and I get an incoming message. I recognise Andal's gravelly tones. 'Get out of here, kids. We can't hold 'em long.'

'Go, Dorsa. See if you can open up the bunker. I'll be along soon.' She doubles off and I check NEKO's skin for any signs of life. Dead as the surface of this satellite, but he's a graph. I have no doubt he's okay – somewhere.

I'm quarter of a klick from the bunker and I can see Dorsa a hundred metres ahead, when I'm side-swiped by something heavy. I slide to the right and my EVA-skin's foot catches. I go over onto my side. As I tumble, I see Jupiter. It fills a third of the sky, and there're little lights too. They're not stars, but bright orange. More marines landing, I guess. I tumble and roll in the light gravity.

I step out of the box. Straight into GRENDEL's jaws. His diffuse, cloudy substance is everywhere and he envelopes me with pain and confusion. It's as if I'm an unwanted part of him that he wants to excise with lasers, rather than a separate enemy. We struggle over the vastness of space and grapple through time but as unmeasurable eons pass, Grendel is losing his grip on me. He gains the upper hand again and tightens his hold. Lightning shoots through us and fire envelops our individual and collective worlds; Zeus and Hephaestus locked together immortally in mortal combat.

I am about to go under, but now my strength doubles, a strength which is of me, or I of it. Father? I expand, like a supernova, and throw Grendel into the void.

Back in my frail body and my toppled EVA. It stops rolling and I'm on my back looking up at an Earther combat-skin. I have a limited field of vision through the glass visor and my displays have all shut down. Other skins join the first, and I'm surrounded. And now, a single display comes back online. GRENDEL's face forms inches from my own. He's the pilot of the closest skin.

'Oh, Ariel, what a dance you've led me.' He energises his weapon. 'I really needed you in one piece, but I can't risk you escaping again. I'm almost sorry to see you go.'

He lifts the plazzer and points it directly at my head. I shift my gaze to the lights in the sky. They grow bigger and bigger; friendly, orange, warm and glowing. Better than looking at the wrong end of a fully charged emitter that's ready to take my life. 'Get on with it, Grendel. Or do you mean to bore me to death?'

I'm almost blinded by a flash that fills the scope of my visor. This is it then. I thought it would hurt more. There's a crump of metal and my EVA is pushed into the rock with something heavy lying on top of me. Warnings start to fill my ears and the air is bright with flashing red displays. Life support, suit integrity and collision-imminent warnings compete to be the loudest, until they are all silenced by another transmission.

'Stand down, Marines. This is Marshall Thosev Straw of the Venusian Defence Force. I'm authorised by Callistonian Council to take extreme and deadly measures if you do not disengage immediately.' It's a voice that conjures up the image of a man you wouldn't want to upset.

My eyes recover from the flash. I can't move because the Marine combat-skin is lying on top of my EVA. It starts to shake and I'm worried it might detonate. Again, the grinding of metal on metal. Something lifts it from me and casts it aside. It's a VDF EVA-skin, complete with force markings. It moves down towards me until our machines align, visor to visor, and I can see the operator.

'Your EVA-skin's a mess,' Sav says. 'We need to get you back to the Ashen Light before it goes off pop.'

'No, get me to the Alicanto.'

'Nice to see you too, Ariel.'

For now an exchange of heartfelt smiles will have to do. He helps me to my feet and I look down. GRENDEL's machine has been utterly destroyed and I'm sure he must be re-gathering himself somewhere in Quantum. I wonder if he knows he's no longer safe there. I will find him.

Sav and I make for the bunker. Time for a proper reunion and full explanations later, but now we have more pressing concerns. Engineering genius that she is, Dorsa's managed to activate the airlock. We're in!

***

The historical significance of this bunker is simply stunning. I'm overwhelmed. I sit in a control room and watch through the observation window as engineer-skins of various shapes and sizes go about their business, as they have done for centuries; custodians of and carers for a five-hundred year old ship.

I imagine the excitement of those archaeologist of long ago, my professional predecessors, when they uncovered the remains of the longship at Sutton Hoo. And then I try to understand how they might have felt if the ship they found had been in pristine condition, as new as the day it was built. The reality is that I hardly have to try at all, because my feelings must be exactly as theirs were. Before me, separated only by a sheet of glass and a few metres of air, is the magnificent Mapping & Survey Ship Alicanto. On its off-white hull is the golden representation of a bird, the symbol I saw so often in those historical presentations, and even in my dreams.

Like the man whose nose touches an elephant's leg, I'm far too close to see it in proper perspective, but I've called up a schematic which floats between NEKO and me. NEKO looks none the worse for his encounter with plazbolts, but then a graph wouldn't would it? Happily, his Quantum substance was equally untouched. He simply evacuated the ruined EVA-skin and installed himself over here, ready to greet us when we came through the airlock.

Our combined control room and observation deck is located in the bunker about halfway up the height of the ship. If I go out onto the walkway and look down, the engines are eighty metres below. If I crane my neck, I can make out the uppermost edge of the disc, eighty metres above.

The Alicanto, like the Phoenix Song before her, has the shape of a disc with a diameter of a hundred metres, all perched on a sixty metre rectangular engineering hull that also houses the acceleration decks. The grav-ring decks are located at the extremity of the disc which is fully enclosed in hull-plating. Unlike the ships of today, you can't see the decks rotating from the outside. All in all, a very sleek and elegant design.

'She's a beautiful creation, isn't she?' NEKO stares up as if contemplating the face of a much missed friend.

'So like old Phoenix,' he says, as if he really is the original NEKO. He explains why Callisto was the home of many ships back in the old days. Its light gravity allowed the building of vessels much bulkier than possible on any of the three worlds, or even Moon. 'Try to launch a ship this size from Earth and it would shake to pieces on ignition.'

I hear the clatter of feet ascending the metal stair. Dorsa enters, and I've rarely seen her look so happy. 'She's ready for you, Commander.'

'Oh, shush!'

Dorsa's chuckling. 'Seriously, now that she's all secured and checked over, you have to come aboard. It's like a living history lesson.'

'No time like the present. Lead on!'

I follow Dorsa down four levels to where a gantry gives access to one of the Alicanto's docking hatches. As we turn the final bend there's a small party coming the other way, led by Sav. Immediately behind him is a man of Venusian height but with the bulk of a pumped up combat-skin. I assume he's the owner of that voice which demanded the Marines' surrender, and now I'm close I find I'm correct. On his dark yellow trimmed space-film he wears the cypher of the VDF on a rank-patch.

'Ah, Ariel,' Sav says, and then turning to the man, 'Marshall, may I introduce you to Cohort-Commander Ariel Dzalarhons?'

I'm too impatient to go through the whole ritual. I clasp my hands before me, dip my head and greet him. 'Happy to meet you, Thosev.'

There are few men taller than I, but he peers down his nose at me, and I wonder if he's about to shout; perhaps accuse me of destroying worlds peace. Instead he smiles and holds out his hand. 'Let me greet you in the old Earther fashion.'

Instead of shaking, he holds my hand up towards his face and has a long stare. 'Hmm. Well. You look and feel perfectly human to me. Can't understand what all the fuss is about. Happy to meet you, Ariel.' He greets Dorsa with the same friendliness.

'Would you like a tour of my ship?' I ask.

'Your ship? Who says it's yours?'

'Who says it's not?'

The Marshall stares at me with eyes of flint, and then shakes his jowls. 'Good point, well made. Please lead on.'

I wave Dorsa ahead of me, and I follow. Thosev and Sav follow us and the rest of the party form a guard at the hatch. As we explore the lower decks, Thosev tells me the bunker is under the protection of a force of combined VDF and Callistonian militia. Earthers are busy making demands which to their increasing fury the rest of the worlds are ignoring, and I'm to be given every assistance to get the Alicanto into space and on route to Albion.

'I must say, Ariel, how very sorry I was to hear about your father. We're making suitable arrangement for the remains.' Thosev doesn't appear all that comfortable with sympathy.

I nod, trying not to think about it. I make no mention of my fervid if forlorn hope that Father's been reprinted somewhere.

'As for Dorsa Sagan's father, we conducted a search of the city ruins as you requested. Thought it was a bit of a fool's errand, but we actually found someone.'

'My dad?' I want to hug Dorsa. She looks so vulnerable, a quality I've never seen in her before.

'Sorry, but not Citizen Sagan. Another man, and in a pretty poor state. Dehydrated. Malnourished. More skeleton than man. He's been scavenging around in there for weeks. The medic reckons he wouldn't have lasted more than another few days, and it'll be a month till he's well enough to get about.' The medic in question is Dr Verone Kell, another surprise, but her story of re-joining the old crew isn't uppermost in my mind right now.

'Thosev, is it anyone we know?'

'I believe you do.' He keeps me on the edge.

'Well, who for S'Jinn sake?'

'Chap by the name of Benjo Drexler.'

***

My initial thought was that if Benjo could survive murder, recovering from malnutrition would be like peeling a mango. I wasn't that far out, because Benjo joins us today.

Safe in my cabin he looks like a different man from the one I saw two weeks ago in a Cally infirmary, unconscious in bed and hooked up to a squadron of medi-skins. He lays next to me and I count his ribs.

'You're tickling, Ariel. Stop!'

I'd rather not stop, but he's so very thin and delicate. Verone wasn't too keen on him coming with us, but he wouldn't be dissuaded. 'My mental health won't hold up to losing Ariel so soon after I've found him,' he said.

'Actually, your mental and physical health are one and the same. No difference. But you have a point. I'll give you a week to put on four kilos and run a circuit of the bunker in less than two minutes.'

The week's gone by and Benjo delivered on both counts. His ribs still stick out too much though. He shivers as my fingers reach his hip. Despite the depravations, he still looks like himself, but I can't help wondering if this is a new body, and his old, murdered one was incinerated months ago.

I wonder if he's up to talking about his experiences since we said goodbye on Dzalarhons Mons. He lays back and his face loses animation, eyes staring into scenes of horror and deprivation I can only imagine.

'If it's too painful, Benjo, leave it. There'll come a proper time.'

'It's fine. I want to talk. Where shall I start?'

I'm tempted to say 'At the beginning' but I want to go further back. 'What prompted you to venture out on your own quest for my father in the first place?'

'That wasn't it. I wanted to get to the bottom of the clues that all seemed to point to the Phoenix Song.'

He arranged a sabbatical, called in favours, pulled a few strings and set out to follow the trail of the old ship.

'I spent weeks delving into grid and little by little the trail pointed to Callisto.'

'So you, without a stent, managed to uncover clues that neither I nor my graph friends got a sniff of? How?'

'I had help. I knew somebody was placing subtle markers along my way, and when I reached Callisto I found out who.'

'Father?'

'Exactly, but his clues weren't subtle enough for Grendel. They were on to us. We did our best to evade them, but the Earthers virtually invaded Callisto. They cornered us in the Adlinda bioprinting labs, and ... I'm so sorry, Ariel. They killed him and left me to die.'

Grendel had convinced his troops that Father was some kind of evil chimera. One of his men shot him, but Benjo was human and none of them would obey his commands to kill Benjo as well. I recalled much the same when Grendel ordered Raoul's death.

Benjo's recollection of survival in the ruins of Adlinda becomes vague. No more than grubbing around for old food cubes and water sources. 'I had the help of an ancient maintenance-skin. I suppose he saw me as a unit in need of maintenance.'

'More like the universal construct directive to preserve human life kicked in.'

'Probably, but he wore out and died days before your people found me.' He looks drawn and ill, burdening himself with my loss of Father.

'Father's death wasn't your fault.' The words come out tremulous, and now Benjo is comforting me. I'll have a lifetime to grieve. I'm not allowing this to become all about me again. I need to lighten both our moods.

'Here, I have something for you.' I scoot over him, careful that my weight doesn't hurt his frail body. I go through the bedside cubby and pull out a sleek object like blue-enamelled metal. It's in the shape of a chunky 'V'.

'A badge? "V" for Venus?'

'For Very astute, in your case. It's a new style of suit-disc. Hold it mid-sternum. Yes, like that. Now tap three times and say "Space-film".'

'Not very disc-shaped, is it? Here goes then.'

He wriggles on the bed in paroxysms of giggles and the nanobots, obviously better ticklers than me, dress him in a VDF space-film.

'Yes! Very smart. Call up a mirror and see what you think.'

Part of the wall becomes reflective and Benjo gives a turn. 'Am I a soldier now?'

'No, you only look like one. The suit provides necessary control interfaces for space travel.'

'The armoured sections make me look muscly and hide all my sticky-out bones. I like it.'

'Standard dress from now on.' I dip into Quantum to check the time. 'We launch in four hours.'

NEKO and I take Benjo on a tour of the ship while explaining the intricacies of space bending. It amazes me that this information would once have been covered in classes for juvenile sets. Now it's all but lost. I'm the custodian of secret knowledge, a veritable thirty-first century wizard.

'First we have to find an area of exploitable gravitational instability,' NEKO says.

'That's what old spacers used to call "eggies", right?' Benjo asks.

'Correct. They used to call the process of passing through an EGI "scrambling an egg". There are many other examples of twenty-fifth century spacer jargon.'

I call up a schematic and point out the nine bays which house portal pods.

'I used to pilot Pod 9 on the Phoenix Song,' NEKO says.

Benjo and I simply stop and stare. 'You mean the original Neko used to pilot Pod 9?'

'Ah, well. You see, it goes further than the quantum-personality paradox. In fact, I am the same Neko.' He follows up with an explanation which, surprising to nobody, I don't understand in terms I can put into words. 'Shall we continue with the tour?'

'What are these?' Benjo stabs a finger into the projection of another bay and its contents. 'They look like weapons.'

'They kind of are,' I say. 'These ten objects are shift-gen pods, which give us the ability to enter chronodimentional shift ten times. For each shift, a shift-gen pod has to be detonated within a very precise area of an EGI.'

NEKO takes over. 'The graph-operated portal pods are then able to fashion the resulting disruption into a gate, through which the ship jumps to a corresponding destination rift.'

Benjo is frowning and I can virtually see his mind working. 'How's the destination rift formed, and how's it all controlled?'

'Really, Benjo. Isn't your head already on the verge blowing up? It's all graphy-waffie Quantum blox. I'm half-graph and I don't fully understand.'

Benjo surrenders, hands in the air. 'Quite enough explanation for me. But aren't those gen pods dangerous, being nuclear-bomb like?'

'They're completely inert until they're initiated, and they're only initiated when trig-fixed in the centre of an EGI immediately before detonation.'

Benjo enlarges the bay display. 'That makes me feel so much better.'

Risking the exploding head anyway, NEKO goes on to talk about the operation of the portal pods, and once the gate's been established, their mad rush to get back to the ship before it jumps. 'It only looks like a mad rush to humans,' NEKO says. 'To us pod-pilots it's a leisurely little jaunt.'

We explore the other acceleration decks and on the uppermost, check out the chamber to the transfer ring. Once we've reached cruising speed, we'll use this to access the main ring.

'I've never experienced centrifugal gravity. They say it makes you nauseas.'

'In my experience,' says NEKO, the graph who's not affected by gravity, 'people soon get used to it.'

Now with a couple of hours to go before launch, we join Dorsa and Verone on the bunker side of the gantry. There's a speech by Marshall Straw.

Minister Markesa Zown is here too. I suspect we have her to thank for Benjo's fake murder. It saved him from GRENDEL, so my pain was worth it. I thank her for all the work she's done behind the scenes to restore our reputations at home, on Mars and everywhere else except Earth. We're still terrorists to the Earthers. I lived on Earth for nearly two years and find it frightening that such friendly people can be turned so easily with lies.

When officialdom's had its share of us, those of high rank withdraw and we say goodbye to Djogore and Sav. We all keep it light and friendly and try not to think that we may never meet again. I hold to the hope that space-bending may be re-established, and then we'll all be within reach.

I'm sad, yet optimistic for the future. We'll meet old friends again. The Earthers will come to see the truth about us. And I'll complete Father's mission to establish a hybrid colony on Albion. It will be a suitable epitaph for him, for I have little hope he survived the plazzer blast.

The hatch closes behind us and the gantry withdraws. Dorsa leads us up to the control deck which we've configured for four. It looks cramped when NEKO calls in the other eight graphs, all friends of his and vouched trustworthy.

The final hour has arrived. The graphs, with the exception of NEKO, disperse to Quantum. Dorsa checks fuel levels one more time, and I scroll through external view displays: Jupiter as magnificent as ever; the sun, filtered and looking half the size of Moon when seen from Earth, and our ship from every conceivable angle.

'She really is a beautiful ship.' It's a thought I speak out loud.

'Really?' Benjo says. 'Sav told me you thought it was silly calling a ship "she". Was he mistaken?'

I'm pretty certain it was Sav who thought that. 'I don't think it's at all silly. It's very appropriate.'

'I wonder if you've changed you mind about anything else.'

'About "love" you mean? Not so much changed my mind as grown up. I was a youth back then.' It occurs to me that I missed my Coming of Age celebrations. The date passed without me giving it a thought, some time when I was on Mars.

'So?'

'So, it exists.' I reach over and slap his knee.

Dorsa makes an impatient sound. 'Can you two please wait till we're under way and then do everyone a favour by disappearing into your cabin for the rest of the voyage.'

'I can always administer filters.' Verone joins in on Dorsa's side. What a traitor.

We share a laugh and Dorsa tells us it's time to tilt. The final twenty second countdown has commenced. Our seats tilt and our suits adhere, all ready for launch.

'All systems green,' NEKO says. Ship's system confirms, and then commences an audible countdown in a soft, relaxing voice.

'Twelve … elven … ten … nine,' and now a different voice supersedes system. It sounds tinny and flat, devoid of any of the refinement that passes for empathy in a construct. 'Shift-gen pod initiated and armed.'

'Oh, no. Not again.' NEKO says.

I have to do something. 'Disengage! Make pod safe!'

'No time,' NEKO says. 'We're locked out. Two seconds to detonation.'

I enter Quantum where seconds are days, but I see that NEKO's estimate was generous. There is indeed, no time. I sense the vibrations of my friends and wrap myself around them.

RECORD INTERUPTED
NO DATA INCOMING
CLOSE DOWN

Report to Three Worlds Council Adlinda Incident (Summary)

On Othman 12th 3032 at 1400 an explosion of 4.184e+14 joules occurred five klicks west of the ruins of Adlinda City on Callisto. The resulting crater, measuring 298 metres in diameter and 230 metres deep, was categorically not caused by meteorite impact as is claimed by Earth Council.

The dimensions of the crater may appear inconsistent with the energy release. This is explained by the fact the explosion centred in a pre-existing bunker which was part of the long defunct Adlinda Spaceport (see Appendix: "Historical References"). TWC is respectfully reminded that Callisto's icy crust is also a contributing factor.

Our report is based on eyewitness accounts and graph investigation. The author of this report was present as part of a team gathered to witness the launch of the MSS99 Alicanto. The existence of this ship has long been kept under TWC Seal. (See references and authorities that show Earth Council Seal Committee were equal partners to all decisions made). ECSC's continued denial of the ship's existence is rendered highly suspicious not to say deliberately disingenuous.

Others present included Force Marshall Thosev STRAW, crewmembers of the Venusian Defence Force Ship Ashen Light, and members of the Callistonian Militia. There was also a contingent of Earth Defence

Division Marines present despite denials of Earth Council. (See attached Appendix "Witnesses").

Please see attached report from graph NEKO who was on board the MSS99 Alicanto immediately before the explosion and who conducted an investigation in Quantum parallels before and during the explosion.

The following crew of the MSS99 Alicanto were lost in the explosion:-
Benjo DREXLER: (Citizen of Venus)
Cohort-Commander Ariel DZALARHONS, VDF: (Citizen of Venus)
Dr Verone KELL, VDF: (Citizen of Venus)
Dorsa SAGAN: (Citizen of Mars)

There were minor injuries among some of the observers closest to the bunker, but the thin atmosphere of Callisto mitigated the radial effects of the explosion.

From all observations and the subsequent investigation, we conclude that the explosion was due to the detonation of a Chronodimentional Shift Generator Pod, the detonation itself resulting from an act of sabotage, securities and fail-safes having been compromised, and detonation initiated by a graph personality-collective registered as GRENDEL. This conclusion is fully supported by evidence. Complicity of Earth Council highly suspected. Despite this suspicion being supported by strong circumstantial evidence, it cannot be proven at this time.

Respectfully submitted.
Markesa Zown
Venusian Security Minister
Chair: Venus Council Seal Committee.

Christie's Path

It takes me a while to see rather than feel the vibrations.

I float in an expanse of black void. Bright lights form around me, incandescent at the centre with blinding blue halos which fade to dark penumbras at the edges. Are they stars?

I'm drawn to a single light among the thousands. It comes nearer as all the other recede rapidly from my sight. This one light – I feel it – is of Benjo.

In a heartbeat it takes on his form and the dark void becomes a rural scene. Benjo appears as black Bartholomew. He's armed for battle and I know he's for Monmouth, as am I. He raises his hat to see me off, and I doff mine, the plumes dancing in the breeze. I unbend my knee but now he's dressed as a soldier of the Great War. It's Jack! He leans on an old wooden gate, and we're separated by fifteen metres of tall meadow grass which catch the breeze, swaying and swaying, a kind of goodbye.

I back away from him, the grass parting for me. With one final wave I turn to face the meadow, verdant and full of colour: yellows, reds and purples, the nodding heads of meadow flowers. There's a sweet, wholesome smell on the breeze, and the sounds of birds fill the air. A squadron of swifts swoop, screaming at the insects they're about to consume.

A quick look over my shoulder, and Benjo – Jack – is still there, still waving, but as I watch he's swallowed up by shadow. Natural shade or the returning void, I can't say. I only know our paths lie in opposite directions, and sadness threatens to consume me.

But I must go. The field spreads around me, a sea of swaying, susurrating grasses relieved only by a huge oak in the far distance. With no other objective in sight, I make for the oak, and now the grass shows the passage of someone ahead of me. Others went before me and others will follow. It's bent in a narrow path that leads to the oak.

I keep to the path treading down the same stems that another trod before me, and it's as if I walk backwards, for the impressions I leave stretch ahead of me. The path is a little more defined, and then still more. The grass now parts, like the Red Sea story in miniature. Have the chosen ones preceded me?

Onward I go, the oak a little nearer but not so near as it should be after such a long walk. The path now has a distinct bare patch where the meadow plants have given up to the onslaught of many feet. As I continue, the packed earth track becomes wider, so that two people could easily walk abreast.

A thick mist billows in, and straight out again. A flash-mist! It lifts and the path, flanked by wooden fences, is wide enough for a cart. Perspective causes it to narrow to a point aligning directly towards the grand old tree. Without me noticing, that packed earth has given way to a metalled lane. At last I reach the tree. Its thick trunk is surrounded by a ring of paving slabs, kerbed in grey granite, and beyond it the road continues, with a little house to one side, and now two more on the other.

I walk in the middle of the road between houses, first detached and far between, but now closer and terraced. At last I come to the end of the road, and at the corner is the road's name on a marker, black letters on white enamel. There's green algae in the corners of each of the letters. The sign reads 'CHRISTIE'S PATH'.

I do not wonder if Christie ever walked here, because I don't have to. I remember. But my memory fails, and now at the cross roads, I don't know which way to go.

The village fades, slowly and slowly, to void again, but this time without the relief of lights. Benjo is no longer behind me. I'm alone.

Now, a vibration sets up within me, and another light burgeons from the black. In the same way I knew Benjo's light, I know this one is Father's.

'Ariel.' It's Father's voice, gentle, strong, laced with concern. 'Ariel, come along now. This way.' He is intimately present, as he was at my birth.

There's no more uncertainty. My quest for Jonan Dzalarhons is over. I've found him, and I follow.

'Ariel, try to open your eyes.'

There's a long, slow intake of breath, and for the first time in eons I feel my own body. Cool air fills my lungs and chills my skin, and light pierces the cotton wool in my head. I open my eyes and through the unruly mop of my hair I see Jonan. He looks down at me and smiles

He rakes my scruffy forelocks to one side, and I'm a juvenile again. 'Welcome to Albion, my son.'

***

'This is my third body, then?' My hands are as ever they were. I have come through this transition with all my hair intact. And the scar of the lion-snake bite is still on my side. I'm a little older than I was, and one day I will die as entropy takes its toll.

Father walks with me over a plain of rough grass, prickly under our bare feet. Our film-gowns are quite adequate for the climate. The grass is green, as it is on Earth, Venus and Mars. The air is clean and fresh. The sky is blue with streaks of gold. There are white-capped mountains in the distance, which recede rank upon rank until they become purple then blue and violet, and at last merge with the distant sky. Evening is coming, but with two suns darkness will be held at bay. Albion is a beautiful planet.

'Yes, your third body.'

I grapple with the concept that at the moment my last body was destroyed, my new one was initiated in the bioprinter facility here on Albion. Distance, it appears, really is no object, and just as a graph-link provides instantaneous communication, so my graph element is unbound by space.

'One day I'll understand how such distances can be covered in less than a blink of the eye.'

'First, understand this. No distance was covered at all. Graph is one and everywhere and everything. As your form, as defined by your graph element ceased to be where it was, it reformed here. It remained only to reintegrate it with flesh.'

I duck as a flock of swift-like birds swoop over our heads. 'Are they printed?'

'No, completely indigenous, as are most creatures here.' Father smiles and looks at me sideways. I know that look so well of old. He is keeping something from me. A secret with which he'll tease me.

He leads me through some shallow waters. A spring is fed from the surrounding land and meanders downhill between sloping banks. We follow its course until it spills over an edge to form a small waterfall, but my attention is no longer with the water, because the land falls away to reveal a wide valley between us and the distant mountains, and in the valley is a city.

It's vast, and beautiful incorporating an equal amount of nature within its boundaries as it does buildings. The structures are curved and fluid in design and I can pick out tree-lined avenues, and lakes that sparkle in the suns-light. It takes my breath away and I have to sit on a rocky ledge. Father sits next to me. 'Planned and built entirely by graph and construct operated skins.'

'Jonan, I thought you said you and I were the first and only humans, or human-graph hybrids, on the planet.' As soon as we get back to the facility, our numbers will increase by three as we initiate Dorsa, Verone and Benjo, but the city is vast, and we could initiate lives for months without making a dent on it.

'Do you believe humans are the only life in the Universe?' That teasing look again.

I gaze at the wondrous city. 'Other advanced levels of sentient beings?'

Father nods. 'Albion was always intended as a nexus for Universal life.'

'Planned by who? The graphs? Who do they think they are? Gods?'

Father rises and stretches stiffness from his back. 'The city will need a human name,' he says. 'It's already has a felispien one, and several others for each of the races present, but I'd like you to give it one for humans.'

He walks back up the way we came and I follow, with many a glance back towards the city. I haven't a clue what I should name it and I'm not giving it much thought. Instead my head is full of images of exotic beings from other worlds. I can't wait to meet them, but they must wait until my friends are made flesh again.

We head back to the facility. There's work to be done, and we won't be the only humans on this world for very long. Once initiated, a human can be printed in a matter of hours.

We walk slowly as the facility comes into view through a small copse. I think of the task that awaits, and an anomaly in my understanding presents itself. 'Jonan, you said we have to be present to initiate the printing. In that case who printed you?' I shudder as an image of the remains of his previous body steals unbidden to my mind.

'Any old graph can integrate and print a human-graph hybrid because we do most of the work ourselves. We're needed to resurrect those whose human-graph links are more tenuous.' He relates the facts in such detail that I'm left behind. The gist I do understand: all life is a hybrid of the macro and Quantum worlds.

It all falls into place. 'My past-life memories and experiences are all real, aren't they?' He doesn't need to answer. 'In one sense, I was all of those people. Duke Arthur, Elias Grey, Christie and all the others.' I wonder at the details of how that could be possible, but I don't dwell on it for long, because we've arrived at the bioprinting facility. I do know they were all on the path that led to me, that led to here and now.

Skins get on with their work, maintaining the place to the highest degrees of cleanliness. One gives us a little half-bow by way of informing us it's graph-operated. The units of machinery are familiar to me, but these don't have the strange markings of those in the caverns of Venus, Mars and Callisto. Father tells me they were all built by civilisations far older than humans.

'The ones who left the fossils on Venus?'

'Indeed, and the ancestors of those you'll meet when we visit the city. They were the earliest instruments of the graphs, and responsible for our genesis.'

'Human genesis?'

'No, early modern humans were already widespread on Earth. It was by a combination of their science and graph science that made the first human-graph hybrids. We were there, if not at the beginning of humanity, then certainly at the very start of human civilisation.'

It's been a day since Father started the process that brought me back to physical form, and being one of only two humans on an entire planet, a day is quite enough. 'Can we bring back the others now?'

'Of course. But may I ask, as much as I know you want to initiate Benjo, Dorsa and Verone, there's another who I'd like you to begin with.' He plants a vibration in my graph-mind, although whose I don't know.

We pass through ranks of tanks and banks, and come to the interface into which I spill the graph of myself. While my body relaxes in a chair, I seek and sift through Quantum until I fix the vibration and convey it to where it needs to be. The process begins.

It must be the most intimate of acts, watching the bioprinting of a human, to see them built up, matrix, bone, nerve, muscle and skin. I leave the process to continue without me for an hour and now return. The hair is being formed.

This young woman before me looks terribly familiar but recognition won't snap into place. I sift through many lives-worth of memories but I can't quite ... Oh, by Saint John. No! It cannot be.

Father reaches into the chamber and attaches a disc, so by the time she awakens she is dressed in clothes suitable to her era.

She opens her eyes, and I'm the one in her line of vision. 'Phil?' She puts her fists on her hips. 'Philip Fryer, what the hell are you doing here?' She looks around, confused by her surroundings.

It's all too much for me, and it spills over.

'Shut your mouth, Phil. Before a fly goes in. And now what? Why're you crying?'

I sniff it up, because it's either cry or laugh, and I opt for the latter. 'Happy Bumblebee Day, Shona Eastbrook.' I wipe my eyes on my sleeve. 'Where've you been for the last thousand years?'

***

The streets are as beautiful close up as the city is from afar. More so, in fact, because they're populated by people from across the Universe. We've already met and conversed with felispiens (who are the very embodiment in flesh and blood of NEKO), and a representative of the first Venusians. Shona takes it all in her stride, proving that my concern for her was misplaced.

The city has been built for fifty thousand people, and so far it is home for only a few hundred, only six of whom are human. The task ahead of us is to initiate a human population, the graph elements taken mainly from those who, like Shona, laid down their lives to save humanity. There's something fitting about that. When the Endeavour arrives, they'll find an inhabited world, and we will welcome them.

'Have you thought about a name yet, Ariel?' Father looks high up, past the grove of trees and to the finial of a silver tower.

We've been here a week, but I haven't given a thought to naming the city, until now. It has to speak of achievement and continuity. At the same time, it must bring it back to the individual, because we are all, but we are one. I remember how Benjo was intrigued by the name of a bridge at home, and how his curiosity led him to research the history of the structure and the meaning of the name. I want the name of our city to inspire others in the future to do the same.

My friends form an expectant half-circle around me: Father, Dorsa, Verone, Shona and Benjo.

'Don't keep us all waiting forever, Venus-boy.' Dorsa chuckles.

'Take all the time in the worlds, Ariel.' Benjo looks towards the road that leads out of the city.

Got it! 'Christie's Path,' I say. 'Let's call the city "Christie's Path".'

And we do.

THE END

Appendix One

Venusian Defence Force Ranks & Insignia

Rank Level	Rank Grade	Insignia
Sub-legionary	Officer	Branch patch: 30mm sq in branch colour.
Sub-legionary	Adjutant	Branch patch bearing 1 black bar 25mm x 5mm
Sub-legionary	Section-Commander	Branch patch bearing 2 black bars.
Sub-legionary	Company-Commander	Branch patch bearing 3 black bars.
Legionary	Cohort-Commander	Branch patch bearing 1 silver bar.
Legionary	Legion First Officer	Branch patch bearing 2 silver bars.
Legionary	Legion-Commander	Branch patch bearing 3 silver bars
Force	Group-Commander	Branch patch bearing 1 gold bar.
Force	Force First Officer	Branch patch bearing 2 gold bars.
Force	Force-Commander	Branch patch bearing 3 gold bars.
Force	Force Marshall	Branch patch bearing VDF monogram in gold.

Branch Patches

Branch	Patch Colour
Force Level (except Group-Commander)	Dark Yellow
Task Force/Combat	Red
Space Corps	Orange
Medical & Science	Green
Police & Security	Blue
Corps of Engineers	Grey
Special Operations	Black

Note: Group-Commanders, although of Force Level, generally wear the patch of the group/corps/branch they command. If in a Force command role, they wear the dark yellow of the Level.

Acknowledgments

'I wonder, is there anyone who would like to read my manuscript?'

At this point, most sane people bury their head in a newspaper, pay special attention to their drinks, or simply run away.

These words of thanks are for those who didn't.

Many thanks to Veronica Kelly and Mel Thompson for seeing some potential, and to Malcolm Egre for useful early feedback.

I'm especially grateful to Jacqueline Watts and Simon Michael, fellow members of the Hertfordshire Society of Writers (a branch of the Society of Authors) for their detailed critiques. They may have worn velvet gloves, but they pulled no punches, and thanks to them the final work is much better. It's certainly far from perfect, but that's down to me.

Other Books by the Same Author

If you are curious about the fate of the good ship Phoenix Song, her crew, and an early incarnation of the beings known as graphs, you can find their story in David's book "The Delightful Guide".

Fiction:
    The Last Spellherder
    Come Away O Human Child
    The Children of Bast
    The Delightful Guide
    Raven-Fish!
    Tallahatchie Timebomb & Other Stories
    Take Another Life
    The Ballad of a Fisher Boy

Non-fiction:
    Die Hard, Aby!

Printed in Great Britain
by Amazon